A PLUME BOOK

SOMEBODY ELSE'S DAUGHTER

ELIZABETH BRUNDAGE is the author of *The Doctor's Wife* and holds an MFA in fiction from the Iowa Writers' Workshop, where she received a James Michener Award. She lives with her family in upstate New York.

"Riveting...very moving and completely involving...Brundage is a brilliant novelist."　　　　　—Richard Bausch, author of *Peace*

"A taut tale of suspense rounded out with sharp observations on parenting, adoption and the fraught business of keeping up appearances."　　　　　—*The New York Observer*

"A terrific fast-paced summer read."　　　　　—*Library Journal*

"Marvelous...This second finely crafted novel is superior in its superbly balanced character development...*Somebody Else's Daughter* is topical and relevant."　　　　　—www.mostlyfiction.com

"A dark, disturbing novel that was difficult to put down."　　　　　—www.blogliterarily.com

ALSO BY ELIZABETH BRUNDAGE

The Doctor's Wife

Somebody Else's Daughter

Elizabeth Brundage

A PLUME BOOK

PLUME
Published by the Penguin Group
Penguin Group (USA) Inc., 375 Hudson Street, New York, New York 10014, U.S.A. • Penguin
Group (Canada), 90 Eglinton Avenue East, Suite 700, Toronto, Ontario, Canada M4P 2Y3 (a
division of Pearson Penguin Canada Inc.) • Penguin Books Ltd., 80 Strand, London WC2R 0RL,
England • Penguin Ireland, 25 St. Stephen's Green, Dublin 2, Ireland (a division of Penguin
Books Ltd.) • Penguin Group (Australia), 250 Camberwell Road, Camberwell, Victoria 3124,
Australia (a division of Pearson Australia Group Pty. Ltd.) • Penguin Books India Pvt. Ltd.,
11 Community Centre, Panchsheel Park, New Delhi – 110 017, India • Penguin Group (NZ),
67 Apollo Drive, Rosedale, North Shore 0632, New Zealand (a division of Pearson New Zealand
Ltd.) • Penguin Books (South Africa) (Pty.) Ltd., 24 Sturdee Avenue, Rosebank, Johannesburg 2196,
South Africa

Penguin Books Ltd., Registered Offices: 80 Strand, London WC2R 0RL, England

Published by Plume, a member of Penguin Group (USA) Inc. Previously published in a Viking
edition.

First Plume Printing, April 2009
10 9 8

Ⓟ REGISTERED TRADEMARK—MARCA REGISTRADA

The Library of Congress has catalogued the Viking edition as follows:

Brundage, Elizabeth
    Somebody else's daughter / Elizabeth Brundage.
        p. cm.
    ISBN 978-0-670-01900-7 (hc.)
    ISBN 978-0-452-29537-7 (pbk.)
    1. Adopted children—Fiction.   2. Berkshire Hills (Mass.)—Fiction.   3. Psychological fic-
tion.
    4. Domestic fiction.   I. Title.
    PS3602.R84S66   2008
    813'.6—dc22   2007042807

Printed in the United States of America
Original hardcover design by Carla Bolte
Set in ITC Garamond Light

For my parents

There is no revenge so complete as forgiveness.

—Josh Billings

Summer, 1989

We left San Francisco that morning even though your mother was sick. It was a pretty day, the sun shimmering like a gypsy girl's tambourine. I thought it would be good for her to get out into the sunshine because it had been a long few weeks of rain and her skin had gone gray as oatmeal and she had this dull look flaming up in her eyes. You were sleeping in your little rocking seat and I had your things all packed. We didn't have much. It was time to go, but Cat wanted me to wash her hair first, said she couldn't go out looking like that. Holding her head in my hands I could feel her bright with fever. From behind, she looked like a healthy schoolgirl, just her sweet body and that long yellow hair. Then she'd turn around and you'd get pins in your heart. I wrapped her head in a towel and said, you take your meds today, Kitty Cat, and she nodded with her long face, the kind of woman you see in the museum up on the old canvases, a woman washing clothes or out in the fields, a strong body with large capable hands and this wisdom in her eyes because she knows more than you. She hated the idea that she was sick, and even with you so small she was still shooting drugs. Dope kept her comfortable. It had always been her favorite thing to do and that's the truth. You could see it just after she'd put the needle in, like an angel her face would go hazy and beautiful like so much fog. She dreamed of horses, she said. She told me she'd come into the world wanting to ride, wanting to be near the big dark creatures. Horses understood her, people made her nervous. This was your mother; this was the woman I loved.

We made you one night in a broken house, your mother riding my hips and howling with pleasure, and then six weeks later she's throwing up and wanting strange foods from the Iranian down on Willard

Avenue. Months passed and her belly went round and tight. At the clinic they said she had a weak heart and HIV. Maybe her baby wouldn't get it. They didn't know. They gave her some pills and told her to come back every three weeks. She quit dope that afternoon, and took the pills and started going to church. She told me she had begged Jesus for a miracle. She believed in miracles, she said; she believed in Jesus. She liked to light the candles and sit in the darkness and think and then she'd get down on her knees and press her palms together. I'd watch her sometimes in the trembling blue light, among the other whispering strangers.

This one day we were walking through the park, leaning and kissing, that smell at the nape of her neck, the nape, like vanilla, like I don't know what, heaven, and then she's down on all fours in labor and this crowd comes around and she's white as fucking God and the next thing I know we're in a taxi with this Pakistani barking orders and I'm just wondering how we're going to pay for it. At the hospital they gave Cat a C-section on account of the HIV. They let me stand there and hold her hand and when I saw you for the first time I started to cry, I couldn't help it. You were bundled in a little blanket and you had on a little hat and you were the most amazing thing I had ever seen. I handed you to your mother and she was trembling and a little frightened and it made me want to crawl up next to her and hide my face in her heart. The nurse explained that there was a chance you'd be all right; they wouldn't know for a few months, we'd just have to be patient. I promised Cat that everything would be okay, I'd make sure of it, but she shook her head. "I'm sick," she said.

They made her talk to a shrink. I waited out in the hall and I could hear her crying. I didn't know what to do. I went down to the waiting room and bought a candy bar and sat there. There were some old books on the table, old paperbacks. One had a girl on the cover who looked like your mother. The book was *My Antonia* and I vaguely remembered reading it in high school. Later, I gave it to her, and she snapped it out of my hands and told me to leave her alone. We had this thing between us; she didn't think she was smart enough for me, which of course wasn't true; she was the smartest person I ever knew, the kind of smart you don't get in school. I'd gone to a fancy prep school where my father was a teacher. I'd grown up in a crummy faculty house with people coming and going, writers mostly, nasty drunken poets who always ended up sleeping on the couch. It was one of those poets who turned me on to dope, among other things. "We're calling her Willa," your mother declared when I walked in that night. She was sitting up in bed, her eyes shining, holding the book in her shaking hand. I could tell she'd liked it, and we named you after its author. We brought you home and the very next day they sent someone over from Child Services and it was that same woman who suggested we give you up. She brought two cases of formula and some diapers. She looked around our apartment, her eyes grim. Cat served the woman tea in one of her mother's old china teacups, it had little rosebuds on it, and your mother had saved it for a long time, keeping it carefully wrapped in newspaper so it wouldn't get broken, but the woman wouldn't even touch it. She kept on us, trying to persuade us to let you go, to give you a better life, but we put her off.

I tried to find work. I could get work here and there. For a little while things were good between us, and Cat was all right and I sometimes forgot that her blood was tainted. She would do things, buy peaches, and there they'd be, fat and round on the counter, or she'd make a meal and set the table, like we were a real family. I don't know; I couldn't deal with it. It was a time in my life when I didn't know any better; I didn't know who I was. Sometimes I wouldn't come home for a few days and it would be just her and you and she'd know when I walked in stinking of dope, the whole thing, the cigarettes, sometimes women, and she'd just hold me because there was nothing else to do. I know it sounds pathetic to you, who we were, but it's the truth and I can't change it. There's a vivid transition when you come in from being high, and the walls have this mustard tint like old tapestries, and your body feels drained, beat up from the inside, and everything feels like a déjà vu, like you've made this big circle and instead of moving on you're right back where you started. I don't know, it's hard to explain, and I'm not good with words even though they shoved Tolstoy down my throat at Choate and fucking Whitman—I have a box of quotes someplace—I'd even memorized some of it—fucking useless information. Anyway, later on, weeks, maybe months, she started feeling sick and it was like crashing into a wall of bricks, and for a long while you see the pieces of your life floating all around you, the burning embers of your totally fucked-up world, and it comes to you that you haven't made much of your time, and you haven't done all that much and it's almost over. It's like you can hear them cackling about you up in heaven, the big mistake you've turned into.

By then I had found a job working construction. I've been up on rooftops, looking down on the clay-colored buildings, the dark alleys where you see things you shouldn't, people pissing in the gutter or puking or sharing secrets. You can see the steep hills and the trolleys with their little bells. I've been up on buildings in the pouring rain. Sometimes it comes down so hard you get the feeling it is God Himself drumming upon your back. When you work on buildings, you see things. I have looked into the rooms of strangers. I have touched their things, unfolded their letters. I have run my hands across their glistening tabletops, their ivory piano keys. I have changed the hands on their clocks just enough to alter the passing hours of their days. I have lain down on unmade beds, breathing in the dank sweat of a stranger's dreams, and I have used their toilets, read their magazines, and sipped from their open bottles of wine. I have been on bridges; I have hung from cables like a paratrooper, like a secret agent in some espionage movie. I have danced in the sky like a marionette, swinging from cables over the dark water of the bay.

I have been lucky in my life to know freedom, unlike your mother who was a prisoner of her fate. Simple things didn't interest her, whereas just the sunshine could keep me happy for days on end, just a walk on the street, out in the air with the smell of the wharf, the fish smell that is life in my nostrils. The sun on the crown of your head like a father's hand, this is what I want you to remember about me, that no matter what, my hand is there with the sun in your hair, heavy on your head, guiding you. There is pleasure, for me, in cupping water from my hands, the cool water bringing life. Like when you are trembling over something or feeling dead inside and you end up in a gas station bathroom that stinks of the body and maybe you are so doped you can hardly see and all the dirty blue tiles smear together and then you put your dirty hands under the running water and you marvel at its clarity and it stops you there, it stops everything, and for a moment you can't move. It's a small thing, something that has occurred to me over time. The sense a man will have of being a small part of things. There is freedom in knowing your place in this world. Your mother never really knew where she stood and it was like a net over her head and she could not wriggle free of it.

You're probably wondering how we met. I like to think of it this way: We first met hundreds of years ago when I was a boy in the deep fields of Ireland and she was yet a young lass with flower petals in her hair. I swept her up on my horse and we rode away like that. I had her for the first time in the cold open space of a castle. I knew her, like some princess of the wild. I grew up in this world with her stuck in my head from another time. She was my phantom limb. I could sometimes see her in dreams, opaque, violet, but I could never reach her. I searched for her. I waited three centuries. And then, finally, she was there.

It was a crack house on Washington Avenue in Chinatown. I don't exactly know how I got there, but I was on the floor to my best recollection and I looked up through the intense smoke and there was this girl, this sea urchin, this exotic flower, this *ghost*. She didn't have any tits, so skinny you could push her over with one finger, and her nose running snot and the woozy yellow eyes of an addict. But lips warm like a good supper somebody makes you out of kindness, when you haven't eaten for days, and you've never tasted food so good, and the feeling in your belly of being full, like when you were a kid.

This was Catherine—Cat. This was my woman coming toward me through the smoke. We fell in love over the broken streets and in and out of the rain and sunlight and the music pouring out through people's windows. We lived in this condemned building with rats and black slippery birds and we just kept shooting drugs and fucking and drifting down the streets and boulevards and finding things in the trash and kissing in the hollow corners of the city or standing in somebody's doorway behind the falling rain.

I knew her love for the drugs was stronger than her love for me, and I knew it would catch up someday and I knew it would destroy her. She couldn't help it, she couldn't control it. Then she'd cry over her guilt. She'd put her hands over her ears on account it got so loud in her head, like horses stomping on her brain, she said, and I'd have to hold her. I'd just have to hold her.

Let me tell you about love. Love is a kind of madness and you would follow it anywhere, you don't care. We fucked, that was me and Cat, fucking, not the lame pretense of making love. And she had this beautiful yellow hair, and she smelled earthy, you know, like geraniums when you get down close to the stems, and she tasted like sunlight, hot in your mouth and a little bitter, and the rest of her like seawater. You fuck because it's your freedom, and that's what we did, and that's how we began. Cat with her pretty knees and those little skirts she used to wear when we first met, from school, those creamy yellow skirts, button-down shirts with collars, *St. fucking Brigid's,* and her underpants—that's what I remember from the beginning—the butterscotch smell of those underpants. When we met in that house, it was the Inferno, all the animals swarming and lurking and sniffing, and you couldn't get up, you'd be sitting there in the smoke and you'd say to yourself, come on, man, get up, get the fuck out of here, but you'd ignore it and just stay and have more and do more and then you'd find yourself rolling through somebody's shit, with their fucking pubes in your teeth and lice up your neck. But you couldn't walk away, you couldn't give it up. It still had you by the balls.

But this is not a story about drugs. And it's not a story about me and Cat, because Cat is on her way out of this story. Cat is going to die; I think we both know that. You can smell death on your woman, like grease—not the kind you eat—the murky black oil that drips out of your car and makes a puddle on the ground. The black oil that stains your fingertips. She started to have that smell all the time. She went back to dope like a repentant lover, unraveling the tinfoil like some priceless gift, the apartment smelling of burning wax, of scorched pewter. She had crawled back into its warm lap on her hands and knees. One afternoon I came home from work and found her sprawled on the bed like a dead woman, with you on the other side of the room, screaming, your tiny hands brittle with rage. She'd put you in the laundry basket atop a soft pile of clothes. There were notes from the neighbors shoved under the door, threatening to call the police. I found the lawyer's card on the table. Under his name in fancy script it said *Private Adoptions*. I woke her up and held her in my arms and she wept. "I just wanted to do something right," she confessed. "For once."

The lawyer had told her a week, maybe two. And maybe the waiting was the worst part. Cat wrapped herself up in death. She was ready for it. She'd sit in the chair by the window, looking down at the people on the street. You could hear their voices rising up. Laughter or somebody shouting. Her skin had gone yellow. Sometimes I could get her to go down to the wharf and we'd walk around and I'd hold you up on my chest like a little kitten and even the wind could make you cry, even just the wind. She'd have this blank, frightened-foal look that made my heart weary. I'd have to take her to the clinic sometimes, rows of orange seats, and I'd make a cradle for you on my legs and people would hunch over and look at you out of their ruined faces. A week later the lawyer called to say arrangements had been made. I thought I'd made my peace with it, but I went into the bathroom and threw up my supper.

We left that place, that awful apartment, and we owed the bastard landlord plenty. I helped Cat into the car and buckled your little car seat in the back. I remember the sunlight, bright as Dunkin' Donuts at three o'clock in the morning, when the smell lures you in off the street and you sit down at the counter and they put the coffee in front of you and you think to yourself: There is nothing better than this. The heavy white cup in your hand.

I drove straight to New England, only stopping to use the toilet or buy some food. Cat slept most of the way, waking only to feed or change you. I tried to get her to eat. I had some applesauce and peanut butter and I made her drink some milk. What she needed was a hospital, not some car ride across the country, but she wouldn't let you go until she met them, your future parents. It was all arranged. It was the only way she would give you up.

I want to tell you about the drive, the way I felt. The hours passed slowly, unraveling in a blur, almost like a dream. Sometimes it rained and you and Cat were sleeping and I'd listen to it pounding the roof of the car. I knew I was losing you both. It was the end of something and it made me feel desperate. I remember driving through this town with its dark corners, looking to score. We lost a whole day with me fucked up out of my mind and you screaming in the backseat and Cat hardly moving.

They had a farm in Massachusetts and Cat liked the idea of you growing up someplace pretty, and they had horses, which clinched it. We pulled up this long driveway and my body began to shake a little. It was a mixture of feelings, both awful and good but mostly awful. The rain was coming down hard and I stopped for a moment and put the window down and just listened to it. There is nothing that compares to the sound of a hard rain.

We got up to the top of the driveway and this house appeared, this fucking mansion. They saw the car and came out with umbrellas. Cat wasn't doing well. She started to wheeze like she couldn't breathe right. She couldn't bear it, the whole ordeal; she didn't want to get out. We sat for a moment looking through the fogged-up windshield with the wipers going back and forth, back and forth, and them standing out there in the rain under umbrellas, waiting, and Cat took my hand. She took my hand and she squeezed it. Then she said, "You take her."

She couldn't get out of the car. She just didn't have the strength. And I could feel her slipping away from me. It worried me. It worried me so much. I got out and gave the people a little wave to let them know everything was on like we'd planned, and then I opened the back door and took you out. Cat wouldn't turn around and I understood that she couldn't. The woman who would become your mother ran over with the umbrella, her blue eyes filling with tears. I could see she wanted you like nothing she'd ever wanted before. I could see a lot of things about her in that single moment. I could tell she had suffered in her life and that you were a gift to her. She gasped out loud, putting her hand over her mouth, and touched your head. The rain fell harder, harder than I'd ever heard it before or ever would again, and we ran into the house. I could feel them wanting you so bad. I shook his hand. I don't know what else to say about him. At that point I couldn't really look at him. She smelled like lilacs, I think. Anyway, I took you out of your seat and held you up like the prize that you were, and kissed you on your little forehead, soft as a flower petal, and then I handed you over to her.

They made me sign some papers, and I had to go out and get Cat's signature. Cat said, "Are they all right? Are they good people?" And I told her that they were. And she signed. I left her there in the car to bring in the papers, and I remember feeling the distance between the car and the door was like a whole country, and I did not belong in either place anymore.

When it was all over, when everything had been signed, they walked me out. The woman was holding you close, her back curved like a shield around you. You had started to fuss and she took you inside to give you a bottle, but I didn't think you were hungry. It was another kind of hunger, and you couldn't satisfy it with milk or food, and I knew in my heart it would linger and I found myself wondering if you would eventually get used to it.

The rain had stopped and the sun started shining and the whole car dazzled with raindrops. The windows were all fogged up, and I couldn't see Cat and I had a feeling, like I already knew—and then I thought maybe that's why the sun had come out, that she had made it happen. Even so, I went along with the man and brought him over to the car to meet her. I genuinely liked him and, even though my heart was busted open, I trusted he would be a good father to you. When I opened Cat's door, I saw that she was gone. I guess I started to cry, I don't know, I can't remember, but I took her into my arms and held her there while he went in to call someone. My heart was busted apart. Once it had played music, but now it was smashed on the ground and all the springs had jumped out and were wobbling. Now it made a dull whine.

I held on to her, feeling her body go cold in my hands, and time passed, minutes, maybe hours, and I told her that I loved her, I adored her. Be patient, I whispered. It won't be long before we meet again.

Part One

⌒

Prone to Depression

[sculpture]

Claire Squire, *50 Year Warranty,* 2004. Beeswax and microcrystalline wax on metal stands, vacuum cleaner parts, horsehair, 66¼ x 62 x 26 in. The Museum of Contemporary Art, Los Angeles: gift of the Wellman Foundation.

The sculpture depicts a woman, whose spinal chord is formed out of the hose of an Electrolux vacuum, whose pelvis and coccyx region is formed from the triangular-shaped metal floor nozzle, whose pubic area is formed from the brush attachment, whose nipples are canister wheels, and whose stomach is the bulging vacuum bag, bursting with debris.

The sculpture typifies the artist's assertion that the female body is interpreted as little more than the sum of its parts.

1 ∽

Claire waited out on the porch for a long time, wrapped in her ratty gray sweater. It was cool for August and all of the trees were moving and the wind jangled the chimes in the darkness. It made the flag whip around on the pole. The flag had been there for as long as she could remember. She'd been the one to lower it to half mast when her mother died, the taut rope trembling in her small hands. Her father had stood there with her, smoking a cigar, looking up into the bright sky, watching the flag snap and twist. Now she was losing him too.

She grasped her hair and twisted it into a braid. People always said her hair was her greatest feature, but over the years she'd been reckless with it, contemptuous of anything that made her beautiful. She had no interest in being beautiful. It was her work that made her this way, and all that she'd been through that drove her to it.

She looked out into the darkness where hundreds of fireflies flickered like the lights of alien spaceships. Tiger lilies stretched over the porch railing like the greedy hands of children. Her mother had been the one to plant them. In her straw hat and wooden clogs she'd go out before breakfast and tend to the beds. Her mother had told her that lilies were nearly invincible. You could neglect and abuse them all you wanted, but somehow they always found the strength to uncurl their fists and bloom. It began to rain, splattering the floor of the porch. The air was damp and she could smell the wet grass, the earth. It was a smell she had known well as a child, growing up here in the country. She felt a chill all through her body and went inside. Her son had fallen asleep on the couch with his boots on. The boots were big and black, what he fondly called his prison boots, purchased at a vintage store on Melrose, and he was immeasurably proud of them.

Gently, she untied the laces and pulled them off, then covered him with a blanket. In the tender light she could see how the room had been abused over the years by a steady traffic of strangers. It looked like there'd been a party and no one had bothered to clean up. Glasses left behind on the piano, the coffee table, the radiator. Ashtrays full of cigarettes. Out of habit, she picked up the empty glasses, balancing the ashtrays on the rims, and brought them into the kitchen and set them down on the counter. There was a bottle of vodka on the counter—she thought perhaps it would make her feel a little better. It was good vodka, expensive. She poured a glass and sat at the round table, which was laid with her mother's blue cloth from Provence. The cloth was worn now, and there were a few cigarette burns. Claire had the sudden memory of finding her mother, a perennial insomniac, down here at three o'clock in the morning, drinking sherry and playing solitaire, a cigarette between her lips. She lit her own cigarette and drank the vodka and looked around the unchanged kitchen. There were the same warped cabinets that never stayed shut, painted a butter-knife gray, the shelves stacked with mismatched plates and teacups, the black-and-white tiled floor, the enormous porcelain sink. The pine secretary with its green velvet desk, crammed with old cookbooks. She opened the desk and found a stack of bills and wondered who was keeping his books.

The vodka burned her throat. She drank and waited, hearing the rain. It was a quiet old house; it wasn't hers. She was a stranger here.

Sometime later, maybe an hour, she felt someone's hand on her shoulder. She'd fallen asleep at the table. It was early still, the sky white, nude. The rain had stopped.

"You fell asleep," a woman said in a Jamaican accent. "I've made the assumption you're not a criminal."

Still, she felt caught. Ashamed, she pulled her sweater around her. "I'm his daughter. I grew up in this house."

The woman examined her face as though she were looking for proof. "He's very sick," she said. "I'm his hospice nurse."

Unwittingly, Claire started to cry. It was the last thing she wanted to do in front of this stranger, but she couldn't seem to help it, and they were old tears, they'd been waiting to come out for a long time. The nurse sat down at the table. The sky suddenly looked bruised and it started to rain again and you could hear it beating on the ground.

"I haven't been home for a long time," she said. "We weren't close."

"It doesn't matter," the nurse said. "It's good that you're here, now." She stood up and held out her hand. "Come, we'll go up. He's been waiting for you."

They climbed the stairs, and she entered the cold, blue dream of her father's death. It was very quiet. The air smelled of alcohol and Clorox and burned toast. And when she passed the opened windows she could smell the earth too and she could smell the rain. She sensed that strangers had been here, a parade of friends and caretakers, the kind souls who understood what death was, who nurtured it like a garden of delicate black flowers.

There was a draft in her father's room, the window was cracked. Beyond the dirty glass was the yellow field, the ruined garden. Lilacs trampling the fence.

"Isn't he cold?" she asked the nurse.

"The fresh air is good."

"Can he hear us?"

"Yes, I think so." Claire swallowed hard; she would not cry her guilty tears. She sat down on her father's bed and looked at his face. It was an old man's face. His blond hair had gone white. His chin pointy, his broad cheeks hollow, his mouth fixed in a gargoyle's grimace. His eyes dim, colorless. She put her palm to his cheek. His skin was warm, damp.

"Look who's here, Mr. Squire. It's your daughter, Claire. She's come home."

"It's me, Daddy," she muttered, taking his hand. It was soft in the way a child's hand is soft, before it has learned to be hard. She heard the door settling into its frame and realized that the nurse had left them alone. The room seemed to close in on her. This was her parents' room. The paint-chipped radiators with clanging pipes. The yellow window shades. The Chinese dish on the bureau where her mother had kept her earrings. The Tibetan rug her mother had dragged back from one of their trips. Claire remembered one of her birthday parties, she was eight or nine, all her friends sitting on the steps in party dresses, the lovely Turkish runner, and her mother in a handmade apron, wearing her trademark red lipstick. *Say cheese!* The big windows full of sunlight, pussy willows pressed up against the panes. Something good in the oven. Pink icing on the cupcakes. And her father, in one of his camel-haired sport coats, getting all the girls to giggle and blush.

Her father's chest expanded then deflated. "I'll just sit here with you, all right, Daddy?"

He closed his eyes then opened them again. She held his hand tighter. She sat with him for a long time, looking at his face. Maybe the nurse had been right, she thought. Maybe the past didn't matter now. What mattered was this moment. This moment right now and the one that came next. His dying was a bridge she could cross, and he was waiting for her there, on the other side.

2 ✺

For lunch, the nurse made soup, the chicken bones like babies' fists floating in broth. Claire couldn't bring herself to eat. After lunch, she took Teddy up to see her father. Her son stood in the doorway like an uninvited guest with his long arms and legs, hands shoved in his pockets. She nudged him gently, taking his arm. "It's okay," she said.

They went to the bed and looked down at the old man. Her father's face hadn't changed. His eyes stuck on the ceiling as if someone had Velcroed his gaze. "He's awake?" Teddy asked.

"Yes," the nurse confirmed. "Your grandson is here, Mr. Squire." The nurse tugged on the old man's blanket as if to straighten it, even though it was already perfectly straight. Her father looked like a Kewpie doll in a giant's pocket.

The wind rushed against the house, the screens. The window shades slapped their frames. You could hear the chimes outside. Everything seemed to be moving, but her father was still, his arms at his sides. Claire sat on the bed and took his hand. His fingers were tapered, his fingernails wide and flat like seashells. She had never looked at his hands so carefully. He had lived a long time with his hands and now they were useless. "Dad," she said. "Teddy's here."

Teddy hunched over the bed, his arms crossed over his chest. His face pale with worry, doubt. "He doesn't see me."

"He hears you. He knows you're here."

He left her there with her father. She could hear him going outside, the slam of the screen door. A little while later she could smell his cigarette. He was angry at her, she knew, for keeping him away from here, for refusing her father's charity, and he'd had a shitty life because of it.

She sat on the bed, moving with the guarded solicitude of a stranger. "I could tell you how hard it's been for me," she spoke softly. "I could tell you all that. But I won't." She squeezed his hand hard. "We've hurt each other enough, haven't we?"

Abruptly, his eyes closed. She watched his face, wanting to believe he understood her. His eyes were half moons, slippery, gray. She waited for him to open them, a confirmation of some kind, an apology, but they stayed like that, shut tight.

Later, they walked in the rain. They took umbrellas and crossed the back field. She showed him the old greenhouse, the windows shattered, the grass inside waist high. It was a fragile place, she thought. "There used to be flowers here," she said.

They went down the sloping lawn to the pond and you could see the clouds on the black surface and all the upside-down trees. Moss like spilled paint at their feet. They crossed the tennis court with its torn net, cracks sprouting weeds. The empty pool full of leaves. Overturned Adirondack chairs left out in the grass like some breed of extinct animal. She pictured her mother walking beside her in one of her party dresses, her father in a tuxedo, their shoulders sprinkled

with confetti. Claire had never even come close to having a relationship like that. There had been Billy, Teddy's father, but that had been
a short-lived, drug-induced adventure that had lasted a month. And
she'd messed up that relationship too.

The years had piled up like dull books. Pages of anger and resentment. She'd rip those pages out if she could. Maybe she'd gotten lost,
she thought. It happened to people, it had happened to her. She'd
made mistakes; no one had to tell her. Her lousy judgment when it
came to men. She knew. But she wouldn't take all the blame for it.

She took Teddy out to supper at a café in town. She drank vodka,
watching him eat. They went to a movie at the tiny theater, a French
film with subtitles. Driving back to the house they let the windows
down. Horses were running in the darkness. Teddy made her pull
over so they could hear them. It was a sound, a kind of fury.

The house was silent. She crept up to her room and got into bed.
Listened for a while for Teddy; didn't hear him. At last, she succumbed to sleep, a murky deluge, sewer-tepid. Hours later, the nurse
woke her. Birds were screaming at one another across the field. "He's
gone," was all she said.

They buried her father in the town cemetery, next to her mother. It
was a small gathering, mostly people she didn't know. People her father had worked with over the years, some of whom had driven up
from the city. Skinny, beautiful women in black dresses and high
heels. Men poised in their suits, holding flowers. Claire smiled at them,
grateful that they'd made the trip, but their eyes came back empty. *We
didn't know he had a daughter—he never mentioned you.*

Teddy took her hand. At seventeen, he had a man's hand and
when she stole a look at him she saw a full-grown adult in his
new suit. Even under the circumstances, she couldn't help feeling
proud of him, admiring him in the suit, grateful to him for behaving
himself. For being kind to her. You couldn't teach kindness, she
thought. It was something you were born with. People either had it
or they didn't. He took her hand and squeezed it, a ritual of theirs—
something that they had not done for a very long time—a signal that

meant *I love you*. When he was little, just doing ordinary things like going to the supermarket, she'd take his hand as they crossed the parking lot and squeeze it and he'd squeeze hers back. *I love you too, Mommy*. It came to her that one day she too would die and be buried here in this field. She glanced at Teddy, who had spotted a lone dandelion in the grass. He leaned over and pulled it out and blew the fluffy white spores into the wind.

The rain fell. Edith Piaf on the turntable. She had to order more liquor from Hardy's. People drifted through the rooms, looking at the photographs of her father and his friends. After everyone left it was just her and Teddy. Silently, they ate a meal of spaghetti and she drank from a bottle of Turley, one of her father's favorite wines. She gave him her father's watch, his wallet. He put the watch around his wrist and held it up for her to see and smiled because he was proud to have it. He examined the wallet. It was old, battered. He breathed in the smell of it. They went upstairs to her father's room. There was the empty bed, the sheets stripped. There was the open window.

The following afternoon, her father's old friend and attorney, Irving Lubin, came to see her. They sat in the kitchen. She poured him a drink, vodka. The sun streamed through the old wood blinds, making penitent stripes on the table. Lubin had large, trembling hands. They ate sardines on crackers, doused with lemon. He kept his files in an ancient alligator briefcase that yawned when he opened it like the jaws of an exhausted beast. "Your father was a shrewd businessman," he told her, thumbing through the papers. "You don't owe a penny on this place."

"I don't deserve it," Claire said.

"Oh, I think you do." Lubin looked at her out of his watery eyes. "It's yours now," he said. "Make the most of it." He took out a handkerchief and blotted his tears, then folded the cloth and swept it across his forehead. "I'm an old man now," he told her. "I knew your father a long time."

"He trusted you," she said.

"We understood each other." He looked at her meaningfully. "He loved you very much."

"He had a funny way of showing it."

Lubin nodded. "You've been gone a long time."

"It was easier than being here." She swallowed her drink. She wouldn't tell him how inside her heart she was still a thirteen-year-old girl who'd lost her mother. Her father's way of dealing with her mother's death had been to drink too much, staying out to all hours. Claire had lived on Campbell's soup and tuna fish and Kool-Aid. When she graduated from high school, she went out to CalArts and never planned on coming back.

She'd never asked her father for anything. She used to be proud of it; now she wasn't sure.

Lubin lifted his glass and drank from it, then put it back down on the table methodically, like a chess move. "After his second stroke he called me. He wanted me to sell his old truck. I came over to get it; he was in bad shape. He could barely talk. I had to get right down to his ear. He knew he was going to die. He told me he had one request. Just one." Lubin looked at her. "He wanted you back here, Claire. He wanted you here in this house. He wanted the boy at Pioneer."

She watched as he fished through the files, licking his big thumb, his tongue quick as a toad's. At last he found what he was searching for and handed her a letter with the private high school's letterhead across the top. Both her father and she had attended the school. "He took the liberty of enrolling Teddy. His tuition's paid."

She studied the letter. "I don't understand."

"He wanted to give you something. He wanted to do something important for the boy. He thought if he paid his tuition, you might consider staying."

"My son isn't the prep school type," she said wryly.

"Your father built their gymnasium, sweetheart, I don't think they're too concerned about his academic record."

She shook her head, incredulous. "What did he think? That I'd just drop everything and move back here?"

"Something like that." The old man studied her carefully.

"It's not that I'm ungrateful," she wanted to clarify. "I *am* grateful—

you have no idea. It's been very hard for me. Raising Teddy. My work, my sculptures, they're expensive to build. It's been difficult." She finished her drink, trying not to cry. "I just wish he'd tried harder when he was alive, that's all I'm saying. I wish we both had."

"I can appreciate that."

"The awful thing is, if he hadn't gotten sick we probably never would have come back here." She started to cry. "I've been such an idiot, Irving. *Such an idiot!* He missed so much. *Years.*"

"I know he did, honey. You both did."

Claire nodded; it was the truth.

Lubin closed his briefcase and patted the leather top affirmatively, his business complete. Then he stood up and put on his jacket. "It's a good life here, honey."

Claire walked him to the door and he turned to her and took her arm and kissed her forehead. "I know it's hard to see it, my dear, but this is your father's apology. Maybe he couldn't do it when he was alive, but he's doing it now."

3 ∽

Nate Gallagher woke in his Brooklyn apartment, his bedsheets soaked with sweat. She had come to him again in a dream, cradling a swaddled infant in her arms. He went to work that morning in a fog, riding the subway with the detached preoccupation of a condemned man. He spilled coffee on his trousers in the teachers' lounge, and during his first-period class, entirely forgot the content of his lecture, staring out at the sea of faces with a bewildered gaze of apology. As he was leaving work, there was a freak electrical storm and it began to hail. He pulled up his coat, an old lumber jacket he'd bought used, and ducked into the public library for shelter and wasted an hour in the lounge near the magazine racks. A copy of *Academic Monthly* caught his eye. When he was a boy, his mother had had a habit of perusing the job listings in the back of the magazine and he would sit with her in the living room of their borrowed house, entertaining the possibility of moving to some other place, someplace far away like Montana, where there was open space and less of what his mother called the burden of judgment, even though they both knew that his father would never leave Choate. *Splendor in the Berkshires* read the headline of one of the current job listings. The Pioneer School, which billed itself as a prestigious college preparatory school, advertised the need for a writing instructor. It was only for one year, filling in for a teacher on sabbatical.

On an impulse, he sent a letter to the Head, with a copy of his résumé and references, and two weeks later, the Head's wife, Maggie Heath, called him. "Nate Gallagher?" Her voice came as an accusation. She identified herself, explaining how she'd gone to Choate and how Nate's father had been her favorite teacher.

Nate's father had been something of a legend in those days, hamming up his professorial image with a wool vest and tartan beret. With his lilting Irish brogue, he could transform even the most pedestrian prose. He was famous for his recitation of *Beowulf*, a highlight of the spring semester of sophomore year. But when it came to his own family, he had little patience for the routines of domesticity, or for the unexceptional qualities of his only son.

For a variety of reasons, Nate had never graduated from Choate. He'd gone to San Francisco and met Catherine; two years later she was dead. At a loss, having nowhere else to go, he drove back to Wallingford and appeared on his parents' doorstep. Nate stayed there for several weeks, holed up in his mother's sewing room, drinking as much whiskey and swallowing as many pills as his body would tolerate, until his mother shoved something under the door. An application to Yale. "Your father has made a phone call to the dean of admissions," she whispered. "They're willing to take you if you get your GED."

The next morning, Nate left the house and drove to New Haven, but not to attend Yale. Instead, he passed his high school equivalency and enrolled in the community college. He fumbled through that first semester, until an English professor praised one of his short stories.

He kept his writing to himself, but put all his spare time into his work—that's what he'd begun to call it—his *work*. In his mind, writing was a way of reaching Cat, a way of finding her again and again inside that made-up world. He didn't know where it would take him, or whether he would make his living at it, but, like some essential nutrient, it seemed to keep him alive. To support himself he earned his teaching certification and secured a job in a sprawling public high school in Brooklyn, teaching suspicious, intolerant students how to make sentences. Everything about his life there, where he lived, his neighborhood, the constant alarming insinuation of strangers—once he'd been mugged at gunpoint—had turned him into someone else, someone he barely recognized. On the streets, he had learned to be invisible. It was a kind of exile, a place he'd banished himself to. There were the tenements, bristling with barbed wire. Windows were barred up to the rooftops—it occurred to him that he too was a prisoner. His gloomy apartment, the dim corridors of the high school where he taught, the numb and indifferent students, his taciturn colleagues, a routine of futility, of compromise. Over time, it had worn him down.

On the day of his interview at Pioneer, the Head, Jack Heath, gave him a tour of the 350-acre campus, loaning him a pair of thigh-high muck boots for the expedition. It was early March: the beginning of mud season in the Berkshires, although, Heath reminded him, it was not uncommon to see snow into May. On the tour, Heath explained that the school had once been the summer home of Eliot Chase, a nineteenth-century entrepreneur. The property abutted the state forest and had been a working farm for a century before it had been turned into a school. Heath had been Head for nearly seven years and implied, in a voice teeming with pride, that when he'd arrived on the scene the school had nearly fallen to ruin. "I had to chase a cow out of one of the classrooms!" he told him, his eyes bright with the memory. "I saw this place as an opportunity," Heath said wistfully. "To start something new, you know, to make changes, to fix it."

"Is it fixed?"

"I like to think so. When we first came, the kids would come to class barefoot. We'd catch the teachers getting stoned in the woods. Now, they're a whole different species of animal."

"How'd you turn it around?" Nate asked.

"In a word?" Heath grinned with pride. "Uniforms."

Heath himself was the image of a prep school headmaster, what Nate's mother would have called a usual suspect. Khaki trousers, a cable-knit cardigan (unlike a crew neck, the cardigan made a more progressive, even *evolved* impression), a red bow tie (which Nate interpreted as a coy, Republican gesture), and bookish, wire-rim glasses. Less typical was the loosely knitted persimmon scarf that his wife might have made him for Christmas. The ruddy flush in his cheeks was either good health or alcohol, Nate couldn't decide which. Nevertheless, he suspected that Heath's overall package dazzled the mothers.

"I met your father, once," Heath told him. "What a great character."

"He certainly was," Nate said. "He's not doing so well now. He can recite *The Duino Elegies* by heart, but ask him what day of the week it is . . ."

On the first of August, Nate caught an express train from Penn Station to Hudson, New York. He carried a single suitcase. The excursion was two hours long, a picturesque journey along the river, and when he arrived at the station he hired a cab and instructed the driver to take him to the nearest used-car dealership. The driver knew of one in Canaan, some twenty miles away. In just a few minutes they were in the country, fields of corn and alfalfa, desolate old farms. Nate cracked the window, smelling the earth. His eyes burned in the white glare. It was good to be out, he thought. He was like a man who'd been granted asylum, and for the first time in years he felt free.

4 ∞

The time had come to make peace with the house.

It had been two weeks since her father's funeral and still Claire walked around like a disoriented housekeeper as though at any moment the owners would come home and send her away. It was a dark place, shrill with mothballs. Dense mustard carpeting. A hovering gloom.

That morning she tugged down the heavy drapes. Many of the windows refused to open. She had to use soap, coaxing the splin-tered wood to relent. The house had been holding its breath for a century. Now the wind rushed through the screens and sang to her, a sad wheezing song. She pulled out the carpeting, cutting it up with an X-Acto knife. Sweating into the filthy wool. She hauled the stink-ing rug out to the yard, dragging it like a corpse. Then sunlight came and went across the wood floors. She scrubbed the wide boards on her hands and knees. There were mice. Lumpy brown spiders unrav-eled from their webs like spools of thread. She cut oranges into a pail of vinegar and washed the floors. She was a slave to the house. She wanted it to like her. She did everything herself, her body running with sweat, sweat dripping down her arms, her wrists. It was a quiet time. Aside from Teddy, whole days passed and she spoke to no one.

Sometimes she'd pause at the windows. Her father had given her this gift, an ache in her belly when she thought of it. Guilt like a water snake in her bowels. She emptied his closets, the jackets, ties, the bulky overcoats, his *costumes,* he would say, her hands lovingly smoothing the soft cashmere. Sometimes she sensed him standing in the doorway, smoking one of his cigars. She gathered the clothes in her arms, the unruly pile like a screaming child. She would take everything to Goodwill. Her mother's things she would bring to the women's shelter. Even after all these years, her father had never both-ered to clean out her mother's things. Her mother had been exotic; she'd had excellent taste, a dancer's posture. She wore heavy beads and rings, dangling carnelian earrings. There were rows of cashmere sweaters entombed in plastic bags, mothballs spilled out like lost teeth. Her shoes in boxes, old Ferragamo pumps wrapped in tissue paper, never worn. Claire missed her terribly; she'd never stopped missing her.

She wanted to get into the barn, to make herself a place to work. She wanted to get her hands on her women. Her hands thick with plaster, the wet, warm feeling like birth. Nobody knew her. She was all alone. Maybe her father knew. Maybe he was watching her now, following her around, his ghost shuffling down the hall. She could smell his dead man's breath. He had not gone up to heaven. He had stayed down in the house so he could watch her.

The house was a blessing, it was a curse. There was the luxury of walking barefoot through the rooms, across the pale wood floors. The bathroom with its porcelain basin, apricot soap. Sunlight streaming in on her naked skin. And through every window the open fields, the pear and apple trees, the final days of summer. The trees were heavy with their sloppy green leaves. Somehow, she knew this place had saved her life and she wanted to show it her appreciation. In her old jeans and one of her father's work shirts, she pulled down wallpaper, the torn pieces like a puzzle on the floor. Peacock feathers here and there. Monkeys and palm trees and little men in turbans. She sanded and scraped and the whole house began to sing. She let the radio play. Teddy convinced her to paint everything white. In the evenings, they painted together, after supper, as the sky turned from blue to black. He said little to her, but she could see a change in him. No longer the frowning boy. He smiled more, he whistled to the music. When their arms grew tired, they went to bed.

She had first seen the girl on Route 7, walking along the side of the road carrying a plastic bag. She'd been hitchhiking, walking backward with her thumb stuck out. She was a tall girl, maybe twenty, with stringy brown hair. She had a strong face, prominent bones. She saw her once outside Wal-Mart, crossing the intersection, running for the bus. Then she saw her again at Sunrise House.

Sunrise House was a women's shelter in Pittsfield that took donations on Sundays. The shelter was located in a modest neighborhood at the end of a cul-de-sac, set back behind a high hedge of bushes. That morning, as Claire pulled up in front of the small house, the same girl was coming out. Up close she was pale and slim, her hair pulled back in a ponytail. She had on a pink sweater, two sizes too big for her, and walked with her head down. Claire cut the engine and got out and opened the trunk. The girl glanced over her shoulder, warily, and that's when Claire saw the black eye.

Claire turned away, pretending not to notice—not wanting to intrude on the girl's privacy. Yet there was nothing private about a bruise like that, and regardless of what the circumstances had been, witnessing it made Claire want to do something—anything—to help her. When she turned back around, she saw that the girl had crossed the street and was walking briskly up the sidewalk. Claire took the box of her mother's clothes out of the trunk. Her mother's raincoat was on top, an old Burberry with the classic plaid lining—just about the girl's size, she thought, setting it aside. She carried the box onto the porch and placed it on a table under a sign that said *Donations*. She could hear the sound of children playing in the backyard. Back in her car, she pulled down the street and caught up with the girl. She put her window down and asked if she wanted a ride. The girl hesitated, squinting around to see if anyone was watching, her eye a garish purple in the sunlight. When she got into the car, Claire could smell the alcohol they'd used to clean the wound and something else, a kind of musky cologne. Her nose was running; it was red and raw.

"Where can I take you?"

The girl looked straight ahead through the windshield. "I live far from here." She spoke with an accent, either Russian or Polish. "Can you just take me to Lenox? They have a bus."

"All right."

The girl's white pumps were scuffed and dirty. She had high arches, bunions. Round muscles in her calves. A dancer, Claire suspected. She sat with her ankles crossed, her knees turned out, and her hands clenched in her lap like a first grader on picture day. Her purse was small, a child's purse.

"Do you need a coat?" Claire asked, showing her the coat.

The girl looked at it. "You don't want it?"

"It's too small. It was my mother's coat."

The girl examined it. "It's nice. You sure?"

"Of course. What's your name?"

"Petra," she glanced at Claire uncertainly. "Here, they call me Pearl."

"Where are you from?"

"I am from Poland."

Claire offered her a cigarette and she took it, gratefully. "My eye is ugly, yes?"

"Does it hurt?"

The girl shrugged. She gazed out the window, her eyes empty.

"I hope it gets better soon," Claire said, at a loss. "It's a nice day, isn't it?"

"It's too windy," the girl complained.

"How long have you been here, in this country?"

"Two years only."

"Your English is very good."

She jerked her head, arrogantly, as if she didn't care if it was good or not. "I don't like America," she said finally.

"That makes two of us," Claire said.

"What you say?"

"Nothing. Just an expression." They rode for a while in silence. The girl opened her window and let the sun onto her face. "Are you a dancer?"

The girl nodded as if it were a secret. "How do you know?"

"Your feet."

"I was with my company. We came here to perform. You know Jacob's Pillow?"

"Of course."

The girl rubbed her nose. "I can get out here."

"Look," Claire said. "If you ever need work." She wrote down her phone number on a scrap of paper. "I'm a sculptor. You could model for me."

The girl took the paper and got out. "Thanks," she said, taking the coat. She got out, affecting a cool arrogance, and as she climbed the steps of the town hall to wait for her bus she threw Claire's number in the trash. Claire sighed, feeling stupid, useless; the girl obviously didn't want her charity. She stood back in the shadows to wait. The town hall had been built in the early 1800s, a brick building with Corinthian columns, and it occurred to Claire that not much had changed over the centuries since it had been built—women were still getting beaten up by the men who claimed to love them. Driving away, Claire felt strangely anxious—regretting that she hadn't driven the girl home. It would have saved her the humiliation of being the main attraction on the local bus, one that would inspire either pity or deranged satisfaction.

5 ∽

The driver brought Nate to the garage in Canaan, explaining that the owner of the place was a mechanic of distinction who always had good European cars for sale. The mechanic was a wiry Frenchman named Otto, whose tiny paneled office was covered with pictures from his glory days in racing. Otto walked Nate around the small lot, apologizing for his low inventory. He had only two cars for sale: an older Ford pickup and a '97 BMW. "What about that?" Nate pointed to a vintage blue Thunderbird with whitewalled tires. "Now there's a car."

"That's a customer's car," Otto said. "Not for sale."

"Who owns it?"

"An unusual man owns that car."

"Well," Nate said, as though he were impressed.

"I fix all his cars. We're good friends," Otto said, as if trying to convince Nate. "I've been to his house. He has parties with big sweeping tents. Miniature horses. Even monkeys, once. Food, you've never seen such food. Banquets."

"What does he do?"

"That's privileged information, I'm afraid," Otto said. "But he does it very well, I promise you that."

Nate bought the truck and paid the Frenchman in cash. The truck's owner had recently died of a stroke. "He was a meticulous man,"

Otto told him. "Very wise." The man had had a long career as a theater director and lived on a farm in Stockbridge. "It is very sad what happens when we are old," Otto said. "Tragic."

Otto folded the title into an envelope and handed Nate the keys. "It's a good truck," he assured Nate, caressing the hood of the pickup affectionately. "She won't give you any trouble."

Nate shook his hand and got into the truck and drove off the lot. He slid the envelope onto the visor, where he discovered a photograph, a Polaroid, which had been fastened in place by a rubber band. Nate pulled over to take a closer look at it, a forgotten relic of a dead man's life. It was a picture of a girl, maybe seventeen or eighteen, leaning against a tree, holding a gray rabbit, her long yellow hair twisted into two symmetrical braids. She was smiling at the photographer, not just an ordinary smile, Nate thought, but one that suggested some deeper knowledge, a thrilling secret. She was tall, wearing a white peasant blouse and a skirt she might have made herself out of a pair of blue jeans, cut at the seams and sewn down the middle, embroidered with rainbows and hearts and flowers. Someone had written her name along the bottom of the Polaroid: *Claire, Jack Rabbit Farm, 1988.* It was a lovely photograph, he thought, and debated bringing it back to Otto, who might have sent it back to the girl, wherever she was, as a poignant gesture, but abruptly he decided against it. He returned the Polaroid to the visor and secured it under the elastic, where it had been all along, and flipped the visor back into place.

He drove east toward Massachusetts, passing wide green fields and brown barns and large country homes with tennis courts and swimming pools and acres of open land. There were gardens and white picket fences and pumpkin fields and weary, paint-chipped churches and graveyards with crooked black stones. He crossed over the border and took the state road south, into Stockbridge, a quaint little town straight out of the Norman Rockwell paintings that had made it famous. There were historic buildings of whitewashed brick. Old clapboard houses. Window boxes blazing with petunias. American flags snapped and twisted in the bright wind.

The apartment was in a Victorian house on Main Street. It was a brooding old place set back from the road behind an ornery row of lilac bushes. The clapboards were painted a tawny shade of yellow, and there were chalky blue shutters and window boxes. The front porch held an assortment of creaky wicker furniture. Nate rang the little bronze bell beside the door and waited, glancing through the lace curtains. He stood there feeling foolish, then finally stepped inside the empty vestibule. Someone was playing a piano, Chopin. It was coming through the door of a first-floor apartment that had been left ajar. Nailed on the same door was a sign: *Superintendent*. "Hello?" Nate knocked, peering into the apartment.

The music stopped abruptly and another sound took its place—the sound of birds. Nate ventured down a narrow hall into a small living room, the walls of which were lined with towering stacks of birdcages. There were fat white doves and cockatiels and parakeets. The superintendent, a once famous pianist named Larkin—Nate put him in his early nineties—sat at his piano, hunched over the keys as if he and the instrument were having an intimate discussion. He wore a rumpled linen suit with glaring tea-colored sweat stains, red suspenders, and a striped bow tie. On his feet were a pair of black rubber flip-flops; his toenails were thick and yellow as the claws of his birds. The place stank of birds and gritty coffee and ripe bananas and the ash on the old man's cigarette was two inches long.

"Mr. Larkin?" When there came no response, Nate tapped him on the arm. "Mr. Larkin?" He spoke loudly.

The old man jumped, his face flooded with color. "You don't have to shout!"

"I'm Nate Gallagher. I'm here about the apartment."

"Ah, yes, Mr. Gallagher." Larkin struggled out of the chair and extended his trembling hand. "Welcome to Amadeus House."

They shook. "Those birds," Nate said. "They're really something."

"My old lovers," Larkin said. "You don't have to worry, they're good tenants, they know the rules. Come, let's get you established."

Using his cane, he opened a small cabinet that contained rows of skeleton keys and, with surprising agility, selected two for Nate. "The front door is locked promptly at ten," he warned. "If you don't have your key, you'll have to sleep in the yard." Nate followed him up the wide staircase with its shiny black banister, across the spacious landing. Windows with diamond-shaped panes overlooked the front walk. Nate noticed a girl walking toward the door, carrying a stack of sheet music. He wondered if she was another tenant.

"Resident," the old man corrected him when he asked. "No, that's one of my students."

They peered over the banister as the young girl entered the vestibule and walked toward Larkin's apartment. She was wearing cutoff shorts and a T-shirt and had her sunglasses pulled up on her head like a headband. "I'll be down in a moment, my dear," Larkin called down to her.

The girl tilted her head, wickedly appraising Nate. "Who are you?"

"This is Mr. Gallagher. He's a novelist."

Nate bowed slightly. "Well, not officially."

"Not officially what?" the girl said.

"Well, I'm trying to write one."

The girl smirked, raising her eyebrows. "I'm kind of in a hurry, Mr. Larkin."

"Begin with your scales, my dear. I won't be a moment." With his trembling hand Larkin unlocked the door and they went inside. The apartment was large and bright with the oversized rooms of a bygone era. Sunlight fell through the tall windows. Leafy vines clung to the windowpanes, dappling the floor with heart-shaped leaf-shadows. The only furniture in the living room was a worn velvet sofa the color of pears. The bedroom overlooked a back garden with a birdbath and wrought-iron benches. There was a four-poster bed, a large antique dresser, a desk and chair. The kitchen was modest, but neat.

"Satisfied, Mr. Gallagher?"

"It'll do fine."

Larkin gave him the keys and shuffled out. Nate went into the bedroom to try out the bed. The rickety frame protested, the springs squealed. He lay there for a while, listening to the sounds of the house wafting up through the heating vents. The muffled voices of strangers. The opening and closing of doors. Larkin's impertinent student, practicing scales.

The next day his books and computer arrived from the city. He set up his desk in front of the diamond-shaped windows where he could watch the people down on the street. He rather liked his view of the old brick library across the street and the coffee shop alongside of it with its plate-glass windows. There were three other tenants in the house and he came to know their patterns. He shared the second floor with a pair of identical twins, unsmiling sisters who went off to work each morning in nursing scrubs. Often they'd return from work carrying forlorn bouquets of flowers—he would find trails of faded petals on the stairs. He had never met the tenant on the third floor, the only evidence of whose existence was the sound of a cello that wandered down mournfully through the vents, and the startling rattle of empty wine bottles that collected in a recycling bin just outside the door. Nate did not mind the maudlin cello, but on some occasions it influenced his mood and he'd have to leave the house. He'd walk through town, looking into the windows of houses with their lights coming on, families sitting down to supper. Or he'd walk through the cemetery with its Pilgrim stones and think of Catherine, the only woman he had ever loved. Sometimes, he'd go to Hardy's, a dark little bar on Water Street that catered to the townies. It was a drinker's bar and the grim atmosphere suited him, the small lamps on the tables with their crooked red shades, the old books scattered around the place, written by the great writers of the Berkshires—Hawthorne and Melville and Edith Wharton—the dark green walls covered with oil paintings, most of them horse pictures or scenes of the hunt, and the lingering musk-odor of beer and whiskey. They had Ballantine on tap and a pool table in the back. The bartender had an unusual turnip-shaped head and a mustache that resembled a salamander. He poured a liberal glass of scotch, which kept all the regulars, including Nate, coming back for more.

6

One night, against his better judgment, he left the bar and went for a drive. The long black roads were flooded with fog. The broken yellow lines fed his vision like bread crumbs, luring him into some forbidden place. He had no business driving down Hawthorne Road at one o'clock in the morning after drinking half a quart of whiskey, yet he'd been putting it off since the day he'd arrived, and he couldn't wait any longer. Just a glimpse of her, that's all he wanted; maybe it would be enough.

He had not forgotten their road, a dirt driveway up the mountain, a mile long into wilderness. People called it exclusive, living apart from everyone else, being separate—but he couldn't imagine it. *Excluded* was a word he'd use. He crossed over a short bridge, the sound of the river filling his ears like the rain that had fallen that afternoon. The day came back with startling clarity. The eerie yellow light in the car. The baby fussing. The greenish tint to Cat's skin. *You take her,* she had said.

He'd been a different man then.

The fog grew denser near the top of the hill. He shut off his headlights and pulled over and parked in the bushes, then went up the rest of the way on foot. It was like walking through a cloud. At last the house appeared, blurred by the fog. A single lamp was lit on the second floor. A vintage black Mercedes sat in the circular driveway. He heard a noise coming from the dark fields and realized it was the sound of horses. Beyond the white fence he saw a silver horse galloping through the fog. His heart felt tight, like he couldn't breathe, and his eyes went damp. For him, it was a haunted place. He'd waited two hours in the driveway for the coroner, he recalled, hearing the infant screaming inside the house. They'd covered Cat with a red velvet blanket and taken her away in a black station wagon.

Following the wooded boundary of the property, Nate went around to the back and stood in an open field. It was late now and the house was dark. He stood there, conscious of the water seeping into his boots, and of the fact that he badly wanted a cigarette, even though he had quit. The horses had come to the fence behind him and were stamping their hooves. He turned to look at them. The largest was jerking its head. When he looked back at the house he saw that someone had entered the kitchen. It was Golding, the man who'd adopted his daughter seventeen years before, standing in a wedge of florescent light, his hand up on his chest like a pledge as he contemplated what to eat. He looked older of course, Nate thought, he'd put on some weight. Finally, he chose something and closed the refrigerator door. The room went black.

Nate stood there for another moment. His heart was beating very fast. He could hear the wind sweeping across the field. He tried to imagine what it must be like, living here in this place. He could never have given her this life, he thought. And it was what Cat had wanted for her, he understood that now. Cat didn't want their child growing up poor and she had doubted his abilities and he had not proved himself to her. He would have liked to have done that, but never got the chance. That place they'd lived, that awful apartment, roaches big as his thumbs. There had been other babies in that building, he recalled. The Cubans downstairs, the Samoans on the ground floor. He could have done it; he could have raised her—somehow. He could have been her father. But the truth of it was he hadn't wanted to.

He had made her—he and Catherine had made her together—and it had been miraculous, yet he could not appreciate the miracle. He had no claim to her. She was a splinter in his heart, too deep to retrieve no matter how cunning the tool.

Back in the apartment, he fixed himself a drink and sat at his desk and began to work. He had only a small light and it cast an orange glow around the room. The window was open to the quiet street and occasionally he'd hear a couple pass by on the sidewalk below, talking softly to each other. Moths drilled their bodies into the screens and every so often he'd flick them off, sending them reeling into the night. He wanted very badly to write. He had things to say. His journey back from heroin had taken years and it had been an important journey. The madness of that time lingered still. He had decided that writing about it would somehow free him of it. He wanted to write about a man like himself, who had come to a point in his life. He wanted to dig a hole and put the past inside it and cover it back up again. He didn't know if flowers would grow there or not. He hoped they would.

Suddenly tired, he lay down on his bed, admonishing himself for snooping around the Goldings' property like some kind of pervert. He didn't want to think what might have happened if he'd gotten caught. It had been a stupid thing to do. He closed his eyes, trying to revise in his mind his justification for coming back here, for taking a position at the very school the girl attended where he might very possibly be her teacher—the idea that he would come to know her and, yes, perhaps, even become a mentor of sorts, consumed him with both guilt and longing. Yet, he reasoned, he saw little real harm in it, as he would never reveal to her who he was.

In those early weeks before school started he found himself caught up in a routine. He would work on his book most of the day, then explore the neighboring towns in the afternoon. He always took his breakfast at the café across the street. The waitress was named Hazel and she recognized him when he came in now and always poured his coffee without asking if he wanted it and he always thanked her. In a matter of weeks, his status had been apparently raised from tourist to local, which was substantially better as Hazel generally neglected the tourists, who would shift and careen their torsos in an effort to get her attention. The locals were an odd assortment, an interchangeable collection of artists and madmen and a group he called the ex-people. The ex-people generally had money, and some had plenty of it. They had moved from someplace else with the intention of disappearing off the face of the Earth. They wanted to blend in and pretend to be anonymous, although they weren't generally the sorts of people who could tolerate anonymity at all—those people went to places like Idaho and Montana. In Nate's estimation, the ex-people liked to give the impression that they had relinquished the comforts of suburbia for a higher cause—as if they were living on the tundra as opposed to in a community that deprived them of absolutely nothing. Their concept of living the life of the rugged individualist was driving around in a mud-splattered Range Rover affixed with leftist bumper stickers—he had to admit they had a certain appeal. More than once, while hiking in the Berkshire wilderness, he'd heard a voice drilling through the trees like a woodpecker, signifying the approach of an ex-person on his cell phone.

One afternoon, Maggie Heath called and invited him to a concert at Tanglewood, a Mahler symphony. He was to meet her outside the gate. It was a lovely afternoon for a concert, nearly the last of the season, and Nate was glad to go. The sun was hazy, the air humid, the sort of weather that made him want to sleep. Maggie was dressed in a white eyelet sundress, her skin so pale it looked almost lavender. "Well, *hello* there," she said, standing on her tippy toes to kiss him. She stood back, appraising him with motherly concern. "You look neglected."

"Don't be silly."

"The apartment? Is it all right?"

"It's very," he hesitated, "musical."

"I know, I know. The goddamned piano. But it was really *cheap*. You can't *find* apartments around here in August. And you have to admit, it's big on charm."

"No argument there," he said.

"He was a very good pianist, you know. Back in the day." She smiled, and the sunlight brought out the pale blue color of her eyes. She was the kind of woman who was constantly accused of being cute, he thought. Her strawberry-blond hair was pulled back under a pink headband and her skin was covered with freckles; it looked as though someone had sprinkled her with cinnamon. "I've brought a picnic." She held up a little basket.

"Marvelous."

"Come, Jack's waiting. He's over there." She pointed far into the distance, across a sea of blankets. He followed her to their spot on an Indian tapestry and Jack Heath stood up to greet him. "Hello there, Gallagher." They shook hands. "Welcome to the Berkshires. Help yourself to a beer."

The concert was just about to start. Nate took a bottle of beer out of the cooler. It was Guinness, and he was thirsty and it tasted good. Maggie gave him a lawn chair and they all sat down as the music began. Nate stretched out his legs and looked around. Many people had brought picnics; some were already drinking wine. Some of the women were wearing dresses and straw hats. Several people were napping, newspapers spread across their chests, hats across faces. Children ran barefoot throughout the maze of people, jumping from blanket to blanket. There was a large tree in the distance with low-hanging limbs that seemed to beckon the children; Nate counted seven perched on its leafy boughs. There were parents and babies and teenagers and old people and there were lovers, rolled together under the late sun. The symphony had a tone of longing that filled him with a momentary despair and he had to make a conscious effort to smile, wanting to reassure Maggie that he was enjoying himself immensely. He was glad for the fact that he was not required to talk. In dutiful silence, Maggie opened her basket and began to fix him a plate. The basket was neatly packed. He noticed a thin volume of poetry, Sylvia Plath, tucked in alongside the plastic containers. He watched as she fixed him a plate of fried chicken and bean salad and corn bread. Everything about her, the deliberate way she moved, her small body efficient as a gymnast's, her solicitous gaze, the white dress, her prim pink mouth, made him feel somehow lost. It seemed to him that something was being established between them that he felt he had no control of. It unraveled between them while binding them up. He sensed her wanting him to like her, to trust her. He sensed her needing him too, perhaps even desperately. She seemed intent on gaining his approval, in the way that a child would—but perhaps he was just imagining it.

When it was over, he thanked them and said good-bye and Maggie squeezed his hand, gazing up at him. "Don't be a stranger."

7 ✧

The Heaths lived in a small clapboard house on the outskirts of campus. Maggie had called to invite him over for dinner to kick off the school year, which started tomorrow. He turned onto the Pioneer campus then pulled up a narrow dirt driveway that led to the house. Originally one of the guest cottages, it was situated on a secluded bluff overlooking the lake. Under a canopy of ancient oaks, the house had a storybook quality with its lovely stone chimney, green shutters, and bluestone terrace. It was a warm evening and he'd begun to sweat under his blazer. Maggie Heath opened the door with a smile. She was dressed all in pink down to her painted toenails, her hair pulled back in a ponytail, girlishly tied with a ribbon. "You've got some catching up to do," she said, holding up her drink. "What do you like, gin?"

"Whiskey, if you have it. I'm not much of a drinker," he said, wanting to dispel any suspicions she might have based on his infamy at Choate, but it was a blatant lie and she probably knew it.

"Oh, you'll come to value the pastime. The winters here are very long." She poured him a generous glass of scotch. "Come, come sit down. Jack's washing up. He's been at the club all day, playing golf. Do you play?"

"Not well."

"You should go out with him sometime. You'd have some fun."

He doubted that; he wasn't terribly fond of the game. She led him into the living room and they sat on adjacent couches. On the coffee table was a tray of cheese and crackers. A wall of windows overlooked a stone terrace and the lake. The room seemed to simmer with disorder. It had a certain "make-do" quality, as if, any minute, the Heaths might pick up and leave. The couches were covered with Indian tapestries, the sort college students hung on their walls, and books were recklessly shoved on the shelves as if with contempt. There was a goldfish bowl on the table, the water in which had evaporated, only an inch or two remained. A green slime clung to the rim and the poor, lone fish seemed to be struggling for air, tilting onto its side like a slowly sinking boat. Nate had grown up in a house like this, with cheap furniture and books all over the place, and there was something about being with Maggie that brought it all back to him. She was a kindred spirit, he thought hopefully, a sister he'd never had. Looking at her now, he could still see the girl he remembered, serious and determined, but she was thinner these days, and there was something vulnerable about her that hadn't been there before. She looked almost breakable.

"Cheers."

"Cheers."

"You're going to love it here," she assured him. "There's just something about the Berkshires." She delivered the comment like advertising copy. "I don't know what it is, exactly. It's a feeling, I guess." She seemed lost in thought for a moment as she looked out at the lake. He followed her gaze. The surface of the lake sparkled in the sunlight.

"That's some view."

"It *is* nice," she said. Her forehead tightened. "We *do* love it here."

Somehow he wasn't convinced. "You've got some good books. Who's the Pound fanatic?"

"Oh, that would be Jack. At one point he was writing a dissertation on him. He's got a stack of papers someplace." She got up and went to the bar and came back with the whiskey and the gin.

"I didn't realize Jack had his doctorate."

"Oh, he didn't finish." Her voice swelled with doom. "We had our daughter, Ada." She frowned, attempting to explain, pouring more gin into her glass. "He left his program to work."

"He can always go back to it," Nate said, encouragingly.

She nodded politely, but Nate could tell it wasn't in the cards.

"What about you?"

"Me?" She blushed.

"Aren't you some kind of poet?" She'd been editor of their high school literary journal. "You rejected me, in fact," he complained.

"Did I?"

"I've never quite gotten over it." He smiled. "You were good."

"I wouldn't go that far," she said. "I write occasionally. When I'm inspired. *Or* depressed." She said it as a joke, but he found himself believing that depression might be routine for Maggie Heath.

"Inspiration is a fickle enterprise," he said, sounding suddenly like his father. "Depression is a far more reliable source of motivation."

"Sad but true." She laughed.

"I'd love to read them sometime, if you'd let me."

"No you wouldn't. They're awful."

"My favorite kind. Have you published any?" He knew she hadn't.

"Don't be ridiculous." She made a face. "Speaking of which, I loved your stories. Jack too. We're really thrilled to have you here. I hope you're working on a book."

"I'm actually writing a novel."

"That's wonderful. Do you have a publisher?"

"No. Not yet." He looked down at his hands. "Hopefully, one day."

"Of course you will," she said. "You're very talented." She was curled up on the sofa, her bare feet tucked beneath her. "I'm not surprised you turned out to be a writer. It must have been fascinating growing up in that house. All those famous people coming and going."

"Rarely fascinating," he said. "But I'll admit it wasn't typical." In truth, he'd resented his parents' open-door policy—his mother endlessly doting on guests, cooking elaborate meals. As a boy he'd felt somehow in the way. The poets were the worst of the lot. Drunken freeloaders who'd stay up half the night reciting their tortured verses while Nate and his parents squirmed on the couch. There'd been one man—his name was Stevens—a bald, chain-smoking academic in a black turtleneck who was forever posing like his book jacket photo—he'd won some tony poetry prize—who'd turned him on to heroin. Nate remembered the man's convertible, some party in New Haven where they'd scored and the reeling euphoria afterward, under the stars. Once he'd had a taste, there was no good enough reason to stop. Unlike his fellow classmates, the people he got high with were real, flawed just like he was. And there were girls—all kinds of girls; girls who sat at his mother's dining room table in their thrift shop

Pucci dresses or the college girls in their little tweed jackets, who'd come back to campus for alumni weekend—some had begun to publish what Stevens had called horny-girl poems—his father found them appalling—who'd ride his hips all night on his narrow bed and slither out like rodents at dawn, knowing he had to be up for school in the morning.

"Tell me about Brooklyn, the high school there. I imagine it was a difficult place."

"It's a whole different world." He suddenly felt protective of his work there, his students. "They're good kids," he said. "It's a rough place to grow up."

"I know rough," she said with disdain. "Before we came here we were at the Remington Pond School."

"I don't know it."

"Up in Maine. Kids with major issues. We had a hard time. It was hard on Ada." She frowned. "We did six years up there."

"You make it sound like a prison sentence."

"For me it was," she said quietly. "I felt very—" She began to say something, but stopped when her husband entered the room.

"Very what?" Jack Heath walked toward Nate and held out his hand. "Hello, Gallagher."

Nate stood up and they shook hands. "Jack."

"Isolated," Maggie said. "Remington Pond."

"Ah yes." Heath was freshly showered and smelled of aftershave. He had on a starchy white oxford shirt. His khaki trousers were meticulously pressed. "Did she tell you what happened?"

"I didn't want to spoil the evening," Maggie said pointedly. The moment languished. She looked at Nate and explained, "There was an accident."

"A girl was killed," Jack confessed. "We left shortly after that."

Nate thought better than to ask for specifics. "Wow, that's too bad."

"Yes, it really was," Jack said. An awkward silence filled the room. Then a car pulled into the driveway and Maggie looked relieved. "There's Greer." She stood up and went to the door.

"Our chief financial officer," Jack said, then added in a whisper, "Otherwise known as a bitch on wheels."

"I *heard* that, Jack," Maggie called, opening the door.

"You'll see." Heath flashed a grin. "Watch out."

"I stand warned," Nate said as Greer Harding burst through the door behind an unruly bouquet of white daisies.

"For you, darling," Greer said dramatically, handing Maggie the flowers. "I thought you'd like these."

"They're beautiful."

"They've completely taken over my garden."

"Let me get a vase." The women went into the kitchen and Jack wiggled his eyebrows ominously at Nate and whispered, almost like a threat, "She's got the goods on everyone."

"Is that right?"

"I don't know how she does it—it's scary, really—our very own KGB. I'd be terrified if I were you." He smiled at his joke, but under the circumstances Nate failed to see its humor.

The women came back into the room. They were talking about the traffic. "Who's responsible for it, that's what I want to know?" Greer said.

"Yo-Yo Ma's playing tonight," Maggie said. "It's the last concert of the season."

"Good," Greer said. "Now everyone can go home. Those *motorcycles!*"

"Look, aren't they beautiful?" Maggie had put the flowers into a white pitcher and set it down on the coffee table.

"They are indeed," Jack said.

"Greer Harding, Nate Gallagher."

"Don't get up," Greer said.

But he did anyway. "Hello, Greer," Nate said, shaking her hand.

"You weren't supposed to be this cute," Greer said in what he suspected was an uncharacteristically generous tone and then added, considerably less generously, "I just finished one of your stories. You're an interesting man, Mr. Gallagher."

He waited for her to elaborate, but she didn't. "Well, thanks." He tried to smile. "I'm just an ordinary guy."

"I'm guessing you have few ordinary qualities." She held her gaze on him longer than necessary. The back of his neck prickled with sweat.

"What are you drinking?" Maggie prompted.

"Whatever you're having. Anything—as long as it has alcohol in it." Greer dropped onto the couch, apparently more than comfortable in the Heaths' home. "A good deal of alcohol, I might add." She had on a white tennis shirt and chinos and her silver hair was cut short, like a man's. She'd taken off her shoes at the door and was barefoot now; he noticed she was wearing a toe-ring. There was something frightfully attractive about her, he thought. "Where's Ada tonight?"

"Out in the rowboat somewhere."

"Good for her. It's a perfect night for it."

Maggie handed her a drink. "Cheers."

"Cheers, darling." They clinked their glasses. "I have an announcement, in fact. We have a new student."

"The Squire boy?"

"That's right. Edward Squire—Teddy. His mother called this afternoon to say he'd be starting. She left a message on the machine."

"Talk about last minute," Maggie said, displeased.

"He's a legacy," Jack told Nate. "The grandfather passed away a few weeks ago, died of a stroke. He was well known in the area."

"*That's* an understatement," Greer said. "He was notorious."

"He was a great director," Jack clarified. "With the theater festival here. They live up on Prospect Hill. One of those big old houses."

"With major hedges, I might add," Greer said. "Very tall, very thick, very very green. The wife's money, you know—they were in cosmetics. Shampoo, I think. Anyway . . . she's long dead. Now *that* was a tragedy."

"The old man built our gymnasium," Jack added.

"Guilt can be very motivating," Greer said, raising her eyebrows with relish.

"She's a single mother," Maggie proclaimed the fact like a curse.

"An artist," Greer confirmed. "We have no information on the boy's father."

"Apart from all this fascinating gossip," Jack said wryly, "they're a marvelous addition."

"The boy's grades weren't so marvelous," Maggie said. "His test scores . . ." She shook her head as if they were too awful to utter.

"He does have something of a checkered past," Greer conceded.

"Test scores aren't generally conclusive," Nate said. There was a brief pause as his comment lurked among them like a foul odor, informing him that dissent of any kind among this group was not favorable. He cleared his throat as if to clear the air.

"Well, for *his* sake," Greer said at length, "I sure as hell hope not."

They took their drinks out onto the terrace to watch the sunset. They sat in the wrought-iron chairs watching the sun's gradual descent behind the trees.

"Look at that. The leaves are already starting to change," Greer said.

"It's beautiful here," Nate said.

"Maybe it'll inspire you, Gallagher," Greer said.

"No doubt." He looked over at Maggie and tipped his glass at her. "Here's to inspiration."

"And poems about the changing leaves," Maggie said wistfully.

"God, there must be thousands," Greer said.

"Good old Robert Frost," Jack said. "Let's have a toast to the old boy."

Nate was feeling the whiskey now. It was amazing what a glass or two could do for an evening. Someone nearby was having a fire and the air smelled of wood smoke. Loons were singing to one another across the lake. He couldn't imagine a more pleasant setting and he felt good sitting there with the three of them and he thought that perhaps they might all become good friends. He didn't have many friends in the city. Aside from an occasional beer after work with some of the other teachers, he didn't go out much, and on weekends, if he wasn't visiting his father, he was alone.

"I saw geese this morning," Maggie said. "They were flying some-where in a triangle."

"They're so goddamn organized," Greer said. "Try getting our stu-

dents to do that."

"The sign of an early winter," Jack said, finishing his drink.

"Perish the thought." Greer shuddered. "I get goose bumps just thinking about it."

Two girls in a small boat were rowing to shore. The sun was low behind the trees and you could see their long shadows stretching across the lake's surface. The girls were in silhouette.

"There's Ada now," Jack said.

"Who's that with her?" Greer squinted down at them. "Is it Willa?"

"Last week they weren't speaking, *this* week they're best friends."

Greer laughed. "Ah, the social pecking order. It's terribly hard keeping track these days, isn't it?"

"Terribly complicated," Maggie agreed.

Willa. Nate's throat went dry and the air seemed impossibly warm. Keeping her name had been part of their agreement; it was what Catherine had wanted.

Although he'd anticipated this moment a million times, trying to predict its outcome, he was still not prepared for it. He put down his drink and wiped his sweaty hands on his trousers. What if she should know him somehow? Even worse, what if she *resembled* him? Yet, even if she *did* resemble him, he reasoned, nobody would draw any conclusions—it was the furthest thing from anyone's mind, including hers. And of course she wasn't going to *recognize* him—she'd been an infant! Still, he felt foolish for coming here. It had been a terrible idea, a mistake. What had he possibly been thinking?

He held his hand over his eyes to cut the glare and studied his daughter for the first time. Even from a distance he could see how closely she resembled Catherine. Just the way she was sitting in the boat, angular and poised. The Heaths' daughter, Ada, had gotten out first and was directing the boat toward the shore. They were laughing. Then Willa stepped out, coltlike with her long legs. Her hair was long, auburn, the same color as his. The girls were wearing cutoff shorts and bathing suit tops and they were laughing hysterically, playing some kind of push-me pull-you game. Willa fell backward into the water and laughed some more and Ada took her hand and pulled her up only to be pulled down all over again by her friend. Now they were both in the water, laughing and splashing each other, rolling around like lovers.

Apparently annoyed, Maggie stood up. "Girls! Come in and get changed. We're having dinner in ten minutes." The girls looked at Maggie and then at each other and burst out laughing all over again. "Hard to believe they're juniors in high school," Maggie said, displeased.

"They look like they're having fun," Nate said.

"Too much fun," Greer remarked sourly.

"They're apparently very good friends," Nate said, hoping to prompt more information.

"Willa's father's one of our trustees," Jack said. "He's a very generous man."

"Exceptionally generous," Greer clarified. "He's made buckets of money in advertising—commercials, I think. The wife collects thoroughbred horses."

"Willa's somewhat . . ." Maggie paused, trying to find a tactful adjective, "confrontational."

"She's adopted, you know," Greer confided, and the phrase seemed to hover in a cloud of ambiguity. "Not that that has anything to do with it. We have lots of adopted kids at Pioneer—truthfully, it's how we maintain our diversity."

"Willa Golding's a fine girl," Jack said definitively, closing the subject.

"Yes, she is," Greer said. "No argument there."

Soaking wet, the girls ambled up the incline in their awkward, teenaged way, and said hello to the adults. Nate's heart began to pound. He could feel the sweat rolling down his back. He stood there, waiting to be introduced, his hands clammy. She was taller than her mother had been, and lean. He recognized Ada as one of Larkin's piano students. Heath stood up and made the introduction. "Girls, this is Mr. Gallagher. He's to be your writing instructor."

"How's that novel coming?" Ada asked in melodious flirtation. She had the same face as her mother, sprinkled with freckles.

"Do you two know each other?" Greer frowned.

Nate explained the Larkin connection, relieved to have an explanation for the idiotic grin on his face.

"You're writing a novel?" Greer said.

"He's *trying* to write one," Ada answered importantly.

"Well, good for you," Greer said. "Nate, this is Willa Golding."

"Hello," Willa said, and reached out to shake his hand. Her hand was cool, her fingers long and tapered. He instantly remembered her grip as a baby, the way she wouldn't let go.

"Hello, Willa." Their eyes met and she grinned and for a crazy moment the world stopped.

Maggie's voice shattered the moment. "Go get out of those wet clothes, girls." She ushered the girls into the house. "I'll get dinner started. Look at that, it's already getting dark. I hate that, don't you? All of a sudden it's fall and I was just getting the hang of summer."

"Let's have a toast," Jack said, holding up his glass. "Here's to you, Gallagher. Welcome to Pioneer."

"Hear, hear," Greer said, and they lifted their glasses and drank.

Maggie served trout with roasted potatoes and salad and corn bread. The food was delicious, but Nate could hardly taste it. The girls sat off to themselves on lawn chairs, holding their plates on their laps. Everything about Willa spoke of Catherine. The way she moved, her voice, her mannerisms—if only Cat could see her, he thought. How incredible just to be near her. It was as though he'd been revived from a very long sleep. The world seemed brighter, astoundingly vivid. He was awake! Her presence dazzled his senses, the long hair, the bones of her face, the white teeth. She was, in all her full-grown femaleness, magnificent—and she had come from him—*she was his flesh and blood!*

The girls excused themselves and went inside. It was dark now, and a layer of mist covered the surface of the lake. Maggie brought out scones that had been baked by the school's chef, who'd trained at the Sorbonne. "All the interesting people retire to the Berkshires," Maggie said. "We're so lucky to have him. Of course everything's organic."

"Organic," Greer said wryly. "That's an operative word here at Pioneer, Gallagher. Consider it a metaphor for our clientele."

"The Patagucci set," Maggie said. "You know the clothes? It's the uniform of choice, a kind of subliminal dress code. Of course we're all slaves to it."

"Ah, the salubrious allure of the Berkshires," Greer said like a travel agent. "Don't panic, it's organic."

They all laughed.

"What's underneath is all the same," Jack tried to explain. "We've got our share of doctors and lawyers, trust fund babies, and entrepreneurs. And we've got a handful of Wall Street folks. But people don't come up here to get in the limelight. It's just the opposite. They come up here to get out of it."

"It's not just that," Maggie said. "The people who come up here to live are looking for something they can't find anywhere else."

"Utopian longings," Greer said.

"Whatever it is," Jack said, "it's keeping us in business."

They drank their coffee and ate the scones and the moon rose full and bright over the lake. Nate decided that Maggie was right: There *was* something about the Berkshires. They sat out there for another hour, and then Willa's mother came to pick her up. Nate stayed where he was and watched the mother and daughter from a distance through the French doors. Candace Golding was taller than he remembered her, an equestrian in jeans and paddock boots, a sweater tied with casual perfection around her shoulders. The long black ponytail was gone, as was the bewildered pleasure in her eyes. Now her eyes were clever and sharp and her hair was cut short and blunt at her shoulders. Maggie hurried over to her and handed her a little bag of scones. Willa appeared with her enormous satchel—it seemed to contain the entire contents of her closet—and kissed her mother's cheek, and all four of them talked a little more. Willa looked out through the glass doors and called out her good-byes. She met his eyes and waved and he raised his hand, like a flag, and waved back.

"Good night, Willa!" he called. *Sleep tight.*

8

The Squire boy had been assigned to Maggie as an advisee. At first glance, he appeared to be polite, almost reticent, but among his fellow classmates an arrogance surfaced, a slippery bravado that thrilled and charmed the others. Maggie had tried to get to know him during advisee lunch every Tuesday, but he gave her little to work with. When she'd asked if his father would be coming to any of his soccer games—the boy was a capable athlete—his face went sullen and he shook his head. It wasn't his fault, she supposed. There were issues there, in the genes. The grandfather, for one. According to Berkshire folklore, Eddie Squire's behavior had been so outrageous he'd been asked to resign his membership in the country club—and that didn't happen very often, especially when there were deep pockets in the mix. And the boy's mother—well, Maggie would have to reserve judgment about her. "Give them a chance," Jack had said in one of his more generous moods. "The boy will come around." But Maggie knew it was too late for him—it was harsh, perhaps—yes, she knew it was—but it was the truth.

Experience had taught her that kids showed their true colors in grade school. You could always spot the ones who'd end up at the better colleges—the likelihood presented itself as early as fourth grade—you saw it in a child's handwriting, in the neat formation of cursive letters, their ability to reason and solve equations, and in the articulation of thoughts and ideas. The children who couldn't grasp concepts in the early grades generally had some form of a learning difference—that's what they called it these days—*she* called it a disability. A small percentage of their students had some form of a learning disability, but they generally made it clear during the admissions process that their school was not suitable for children with disabilities. When parents were adamant that their children could get along all right, Pioneer recommended testing, but the parents interpreted the results the way they wanted to, in some cases claiming that the testing provided only vague parameters of a child's intelligence—if they tested significantly above average, the parents clung to the numbers as sacred evidence of a child's brilliance. If the child tested in the average range, which was usually the case, the parents maintained that the numbers were simply an arbitrary consequence of the child's mood that day. So what good was any of it? Under the giant umbrella of dysfunction, the parents found ways to rationalize their children's myriad issues: the ADD and dysgraphia, the dyslexia and processing disorders, the names of which, in the age of euphemism and rationalization, anointed their children as unlikely warriors, members of an underdog class of students whose brilliance was so dynamic and extreme—akin to Einstein's—that no ordinary high school teacher could recognize or identify it. Many of their students took drugs, not just one prescription but sometimes two or three—the school nurse had a lengthy list on file and dutifully dispensed them as instructed. There were drugs for sleeping, drugs for waking. Drugs that quelled depression. Drugs that made the kids more focused or more alert or more relaxed or more able to demonstrate self-control. In most cases, Maggie didn't approve of giving drugs to children, she didn't care what the doctors said, but she kept her opinions to herself, it wasn't her place to judge. But she *did* judge, she couldn't help it. In her mind, the drugs said more about the parents than the children. Over the past ten years there'd been a marked rise in the routine dispensing of drugs like Prozac and Ritalin, yet Maggie wasn't always impressed by the results they promised. To some degree she could understand the parents' anxiety—nobody wanted to hear that their kid was lacking in the brain department— but instead of facing up to the fact that their kids weren't destined for Harvard, the parents squirmed around the reality and turned it into something else. Over the years, during interviews with these sorts of parents, Maggie had observed a growing phenomenon among the applicants to Pioneer. They were all geniuses.

But Jack looked at things differently. Jack was a businessman.

When she'd mentioned the boy's reading and writing difficulties to him one afternoon, waving a stack of papers in his face, Jack had shrugged and said, "How is he doing in math?"

"All right," she admitted, "but look at these, Jack. They're unacceptable. He needs help."

Jack glanced at the papers and tossed them down on the desk, irritably. "What's happened to you, Maggie?"

"What?"

"Where's your 'I can teach anyone' attitude?"

"This is different. We aren't equipped to deal with his issues."

"You don't get it, do you?" He took hold of her shoulders and directed her toward the window. "You see that building? Whose name is on that building, Maggie?"

She looked out at the Squire Gymnasium. "He doesn't belong here," she insisted. "And you know it."

"I'm sure the boy has other strengths. Find out what they are."

She shrugged him off and started toward the door, but he caught her wrist and held it harder than necessary. "You don't seem like yourself these days."

She looked up at his benign face, his sea-glass eyes. "I'm fine."

"Could have fooled me."

"I just want the best for the boy."

"Sure you do," he said, letting go of her. "Get him a tutor."

Something was happening to her and Jack. It had been happening for a long time. She couldn't discuss it with anyone—she didn't dare. She didn't have any friends, really, and the only person she might confide in, her sister, Tess, was off in Africa somewhere with the Peace Corps. Instead, she focused on routine, the predictable unfolding of her days. Mornings, she got up, made breakfast, put in a load of laundry, and the three of them went off to work. She was proud of their daughter, who was an excellent student and knew how to follow the rules. Maggie would observe some of her daughter's classmates, noting their obvious peculiarities, their blatant insecurities, and be glad that Ada had escaped such problems. It was a tribute to her and Jack, she knew, and she took great pride in their parenting. But recently, Maggie had observed a change in the girl, and she suspected it had something to do with the Squire boy. Most of the girls were in love with him. He was new, for one thing, a novelty, but there was something else about him, something *sexual,* a wily dynamic, that was irresistible to them. Watching the kids in the cafeteria during lunch period, Maggie had detected an attraction between the boy and Willa Golding that could not be ignored and she knew that, before long, it would have an effect on Ada. Maggie was well aware of the fact that she had no business having an opinion about the personal relationships of her students, but she didn't like the possibility of her daughter getting hurt and she was nearly certain that she would be hurt; it seemed inevitable. Like Maggie, Ada was plain and unexceptional in the looks department. She tended to carry weight around her middle, and had stubby fingers— peasant hands, her mother called them. Her hair was a dull shade of cornmeal, and her skin was pale, sallow almost, and sprinkled with freckles. She had Jack's nose, flat and prominent as an Eskimo's, and two lumps, tablespoons of flesh, that represented breasts.

For as long as she could remember, there had been a rivalry between Ada and Willa Golding. The girls had attended the Children's School before coming to Pioneer, and had been competitive students, although Ada always got better grades. They had been good friends for a long time, even though they came from significantly different backgrounds. Money, for one thing. Willa's father had plenty of it. And they were Jewish. In fact, Willa was Ada's only Jewish friend. They didn't have many Jewish families at Pioneer, but that was changing. For a long time, Pioneer had a Waspy reputation. Most of the Jewish families in the area sent their children to the public school. But since 9/11, more and more New Yorkers, many of them Jews, had moved up to the Berkshires and had established themselves as full-time residents. Nearly all of them sent their children to Pioneer, which had the reputation of being as good as the private schools in the city, without the high tuition or the grotesque pressure of getting admitted.

You could always tell the newcomers—the immigrants, Jack called them—who had escaped their complicated lives in New York and absconded to the Berkshires. In a fury of romance, they'd buy impractical country homes on acres and acres of glorious land, only to discover months later that they had no closets in which to store their towels and their kids would rather play with their insipid electronic gadgets than run through the grass picking up ticks.

The temple had acquired so many new members that they'd had to build a new synagogue, and the Goldings had helped to fund it—there'd been an article about it in the *Berkshire Eagle*. Four years ago, they'd attended Willa's bat mitzvah, an extravagant affair at the country club. Maggie had spent half her paycheck on a new dress for the occasion, not to mention a gift. The Goldings had hired an expensive band from New York; all of the performers had been black. The guests, all of whom were white, had danced all night, gyrating in their party clothes, and the windows in the hall went opaque in the rising heat. Jack had played his usual role as ambassador to Pioneer, shaking hands, patting the men on their backs, joking about their golf games, and when the other men asked their wives to dance, Jack asked Maggie, holding her gently at a distance as the music pounded in their ears, a primal beat, and the bodies all around them shimmied and shook. It had been a long time since they'd danced together, she couldn't remember the last time, but before long Jack lost interest, distracted by another Pioneer couple, standing awkwardly on the sidelines. She followed Jack, but one of the dancers from the band wrapped a feather boa around her neck and pulled her back onto the floor. He took her hand and swirled her around and a burst of joy sprang from her mouth. He pulled her close then spun her around again and she felt his warm chest against her own. It thrilled her to be held like that, it made her feel like a woman again—desired—and it stirred up other emotions too and her eyes glazed over with tears.

She excused herself and ran into the bathroom, her skin flushed, a shimmer of sweat on her forehead.

There'd been a party for the kids that night, and Ada slept over at Willa's. On the drive home, Jack seemed preoccupied, staring through the windshield, mulling over some despicable notion. When they got home, he insisted she have a drink with him and fixed her a gin and tonic. They sat at the kitchen table drinking and she watched her husband transform into someone else, a version of his monstrous father, and he told her that at the party it had occurred to him that his father had been right about the Jews after all. "They just can't help themselves," he told her. "The way they spend money. Like pigeon shit, it's everywhere you look."

"They wanted it to be special for Willa," she said.

"Oh, it was special all right."

"It's their money, they can spend it any way they want." She got up and started for the stairs.

"I never knew you were so light on your feet," he said.

"He was a good dancer."

"I saw you out there. Don't think I didn't."

"I'm going to bed. You're drunk."

"Come over here."

"Good night, Jack."

Jack nodded, prudently, and finished his drink. Then he got up and rumbled toward her and caught her wrist and held her there so she couldn't move. "I saw you," he said. "I saw your face."

"Jack."

He pulled up her skirt, rifling through the layers of fabric to her control-top panty hose, but she twisted free and ran up the stairs to the guest room and locked the door. She lay awake all night, convincing herself that it wasn't his fault, the way he'd turned out. Growing up with that awful man had done it to him. Her husband's fascination with money and the people who had it—*real* money was what he called it—had been in his head since childhood, when he'd stare out the window of his mother's station wagon at the pretty houses in whatever town his father was based in, wondering what it might be like to live in one. To Jack, money was the school yard bully, sticking out his tongue, taunting in maniacal singsong, "You can't get me, you can't get me."

Jack was still chasing him.

Thunder woke her at half past six on Sunday morning. She sat up in bed, alone. The house smelled of coffee; Jack was already up. The bedroom glared with brooding indifference and suddenly it began to rain. The rain fell heavily on the roof and ran through the gutters. She pulled herself up and sat on the edge of the bed. She felt light and empty. She remembered how hungry she'd been the night before and how she hadn't succumbed to it, reciting her reasons methodically, like a prayer. Now her belly was flat and she could feel the bones of her torso pushing through. Rising from the bed, she felt a little weak, as though she had finally recovered from a prolonged illness, but of course that wasn't true, she was in perfect health.

Pulling on her robe, she went down to the kitchen to find her husband. The house glimmered with silence. A watery, greenish light filled the living room as the rain poured down the windows. She stood there for a moment, looking out at the lake, its surface dimpled like a sheet of hammered tin. Mozart was playing softly in Jack's study, but when she looked in, expecting to find him hunched over his work, the room was empty. The lamp was lit and a cup of coffee sat on the desk. The window was open and rain was splattering on the windowsill, sending sparks of water onto a stack of papers just below it, the applications for the Sunrise Internship. The Sunrise Internship was awarded annually to the brightest female student at Pioneer and was especially impressive to colleges. Two afternoons a week, the student volunteered at Sunrise House, a women's shelter in Pittsfield. Bette Lawton's application was on top, which suggested, perhaps, that Jack had chosen her. There was no surprise there. Certainly, Jack would give the internship to her. Ada, whose grades were nearly as good, would undoubtedly be second on the list.

Maggie shut the window, absentmindedly taking a sip of Jack's coffee, which was nearly cold. Under the applications was another stack of papers, an enormous unruly pile—she didn't have to look at it to know what it was. Jack's unfinished dissertation on the poet Ezra Pound, a man Jack obsessively marveled, was a relic he resurrected from time to time, when he was in one of his states. Like an unrequited love affair, the manuscript comprised years of study that had amounted to absolutely nothing. For the past twenty years, Jack had carted around the unwieldy stack of papers, promising her— *threatening her*—that one day he'd finally finish it. Although neither of them would ever speak of it, the manuscript had become a symbol between them of their ultimate failure as a couple—of dreams turned to dust. She was a failure just as much as he was. When he'd had the affair with his thesis adviser, a woman ten years his senior, Maggie had wanted to leave him and he'd begged her not to.

She'd caught them one miserable evening—he hadn't come home for dinner. It was her first Mother's Day, and she'd made a special meal. She'd waited over an hour, and when he didn't show up she walked over to campus to look for him, carrying little Ada on her hip. The PhD students had offices on the fourth floor of the Classics Building, tiny rooms behind shaded glass doors. The building had emptied out for the weekend and Maggie climbed the stairs with growing anticipation, hoping to surprise him, imagining the pleasant disruption, but as she turned down the corridor under the dim, failing lights, another feeling took hold. Sweat prickled under her arms and Ada began to fuss. Approaching his door, she could hear them, a chorus of unbridled pleasure, and although the glass was shaded it wasn't hard to tell what they were doing. As a result, the adviser resigned her position, and Jack had been asked to leave the program.

She heard his car pulling up in the driveway. He was carrying a brown paper bag from the grocers. He came in and looked sorry to see her. "You're up early."

"The rain woke me."

"It's miserable." He took a carton of milk out of the bag. "We were out."

"I meant to market yesterday," she apologized.

He grunted and his eyes seemed to say *like everything else you meant to do.*

He poured himself a cup of coffee, then carelessly added three teaspoons of sugar, spilling some of it on the table. The white grains reminded her of an hourglass—all the hours she had been with him since the day they'd married—and she wondered now why she hadn't left him. For all these years the question had persisted in her mind. It was always there, creeping up on her. When he ate noisily, it was there, when he slurped his coffee, it was there, when she picked up his laundry, it was there, and when he woke her in the night for sex, it was there too. But a woman in her situation, with a reputation to protect, couldn't just pick up and leave her husband. For one thing, there was the school. People in the community looked up to them. They represented grace and civility and what's more, people trusted them with their kids. You had to earn that trust, and both she and Jack had spent years cultivating it. And second and perhaps most important, divorce wasn't good for children. Almost half of the students at Pioneer came from broken homes, yes, that's what she called them, politically correct or not they were still broken, and you could see the strain in their faces. You could see a lingering malcontent, as though they'd been cheated somehow. Raising children took two parents, she'd always believed it, and Ada adored her father. In Maggie's mind, divorce only refuted the vital premise that what is started must be finished. Sticking something out, for better or worse, was no longer a prerequisite to having a meaningful existence, and quitting no longer brought on castigation—*whatever makes you happy* seemed to be the popular reasoning—why, then, couldn't she adapt it to her own situation. She couldn't help thinking that divorce, with its brawny spectacle, was the definition of personal failure. "I told you so," she could just imagine her mother's response. She'd never wanted Maggie to marry Jack in the first place. Her mother had said to her, "There is nothing redeeming about being a schoolteacher's wife. You'll be darning old socks for the rest of your life." Maggie had never told her parents the real reason why Jack hadn't finished his PhD. Instead, they'd celebrated Jack's first job at St. Timothy's, a Catholic military school in Hadley, where he'd taught Latin for four years before taking the job at Remington Pond.

She'd made her bed, she decided. And she was lying in it.

Later, in church, she took his hand, wanting to let him know that she was there if he needed her, but he hardly seemed to notice her. She had known for some time that he wasn't himself. There were little things; the drinking for one, ice trays in the sink every morning and the rinds of lemons and limes. She would find him late at night in his office, staring blankly at his own reflection in the black window. It was a known fact in their calling—she still believed that's what it was, a calling—that after seven or eight years in one place it was time to move on. Working with the same people, the same trustees and parents year after year could drag you down. Ultimately, like some shopworn piece of merchandise, you wore out your own authority. But aside from a few of his standard complaints—the kids weren't as clever or as polite or as empathetic as they used to be *and neither were their parents*—Jack had remained optimistic until now.

Father O'Rourke paused a moment and people shifted on the hard pews and coughed and blew their noses. Jack looked glum and preoccupied. She looked around at the congregation, many of whom she knew, and wondered: Are *they* happy? It was true that her life had become an elaborate fabrication, she had finally admitted it to herself, but she had no other solution for getting through it. It wasn't easy being in her position as "first lady" of an elite private school. She tried to ignore her feelings—it was selfish to dwell on herself—but she couldn't seem to do that anymore. A dark mood had wrapped itself around her and would not let go. As if reading her thoughts, her husband glanced at her abruptly and she quickly wiped her tears and shrugged apologetically. He gave her an ominous look, and turned his attention back to Father O'Rourke. Maggie always cried in church, she couldn't help it. It was the only place that moved her. It was the only place where goodness actually seemed like a viable possibility. And nobody saw her. What did he care? She couldn't even begin to imagine how her husband felt about their life together. They didn't talk about it. There were many subjects that they avoided. Sex, for instance, was a conversation that seemed too daunting to bear, and their infrequent intimacy, always initiated by Jack, verged on the

perverse—of course she could speak of it to no one. It was a side of her husband's personality that she didn't understand, and yet she knew that for him, marrying someone like her had been an error of judgment. Somehow, though, it made her feel guilty. Like she wasn't enough for him in some way—and she rationalized his treatment of her as punishment for all she simply couldn't be. The last time he'd taken her by force, and she'd bit him on the hand. He'd had to wear a bandage all week, which inevitably summoned the concern of the parents, the mothers in particular, who gushed and fawned all over him, pitying his alleged encounter with a rusty lawn mower.

She didn't know why Jack did those things to her. She didn't understand it. She didn't know why he didn't love her more. She was a good wife; at least she tried to be. Her housekeeping might leave something to be desired, she knew, but there was a certain semblance of order because of her—the stacks of mail, the dishes, the laundry—Jack wouldn't be caught dead doing laundry—and she was an excellent cook, everybody said so—but perhaps they were lying to her. You couldn't be sure what people *really* thought. In the classroom she was at her best, she gave a hundred and ten percent to those kids, even the ones who were trouble. Even the ones that couldn't do the work, like the Squire boy, and the kids genuinely seemed to like her—*of course they did!*

After Mass, everyone went outside on the lawn. The rain had stopped and the sun glared through the heavy clouds. The wet grass seeped into her shoes, and she felt a chill, but it was too early to leave. Across the lawn, Ada was standing with Monica Travers. Monica had come to the school last year, after being thrown out of Nightingale in Manhattan for photographing herself naked and transmitting the image across the Internet. The girl's mother, Greta, was an editor at some la-di-da fashion magazine in the city—divorced, of course. Maggie had warned Jack that it was a mistake to accept her, but he was always a step ahead of her, and sure enough, two months into the school year, the girl's father dropped ten grand into their discretionary fund.

Ada draped her arms around Monica like they were best friends, although Maggie knew differently. It was all an act of course. The girls with their silly games. Monica had started a trend at the school of wearing very dark eyeliner and, as a result, many of the girls walked around like versions of Cleopatra. Ada's complexion looked sallow, and she had broken out in pimples; Maggie thought she might have her period. They never discussed personal things. Over the course of the year, her daughter had contracted a randy conceit, rolling over the waistband of her plaid skirt to raise it up an inch or two—they had spoken to the girls about such behavior and still they continued to do it. At least she hadn't gotten her belly button pierced like Willa Golding. When that had happened, Jack grounded Ada for her friend's mistake. There had been quite a scene between the two of them. Jack had warned Ada that if she ever did anything like that he'd send her to a place like Remington Pond, with all the weird kids. In his rarer moments of reflection, he would relay lectures by his father, a failed army chaplain, who would stand over his son shouting: "Sheep or shepherd, son. It's either, or. There ain't nothin' in between!"

The way Jack saw things the kids in Ada's class had caught a virus of the mind, the cure for which no parent could supply. In his determination to "treat" the virus, Jack organized a lecture series on a variety of subjects from drugs to eating disorders and enlisted Father O'Rourke, who gave a lecture on abstinence to the students, presenting them with a selection of chastity rings that could be purchased through the church—much to the uproar of many of the parents, who called Jack's office to remind him that their school was a secular institution and that his abstinence campaign was out of line. But the rings were pretty, fourteen carat gold, and almost *all* the girls wanted one regardless of their religion, whether they had boyfriends or not. Maggie had agreed to pay for Ada's, which had the saying *Faith* written on it. Willa Golding, of course, had refused to buy one, gliding across campus with an air of superiority as though she were above such commitments, and her father was so irate he had threatened to pull her out of the school, but Jack's glib, sensible explanation satisfied him in the end. "Sheep or shepherd," Jack told her, victoriously. "People just need to be told."

The wind was picking up, a shower of yellow leaves. Ada gave Maggie a little insouciant wave and started down the hill with Monica, into town. "Be back at five for supper," Maggie called, but Ada didn't turn around and the words stayed in the air like balloons at a party where nobody showed up.

The church bells were ringing. She felt a headache coming on. The air was damp, cold. She wanted to go home and make a fire and read the paper, but Jack wasn't ready to go. Across the lawn, he was talking to a couple from Pioneer—the Madisons. The wife had a compact, angular build like Gumby, with short legs and arms. Jack was his usual gregarious self. He wore his good nature like a well-tailored suit and people liked him, they liked his wavy brown hair, the way his mouth turned down at the corners with a self-deprecating frown, the way his blue eyes reeled in the impressionable eyes of the mothers, who hung on his every word in their Patagonia jackets and muck boots, and when Maggie was in a more suitable frame of mind, behaving herself like a good little wife, she was terribly proud of him.

Hunger churned in her belly and she felt herself weaving on her feet. She imagined dropping to her knees and pulling out the grass. She felt on a very precarious edge. She stood there, letting the feeling wash over her, taking comfort in her control over it, indulging, for a precious moment, in its vicious clarity.

9 ↭

Teddy Squire played cards. Poker. He had told Willa he was good at it. This one night he took her to the Men's Club in Lenox to show her how good he was. It was early in the semester and she didn't know him very well, but she had a feeling when she was with him, like she could trust him. He seemed different than the other boys; he didn't care what anyone thought.

The Men's Club was in a rambling, clapboard house down a long dirt drive overgrown with trees, and Teddy told her you could get whiskey for seventy-five cents a glass and they didn't card you. There were cars parked here and there and a small yellow light over the door, twitching with moths. He rode her there on his bicycle, letting her have the seat while he pedaled standing up. It was an old three-speed bike, with wobbly tires, and he was sweating in his leather jacket. The jacket had been his grandfather's and it had been worn in many different plays by various actors including a modern version of *Othello* and before that it had been worn by fighter pilots in World War II. The jacket looked good on him, she thought, it made him look tough. Teddy and his mother had moved back to Stockbridge that summer, into the grandfather's house—he had described their journey as a pilgrimage of debauchery, driving across the country from one seedy bar to another, like a game of connect-the-dots. Willa had seen his mother once from the school bus window, standing at the end of the driveway in her nightgown, an alpaca shawl around her shoulders, her long yellow hair spilling in all directions. When Teddy had stepped onto the bus, she'd raised her hand in a solemn wave. He'd told Willa that he didn't know his father. His mother didn't like talking about it. It was something they had in common, the mystery of their roots.

Teddy leaned the bike against a tree and took her hand. "Trust me, okay?"

From inside the dark foyer, she could see a large room that might have been the living room when this place was a real house. Two pool tables were set up, crowded with groups of men playing teams. There was a bar, but it wasn't crowded. Maybe one or two women in the whole place. Teddy led her over to the bar and asked her what she wanted. Willa stole a look at the bartender, who had the shifty indifference of a rat, and before she could answer, Teddy ordered her a beer. He drank whiskey and they stood there for a minute, drinking, and she watched his beautiful face. He had found someone across the room to look at. A man was sitting alone at a small table. He had on a lumberjack's coat and a blue skullcap. Even in the dim light she could make out a burn along the side of his face. The man turned slightly, as though he sensed their gaze, then he drank down his drink and walked out. "What happened to his face?" Teddy asked the bartender.

"Burned his mother's house down."

"How come he's not in jail?"

The bartender shook his head. "The jury felt sorry for him. He's a freaking retard."

Teddy asked the bartender if he knew where Rudy was and the bartender nodded toward a back room. Willa followed Teddy through a narrow, galley-style kitchen, the counters of which were cluttered with dirty plates smeared with cake frosting and stained teacups, into a dining room that had a single round table laid with a white cloth. Four men were sitting around the table playing cards. She recognized the one called Rudy because he worked for her father. He was the stable manager at their barn.

Rudy appraised Teddy, his eyes glittering. Under the leather jacket, Teddy had on his school clothes, a blue oxford shirt and chinos, and Willa could see this information registering in Rudy's brain. Then he looked at her, taking his time about it, which was something he'd never dare to do on her father's property. She could feel her nipples go hard under her shirt and she crossed her arms over her chest. Rudy's smile was tainted with mockery, and he jerked up his chin like a horse shaking its withers. To Teddy, he said, "You in this round?"

"I'm in."

"Pull up a chair."

Teddy sat down at the table and Willa took a chair against the wall. The chair had a red vinyl seat that was ripped and you could see the stuffing coming out of it. Staring down at her from the wood paneling was a big, old moose head, its dead eyes gleaming. All over the walls were pictures of men at tables smoking cigars. It made her think of her father, who smoked cigars regularly. It was something men did together, she realized, and it was at once dirty and lovely. She couldn't compare it to anything women did when they were alone together, and in a strange way she envied the men with their dirty cigars. The air smelled of old cigars and dust, and now and then one of the men ground out a laugh. She watched Teddy with his pretty wolf eyes and felt her heart go tight. He took out some money and bought some chips and she could see the money piled up in a bucket at Rudy's feet. The chips made a thrilling sound as they clattered into a pile in the middle of the table. Rudy dealt out the cards and the room went quiet.

Teddy looked over his hand. He seemed confident, she thought. He wasn't a loser like her old boyfriend, Marco. Marco came from money and had good clothes, but he was a loser and she was exceptionally grateful she hadn't slept with him. Marco would be begging his rich daddy for money all of his life, whereas Teddy would make his own. There were things Willa knew about people. Once, a psychic had told her that she had a third eye. And she knew about Teddy. Life would be hard on him. People wouldn't understand him like she did. The teachers didn't. He was always in Mr. Heath's office for one thing or another. One time she walked by Heath's office and saw Teddy in the "disciplinary" chair and Mr. Heath offering him a piece of hard candy. Mr. Heath was like that. He would offer you hard candy instead of reprimanding you and give his sheep or shepherd speech, then you'd feel guilty and confess your sins. There was something about Teddy, she didn't know what it was, but it got to her. Something happened to her body when she thought about his hands or his beautiful shoulders or his crooked smile. Her body went damp like a wet leaf, her tongue prickled for the taste of him.

The men played a couple of games and most of the time it was Rudy who won, but Teddy didn't look worried even as he dug deep into the pockets of his jeans. One of the men—his name was Dale— frowned and shook his head and put more cash into the bucket.

"Don't you fret, Dale," Rudy said cheerfully, helping himself to the chips in the middle.

Dale grunted.

"Money don't mean that much," Rudy said. "You think it does, but it don't. Not really it don't."

One of the other players snorted and tossed down his cards. "Who died and made you Oprah?" The man was in his work uniform, a gray shirt and trousers. Over his left shirt pocket were the words *State Line,* and under that his name, *Harv,* was stitched in blue thread. "You're full of shit, you know that, Rudy?"

"Let's say you win tonight. What you gonna do with that money? You gonna pay your bills with it? What about you, Dale? You gonna go pay the electric company and whoever the fuck else you owe?"

Dale's face turned a little yellow. One of his shoulders rose in a half-shrug. "I would, probably."

But Willa could tell nobody believed him. She looked over at Teddy, who had taken out his package of Drum tobacco and was rolling a cigarette.

"Poker's like sex," Harv said. "You gotta know when to pull out."

Everyone laughed.

"And never overestimate the beauty of your hand."

More laughter around the table.

"Money's just a souvenir of the game," Rudy said. "It's not the reason you play, not really it ain't."

Harv shook his head. "If it's not for the money, why do it?"

"For sport, my friend. Fun and Games."

"There's nothing fun about losing," Harv said.

"You must like something about it," Rudy said, "'cause you're doing an awful lot of it."

A crescendo of laughter. Harv nodded deliberately, like he was used to being the butt of jokes, then folded his hand. "I see your point."

"You're full of shit," Teddy said. "Sorry boys: I got a pair of queens, ace high."

Willa watched as he helped himself to the pot.

"You've just got a bad case of beginner's luck," Rudy told him.

"Whatever you say," Teddy muttered.

"We used to play a lot of poker in the joint."

The information seemed to impress Teddy.

"It passed the time," Rudy said. "But we weren't playing for money. We played just to get through the day. It's what kept us going. It was a reason to get up every morning." He sat back in his chair and lit a cigarette and looked over at Teddy. "I guess you can't relate to that, can you, Junior? You rich kids just think you got it coming, don't you? The world owes you a fucking shoe shine."

Teddy shrugged. "You don't know me."

"Don't I?" Rudy looked right at him. A cold silence filled the room.

"Show him the teeth," one of the men said in a ragged, smoker's voice. He was the oldest player at the table, wearing a brown suit and a bolo tie that he might have carved himself out of wood, in the shape of a horse. Willa noticed that he'd twisted the ends of his mustache like the cowboys in old movies.

"Prison wampum." Rudy laughed knowingly.

"Tell the boy," the old man said.

"We used to do some crazy shit in there," Rudy said. "We didn't have any money, so we'd play for teeth. This here's the only game I ever lost." Rudy grimaced, showing his teeth, and pointed definitively to an empty black space. Then he leaned back in his chair so he could get something out of one of his pockets. He pulled out a pill canister and shook it and everybody could see that it was full of teeth. "I won a lot of games in there." He set the canister down on the table. "That's my good luck charm now." He held it up again and shook it like a rattle then let out a whooping laugh. "You play a couple of rounds of prison poker and you understand what it really means to win."

"Not a game for pussies," the old man said.

"You gotta have some real fucking balls to play prison poker," Rudy said, looking right at Teddy.

Willa shot Teddy a look that begged him to get up and leave, but he ignored her and lit his cigarette. Harv tapped a little bell on a side table and a few minutes later the bartender appeared with more whiskey. They played for another hour and Teddy started winning every hand. Every time he won, Rudy's face twisted up a little more, like a wrung-out rag. Then Dale backed out his chair and got up. "I'm all done here."

"Whatsamatter, Dale, you broke already?"

"Junior here's cleaned me out."

"He got lucky is all," Rudy said. "That's poker, my friend."

Dale shook his head. "I got to get home."

"You gonna turn into a pumpkin?" Rudy barked a laugh. "Sit the fuck down."

"Rudy, I got—"

But Rudy cut him off. "Sit."

Dale sat back down, his face grim.

"Now what's Becky gonna say about this, you show up empty-handed?"

Dale shrugged.

Rudy reached over in a fatherly way and put his arm around Dale. "You know she don't like you gambling. She don't want to see that. We've been over that ground before."

Dale nodded his head. "I know it."

"You want her to walk out on you again? That what you want?"

"No, Rudy."

"I'm gonna give you a chance to turn things around." Rudy looked over at Willa. "Shut that door for me, darlin'."

"What?" she said, but she'd heard him perfectly.

Irritably, he slapped the air with his hand and she got up and shut the door, knowing instinctively that Rudy wasn't the sort of man you refused. Her legs felt rubbery as she returned to her seat.

"Let's play one last hand for Dale," he said. "Winner takes all this." He picked up the bucket of money and set it down on the table. Like a starved man, Dale licked his lips at the sight of it. "But let's turn it up a notch. Make it a little more interesting for our guest over here." Rudy looked at Teddy. "You ready to be in our club, big shot?"

Teddy shrugged.

"You think you're man enough?"

"Try me."

"Consider it your initiation."

"I don't get it."

"Prison poker. Right here, right now."

The men around the table snickered, shaking their heads. Willa tried to swallow, but her mouth was too dry.

"Now if you lose, we take your tooth, understand?"

At length, Teddy said, "What if I win?"

"You get all this." Again, Rudy picked up the bucket of money and put it down. "There's around three grand in there. You can buy your girlfriend a present." Rudy glanced over at her and held his gaze a moment longer than necessary and it made something quiver in her belly, as if her insides were being tickled with a feather. "She *is* your girlfriend, isn't she?"

But Teddy didn't answer him and she felt a burning in her chest.

"Of course I'm rooting for Dale," Rudy went on.

A smile flashed across Dale's mouth. His grim eyes brightened whenever he looked at Rudy, and Willa could tell he looked up to him like a brother and always ended up paying for it in the end. It was time to go, but Teddy wasn't moving. Surely this was a joke, she thought. Any minute one of them would burst out laughing, but the minute passed and nobody did. They all just sat there, waiting for Rudy.

"We have to go, Teddy," Willa said.

"She's talking to you," Rudy said almost hopefully.

Teddy glanced over at Willa and raised his chin a little and looked into her eyes and the look made her quiver.

"You willing to lose a tooth, son?" Rudy said.

"Teddy, *please*."

"Deal the fucking cards," Teddy said.

"Well, all right then," Rudy said. "You're either stupid, or you've got some fucking balls. Now who else wants to play?"

Willa looked at the men around the table. Dale had a ferret face, with a pointy chin and beady little eyes, and he was scrawny and stoop-shouldered. He was staring at the pile of money like he could almost taste it. He nodded at Rudy to deal him in. The man named Harv nodded too. "I'm in." Then the man in the bolo tie took out his false teeth and said, "I'm afraid I don't qualify, gentlemen. I guess I'll sit this one out."

Rudy shuffled the cards and dealt them out. Willa watched their faces as the men studied their hands. Rudy had thick, wind-burned skin and cold black eyes. She could remember the first time she'd seen him, pulling onto the farm in a banged-up Chevy pickup. Willa knew the horses didn't like him on account he always wore spurs and readily used a crop, nor did the South American boys who came to work in the barn and would do anything he asked just to keep their jobs, but her father had said he was the best barn manager he'd ever hired. Her mother had told her that Rudy had grown up an orphan and had gone to reform school as a boy, and then on to prison as an adult for nearly beating someone to death in a fight. Once, Willa had snuck into his quarters over the barn and found a stack of library books by his bed, all of them biographies of famous men. It was hard to imagine a man like Rudy reading about Jefferson and Washington, but he did.

It was already eleven o'clock; her parents would be looking for her by now. She tried to catch Teddy's eye, but he was fixated on his hand. Leaving was the thing to do, but how would she get home? She would have to call her father, and she didn't want him knowing she'd spent the better part of the evening in a place like this. The men at the table were quiet and when the bartender came around with more drinks nobody seemed to notice, but they all picked up their whiskey and sipped. Under the table, Dale's foot was shaking, but Teddy seemed calm, as if he was resigned to whatever came next. It made Willa wonder again about Teddy's father and what had become of him, whether the mystery inspired Teddy to do things like this, to take risks.

They played out the hand leisurely. Willa sat in the chair, her sweaty hands tearing up a paper napkin, letting the pieces fall down to the floor like snowflakes. "I'm gonna fold," Harv announced. "I got a whole lot of nothing." He threw down his cards like they were poison. Rudy gazed over his hand at Dale, then at Teddy. He tilted his head back and forth as if he was trying to make up his mind. "Aw, shucks, boys," he said a bit too happily. "I'm gonna have to pull out too."

Teddy looked up for a moment and their eyes locked and Rudy grinned wickedly. Dale was clutching his cards. Teddy lit a cigarette then handed it to Dale who accepted it like a man about to go before the firing squad. Then Teddy lit another for himself. "What do you got?" he said to Dale.

A smile lit the corners of Dale's mouth as he laid out his hand, a full house. He sat back carefully in his chair. "Beat that," he said.

Teddy sighed—with relief or regret, she couldn't tell which. "Well, that's a really good hand, Dale. Really good."

"You see that?" Rudy reached over and slapped Dale on the back.

Then Teddy laid out his hand. "But I got a straight flush."

Dale let out a gasp, as if he'd been hit from behind. His eyes went bright and watery.

"I guess this just ain't your lucky day," Rudy remarked without emotion. Then, in the voice of an undertaker, he said, "Walter, go get me my pliers."

The old man in the bolo tie left the room and Willa wondered if she should go after him and try to stop him. But she didn't move, her body suddenly enervated, as if she couldn't even stand. "Now wait just a second," Dale said, holding up his hands like a man under arrest. He stood up and backed away from the table, but Rudy grabbed him, gripping him around the back, and, in a kind of awkward dance, led him across the floor. "Come on, now, Dale," Rudy said almost gently, "you knew the rules." Dale wriggled free for a moment, but Harv, who was beefy and strong, wrestled the thinner man down to the floor. Under their powerful hands, Dale writhed like a trapped animal, pleading for them to let him up, his spit flying out of his mouth like sparks from a fire. "Don't do it, Rudy!" he cried. "Please!"

"This isn't right," Willa insisted, standing up with her hands on her hips, her heart thumping so hard it hurt, but nobody seemed to hear her. Teddy just stood there watching Dale with a troubling fascination. Willa wanted to walk right up to him and slap the look off his face, but she didn't dare, and then Walter came back with the pliers, which looked rusty, and handed them to Rudy. By now you could smell Dale's sweat and he'd begun to whimper.

Rudy handed Teddy the pliers. "Here you go, Junior. Winner does the honors."

Teddy put the pliers down. "Keep your money. I can't do that."

Rudy grabbed hold of him in the same way he'd done to Dale and shoved him across the room. Teddy fell into some chairs. He pulled himself up. A cut had opened on his forehead. Furious, Teddy shoved Rudy back, but Rudy was quick and before Willa knew it he'd twisted Teddy's arm up behind his back. Pinned like that, Teddy's face turned crimson and she could see a ribbon of sweat up the back of his shirt. Rudy went up close to his ear, intimate as a lover. "You'd be amazed at what a man can do when he doesn't have a choice."

"I don't want the fucking money," Teddy whined, and she thought he might be crying. "I don't fucking want it."

"You gonna show me what you're made of, rich boy? Huh? We're into this thing now." He let Teddy go and again handed him the pliers. He gestured to Dale, who was cowering on the floor under Harv's hands. "Now get it done."

"Please don't," Dale implored Teddy. "You can't do this to me. *Please.*"

Incredibly, Teddy straddled Dale's hips while the other men held him down. "Hold still now," Teddy ordered, his voice eerily tender, but Dale clenched his teeth defiantly, and the more he refused the more determined Teddy became. "Son of a bitch! He won't open his mouth!"

"Jesus fucking Christ," Rudy said, crouching down at Dale's side. "Don't be a fucking pussy." Using his hands, Rudy manipulated Dale's jaws so that Teddy could get the pliers in. Dale's eyes flared white as Teddy grasped hold of a back tooth and began to pull. Horrible noises curled out of Dale's throat. From where she sat Willa could see that the sole of Dale's boot was coming off and she could see his red sock underneath. Teddy's face had gone white and Rudy was standing over him, overseeing the extraction from above, a passive expression on his face. He was a man, she knew, who had grown accustomed to witnessing terrible things. Behavior like this, she imagined, was an acquired habit. Dale began to scream and Teddy pulled the pliers out like he'd been bitten by a snake and he shook his head and threw them down. "I can't get it, I can't do this." He shook his head again, waiting for Rudy, and Rudy nodded. "But you tried, that's the important thing. You put the effort in." Then Rudy picked up the pliers and with savage determination finished the job.

They let Dale up and he staggered, holding on to his mouth in pain, and she could see tears glittering in the corners of his eyes. His hand was covered in blood, thick as a glove. He walked by Rudy like an invisible man, but he gave Teddy a cold look and shoved him out of his way, leaving a handprint of blood on his school clothes. Rudy fished in the bucket for a twenty-dollar bill and stuck it in Teddy's pocket. "Here's a little something for your trouble."

But Teddy snatched it out and dropped it on the floor.

Outside, behind the house, Teddy puked up his whiskey. He leaned up against a tree, shaking his head. "I'm sorry," he said, "you shouldn't have seen that."

He rode her home, sweating out the whiskey. The air was colder now, but she felt numb to it. The moon was high and keen. You could smell wood smoke in the air and she knew before long there would be snow. She wondered about Dale, where he lived and what it must have been like being down on that floor. She'd never been held down by anyone and she imagined it must be the worst thing to endure. Just imagining it made her skin go clammy. It made her hate Teddy a little for what he'd done, but the hate was twisted up with other things, things that made her chest and thighs and belly warm, things she did not understand nor could she explain.

When she got home, they stood in front of her father's enormous house. He had his hands in his pockets like a little boy. "I'm really sorry, Willa."

"I know."

"Forgive me, okay?" He looked at her a minute more. "Later," he said, and rode away.

Behind her, the door opened, and her father stood there waiting. He would want an explanation, she knew, and after she lied to him, fabricating a story about studying all night for a Latin test and losing track of the time, she would kiss his forgiving cheek good night, and crawl into bed and weep with gratitude that somehow God had given her this life—these parents, this house—her beautiful horse—and that, at least for now, she was safe.

10 ∽

The man with the burn on his face was named Luther Grimm. People said he'd burned his mother's house down for the insurance money and had gotten caught, but for some reason nobody could figure out why they'd never convicted him. He was harmless, people said, slow. His mother had gotten hurt in the fire, she was an invalid now. They lived in a small house across the railroad tracks, a mile or so from Teddy's grandfather's house, through the woods and down the hill. Sometimes in town Teddy would see Grimm's truck with the dog chained up on the back of it. It was a brawny animal with short muscular legs. If you got anywhere near that truck the dog went ballistic, barking like crazy and foaming at the mouth. On several occasions when Teddy went walking through the woods behind his grandfather's house, he'd hear the dog barking and it was not an ordinary dog's bark, he'd decided, but one shrill with desperation, a frantic yodeling that gave him a stomachache.

One afternoon after school, on his way home from Marco Liddy's house, where he'd gotten exceptionally stoned and eaten most of the contents of the Liddys' SubZero—Marco's mother was a pastry chef—he heard the dog barking and decided to go down to Grimm's house to have a look. The woods were a jumble of overgrowth. Prickers coiled up from the ground, sticking to his jeans. He crossed the railroad tracks then shuffled down an incline through piles of leaves. He made a lot of noise walking through the leaves and the dog started to howl. Teddy stood on the edge of Grimm's lumpy yard and saw that the dog was chained to a tree. The driveway was empty, Grimm was not at home. The dog was barking and jumping around, yanking the chain, which was the length of a jump rope. Teddy had read up on pit bulls and knew they were, in some circumstances, dangerous, but part of him believed he could save this dog from its miserable fate. The dog kept yanking the chain and the more it yanked the more irritated it got and the louder it barked. You didn't put a dog like that on a short chain, Teddy thought, unless you *wanted* to irritate it.

He didn't like it when people were cruel to animals. There was a lot of cruelty in the world, you saw evidence of it every night on the news, you saw it on those cop shows, when they'd catch someone and maul them to the ground and snap on the cuffs. Even in his own life back in L.A. he'd seen things. And he'd witnessed a kind of brutality in himself that night at the Men's Club. What he'd done to Dale, the way it had felt holding him down. He'd been in fights before once or twice, but this had been different. It wasn't something he could explain and he wasn't proud of it and every time he thought about it he felt sick.

Teddy surveyed the muddy yard, Grimm's house. Most of the paint was peeled off and the window curtains were yellowed and drooping. Just behind the house was a ramshackle well with a little wooden roof over it. Teddy gave in to his curiosity and crossed the yard and looked into the well—a funnel of darkness—then climbed up onto the back porch, which had all sorts of junk stacked on it, rusty old tools and broken machines with buttons and levers, and by now the dog was barking like crazy and there was foam dripping out the sides of its mouth. Teddy peered through the window in the back door. He saw a kitchen that was surprisingly neat. A short dog crate sat under the window. There were pictures of Jesus all over the place, on the walls, the tables. A short hall led to another room where he could make out a hospital bed pushed against the wall. Grimm's mother was in it, which creeped him out. He couldn't see her face, only the back of her head, a nest of white hair. A TV sat on a rolling cart beside the bed, playing a game show. It was turned up so loud that the flimsy walls of the house trembled with the sound of applause.

Teddy heard a truck coming up the road. It was Luther Grimm's truck and it was turning into the driveway. Teddy jumped down off the porch and slipped out of sight behind the garage. Grimm and another man got out of the truck. Dale.

Dale's mouth looked crooked, his cheek swollen. The dog caught their attention, jerking and barking and squealing. Dale looked around the yard, furtively, like a man planning his escape. Grimm walked over to the dog. "What's your problem?" He kicked the animal lightly in the belly. The dog wrestled with Grimm's boot, nipping at it, growling playfully. "He's still a puppy."

"Don't look like no puppy to me," Dale said. "You ever fight him?"

"Fight him? No."

"Well, you should. You could make some money."

"He could get hurt."

"He'd like it," Dale said. "A dog like that. You should think about it."

"He's just a puppy," Grimm said again, and kicked the dog once more, this time a little harder, and the dog growled and tumbled back.

"He ain't gonna be a puppy long," Dale said.

The dog got up to run after them, but by now they were near the porch, and he jerked once more on the chain and yelped. Dale laughed at the dog, an exaggerated guttural laugh, and Grimm laughed too, and they went into the house. The dog walked around in a circle, then lay down and whined.

Teddy felt sorry for that dog. If he wasn't so afraid of it, he'd steal it.

He walked back up the hill into the woods, crossing over the tracks. He wondered what Dale was doing hanging around with Luther Grimm. Whatever it was it couldn't be good, he thought.

The sun came pouring through the trees. You could hear the trees on their old trunks. They whined just a little, whispering their worries to one another like old men in church. They were old and tired and had been standing for centuries and had had enough of it. He could smell the earth and the dry leaves. He came to the field and crossed it and he saw a hawk flying with its brown wings spread wide. It flew wide and slow. Hawks were the smart birds. They knew things. They knew people were stupid. Teddy hoped his mother was home. He wanted to tell her about the dog. He wanted to sit across from her beautiful face and tell her about the dog and about Luther Grimm who'd burned his mother's house down. But his mother wasn't home. She'd left a note. She'd gone to the city for art supplies. He wandered the big empty house. The rooms glimmered with sunshine. They smelled dusty. It was weird to think she'd grown up here. He compared it to the series of dumpy apartments in L.A. where he'd spent the majority of his childhood and it pissed him off. He had a whole lot of reasons for being angry with her, but at the same time he wasn't angry at all. He loved her fiercely.

He took his bike and rode to town. He met up with Willa at the Pizza Shack. Willa had on black eyeliner. He could smell her lipstick and something else, an earthy musky scent that turned him on. He wanted to push himself against her. They each had a slice, sitting at the counter. The TV was on and there was stuff about the war in Iraq. The war was like white noise, people hardly noticed it. You could still eat and watch the report. You could still eat and see bodies piled up along the road like dead pigs in burlap. You could see men with machine guns and still swallow your food.

What would happen next? He could not imagine a future—what that meant—because he had started to doubt the possibility that there'd be one. The way he saw things, the future was tainted food that you unwittingly swallowed because people told you that you'd starve without it, but at the same time you knew it would make you sick. Maybe not right away, but it would work through your body like a virus and once you got to your future, you'd be on your knees, begging God or whoever the fuck was up there for mercy. Because no matter what, everyone was guilty and would suffer the consequences. He looked back at the TV and saw tanks on a deserted road, a correspondent in a khaki vest. The future was unknown, the reporter was saying. It wasn't anything you could count on.

"You want to play some games?" Willa asked. "I've got change."

"Sure."

They walked around to the video store and went down into the basement where they'd put all the games. There were some other kids there from school. She wanted to play the car-racing game. She liked to sit in the leather seat. "Alas, my throne," she would say in her Shakespearean accent, swinging one leg over like mounting a horse. He stood there next to her for a while. Watching her yanking on the gears, her foot pressing down the pedal, did something to his insides. She raced an eighteen-wheeler truck and it buzzed her out. He could see it in her eyes, they went dull and glassy. He played one of the paramilitary games, shooting at gangsters, but couldn't kill enough of them to get a free game. "I need a smoke," he said, and left her there with the game and walked out without turning back. It was almost five and the sun was going down and the air was getting cool. There were some people hanging out at Bev's, eating ice-cream cones. Little children chased one another up and down the breezeway. He saw Ada Heath coming out of the bookstore. She was with this other girl, Beth, who was chunky and always had too much spit in her mouth. He watched them laughing on the street. He wondered what could possibly be so funny. Willa came out and they walked down to O'Brien's for more cigarettes. It was getting dark and he told her he wanted to go home.

"Can you give me a lift?" she said.

"I guess so."

"You *guess* so?"

"You can have the seat, is what I meant." He grinned at her.

"Chivalry is not dead." She took his face in her hands and kissed his cheek like a mother.

They rode down Main Street with its white houses and crooked shutters, its front porches and rocking chairs, its pumpkins and brittle mums. He saw boys making a fort in a pile of leaves and a girl on a tree swing, pushing her heels to the sky. He saw an old man sweeping the sidewalk. Lights were coming on in the windows. He could see people in their houses, a woman setting the table, a family sitting down to supper, and he felt something pull in his chest, a kind of longing he'd never felt before, and it made him want to hold Willa. It made him want to lie down with her someplace and just look at her.

She lived down the road from his grandfather's place. When they finally got there he was covered with sweat. It was nearly dark and fog had settled over the fields. It gave him a feeling, like another kind of ocean, like he was small. "Come in," she said.

He followed her into the house. The place was like a museum. Everything in place. Everything in order. The floors were shiny and clean. He didn't know where to put his feet. He could hear music coming from one of the rooms. They went through the kitchen, into the foyer. The music was coming from her father's study, a symphony on the stereo. The door was ajar and her father was inside. The phone rang and the music went down and the door started to close. Teddy could smell a cigar. Willa started up the circular staircase and Teddy followed her, glancing into the father's study. Joe Golding nodded to him as he closed his door. In Willa's room, horses galloped across the wallpaper and she had ribbons all over the place that she'd won in horse shows. They shut her door and sat down on the rug and she put some headphones onto him. It was strange music, like chanting. He didn't know what it was and he didn't ask her. Then she unzipped his pants and made him come.

Once Teddy had Willa Golding under his skin he thought about little else. He did not focus at school. His tutor would point to various sentences, lines of little black marks, and read the words out loud, but he heard none of it. They were words and they made a sound when they came out of her mouth and her mouth made a funny shape when she said them, but none of it mattered to Teddy—it meant nothing to him. He could not interpret the sound. He watched his tutor's lips pronouncing the word *somnolent* and he thought about kissing Willa.

S O M N O L E N T

He could stretch it apart and the letters separated like bread in a puddle, so he saw *TENT* and he saw *TENT ON SAM* and it did not make sense. He saw *TENSION*. And he heard monks chanting.

He had brought his face down to her belly, the soft pillow of flesh, and he had played with her nipples and they had poked up in his mouth like gumdrops.

He wanted Willa. He wanted to be *inside* her.

Romeo and Juliet did not interest him. It bored him silly. He was *stupefied* with boredom. He was *FRIED WITH STUPE*. He was *STUPID and FRIED*. At school, he felt like an outlaw, like in those old Westerns. Like when he'd walk into Mrs. Heath's class everyone went quiet and looked at him expectantly, nervously, like he was about to take out a gun or something. It was weird. Mrs. Heath turned the shade of curdled milk at the very sight of him and he'd think: *This town's not big enough for the both of us!* She would mark up his papers with wild abandon, encircling his terrible grades in red ink like some stamp of disapproval, and he'd have to pretend it didn't get to him, but it did. He told his mother he wasn't doing very well and she shrugged and said, "Just try your best." He didn't know what his best was. He wasn't good at reading and he'd never be good at it and you had to be good at it if you wanted to do well. There was no way around it. When the teachers asked questions in class and the hands would rise up like the flags of inferior countries, he *knew* the answer too; it just took a little longer for it to come into his head. It would fly into his brain like a big clumsy insect, one of those slow-flying cockroaches, and land there, finally, making a spectacle of itself. What did it matter if he was a little slow? They never called on him anyway.

His mind wandered. He'd watch the people at school. They all seemed stuck inside little clouds and he couldn't hear them or understand them. Even when he heard what they were saying, *what* they said made no sense. He would yawn and yawn. They were all talking so much. It was noisy. Talking and laughing and scratching and smiling. He watched the jiggling girls at school. They were flashes of pink. They were this hand or that leg. This foot. This pair of glossy lips. Those tits. Their hair smelled of coconuts. It fell in their faces as they spoke. But Willa was not pink. Willa was a striped cat high up in a tree, ready to pounce. She had little soft paws. She was a dark animal in the shadows. She was a rubber ball rolling through the wide hallways of her father's house, down the stairs, *bounce, bounce, bounce.* Willa bounced and floated. She bounced up and down and up again. She was a fucking Super Ball.

11 ༄

What it felt like sucking on Teddy's penis. He had a nice one and it was friendly, it was polite. She didn't have any trouble making friends with it. She liked its shiny hat. She liked his musky smell. She liked his clothes and wanted to wear them. She liked boy's clothes better than girl's clothes. His clothes always smelled good and fresh. She tried to imagine his mother washing them. His mother didn't have any help like her mother did. Sucking on Teddy's penis was not as big a deal as people thought. It made him feel good and she liked the way he looked afterward with his face ruddy and damp and that beautiful smile he had, one tooth sticking out a little more than the other. Teddy was gorgeous. He was going to be something when he was in his twenties, she knew. But he wasn't as smart as Marco, at least he couldn't seem to get good grades like Marco. Willa didn't know why. He had refused to read aloud in class and nobody said anything, not even Mr. Jernigan, everyone just teetering on their tipped-back chairs to see what he'd do. Teddy seemed smart to her. Smarter than most people. He was always thinking. He had ideas about things. Just the way he looked at something—like some ordinary thing—he'd consider it as though it had just dropped down from Saturn or something. You could tell he was thinking something deeper than most. And things bothered him. Trash on Mount Everest, rude people, careless behavior. Whenever he rode her home on his bike he'd point out all the trash along the side of the road that people threw out of their windows. "How can people be so careless?" he'd say to her. He took it all to heart. She liked Teddy so she sucked on his penis. It didn't worry her much. She opened her mouth and let him in and let him go down her throat till her eyes teared. She wasn't comparing what she did for him to what he did for her—you didn't do that when you loved someone. He might put his head on her belly and breathe her in—she took care to dab some perfume below her belly button—but she wasn't letting him inside her pants and he knew it and he respected that and he didn't even try. She felt like she could be herself with Teddy. They could just *be* together and it was all right. It was quiet and peaceful. They could just *be*.

Mrs. Heath was always getting after Teddy. She was a bitch, and everybody had started to hate her. She was always after the girls for rolling over the waistbands of their skirts so that the hem rested at midthigh instead of at the knee, where it was supposed to be. She'd chase you down in the courtyard and make you lower it while she watched, but with Teddy it was different. Mean-spirited. She came up to him at lunch that day, her face jaundiced and wrinkled like a dried apricot, and explained in a voice dripping with honey that his paper for her class was unacceptable, on something like a fourth-grade level, and how dare he attempt to turn something like that in to her. "Your work insults me," is what she'd said, shoving the paper into his hand. Willa took him into the girl's room to smoke before Chemistry and they stood there together in the way horses will stand quietly, hardly moving. Teddy leaned at the window with his tortured squint, wearing his usual gray wool sweater. It was his dead grand-father's sweater and the sleeves were frayed on the bottom. Teddy was a big husky dog with his pretty blue eyes and pink tongue and if he had a tail it would be wagging, no matter what his trouble. He was a happy dog and she knew he didn't care what Mrs. Heath thought—not really he didn't. Then Ada Heath came in and com-plained, "He's not supposed to be in here, there are rules for Christ's sake, why can't he follow them." Teddy muttered something under his breath and walked out and Willa absorbed Ada's drama like some kind of toxic smoke. Ada rubbed her eyes with her yellow fingertips and bragged about her bulimia. Yesterday she'd done it twice. "Your face is yellow," Willa told her. "Be careful."

Sex was everywhere she looked. The possibility of sex lingered be-tween people like the shadows of trees. She could feel it with Teddy, a kind of heat. She was still a virgin, but she thought about it a lot, trying to imagine what it would be like, how it would feel to have a boy inside her. She didn't think it was such a big deal like everyone said. Her parents had taught her that sex was a natural thing that oc- curred between people who loved each other, it was natural and it was beautiful. Just the word *beautiful* was seductive—but what did it really mean? *Beauty* was a soft word that ached with possibility, pliant as dough. You could not presume to define it, she realized, because the very idea of beauty and all it represented was a subjective thing—*in the eye of the beholder*—but that wasn't really true anymore, it hadn't been true for a long time. The media defined what beauty was. You would look at a magazine and you'd say *that is beautiful.* Or you'd watch two people making love in a movie and you'd think *that is beautiful.* Or *she is beautiful. She had a beautiful body.* But someone had *decided* it was beautiful and made it so. There was *real* beauty like you saw in nature or in babies, and then there was *fake* beauty like you saw in movie stars or women who looked too young for their years or in artificial flowers. Some things *looked* natural and some things *looked* beautiful, but really weren't. It was confusing. It was deceiving. Just the word *natural*—it prickled with artifice. *It looks so natural,* her mother had cooed over Monica's mother's eye job. *So natural.* But it *wasn't* natural, was it? Her mother's boobs weren't natural either. Natural would be sagging, pendulous, weary. But nobody wanted *that* brand of natural. Deception taunted people, Willa thought. It was routine, it was pervasive, and such casual trickery made her furious, but she could never discuss these ideas with anyone, except maybe Teddy, who hated the world almost as much as she did. *Feed them a steady diet of deception and everyone will be happy.*

When she got home from school that afternoon, her parents were fighting in the kitchen. The minute she walked in they shut up, as if she couldn't tell; her mother had begun to cry. They were quiet tears; they were not for sale.

Willa blamed everything on sex. She didn't think that her parents ever had sex. They never touched each other—not even in a casual way. Her dad never put his arms around her mom like you saw married people do in movies. He didn't come in at the end of the day and kiss her hello and vice versa. He never said, "You look beautiful, Candace," like the men in movies said to their wives. Her parents took each other for granted or something. They were just taking up space in the same house. She loved her father and she loved her mother, but it didn't matter to her if they were together or not. Not really it didn't. She had thought about it and decided. Everybody got divorced, eventually. Some people just had more endurance than others. Willa just wanted them to be happy. A wall had come up between her parents. They couldn't talk anymore. In the big quiet house that had swallowed them whole.

12 ᢗᢌ

"Everyone has a broken heart," Nate told his students. "That is the first thing you have to know if you are going to write." He said this mostly to provoke them, to rouse them from their teenaged stupor, but, dramatic as it was, he believed it to be true. The class was comprised of fifteen juniors. They sat around a wooden table on ladder-back chairs. They were all staring at him, forlorn as neglected house pets. He suspected that they were feeling sorry for him.

"You have to become very quiet," Nate told them. "You have to listen."

Marco Liddy, whose father made the widgets for airplanes, shifted in his chair and said in his typically patronizing tone, "And what are we listening for?"

Some of the others stifled laughter. "Voices," said Nate.

"Voices," Marco repeated, and looked around at his mates as though he'd made his point.

"When you write, you might hear some. But you've got to get very quiet."

Willa Golding frowned. The period was about to end. She had things to say, he could see it in her eyes. Questions. She ran her hand through her long hair, her bracelets jingling. He saw in her eyes a longing for something she could not yet define, and he sensed that, before long, she'd search for whatever it was in all the wrong places, just like Cat had.

Journal writing was considered a fundamental practice for new writers and it was included in nearly every high school's creative writing curriculum across the country. This is what he told the students, dispensing a box of composition notebooks around the table, but in truth he saw little benefit in it. He was not in the habit of writing in a journal, nor did he necessarily believe that writing in a journal produced good writing in the classroom. He supposed it allowed students to translate their feelings and ideas onto the page, without the pressure of producing something artful, but in his case, cheap shot that it was, it would bring him closer to Willa, and that was his primary concern. It would take him into her mind. "Your journals will be strictly confidential," he told them.

"What are we supposed to write about?" Teddy Squire asked.

"Anything you want. Anything at all."

"Are we getting graded on these?" Ada Heath asked in a burdened voice.

"No," he said. "No grades on journals. Writing is your freedom. Just go with it. See where it takes you."

On his way out, Teddy stopped to see him. He waited until everybody had cleared out before he spoke. "It's true what you said, the broken heart thing."

Nate nodded. "But, it's a very forgiving muscle."

Teddy looked at him, skeptically. "Whatever." He shrugged, and went out.

On the surface, The Pioneer School was an ideal place. As a visiting writer, Gallagher was treated cordially, with guarded respect. Most of the teachers had been there for years. They were a somewhat eccentric group, the sort of folks he'd grown up with, who lived in dusty little houses crammed with books. Over lunch in the teachers' lounge, they'd discuss a variety of teaching-related subjects. They often discussed ethical issues, in the vein of Theodore Sizer, whom several of them admired. They assured Nate that the school had changed since the early days when many of them had first started. "Since Heath's been the Head," Mr. Jernigan whispered conspiratorially, "it's a very different place. More competitive. The uniforms and whatnot. Many of us here don't support what he's doing. Unfortunately, the parents do."

"Heath has one goal and one goal only," Mrs. Wheaton asserted, then hissed the word, as if it were profanity: *"Money."*

The kids were different now too, they argued. The world had made them so. They blamed the television, the Internet, the iPods. Even the drugs were different. You couldn't trust the drugs anymore. "Not like in our day," Jernigan said. "Now, who knows what they're getting?"

The parents too were different. "In your face," Jernigan complained. "I get phone calls at all hours."

"It's the money again," Mrs. Wheaton said. "They pay more, so they expect more. Yet, it guarantees them nothing."

"Yes," Jernigan agreed. *"That's* the betrayal."

"There's nothing worse than that," Mrs. Wheaton confirmed.

"Suddenly, little schools like ours are out of favor with the Ivy League. They want the public school kids. They're under the impression that they work harder."

"Myths!" Mrs. Wheaton said.

"It's all nonsense of course," Jernigan said. "I feel for the kids, I really do."

On the few occasions that Maggie Heath took lunch, Nate would sit with her out of a sense of brotherly obligation. She ate in a kind of disconsolate haze. One had the sense that if she moved too fast, or too abruptly, all of the thoughts in her head would spill out onto the floor, only to be swept up later by the janitor and thrown in the trash. She was a woman, he thought, with little confidence in herself. There was an ambiguity about her that made him anxious. Occasionally, he'd see marks on her body in curious places. Raw-looking rings around her wrists and ankles; he found them disconcerting. She scarcely ate. She'd take a brown bag out of her briefcase and proceed to empty its contents on the table: a can of vegetable juice, a Baggie full of carrots, a small triangle of cheese, three crackers. And she seldom finished it. She'd put everything back into the bag, relieved, it seemed, that the lunch period was over, and dump it in the trash.

Sometimes, after work, they'd go running together. They'd go down by the lake. There was a trail around the lake that attracted many runners. The lake was seven miles around, but their route was only three. Maggie was easily winded, but refused to slow down. She'd get a look in her eye of feverish determination. In truth, he would have preferred to run alone. There was something draining about being with her, and he found himself worrying about her more than he should. Somehow, their history at Choate, vague as it was, had encouraged a siblinglike bond, and neither had refuted it. When he'd ask her, casually, "Is everything all right?" she always gave him a winning smile and said, "Why shouldn't it be?"

As the weeks passed, Nate detected in Maggie a growing animosity for Teddy Squire. She seemed highly critical of the boy, more than most, accusing him of being lazy and insolent, two qualities that Nate frankly saw in her own daughter, Ada. Perhaps not lazy, but Ada had something of an attitude. He sensed that the faculty members walked on eggshells around her, and graded her accordingly, allowing her more than the benefit of the doubt—but, then again, perhaps *he* was being ungenerous. Everybody knew it was the social kiss of death to be related to the Head of School—and somehow Ada seemed to hold her own. He knew she was friendly with Willa, but he also knew that, now that Teddy Squire was in the picture, Willa was less than devoted to her.

Nate couldn't relate to Maggie's criticism of the boy. In his estimation, Squire was bright, observant, acutely aware of his surroundings. Yes, his handwriting was chaotic and he had trouble forming a decent sentence, but his ideas were unique, different from the other kids', more exacting, more deliberate. On the rare occasion when he spoke up in class, it always turned the conversation in a surprising direction. The kids would sit up taller in their chairs.

Nate wasn't worried about Teddy Squire. He was going to be just fine.

The trees were turning colors, blazing with red and gold. The lake had taken on a somber hue, a foreboding of what winter might bring. After their run, Nate and Maggie would say their good-byes and he'd walk through town on the way home and buy something to cook for dinner in the small grocery on the corner, a steak or a piece of fish, a good bottle of wine. While his dinner was cooking, he'd have a drink in the empty living room, in the salmon light of the setting sun, and think about the book he was trying to write and how badly he wanted to write it. He ate in the tiny kitchen, listening to the blaring sound of Larkin's television, scandalous news shows dishing out the perilous travails of ordinary people like gruel in a soup kitchen. He'd read over the journals of his students, coming to know their specific likes and dislikes, their tastes in music and fashion, their ideas about politics even, their fears and dreams, and in the process he came to know Willa, which only reaffirmed in his mind that Catherine had been right, after all, to give her up. Nothing had been spared in raising her, it seemed; she had a privileged life with the Goldings. And in her face, her bright, dazzling eyes, he saw that she was happy.

Coming up here had restored him on some fundamental level. He could remember the month or two just after giving her up. He'd lost Catherine; he'd lost them both. He remembered that sharp little pain in his gut. He'd have nightmares and wake with the baby's screaming ringing in his ears. There was nothing worse than not knowing how she was—not being able to call and check. *His child was out in the world—with strangers!* Not knowing if she'd been fed or changed or hugged sufficiently. Wondering if she'd experienced any confusion—if she'd known, in her tiny little mind, that her mother was gone—her *real* mother—and that this new mother was there to stay. Had she missed him at all? The way he used to carry her up on his chest like a little kitten? His big hand on the soft crown of her head. When they'd walk on the pier with all the sounds and colors and he'd hold her up so people could see—the fishmonger with his glass eye, the man selling umbrellas, who'd touch her cheek with his crooked, tobacco-stained finger, cooing at her like a pigeon, or the fat lady bartender with her frilly neckline who'd always ask: "How's my little sunshine today?"

You couldn't go back that far; your brain didn't let you. Which he knew was for the best. Because there were other things she'd remember too. The apartment, her mother comatose on the bed, her teeth black as licorice. Her sour milk smell. The look in her eyes, of terror.

Cat was dead; she'd been dead for sixteen years, and his life was finally, at long last, just beginning.

13 ⟋⟍

They were drinking in the Union Cemetery: Willa and Teddy Squire and Ada Heath and Monica Travers and Marco Liddy and Bette Lawton and her sister, Darcy, who had a turnip brain and had to be coaxed into the cold field with a bag of Hershey's Kisses like a dim-witted nag. Monica dared them to find the Weeping Angel, a statue on one of the graves whose hands had been severed at the wrists. It was said she wept tears of blood whenever there was a full moon, and there was a full moon tonight. Legend had it if you touched the statue you got cursed, and there were stories to prove it. One man had crashed into a telephone pole just outside the cemetery gates and died instantly—his car horn had woken the caretaker. Willa was superstitious and believed in things like legends and curses, and it was why she'd kept her distance from the statue all her life, but tonight they were all stoned and drunk and happy and nothing bad was going to happen, that's what Teddy was telling her as he cored an apple and stuffed it with pot and lit it up like a pipe and passed it around. It reminded Willa of the film they'd seen in Cultural Studies about Aborigines. They'd had a substitute and when she left the room they'd had a spitball contest to see who could hit the nipples on the naked women of the tribe. It had been an intensely juvenile thing to do, even the boys admitted it, but Teddy Squire had a way of transforming even the most insipid behavior into a life-altering experience. Teddy laughed suddenly, like water splattering, and handed Willa the pipe and she took a hit, letting the sweet smoke quiver inside her. She didn't really like to smoke, but they wouldn't trust her if she didn't. They'd turn her into someone else.

They linked arms and marched across the field like some crazy infantry, chanting: *Left, left, left my wife with forty-eight kids, right, right, right in the middle of the kitchen floor,* and it was so cold you could see your words like smoke on the black air, and there was the jangle of stolen whiskey bottles and the yellow moon screaming above them, taunting the spinning earth as if any moment they would all fall off and be sucked into oblivion. *Oblivion* was one of her SAT words: *The quality or condition of being completely forgotten.* It was how she felt sometimes. Not just forgotten, but *completely* forgotten. It was a feeling she had from time to time and she thought it had something to do with being adopted. The mystery she carried around was *her* birthmark. She didn't know much about her biological parents, except that they'd been very young, and that her biological mother had died. She'd had a weak heart, but she'd been very beautiful. "You look just like her," her mother had told her, smoothing back her hair behind her ear the way she always did. They'd been students or something, out in San Francisco. They'd been the ones to name her; it was part of the agreement, that she kept her name.

She was cold and wanted to go home, but she couldn't leave now, they'd think she was afraid. She *was* afraid. She didn't like cemeteries, they gave her the creeps, and when she thought about death, its vacant intangibility, she felt a wild rush of helplessness. Sometimes she pictured herself in a coffin under the ground, her hands folded across her chest, the white satin enveloping her like snow. A girl from school had almost killed herself and Willa knew it was a stupid thing to do, even though sometimes she wondered what it would be like, just lying there, waiting to get pulled into heaven. Sometimes, when she looked in the mirror, she tried to imagine her dead mother's face and on some occasions could even believe that she saw her there, shining through like a ghost. It would freak her out and she'd have to look away. She didn't know anything about her biological father or his whereabouts, but her father had told her when she turned thirteen that he'd do whatever he could to find him, if that's what she wanted, and she'd been so touched by the gesture that she'd put the thought out of her mind after that. Somehow, knowing where he was didn't matter as much to her—he hadn't been the one to carry her for nine months and give birth to her—it was different for men. And men could be such assholes.

It was how she felt about Teddy Squire—he was hard to know. Sometimes he seemed indifferent to her. She had to be careful. He wanted things from her. Sex. She could tell; she could *feel* it. She wasn't sure; she didn't know what to do about it. She wasn't certain about anything, except maybe riding Boy, but it was impossible to explain how she felt to anyone—that was one thing she and her mother had in common: horses. There was nothing that compared to being on a horse. The wind rushing through your hair, the horse's sweat mixing with your own, the smell in the air when you rode. And the sound that galloping made as you crossed a field. That sound alone was a kind of drug. But the feeling she got—of being totally free. Freedom was her drug, not stupid pot. Not pills. She felt connected to her horse. She knew he loved her and it was *real* love, not love because you got something for it. It was her own private feeling and they shared it when they were together, especially after she rode him, when she brushed him in the cold quiet of the stable. You couldn't have that quiet love with a real boy, she thought. But with horses it was different.

Monica started running and then everybody started running. Monica with her perfect boobs, her murderous black hair, eyes that glittered with secrets. Willa was flat-chested and didn't have any secrets. Monica was smaller than her and curvy and slim-hipped and had her own account at Gatsby's. She was a prep; she bought Lacoste T-shirts at seventy bucks a shot, and wore them a size too small so her belly showed, even though it was against school rules. She had a way of making you do things you didn't want to, like drinking somebody's bourbon. Monica had moved up from the city with her mother because her father had fallen in love with somebody else. They lived in an old cottage full of unpacked boxes. People thought she was cool because she was from the city, and she had this power over them. Even Teddy, who was no less susceptible to big boobs than the next boy, couldn't resist her.

They found the statue in the deepest part of the cemetery, among the crooked Pilgrim stones. The statue was taller than she expected, over six feet, draped in robes of cement. Her severed wrists, which ended in stumps, seemed to tilt up toward the heavens. Great wings were attached to her back. Her long hair twisted snakelike down to her hips. Her breasts were perfectly round. Willa wondered about the stonecutter who'd made her, if he'd fashioned her after the dead woman in the ground, or after his own fantasy of a woman. The grave read *Beloved Wife and Mother,* but this woman didn't look like anyone's mother.

Teddy came up to her ear, his breath a warm hiss. "Want some more?" He held up the apple and she shook her head. He ran his fingers through her hair. His fingers had cuts from Shop and the Band-Aids were catching in her hair. He was making a box for his mother for Christmas, with an owl carved into the top. Mr. Jernigan, who taught the Shop class, had made a big fuss over it, saying that his mother was lucky to get such a fine gift. Teddy didn't talk about his father much. She knew he lived someplace far away, out of the country perhaps. Teddy's mother was beautiful and cool and she was an artist and Willa couldn't understand why she'd left L.A. and come to live here, in the most boring place on Earth.

"Who wants to go first?" Monica said in a diabolical, stoned voice. They stood there in front of the statue, looking up at it, everybody's breath like smoke, everybody stuttering in the cold. "Okay, you cowards." Monica took out her pack of Marlboros and emptied all the cigarettes into her hand. Then she ripped one in half. She put them back into a pile so you couldn't see which one was ripped, then held them out like a little bouquet of flowers. "We all pick. Whoever picks the short one has to touch her."

"I have to get her home," Bette Lawson said, tugging her sister's sleeve.

"Fraidy cat," Monica said.

"This is so stupid," Ada Heath announced.

"It's *not* stupid, Ada. It's *exciting*. You never want to do anything, you're so afraid Mommy and Daddy'll find out."

"I am not," Ada said sullenly.

"Are too." Monica thrust the cigarettes out to Bette. "Bette picks first. Then she can go."

Nobody said anything. It pissed Willa off how much power Monica had. Bette's sister, Darcy, who had something wrong with her, nobody knew what exactly but you could see it in her eyes, a squint of confusion, began to cry. Loud, shuddering sobs. "Don't do it, Bette, *please don't!*"

Trembling, Bette reached out her hand and chose a long cigarette. "Not me," she declared to the solemn group. Then everybody else picked, including Willa, who knew instantly that she had lost. Defiantly, she lit the cigarette, and everybody backed away from her, like she had a disease.

"Don't do it, Willa!" Darcy cried. "You'll get cursed!"

"You don't really believe this shit, Willa," Teddy said.

Willa threw down the cigarette and looked up into the statue's face, her indifferent gaze, and wondered how the legend had come about in the first place. Why were women always getting accused of being the evil ones? It wasn't fair. It had occurred to her even when she was little, watching the movie version of *Snow White*. Even in the fairy tales, the female villains never relied on weapons to do their damage—they were far cleverer than that. They relied on deception. Games and trickery. Everything was just another game and you couldn't trust a woman, you couldn't believe a word she said. The statue didn't *look* dangerous, she thought, but perhaps that was its greatest danger. Girls like Monica didn't *look* dangerous either. It was hard to know when you could trust someone.

It made her angry; it made her stomach ache.

Someone pushed her from behind and she stumbled into the statue's cold embrace. Everyone was laughing and when she turned around she saw that it had been Ada who had pushed her and that even Teddy was laughing.

"Cursed," Darcy whispered darkly.

"It's only a joke," Teddy said.

Willa swallowed hard to keep from crying. She hated Teddy for laughing and she hated Ada and she doubly hated Monica. She ran as fast as she could back through the graveyard toward the road and Teddy was running too and she slowed down a little so he could catch up. She wanted him to take her in his arms and hold her, that was the only thing she wanted, but he didn't. He grabbed her roughly and said, "Would you fucking wait?"

She looked at his face, his mouth.

"I want to get cursed too." He kissed her, his tongue sweet and bitter and dry and wet, but she didn't want him kissing her now.

"I can't."

"Come on," he said with an edge of impatience. "You know I love you."

But she didn't know. She didn't know anything. She started running. She ran like a wild horse through the blue cold light of the cemetery. She could hear Teddy chasing her, breathing fiercely, calling her name and telling her to wait, *wait up,* but then it was quiet, and there was nothing, only the wind, and she knew he'd given up, and she suspected that it was the very thing that would be Teddy's downfall in life—that he gave up too easily. She stopped to listen. They were still up on the hill, she could hear them laughing and she knew that the laughter was about her, but she wouldn't go back up there, she wouldn't, she'd just keep going.

It was almost eleven and the road was dark and her cell phone was out of charge. Teddy should have run after her, she thought. He should have cared more. She didn't want to have sex with him anyway. For a long time she had thought she might, they almost *had,* but now that possibility was a dead thing that could not be watered. She ran along the road in the flashing light of the cars, tears coming down her face. *Cursed,* he had said as he kissed her. *I'm cursed.*

It wasn't safe on the road at night. Anyone could stop. Anyone could grab her. Her throat burned from all the cigarettes and she was still a little drunk. But the rest of her was strong. She'd been in track last year, before Monica had come to Pioneer. It was like a dare because Monica didn't participate on school teams. She didn't want Willa running track and Willa had been such a loser last year that she'd quit so Monica would think she was cool. It had been something she'd done for her friend, a symbol of loyalty, and now she knew it had been stupid because Monica didn't do anything for her in return, Monica didn't do things for people.

Walking in the darkness her life suddenly became clear to her. You could hear everything in the darkness. You could hear the grass. You could hear the wind gulping at your neck like somebody trying desperately to tell you something, like someone coming out of the woods in tattered clothes and covered with dirt and a look of terror on his face. A fugitive—that was who the wind was tonight—and he desperately wanted to tell her something. *What?* What was he trying to tell her?

Sometimes, in the wormy dark of her head, she hated herself. It was a deep thick muddy hate, way deep inside of her. She might stick her finger down into the throat of it just to see what came up. Down where it gets narrow and damp, but even that wasn't deep enough. When she was a child and they went to the beach in Montauk her mother would tell her to dig all the way to China and she would try to do it and that's what she meant now, digging so deep into her own misery. You can't find the bottom of it. You can't touch it. Nobody really understood what she was going through. She just felt down. *Down, down, down.* She had taken to wearing black and nobody seemed to care. There was this Goth store at Crossgates Mall and she had bought a black cape, but still hadn't worn it. She imagined herself naked in the black cape and it made her body restless, it made her heart feel rubbery. Her parents had stayed up late the other night discussing their troubled daughter and her father had said in his ultimately casual tone that it was all normal teenaged angst, nothing to worry about, and she'd felt like screaming, *There is nothing normal about me!*

Her parents were having problems. She had seen them apparently avoiding each other all around the house. Her mother would pause, often, at the windows, gazing out at the horses. Her mother was like an old beautiful harp you pulled out of a closet only to discover that the strings had popped. It was her mother who filled the house with strangers. The cook, the cleaners, the errand runners. Her mother had insisted on building the stables and buying the horses and hiring Rudy and the trainer Carlos and her mother spent so much money it wasn't even funny. One day it would run out, Willa thought, and there would be nothing left. And her father wouldn't survive without money. He relied on certain comforts—his weekly massages and manicures, his personal trainer—whereas her mother could survive anywhere, her mother was like some kind of slippery animal, she could adapt. Her mother had been in a foster home. She'd been a sad little girl and she was a sad woman too. Willa felt sorry for her and she loved her desperately. She wanted her to be happy. The only time her mother looked happy was when they rode together. They'd take the horses out on the trails and they'd ride for hours without even talking. They didn't need to talk. Silence was their language; it was something they could share.

But being her father's wife wasn't easy, even Willa knew that. He could be demanding. He could be distant. Her mother had figured out how to be a rich woman. She walked around in the most expensive clothes she could find with her shirt open too low so all the men on the farm could look into the deep crevice of her cleavage and see the lace trim on her bra—but it wasn't for all of *them*. She dressed like that for her husband, but he never seemed to notice.

Willa could remember reading the story of Thumbelina as a child, confused that such a delicate girl could marry an ugly mole, and it reminded her of her parents—her father, like the mole, was dark and hairy with large, brooding features, and he could be rude and unpleasant, especially on the telephone when he spoke to his people in California then complained afterward of their stupidity. Like the mole he had a preference for dark rooms, closing himself up in his paneled study, removed from fresh air and sunlight, smoking cigars incessantly, a proven method of keeping everyone out. It was all about money where her parents were concerned, and her father had

tons of it. She didn't know where he'd gotten it all, but it was there—
it was *everywhere*. And like poor Thumbelina, her mother had crawled
into a hole, far away from everything she knew. Even Willa knew that
you couldn't wash that kind of dirt off your feet once you'd trampled
through it.

Down the road, a car was coming toward her. It was an old-
fashioned car, a vintage convertible with the top down. The car was
turquoise, with whitewalled tires. It looked familiar, and she thought
it might be one of the cars in her dad's car club. She kept walking,
the bright lights in her face. The car came up beside her and for a
moment she thought it was her father, swiftly machinating an explanation for her whereabouts, but it wasn't. It was somebody else she
recognized, Mr. Heath. "Hello, Willa."

"Hello, sir."

"What in God's name are you doing out here?"

"I'm walking home."

"At this hour?"

She shrugged, unwilling to elaborate.

"Get in. I'll give you a ride."

She hesitated for a moment, hoping that by now Teddy would appear, hurrying to catch up and apologize, but he didn't, and she
couldn't help wondering if her Headmaster's fluke appearance was
a cunning harbinger of the Angel's curse. Still, she was cold and
scared and it was better than walking home. She got in and put on
the seat belt, stretching the old-fashioned strap across her lap.

"Cool car."

"It's not mine. I'm in a club—with your dad, in fact."

"What is it?"

"A Thunderbird."

"It's nice."

"I'm kind of a car fanatic. It's always been an interest of mine. Believe it or not, I'm a pretty good mechanic."

It occurred to her that Mr. Heath wasn't his usual tucked-in self.
The tail of his Brooks Brothers' shirt was hanging out and there was
a pack of cigarettes in the front pocket—she wasn't aware that he

was a smoker and smoking was forbidden at Pioneer. A seedy corduroy blazer was jumbled up on the seat between them. His genial boyish charm seemed compromised tonight by the stubble on his cheeks, a sheepish glaze over his eyes. "Ever since I was a kid I've loved them," he went on. "Cars, I mean. I was always good with things like that. Mechanical things."

"Where did you grow up?" she asked him.

"Everywhere." He looked over at her. "I'm an army brat."

"That must have been hard," she said, even though she would move the first chance she got. She would travel; she would live in Paris.

He grunted and shook his head. "As my father would say: Not hard enough."

He smiled, but she saw that it was a sad smile, and it made her sorry for him.

"Let's see what this baby can do." He shifted and stepped on the gas and they drove the dark empty roads. Willa was glad he was driving fast because with all the wind blowing around it was too loud to talk. She stared ahead at the road, her hair blowing wildly about her face. What Mr. Heath was doing driving around at this time of night eluded her. It seemed doubly strange that he hadn't asked her about Ada, who, at the moment, was stoned out of her mind in the Union Cemetery and by now was probably puking her guts out, which was not particularly unusual when it came to Ada, who threw up regularly for sport. The radio was tuned to the local jazz station, a raspy whisper through the speakers. It was Miles Davis, she realized. His tune "So What?"

Heath turned onto Hawthorne Road and sped up even more. He glanced at her and smiled and she couldn't help laughing, it was fun, it was terrific—and they passed all the landmarks she knew so well— the red cottage where Nathaniel Hawthorne had lived and the boys' summer camp on the lake, the little dark cabins along the shore, and the furry evergreens under the cotton-candy moon. They went over the bridge, where a lone man was fishing, then up Prospect Hill with its deep, narrow curves. Heath was driving well over the posted speed limit, looking more like a savvy race car driver than the head-master of a school, and less than a mile from her house a cop pulled up behind them with his siren wailing.

Heath cursed under his breath and pulled over. Willa froze in her seat, her mouth dry. She couldn't help thinking about the little roach she'd stashed in her pocket. She hadn't wanted to take the joint when Monica had handed it to her, and she'd put it out and hidden it and everyone had forgotten about it. Worse, she noticed the neck of a gin bottle poking out from where he'd secured it between the seat and the gears column. Stealthily, he reached around for it and shoved it under the seat. Then he unrolled his shirtsleeves and buttoned them at the wrists. He swiftly retrieved a roll of Lifesavers from his pocket and put one in his mouth. By then the cop was there, his flashlight raised like a weapon.

"License and registration," the cop said.

Opening the glove compartment, Mr. Heath touched her knee. "Was I going too fast?" With the cop watching, he flipped through the car's documents in search of the registration, then handed it to him. Willa's knee throbbed with heat where he'd rubbed it with his knuckles.

"I'll say," the cop said, reading over the license. "Try seventy-five in a thirty-mile limit."

"I didn't think this thing could go that fast."

"Have you had any alcohol tonight, Mr. Heath?"

"Maybe a beer or two earlier with dinner," Heath admitted. "But nothing since then."

The cop studied Mr. Heath's face, then looked over at Willa.

"This is my daughter's friend," Heath tried to explain. "I'm just tak-ing her home up the road here."

Willa nodded and tried to smile.

"A little late to be out on a school night, Mr. Heath," the cop said, dissatisfied. "Why don't you step out of the car?"

"Is that really necessary, Officer?" Heath tossed a glance in her di-rection and the cop frowned.

"Step out of the car, Mr. Heath."

Heath's face went peaked as he stepped onto the pavement. The cop led him away from the car, but Willa could still easily hear them. The cop made him walk along the thick white line bordering the road. Willa's heart thumped as she watched him. Tears prickled her eyes. *The poor man*. She was embarrassed, sitting there. She wished she could just get out and walk home, but that wasn't possible, not now with the cop there. Several minutes passed. Finally, Heath got back in the car, annoyed. "It'll just be another minute," he told her. "He's writing a ticket."

"Okay," she said.

He rubbed his eyes. "I am so sorry about this."

"It's okay. Really."

They sat there in the screaming silence of the car. Heath had broken a sweat. She could see it gleaming on his forehead in the moonlight. "I feel just awful about it."

She didn't know what to say to him. "Don't worry. It's fine." She turned around and saw that the cop was talking on his radio.

"Adults make mistakes too," he said stupidly.

She nodded.

"God knows I've made plenty." He checked the rearview mirror to see what the cop was doing, then sat back and folded his arms across his chest. "It's not easy these days," he said.

"What?"

"It's hard to know."

She didn't really know what he meant, but she said, "It must be."

"Too many choices, that's the problem. Sometimes you get to a point, you know?"

She looked at his face. His eyes seemed distant. "What do you mean?"

He shook his head. "You wake up one day and nothing's the same. It's like you're in the wrong life or something. I don't know how to explain it."

"You mean like you're an imposter?" she asked.

"Something like that." Again, he cracked a smile. "You're like a mime in a glass box, you can't get out, you're trapped. And nobody but you can see the walls. I know it sounds weird."

"No, it doesn't."

"I'm not making any sense tonight."

"It's not good to feel trapped," she said.

"No, it's not. And I don't. Not really. Not any more than you probably do."

Now that she thought about it, she *did* feel trapped.

"We probably shouldn't be having this conversation," he said.

"It's all right."

"Sometimes things happen," he said. "Change comes into your life like a meteor."

"Totally out of the blue," she said.

"Exactly. And suddenly you don't see things in the same way as you did before."

"I get it." She wanted to ask him what sort of change he was talking about, but by then the cop was walking back toward the car with the ticket. Heath sat up a little taller in his seat. The cop handed him back his license and the ticket. "You can go to traffic court to reduce that fee," he told him.

Heath nodded; he looked annoyed.

The cop slapped the side of the car. "Good night, now."

"Good night, Officer."

Heath stuck the ticket in the visor and pulled back onto the road, slowly. The cop pulled out behind them, following from a distance. They went along in silence. She could tell Mr. Heath was nervous, his eyes darting up to the rearview mirror. Finally, with no shortage of relief, they came to her driveway and he turned into it. The cop roared past.

As they climbed up the hill, Heath said, "This is somewhat awkward for me, Willa, but if it's all right with you, I'd like to keep this little incident a secret. Can we do that?"

She nodded that it was.

"Thank you." He glanced at her. "Are you sure you're all right?"

"I'm fine. Really."

They didn't talk the rest of the way. She sat there, at once rigid and exhilarated, her hands clasped in her lap. At the top of the hill, Heath turned into the circular driveway. The house was enormous, a fortress. All the lights were on, making it look warm and inviting, which it wasn't. The grandeur of the house embarrassed her.

"Say hello to your parents for me."

"I will."

As she was getting out, he grabbed her hand, startling her. "We have our secret, now, remember?"

She nodded and he let her go and she started for the door, thinking: *left, left, left my wife with forty-eight kids,* and it occurred to her that she felt sorry for that poor wife, stranded on her kitchen floor; it wasn't anything to be mocking or celebrating, and it seemed to her that so often they did things—people did—without really thinking. The door was locked. She rang the bell, anxious that her parents would insist on coming outside to thank Mr. Heath for his trouble. But unlike other adults who had brought her home, Mr. Heath did not wait until she was safely inside. Instead, he pulled out quickly, stirring up the gravel, and was gone within seconds, before the chimes on the doorbell had stopped ringing and her mother, in her feathery nightwear finery, had answered the door.

Several days later, Ms. Harding, her adviser, e-mailed her with the news that she'd won the Sunrise Internship. Willa had filled out the application the first week of school, but never expected to get it, assuming that Ada, who was ten times smarter than her *and* the Head's daughter, or Bette Lawton, who had a perfect A average, would be chosen. Sunrise House was a women's shelter in Pittsfield, and she would be working there Tuesday and Thursday afternoons, in whatever capacity they needed, whether it be watching the younger children whose mothers were still at work, or washing clothes, or addressing envelopes. She needn't worry about transportation, it was provided by the school. "You should be very proud," Ms. Harding told her.

On the first day of the internship, Mr. Heath drove up in the school's community service van. "Congratulations, Willa," Mr. Heath said to her in his usual jovial voice—part Barney, part Mister Rogers, the Mr. Heath she had known and loved since she was little.

"Thank you, sir. I totally didn't expect it." She climbed into the back of the van.

Heath turned around, his arm hooked over the top of the seat. "I was hoping they'd choose you."

She could feel her face turning colors. To her relief, a group of sophomores climbed into the van. They were doing community service at Solomon's Table, a soup kitchen in Pittsfield. Willa had volunteered there last year as well. She moved all the way over, behind Mr. Heath, making room for the others. She could see his face in the oversized rearview mirror. If you didn't know better, you could almost mistake him for one of the students. He had a boyish look, the way his hair swept over to the side, the way his eyes shone salty and bright. The other kids were noisy and Mr. Heath was talking to some of them and she remembered their conversation in the car, their secret. As if he were reading her thoughts, he met her eyes in the mirror and smiled and she smiled back. It was a brief exchange, but it seemed to suggest that there was something between them, something special that separated her from the others. It was a heavy, uncomfortable feeling, as if she'd eaten a big meal. She wasn't sure what to do about it and hoped it would go away. Maybe she was just imagining it.

He pulled the van out of the school's driveway and headed up the road. She studied the back of his neck. His hair was cut short and his collar was perfectly ironed. She would bet that Mrs. Heath had ironed it herself. Ada had told her that Mrs. Heath did everything for Mr. Heath. Willa couldn't help feeling a little sorry for her. She couldn't help wondering what it was like for Ada, having him for a dad.

It began to rain. On the sidewalks of Pittsfield, people were rushing under umbrellas. She noticed a man jumping in a puddle, his face lit with glee—there must be something wrong with him, she thought. They were on North Street, near the ballet studio where Ada took dance, where she probably was right now, in fact, rehearsing for *The Nutcracker,* which she did every Christmas. Pittsfield was an odd little town, she thought, with its shadowy storefronts. Heath turned down a narrow street by the courthouse. The soup kitchen was on the corner. Last year, Willa had served homeless people at long tables with white paper cloths. This one time she had served a woman a bowl of soup and the woman had grabbed her hand and said, "Why don't you smile once in a while?" For some reason it had upset Willa, and she'd run into the bathroom and cried and washed her hands. Mr. Heath pulled the van up in front. There were some people hanging out on the steps, smoking. "I'll be back in two hours," Heath said, letting the sophomores out. "Be waiting for me in that vestibule."

He got back into the van and pulled out and it was just the two of them. He looked at her again in the rearview mirror. "How you doing back there?"

"I'm good." She felt weird. She didn't know what to say.

"Good for you for wanting to do this," he said. "You should be very proud."

She thanked him, but she didn't feel proud. Not really. She hadn't applied for the internship because she'd wanted to—it was just something you did for your application, so you'd look good to colleges—and all the girls in her class had applied. She hadn't really thought about what Sunrise House was, or what she'd be doing there if she won the internship—and anyway, she'd never thought she'd win it in the first place. It was a women's shelter, she knew that much, a safe place for women to go when they'd been beaten up by their boyfriends and husbands. The whole idea of it, truthfully, gave her the creeps. What she knew about it was from TV and movies. Women were always getting hurt in movies: raped, shoved, beaten, held down—and sometimes, in a certain context, if, for example, the woman was stupid or evil, it made sense, and others it didn't and you felt sorry for the woman and your heart broke for her. Sometimes she would wonder: How did the woman get herself into that situation in the first place? It wouldn't be anything that *she* would do, that was for sure—she'd never be that stupid. The minute she sensed danger, she would be *out!* She couldn't imagine being shoved across a room, or bashed against a wall, or having her face punched in. But she had seen it so many times. She didn't know what it would be like to be near someone who'd been hurt like that; she'd never met a battered woman before—just those two words *battered woman* made her queasy.

Heath took several turns down one-way streets, then turned into a dead-end street flanked with small houses. At the end of a narrow driveway, he pulled up alongside a small Colonial with a front porch. The only thing that distinguished it from any of the other houses was the muddy lot next to it, which had a few parked cars. A high fence enclosed the backyard where she could see the top of a swing set and could hear the voices of children playing. "I have to walk you in this first time," Mr. Heath told her as she climbed out of the van. He took her hand to help her and she remembered the way he'd grabbed her hand that night. Maybe he hadn't meant to be so rough. She tried not to look at him, but his eyes were very blue, almost green, and were impossible to ignore. He smiled and rubbed her shoulders in a fatherly way.

They went up onto the front porch and rang the doorbell. Willa's mouth was dry. She had the same nervous feeling she'd get when she went to the doctor. After a few minutes, a woman answered and let them in. She was a big woman, with moon-white skin and a long black braid. Her dress was brightly colored, putting Willa in mind of a Japanese kite, and on her small feet were red Mary Janes, the sort Willa had worn as a child. The woman had a frowning girl on her hip, hiding her little face in the soft pillow of her neck.

"Now, now, Gracie, just a minute."

Mr. Heath introduced Willa to the woman, whose name was Regina.

Regina stretched out her hand. "Well, now, I am so glad to see you. We feel real privileged to have you here with us, Miss Golding."

"You can call me Willa."

"And who is this beautiful girl?" Mr. Heath asked the child, who refused to show him her face.

"This is Gracie," Regina said.

"Hello there, Gracie," Mr. Heath said, and the little girl smiled.

"Well, now, could that possibly be a smile?" Heath asked the child.

The little girl nodded apologetically.

"Well, you're the only one she smiled for the whole day," Regina said. "Can you imagine that? I wonder what it is about you, Mr. Heath, that makes all the pretty girls smile?"

Mr. Heath blushed. Willa had the feeling that Regina flattered him often. The way they talked to each other seemed practiced and rehearsed.

"It's good to see you, Regina," he said.

"Don't you worry about Miss Golding. We'll take good care of her."

"You always do," Heath said. "I'll be back at six, Willa, dear."

They watched him go out. Regina put down the little girl and locked the door. "He's such a lovely man." She smiled at Willa. "Welcome to Sunrise House."

"Thank you."

They shook hands and the little girl called Gracie wanted to shake her hand too.

"Let's go in here." Regina led her into a small dining room. The round table in the middle was laid with a printed cloth and surrounded with all kinds of mismatched chairs. The surface of the table held stacks of papers and envelopes. She set down the child. "Go on and pick a chair, peanut, and do your coloring while I talk to this nice girl," she told her, and the child tugged out a chair and sat down and started coloring with crayons. Willa watched her make a series of stick figures with red crayon. Regina said, "She didn't want to play outside today."

The little girl glanced up at her suspiciously.

Willa smiled at her, but she didn't smile back. "I don't feel like playing outside either," Willa said.

The girl kept coloring, but Willa saw her lips curl up in a smile and she felt like she'd done something right.

"First of all," Regina said, opening her eyes very wide, "thank you for being here. We all appreciate it a whole lot."

Willa shrugged, feeling a little shy. "You're welcome."

"You're wondering why we picked you. I can see it in your eyes, and your shoulders are all stiff. You can relax, girl. Everybody wanted it to be you."

"I'm not a very good student," Willa admitted.

"Let me tell you something, honey. It's not just about the grades here. We liked what you wrote on your application. Your essay had something we don't see very often—it had heart, and that kind of thing goes a long way around here."

Willa blushed with pride; it was the best feeling in the world.

"You're one of us, aren't you?"

Willa shrugged. She didn't know what Regina meant, but it sent a quiver through her like a small arrow. "I guess."

"I always get a hunch about a person. I had a hunch about you." She looked at Willa with certainty. "Any-hoo, how about a cup of cocoa? Gracie and me were just about to have one, right Gracie?"

"Uh huh," the child said. "With marshmallows?"

"Of course with marshmallows. We make a very impressive cup of cocoa here at Sunrise House."

They went into the small kitchen. It was neat and smelled nice, like banana bread. Willa could see some kids out in the backyard on the swing set. A woman was standing off to the side, watching them. Regina glanced out as if to check on them, then put a teakettle onto the stove and turned it on. While they were waiting for the water to boil, Regina told Willa about the shelter and how it worked. "A woman can come here whenever she's in trouble, and she can bring her kids and she can stay till she figures out what to do next."

"What happens when you run out of space?"

"Usually, thank God, we don't. We have some people we can call on if necessary." Willa thought about her parents' house, how it was four times the size of this place, and she felt a little sick. "During the day, we offer counseling to women," Regina went on. "They can come in and talk. That's a big step for some. Now, for the most part, your job is with the kids. We need someone out there getting the kids off the bus. We might ask you to watch them out on the swings, or do a little art project or something. It's a big help for us. They're nice kids too. Some of them are a little messed up, but for the most part they're pretty good."

The teapot whistled. Regina made three cups of instant cocoa and put the cups out on a tray. "Now where'd my marshmallow girl go?" She pretended she couldn't find Gracie, who was hiding behind her broad back, and said to Willa, "Have you seen my marshmallow girl?"

And Willa shrugged, playing along. "No, I haven't seen her."

Gracie jumped up and down, up and down, clapping her hands. "I'm right here!"

"Thank goodness!" Regina handed the child a bag of marshmallows. The child pushed open the swinging door and held it open with her back, grinning importantly. Then they all sat down at the table with their cocoa and Gracie plopped a marshmallow in each cup. "Well, isn't this nice," Regina said. "I love to have a little cocoa party in the afternoon, don't you?"

Gracie nodded.

The swinging door to the kitchen opened and the woman from outside poked her head in. "Regina, can I talk to you a minute?"

Regina got up and went into the kitchen. Willa sipped the cocoa and watched the little girl color some flowers. She had put a big fat sun up in the right-hand corner and Willa remembered how she'd do the same thing when she was little. All her pictures always had a sun, with long yellow lines reaching down like rays. She heard a car pulling up outside. Through the window, she saw a young woman get out of a taxi, yanking a little boy behind her. The taxi drove off. The woman stood there for a minute, looking at the house. The boy started to squirm and she yanked his arm, walking toward the door. The little boy's lip was trembling, and Willa knew he was trying not to cry. She rang the bell.

Willa waited a moment, expecting Regina to appear, but she did not. Willa got up and glanced into the kitchen, which was empty now, and she could see that Regina was outside with the woman. The bell rang again.

Willa went to the door and unlocked it and let the woman in. "What in hell took you so long," she said, marching into the room. She was young, about Willa's age. She carried a big plastic Wal-Mart bag full of clothes. "Where's Regina at?"

"Outside. Hold on, I'll get her."

"I'll get her myself," the woman snapped. "Stay here, Tyrell." She dropped her bag on the floor and left the boy and disappeared through the kitchen door.

"Hi," Willa said to the boy.

"Hi."

"This is Gracie. And I'm Willa."

"That's a funny name."

"I know it is. Do you want to color?"

The boy shrugged.

"Come over here with us," Willa said, taking his small hand in her own. She led him over to the table and he climbed onto the chair. She put a piece of paper in front of him and gave him some crayons. "What do you want to draw?"

The boy shrugged and wiped his eyes. Willa guessed that he was about four years old. She hadn't spent much time with small children and she worried that she would upset him in some way. The boy's nose was running, making a slippery yellow film on his upper lip. Before she could find him a Kleenex, he wiped it on his sleeve.

Gracie finished her drawing and folded it up like a paper fan and fanned herself with it. Then she fanned the boy and the boy smiled. Willa could hear the women coming inside. Willa felt a little frightened of the boy's mother and avoided her eyes as they came into the room. She was crying and Regina had her arm around her. "Go on upstairs and lie down, Darlene," Regina told her.

Tyrell's mother grabbed her Wal-Mart bag in the same way she had yanked the boy's arm when they'd gotten out of the taxi, and went upstairs. The boy stood up, as if to follow her. "You stay with us,

Lovely One," Regina said to him, and sat down at the table next to Willa. The boy climbed up on Regina's lap and leaned against her ample bosom and sucked his finger. They sat there for a few minutes,

listening to the floorboards creak overhead as Darlene paced the room like a trapped animal. At last it was quiet. Regina said, "Why don't you take them outside for a little while, before it gets dark."

"Okay." Willa took each child by the hand. Walking gingerly, as though the floor had been scattered with glass, she took them out the back door into the muddy yard. The older children were sitting at a picnic table having snacks. It was getting late and the sky was beginning to darken. A stripe of orange ran across the rooftops. She could hear the caw of a crow. Gracie and Tyrell ran to the swings. "Push me! Push me!"

"I'm coming!" Willa said, helping the little boy onto the swing. His jacket was too big. "Hold on now."

She started to push and then she traded off and pushed Gracie too. "It's nice on the swing, isn't it?"

"Look at my party shoes." Gracie held up her feet, but she had on dirty sneakers with Velcro straps. Willa could see a little picture of Cinderella on the side.

"I wish I had a pair like those," she told the child. "You think they'd fit me?"

This made Gracie laugh.

"Can I try them on?"

Gracie shook her head. "Push me!"

Willa could remember when she was little and her mother would take her to the playground and push her on the swings, singing: *He flies through the air with the greatest of ease, that daring young man on the flying trapeze!* Her mother was a good mother, Willa thought a little mournfully, *My mommy!* Then she thought of her other mother, her *biological* mother—sometimes people said *real* mother, which always hurt her feelings. Once, in grade school, a girl had come up to her and said, "You're adopted, right?" and Willa had told her that she was and the girl, who was large and mean said, "It's nothing to be proud of! Your real mother didn't want you!" When Willa had finally gotten home that afternoon, she'd cried in her mother's arms. Candace Golding was the only mother she knew, and if that wasn't *real* she didn't know what was. When she imagined her biological mother giving her up, she felt a hollow pain in her chest. It must have been very hard for her. She couldn't imagine anything in this world harder than that. But she also sensed it had been the best thing for her. And she loved her parents. She couldn't imagine life without them.

"Push us, push us!" the children sang. They were holding hands so they could go at the same time. "Push us, Willa!"

"Okay, okay! Hold on!"

With one hand on each child's back, she pushed them into the sky. The sound of their laughter was like the best kind of music. She felt incredibly happy and she felt proud too that she had made the children happy. She decided that she would adopt when she grew up. She looked at the heads of the two children and confirmed the idea in her own mind. Yes, she would have lots of babies in her house, babies that she made in her body and babies that had been made in other people's bodies, and she would be an excellent mother. Yes, she thought, she would be the *best* mother of all.

14 ∽

It didn't take long for news to spread at Pioneer. Like any formidable institution, idle gossip pulsed through its corridors with the teeth-grinding candor of *The National Enquirer*. In the faculty lounge that afternoon, Maggie overheard Greer Harding telling Lloyd Jernigan that Willa Golding had won the Sunrise Internship. Greer had her back turned and couldn't see Maggie, and Maggie detected the subtlest degree of relish in her voice. Lloyd looked up abruptly and caught Maggie's eyes, and excused himself, muttering a greeting as he made his escape. Greer looked at her, dispassionately. "Didn't Jack tell you?"

"No, he didn't."

Greer raised her eyebrows. "Surprise, surprise."

It occurred to Maggie that she didn't really like Greer Harding—
she was cynical and negative—in fact, she'd never liked her.

The back of her throat began to prickle.

After school, she went into town and bought pork chops then
went home and put potatoes in the oven and made a salad. She sat
at the kitchen table correcting papers. Ada came in around five, red
and sweaty from field hockey practice. "I'm not upset if that's what
you're thinking."

"No?"

"I'm glad Willa got it." She untied her shoes. "Anyway, she's going
to need all the help she can get next year. God only knows where
she'll get in."

"She'll have to work very hard," Maggie agreed.

"Daddy favors her. It's weird. I'm not even kidding."

"What makes you say that?"

Ada looked away, suddenly embarrassed. "I can tell. You should
see the way he looks at her."

"Ada, you're imagining it."

"Maybe." Ada shrugged. "I'm going up." She went up the stairs and
shut her door. Maggie heard the bark of her stereo, then silence, indicating that her daughter had put on her headphones. She would
spend the next several hours barricaded in her room like a soldier on
the front lines, singing out some deranged musician's heartache until
she could almost believe it was her own.

Maggie poured a drink. She took it into the living room and sat on
the couch. The late sunlight poured through the picture window. It
washed the room in a red tint, glinting sharply off the silver frame of
her wedding picture. Her mother had bought her the frame and she
could remember how awkward she'd felt putting it out for people to
see—for strangers—to convince them, perhaps, of her happiness. The
silver frame was too ornate for her taste, but it was the only frame
she owned that fit the picture, an eight by ten. In the picture, their
faces looked pale and tired and their smiles looked false. In her own
eyes she detected the slightest glimmer of fear—ah, but perhaps
she was reading into it. Jack was so much taller than her, and was

clutching her behind her back with one arm, like a ventriloquist. Her wedding dress looked like a nightgown, with a single satin ribbon running around the bodice. *A schoolteacher's wife,* she could hear her mother mock.

Maggie drank the gin and sat there, letting the darkness coat her skin. She felt invisible, numb. The first time he'd hurt her, she'd been pregnant with Ada. It occurred to her that she'd blocked it out, but now she could remember precisely the way he'd held her down, his hand over her mouth, the things he'd said to her, the menace of his voice, and she could remember her reaction, what at first had seemed like play—rough play perhaps, yes, but still—and then swiftly transformed into violence—her mounting panic over the reality that this was her husband, a man she knew and loved and not a total stranger—how the hand over her mouth had made it difficult to breathe, how, at first, she'd fought him, using her fists, her nails, and then her ultimate defeat as his strength overtook her. For reasons she could not understand at the time, and had since intellectualized, she had let the incident pass. Out of love perhaps—for she did love him. His behavior had seemed an anomaly to her, a rude expression of frustration, she'd thought, over her changing shape. But that wasn't true.

Because it continued. When he drank, he could do despicable things, although she could never admit it to anyone. No one knew; not even Ada. It wasn't the type of information she dared to share; it could ruin their lives. It was private, it embarrassed her. She couldn't possibly understand it. He'd leave marks in places no one could see. She didn't know *why* she couldn't seem to stop him. Perhaps it was her guilt that allowed it. Guilt for being an inferior wife—for being inferior, period. She wasn't as pretty as some of the moms at Pioneer. They were bold, polished. When she spent time with the mothers, either at school meetings or parent/teacher conferences, she always felt inferior to them, which she knew was not the case. She knew she was smart, but they seemed so confident, so stylish. Their husbands had made money, fortunes. The women too had been successful. They had worked in the city. They rode elevators to brightly lit offices, they went out to lunch. They lived in beautiful houses that had once been the homes of struggling farm families. Most of them drove expensive cars, Range Rovers and Mercedes station wagons, and they wore expensive clothes and took expensive trips over the holidays, either to Canada to ski, or to Switzerland, or some had homes in Palm Beach or Jamaica. Jack and Maggie rarely traveled. When Ada was younger, they took her to Lake Placid and stayed over in a little inn. Ada had loved going ice skating, drinking hot chocolate afterward on wood bleachers around a fire. Sometimes they would visit Jack's parents, who lived in Virginia, but Ada always got carsick on the way. Once they'd arrive, Jack and his father would start fighting and his mother would go hide in the kitchen. Maggie's mother still lived in Andover, but Jack refused to stay with her and never wanted to pay for a hotel, so they would end up finding excuses not to go. Maggie's mother had never liked Jack, and she supposed Jack knew it—he'd known it all along.

She had learned to live with the way things were. Their intimate relationship was too complex to talk about. She wasn't sexually adventurous. She didn't really *like* sex, truth be told. Sex only happened when he wanted it to, she didn't know the first thing about seduction—she was too terrified to do that. It seemed to be their natural way of being together, with him making all the decisions. She did whatever he told her; she tried to please him. But sometimes he'd just lie there, staring up at the ceiling, vacant, detached. Sometimes he'd even look disgusted by her. She often got the feeling that he'd been with someone else—there were subtle clues, a hint of fragrance, the way he'd come home late sometimes, looking rumpled. Maggie couldn't imagine what he'd do with anyone else. She didn't like to think about it. It frightened her, really. She didn't sleep well with him; she was somewhat afraid of him. There, she said it. It was how she felt. *I'm afraid of him,* she whispered to the dark room.

After the incident at Remington Pond, when Jack had gotten the job at Pioneer, he'd promised her he was going to change. And he did for a while. They'd moved to the Berkshires, into their little cottage on the lake. As the new Head, he'd organized a capital campaign, which raised enough money to restore the old buildings. He hired a savvy PR firm to revamp the school's image, creating a glossy catalog and sophisticated Web site. Jack understood what the parents wanted and they trusted him. They liked his preppy image, the little bow ties, his Amherst pedigree. They especially liked his finesse with a golf club—he had a ten handicap. They wanted certain things for their children and Jack delivered. They wanted all the things that were promised on the pages of their catalog: excellent teachers, challenging classes, the probability of getting into a competitive college, but what Pioneer was selling went beyond that. And it was Jack's specialty. They were selling the dream of an ideal adolescence—as if it were even possible—and the parents were buying.

Nobody knew better than Jack that a person's history defined their future. He'd been shuffled from one army base to another. His father had been a brutal, complex man who'd terrified his mother into submission—Maggie had never predicted how definitively her husband's youth would determine their marriage, and it had. "Children suffer," Jack was fond of stating the obvious. The parents who sent their kids to Pioneer didn't want their children to suffer, not even a little bit, and they were willing to pay top dollar so they wouldn't have to. Whether they knew it or not—and she guessed very few did—they saw Pioneer as a nearly perfect place, and she and Jack were included in the imagery. Suspension of disbelief, you might call it—a way of seeing what you needed to see, not what's really there. And like any convincing set, all the props were in place, the teachers, the students in their neat frocks, and the enchanting campus. When problems arose, and there were few, Jack had a way of talking to the parents, easily manipulating the most disgruntled mind to see things his way—it was a talent he had, she had to admit. Everybody wanted to be near him. He made all the kids feel good—he knew all their names by heart—and, not unlike a seasoned politician, he was always ready with a greeting and a handshake. The kids looked up to him, the staff too. They trusted him. In their eyes, as corny as it sounded, they recognized the qualities of a hero.

No one in the community would ever guess the reality of her

dilemma. In her husband's presence, Maggie felt small and meek and ashamed and in a remote corner of her brain she sensed that he wanted her to feel that way. Still, she could not change it. As much as she knew she should, she also understood that she could not. After all these years with him she no longer had the strength to challenge him; maybe she'd never had it. She had taken his hand as a young woman and let him lead her away from everything she knew. On that day she had relinquished her soul for him, and she could not say why she'd done it. She didn't seem to know. She knew, though, that it had something to do with how she saw herself. When she'd look in the mirror, the image reflected there only disappointed her. Perhaps she felt sorry for him, that he'd gotten stuck with her. That she'd tricked him somehow, into thinking she was more interesting, smarter, than she really was.

There were true acts of terror that had occurred throughout history, great battles fought for cause and purpose. Maggie taught them all in her classes—they'd read *Beowulf* and they'd read *The Iliad* and *The Odyssey*, and each tale described great battles and bloodshed, and those were the things of legends. Maggie had never been forced to endure a war. Wars were fought elsewhere, in places like Iraq and Afghanistan. But the worse form of terror had whispered its way into her own home, and the man whom she slept beside night after night had become her greatest enemy. He was transforming gradually into another being, as if he'd drunk a mind-altering potion, yet there were no claws sprouting from his fingernails and no clusters of hair growing on his hands, no fangs in his mouth. Jack was the most common species of monster, she thought: an ordinary man.

She finished her drink. The windows were black. She heard his car, the slam of the door. His keys on the counter. The crack of the ice tray, the gush of gin. She went to greet him and he nodded dismissively. Like an actor removing his costume, he took off his blazer and tie and rolled up his shirtsleeves. He washed his hands and drank his drink and sat at the table flipping through the mail. She poured herself another and sat with him, watching him, waiting for him to notice her. When she tried very hard, she could still see the boy she'd fallen in love with at Amherst. "How'd it go?"

"Fine."

"You never told me it was Willa."

"Didn't I?"

"That was a surprise."

"She's come a long way. You shouldn't underestimate her."

"I don't."

"Yes, you do."

"I thought Bette would have gotten it. Or Ada."

"They wanted Willa." He looked at her with watery eyes. His face looked depleted, bereaved. He finished his drink.

She went to the stairs and called for Ada, but the girl had her headphones on and couldn't hear her. Climbing the stairs she felt enervated, as if the night from that point on would demand impossible endurance. She stood outside the door and said her daughter's name and knocked. She didn't want to barge in. The last time she'd done that she'd caught Ada eating donuts. When she'd cleaned her daughter's room the next morning, she'd found a collection of empty junkfood bags shoved under the bed. It was a wonder they didn't have mice. The door opened and Ada stood there, the tiniest orange remnants of Cheetos around her mouth.

"We're having dinner," she said.

"I'm not hungry."

"You will come down and sit at the table, whether you're hungry or not."

Ada scowled at her, but did what she asked.

They sat around the table. She served her family dinner. She'd had too much to drink and the table seemed wobbly. She watched as her husband and daughter began to eat. Maggie took a pork chop and some potatoes and some green beans and looked at the plate. The food was nicely presented, she thought. She'd done a good job. It was a lovely meal.

She forked a green bean and put it into her mouth and began to chew. It felt like a piece of rubber, she thought. She used her teeth.

Her tongue always seemed to get in the way. It was a diligent little muscle, her tongue, and her epiglottis too created problems. The epiglottis was a nasty little thing. Slimy and officious. Recently, she'd become terrified of swallowing. It was something she kept to herself. Something she couldn't discuss. As the food filled up her mouth, mixing with saliva, she had to remind herself to let it all slide down her throat into her stomach, where it belonged. Sometimes her timing was off.

"Are you all right?" Jack was looking at her.

She coughed into her napkin. "I'm sorry. I'm fine. It went down the wrong pipe."

"Get your mother some water."

Ada put the glass down in front of her. Maggie could feel her staring with contempt. The girl backed away from the table and went upstairs. A moment later the door slammed.

Jack finished his drink. "It was delicious, Maggie," he said. "Once again, you've outdone yourself."

Part Two

❧

Attention Deficit

[sculpture]

Claire Squire, *Spanking Machine,* 2000. Beeswax and microcrystalline wax, 4 x 14 x 3 ft. Collection of Millie and Wilbur Rice.

Three children stand with their legs spread apart, encouraging the fourth child to crawl through the "spanking machine." The standing children, two boys and one girl, share an almost feral exuberance as they await the girl crawling through their legs. On hands and knees, the girl enters the punitive tunnel, wearing an expression of cautious anticipation.

1

15 ✑

Late in September the fields began to turn from green to yellow. Already there were turkeys. They walked in formation like soldiers, or grammar school children. An ancient Japanese maple shimmered with crimson leaves. Three crows watched over the house from the top of an oak tree. They screeched at the sight of her, gossiping in rude shrieks, swooping across the sky in arcs of sooty bravado.

Claire had made a place to work in the barn, the floor was clear. Already she had begun to light the woodstove, carrying the wood from the pile into the barn. Her arms were strong. When she woke in the morning the sky was pink.

She had sent her landlord in Los Angeles the money she owed him, and had arranged for her work to be delivered. The sculptures had been locked away for over a year and her landlord had threatened to throw them in the Dumpster if she didn't pay. That morning they arrived, it was a Saturday, two Guatemalans in a Ryder truck with fifteen sculptures. Teddy heard the racket and came down to watch. The men hardly spoke English and she gestured emphatically as she instructed them where to pull the truck. When they opened the trailer, she saw her work in a heap, a pile of broken bodies—legs, arms, a foot, a torso. Some of them were nearly intact, crammed into the darkness.

"At least they're free," Teddy said, putting his arm around her.

"Free at last." She had no one to blame but herself.

"You'll fix them," Teddy said.

The men were careful, gingerly carting the pieces down a ramp, placing them gently, apologetically, around the space.

"We should celebrate," Teddy said. "Let's make pancakes."

Ever since Teddy was little, pancakes were the way they celebrated things—little milestones like losing a tooth or learning to tie shoes or whenever she sold a piece. They fed the men and watched them drive away in their noisy truck. Then she went into the barn and inspected her work. The sculptures were battered and broken, crippled, but she would fix them, she would make them better. And then, somehow, she would find a place to show them. It was something she could do, she thought. Her way of making a contribution, if that was worth anything. Sometimes, in her darker moments, Claire doubted the value of her work. It was difficult and consuming and she spent most of her time alone, cut off from the rest of the world. What was she trying to do or say? She would ask herself the question over and over again, but could never find an answer that justified the effort. When people asked her about the work, why her sculptures seemed doomed or sad or perverse, she had a variety of theoretical reasons at her fingertips, but they didn't really mean much to her. The people would nod as if they understood, but they didn't, not really. And often she didn't either. It was instinctual, making art. You had a hunch about something and you went for it. You were like one of those wild police dogs, searching for something—something terrible or something beautiful. Sometimes it worked, sometimes it didn't. Sometimes it made sense to her, and sometimes it made her weary and she felt all of the unsolvable problems of the world filling up her heart like so much rainwater. Still, she felt compelled to do it, to say something, to seek the truth, to find her own way.

The barn was a good place to work. It was better than L.A., with its surplus of glossy criminals. And Teddy was happier here too. For the first time in his life, he seemed interested in school. He had never liked it before, except nursery school in an old church where all the other children spoke Spanish. But after that, in grade school, he had floundered. He couldn't sit in his seat, he couldn't listen. He was *bored*. His teachers were mean. Nobody liked him; he didn't have any friends. It broke her heart, but she didn't have the time or money to be able to change it, and each day, month after month, he became more despondent until, finally, he just didn't go. She'd get calls from the school, where was he, and she'd have to drive around to find him—usually at the skateboard park. "You have to go," she'd tell him, "it's the law," and he'd shake his head and refuse. "I'm too stupid," he'd say. "I can't learn anything."

But at Pioneer he was different, engaged. They were reading *The Odyssey* and his tutor had gotten it for him on tape, and he walked around with headphones, listening to it. One afternoon, he missed the bus and she went to get him at school. She pulled into the circular driveway, around an island of drooping peonies. It was late and most of the kids had gone home. She spotted her son, kissing a girl under an umbrella. The girl was wearing black high-tops with her uniform, a plaid skirt and white blouse. Her hair was tied back in a shoelace. Her arms were draped around Teddy's shoulders, his hands swimming at her hips. Witnessing their intimacy made Claire's heart stop a moment. It was real, natural, *appropriate,* and she was happy for him. In contrast, her own lack of intimacy was abnormal, she knew. It had been years since she'd been with anyone, and it had turned her hard and a little cold.

The girl caught her staring and then Teddy turned and smiled. Feigning distraction, Claire rattled the pages of her newspaper. "Hey." He rifled through his papers to show her his grade—an A. The first in his life. It was from his writing teacher, who didn't believe in grades in the first place. "Everyone got an A," he said. "But still."

He smelled of patchouli, the girl's scent. A moment later, a pickup truck pulled up behind her and the girl got into it. Claire watched through her rearview mirror. The man behind the wheel looked rough, an employee, she surmised. The truck pulled out and the girl waved. "Her name's Willa," Teddy said. "After the writer. Willa Cather?"

"Interesting," Claire said.

"Her *real* mother named her."

"What do you mean, her *real* mother?"

"The one who had her. She's adopted."

"You mean her *birth* mother."

"It was part of the deal," Teddy explained. "They had to keep her name for some reason. Maybe because she died."

"Who died?"

"The mother."

"Really? That's sad."

"Yeah." He shrugged. "That's all she knows."

Claire pulled out onto the road; she knew what was coming.

"She doesn't know her father either."

"You mean her *birth* father."

"Right."

Teddy looked at her, waiting. "What about mine?"

"What?"

"*My* birth father?"

Claire had been three months' pregnant when Billy had called her from Mexico to tell her that he'd gotten busted with some pot and was going to prison for twenty years. "Take care of yourself," he'd said to her. "Hasta luego."

Claire had never told him she was pregnant. It had been an accident, anyway, and to this day he didn't know. Teddy's father may as well have been a sperm donor.

"I've told you."

"Tell me again."

"Your father was a good friend of mine," she said. "We were very young. I was your age. Try to imagine that for a minute."

"I know, Mom. But where is he?"

"We lost touch a long time ago, Teddy."

Unsatisfied with her answer, Teddy crossed his arms over his chest defiantly. "I want to find him."

She didn't have the heart to tell him his father was in jail. "Okay."

He looked at her. "Will you help me?"

"Of course."

She pulled into the driveway and he got out and slammed the door, as if finalizing the decision, and she sat there for several minutes, feeling as though she'd got the wind knocked out of her.

Willa Golding was a brown-eyed, autumn-haired girl with creamy skin and long, elegant limbs. She moved like a horse, a young mare.

He brought her to the house. They crept up to his room and closed the door. They walked in the fields together with their heads down. She lived in a house down the road, Teddy said. You could see the horses. One night he called from the girl's house. It had begun to rain; he didn't want to ride home on his bike. "Come and get me," he said.

Claire was in the barn, working, covered in plaster. She worked like a doctor through the night, tending her broken work. She rinsed off her hands and threw on an old raincoat, her father's felt hat. Lightning filled the sky. The Goldings lived up the hill, a mile from the house. Turn at the white fence, Teddy had said, the long dirt driveway over a wooden bridge. She could see the horses in the field, lit up in the storm, their hides shimmering.

The house sat high in a clearing, all lit up. They were having a party. The windows were fogged. Teddy hadn't mentioned a party. Cars were parked on the lawn. Even from inside the car she could hear the band. Swing music. She pulled the car up under the porte cochere, where the caterers had parked their trucks. There was a side door to what looked like the kitchen—the servants' entrance. The band was playing Cole Porter: "Night and Day." She tried Teddy's cell phone, but he wasn't picking up. She sat there for a moment, feeling undignified in her work clothes, the old coat. The wipers swished, keeping time. One of the caterers appeared at the side door in her white apron. She went to get something out of her truck. Claire leaned out the window to ask if she'd seen Teddy, but the woman shrugged, she only spoke French.

Once more, Claire tried the cell phone. Infuriated, she got out of the car and went to the door and looked through the screen. The kitchen was bustling. What a fancy party they were having. The caterers were hard at work, bringing out trays of hors d'oeuvres and glasses of champagne. Claire stepped inside as the waiters in their penguin clothes took out the trays. The music stopped and some of the musicians sauntered through the kitchen in their black suits and red shirts with unlit cigarettes in their mouths and went outside to smoke. Alone in the kitchen, Claire could hear what sounded like an argument coming from the butler's pantry. A swinging door connected the two rooms, and through the circular window Claire saw a man and woman hissing at each other in the dim light. It wasn't nice to be snooping, Claire thought, but the savage nature of their fight compelled her, and neither of them had any idea they were being watched. They were fighting bitterly, their teeth flashing, their voices sharp.

"Can I help you?" A voice startled her, a French accent.

Claire turned around to face a man, one of the catering staff. Her cheeks burned with embarrassment. "Are the Goldings . . . ?"

But the waiter was unfazed, and nodded toward the butler's pantry. "Parties bring out the worst in couples."

"I'm looking for my son," she explained. "Teddy Squire. He's here somewhere, with their daughter?"

"Wait here."

The waiter returned seconds later. "He'll be right down." He handed her a glass of champagne and motioned to one of the kitchen chairs. Claire sat in the chair in her dripping raincoat, feeling like a servant, trying to stay out of everyone's way. She was on her second glass of champagne when Joe Golding glanced into the kitchen and noticed her, and although he studied her only briefly, assuming, perhaps, that she was one of the catering staff, there was something in his eyes that told her she interested him. He had a brooding, unsmiling face, suggesting to her that he was a man who was rarely satisfied, but now he pushed out his chin and nodded at her, a primal greeting perhaps, but a greeting just the same. And then he was gone.

Two weeks later they ran into each other at a wine tasting, a school fund-raiser. Golding was there with his wife, Candace—everybody called her Candy—but after just a morsel of conversation with the woman, Claire quickly construed that she was anything but sweet. Candace wore a shawl around her shoulders that had a peacock on it, and a heavy turquoise necklace and several bracelets—it was good turquoise, vintage. Her hair was black, cut short, and she wore almost no makeup, only a hint of color on her lips. She was leaning on a cane, wearing an expression of superiority. She didn't initiate conversation with anyone, Claire noticed. In contrast, her husband, Joe, moved like a street vendor, plying his wares. *Come to me! Come to me!* He was the sort of man you couldn't help noticing. Not that he was especially good-looking; he wasn't. But he had a way about him, a presence that made you want to be near him. He gave the impression of being the guy with the bottom line. You wanted answers, you wanted the whole story, you went to him. He had a pickle barrel chest, big shoulders. He exuded strength, a roguish confidence. She could practically smell his money. They were talking to Greer Harding, who was all wrapped up in carnation pink, down to her pink Tod's. Greer made a joke and the three of them started to laugh. Watching them, it occurred to Claire how out of place she felt. Even with all her father's money, she couldn't seem to relate to these people. It was so *high school.* They were in the popular group and she was the outcast. The only person who looked at all interesting was Teddy's writing teacher, Mr. Gallagher, who was standing off to the side like a butler awaiting instruction. He was taller than everyone in the room, and there was something guarded and elegant about him, like those nineteenth-century men in paintings by John Singer Sargent. His hair was a reddish blond and he wore a thick woodsman's beard. His gray eyes were wolfish, keen, yet tainted with suspicion. She had seen eyes like that on the street, a kind of hunger, a weary glimmer. It was what she saw when she looked in the mirror.

The wine presented an amiable distraction, and she went over to the Bordeaux table, where the Heaths were schmoozing with a cluster of parents. Claire couldn't help feeling intimidated by them. They had the authority to judge her son and by extension her—she knew the only reason they'd accepted Teddy was because of her father's money. Truthfully, the whole arrangement made her uneasy, but she also felt it was the best for him. In less than a year they'd be applying to colleges and Teddy needed all the help he could get.

Jack Heath had on his headmaster's uniform, a blue blazer and khakis, the red bow tie, and wire-rimmed glasses. His unbearably thin wife, who was Teddy's vigilant adviser, seemed to be hanging on to his arm for support. She had on a dainty wool butter-colored suit with matching pumps and headband. There was something stuffy and schoolmarmish about her, Claire thought, and they seemed an odd pair, Claire couldn't quite put her finger on it. Pioneer was no longer the hippie farm school that Claire had attended, where grades were almost an afterthought. No, Claire could tell just by looking around the room that these parents expected a lot for their money; they wanted results.

Claire went up to Maggie Heath and shook her hand. "I wanted to thank you," she told her, "for letting Teddy come to school here. Until now, he hasn't been a very motivated student, I'm afraid. We moved around a lot. The schools in L.A. are somewhat difficult."

Maggie looked at her doubtfully, then said, in a less-than-thrilled voice, "We're thrilled to have him."

"Everyone gets a clean slate at Pioneer," Jack Heath proclaimed. "You just leave everything to us."

They talked about the days when Claire was a student there, when Woody Baxter ran the school. "I remember he drove this yellow Karmann Ghia," she told them. "It was always breaking down. We used to go blueberry picking during math class."

The folklore was making the Heaths squeamish, Claire realized.

"Times have changed," he said flatly. "The community. It's a lot different here now."

In a tart, proud-wife vernacular, Maggie Heath began to list the myriad improvements her husband had made since Baxter's retirement, but Claire noted something perfunctory in her delivery. A moment later Greer Harding interrupted Maggie to introduce them to another set of parents. Claire politely excused herself and asked the pleasant bartender for a glass of wine—this time Chianti. Behind the bartender was an enormous mirror with an ornate gold frame, through which Claire could watch the party behind her. The waiter handed her the wine and she sipped it gratefully. When she glanced up into the mirror a second time, another face was looking back. Joe Golding.

She could feel herself beginning to sweat. *You don't love me* *enough,* his eyes seemed to brood, *but you will.*

He came up to her and ordered a glass of wine and they toasted each other silently, smiling like two dignitaries sharing a secret. What the secret was neither would say, but it wasn't going away—a negotiation was in order. Golding introduced himself, taking her hand. He had rolled up his shirtsleeves and his forearms glistened with black hair. There was something intimate in the way he touched her.

"I'm Teddy's mother," she said.

"So that's what you were doing in my kitchen."

"She's very beautiful," Claire said. "My son has quite the crush."

"It appears to be mutual."

"I hope he's behaving himself."

"I wouldn't count on it."

"That's some party you had. That band—where did you find those guys?"

"The Connie Winter's Orchestra," he clarified. "I'm a brass fan. There's nothing quite like the sound of a trumpet. It hits me in all the right places."

"You don't look like the patriotic type," she said.

"I'm a sap," he admitted. "I start bawling whenever I hear taps." He shook his head. "It was a nice party, but I knew there was someone missing." He smiled at her with his gypsy eyes. "Promise me you'll come to our next one."

She couldn't help feeling charmed. "I promise not to wear my raincoat."

"I knew your father," Golding said. "He was a good man. I'm sorry."

"Thank you."

"We played golf a few times. He liked a good cigar. And he was a hell of a director. Nobody did Chekhov like Eddie—the best *Cherry*

Orchard I've ever seen. There were these cherry blossoms everywhere. You came out of the theater—you were covered with them. It was brilliant."

"I know he'd appreciate that." She took a sip of the wine. "This is good."

"Chianti from Tuscany. Very Hemingway."

"Cheers."

They touched their plastic cups. She smiled. The moment lingered.

His wife caught his eye and he motioned to her. "We're all going out for dinner afterward. If you want to join us."

"I'd like that."

Golding kept his greedy eyes on her longer than necessary. "Bring your husband. I'd like to meet him."

Before she could tell him otherwise, he had disappeared.

16 ∽

Gallagher couldn't take his eyes off her. It was her hair that did it, the long yellow braid, the particular angular shape of her face, the fleeting gaze of inquiry. She was older now, and no less beautiful, but it was her, he was sure of it. It was the girl from his truck. The girl in the forgotten Polaroid. Claire.

She carried herself like a woman who knew her own beauty yet could not be bothered with it. Her dress a simple black tunic. Thin silver bracelets around her wrists. She wore small pearl earrings, her neck bare. Her skin very pale, a glimmer of color on her lips. He was much taller, of course, but he was taller than most women. He was just about to introduce himself when Maggie Heath appeared and took his hand. "I want you to meet some of the parents." An expedition ensued through the enormous room with its tall castle windows and heavy mahogany furniture. There were the Madisons and the Liddys and the Sterns and the Fairchilds. "And these are the Goldings," Maggie said, beaming like a proud mother. Nate had anticipated meeting the Goldings a thousand times before this moment, going over their handshake in his mind as though he were replaying a single frame of film—they were, after all, something like relatives— although he ventured the Goldings would never recognize him. He suspected they had blocked him out of their minds long ago, as they should have. He had simply been a liaison to their happily-ever-after. For a few unpleasant hours, they had dealt with the burden of having a dead woman on their property and had even probably been a little grateful for her death—yes, he knew it was cruel to think so, but it was probably the truth. They were all older now. Nate was no longer the scrawny drug addict. Instead of the filthy clothes he had worn that day, he was dressed in a suit and tie and he had a beard now, which grounded him, he liked to think, in the realm of scholars and intellectuals. The Goldings too had changed. The wife, who had a sharp, reliable beauty, was afflicted with a back injury of some sort, and relied on a cane—he'd overheard her telling someone she'd been thrown by a horse the day before. And Joe Golding had grown stout over the years. He looked buffed up, like a good car—fully loaded— but nobody ever bothered to read the fine print. A physically powerful man, he had an air of magnanimity about him that Nate instinctively distrusted. Like an emperor, people fawned all over him.

"Here's the man I've been telling you about," Maggie announced. "This is my old friend, Nate Gallagher."

They shook hands. "Your daughter's a charming girl," Nate said. "A talented writer."

Golding smiled, pleased by the comment. His eyes held Nate's a moment too long. Nate cleared his throat and the wife asked, "What sort of things do you write, Mr. Gallagher?"

"Short stories, mostly. I'm working on a novel."

"Nate's a wonderful writer," Maggie chimed in. "But it's in his blood." Maggie explained about his father. "Nate was a faculty brat."

"Well," Golding said. "I'll have to read your work. Where can I find it? Do you have a book?"

"I'm hoping to have one out soon," Nate said sheepishly. He suddenly felt incredibly foolish.

Golding's wife looked sorry for him, and put her hand on his arm. "You've really inspired our daughter. We appreciate it so much."

"It's my pleasure."

Another couple interrupted the Goldings and Nate gratefully backed into the crowd. He felt a little light-headed and helped himself to another drink. Someone tapped him on the shoulder and he turned; it was Claire. "Hello there," she said.

"Hello."

"I'm Claire Squire. Teddy's mom?"

"Of course." He took her hand. It felt cool and soft, like one of Larkin's doves. "He's a great kid."

She swallowed her drink. "Actually, I'm a little drunk. I'm not used to this kind of thing."

"No?"

"People." She grinned. "They make me nervous."

"Let's get some air."

"What a good idea."

They pushed through the crowd toward the enormous foyer and the wide front door. It was amazing to think that the building had once been home to a single family. The sun was just beginning to set and the air was cool and damp. Her arms had goose bumps, and he took off his jacket and offered it to her, draping it over her shoulders.

"You're the writer, aren't you?" she said. " 'Everybody has a broken heart.' Teddy told me about it. It's true, isn't it?"

"To some degree."

"What about yours?"

"I have my share of war stories." He thought of the photograph of her in his truck, a premonition of some sort. He thought of telling her about it, but decided against it.

"You're very tall," she said. "You're a skyscraper. What's it like up there?"

"What's it like?"

She took off her heels and put her hand on his shoulder and

climbed up on the stone wall and now she was slightly taller than him. Standing there with the wind in her hair she was iconic, a goddess. She smelled of roses. "There."

"How do you feel?"

"Tall," she said. "You must feel terribly superior."

"Just the opposite," he said. "I'm pathologically insecure."

"You can't be. You're much too handsome. You have this sort of nineteenth-century quality."

"It's the beard. I've been told I'm an old soul," he admitted.

"Me too."

He looked at her gently. "I believe that."

"Maybe we knew each other in another life."

She returned her hand to his shoulder and he helped her down and she stumbled a little and he gripped her and for a moment he could feel the ripple of her bones under his hands. She looked up at him and smiled in a shy way and he wondered if there was any possibility that she was feeling about him the way that he was feeling about her. He had an incredible desire to kiss her—but of course that could never happen. It wasn't right, it wasn't professional.

"Have you been teaching long?"

"Almost ten years." He told her about his job at the high school in Brooklyn and she told him about the school her son had gone to in Los Angeles. "This is a whole new world to Teddy. No one's ever taken him seriously before." She paused a moment and looked away and when she met his eyes again they were moist and full of emotion. "Do you believe in fate?"

He coughed. "Fate?" If it had anything to do with her, he did. "Yeah, I believe in it."

She nodded as if she were grateful and then her forehead went tight and she looked as if she were about to say something to him, something important, when a noisy crowd came through the door. It was a whole throng of people, laughing raucously. Joe Golding came up to Claire and took her elbow possessively. Nate couldn't help thinking him arrogant. "We're all going over to Colette's, if you want to join us," Golding told her, then glanced at Nate indifferently. "You're welcome too, Gallagher," he said, his tone very slightly patronizing. Nate was, after all, only an employee.

"I've got to help out here," Nate told him.

Claire smiled at Nate and shook off his jacket and gave it back to him. "Thank you, Mr. Gallagher."

"Sure."

Nate stood there a moment, watching the group wander off into the parking lot. It brought him back to his days at Choate—the way he'd felt then and the way he felt now—separate—different. Unlike the other kids, he wasn't there because of his abilities, and he would walk the paths of campus with his head hanging down, as though at any moment something would fall out of the sky and pummel him. The other kids were brighter, richer, confident. He was a mere tint among their vibrant colors and his father resented him for it. In those days, he'd felt secondhand, shopworn, but when he'd started shooting dope everything was new again. During those months with Catherine, he was *right there*. He'd felt connected to her, body and soul. The days unraveled the way they wanted to, uncontrived, inspired by little more than simple gravity. He could subsist on her tiny breasts, her flesh, her slow oboe voice. But the drugs had made him indifferent, and the world beyond their dark little room—the squealing buses, the strangers in the street, the fish market, the farmer's stands, the open cafés, the airplanes, the abrupt whirl of daylight—did not welcome him. Cat could not depend on him. And, as it turned out, she'd found herself a much more faithful keeper: death.

17 ⁓

Colette's was a swishy bistro on Church Street. It was dusk, the sky violet as Italian plums. The restaurant was jammed, the parking lot full. Luckily, she found a spot on the street. She walked up the sidewalk under the yellow moon. The air was cold on her bare arms and she found herself missing the pleasing weight of Gallagher's jacket on her shoulders. Nate Gallagher was a gentleman, she thought wistfully, reviewing their conversation in her head like the lyrics of a favorite song. She had no business thinking about him in any way that was even remotely wistful and she blamed it on the wine and made a concerted effort to push the idea of him, gentleman that he was, out of her mind.

The others were already inside and had been seated at a table in the back. She had a sudden impulse to back out of the crowded place and drive home, but Joe Golding caught her eye and waved her over and she put a smile on her face. People like Golding didn't like to be kept waiting. They had the attention span of a peanut, and when they wanted something they figured out how to get it, no matter what. It was something the very rich and the very poor had in common.

It was a good restaurant, full of noisy, happy people. White walls, white table cloths, peonies in glass jars. They were a big group, thirteen in all. She took a seat at the end of the table next to Greta Travers, the other spouseless woman. Greta had short, boyish hair and wore very dark red lipstick and expensive gold earrings with tiny sapphires. They were the sort of earrings Claire might have worn for a state occasion, but when she complimented her on them Greta groped her lobes dispassionately, as if she'd forgotten she had them on. Joe and his wife, Candace, were sitting across from them. Greta was telling Candace that she had recently gotten divorced. Her husband, she explained, an orthopedist, ran off with his X-ray technician. "Apparently, she had very good bones." She told the story of her escape from their Tribeca loft, her pugnacious thievery. She'd fled with her grandmother's Spode and wedding silver. "I took the Alice Neel paintings," she said, finally. "They were *mine*."

"What about you?" Candace Golding peered at Claire over her bifocals. "Don't you have a husband?"

"I'm an old spinster."

"Hardly," Candace said, waiting for an explanation.

"I've just never found anyone I wanted to marry."

"Fascinating," Candace said. "It is something of a challenge, I admit. It's certainly not for everyone."

"What's not?" Joe said, turning back into the conversation.

"Marriage," his wife said darkly. "I said it's not for everyone."

Joe nodded noncommittally and opened his menu. "What are we ordering?" He looked at Claire and said, "The food here is fabulous. The chef's a genius."

"They're friends of ours," Candace said. "The husband makes all the breads. He's Italian. Whenever he comes to visit he brings us bread."

"Look at this bread," Joe said, taking one of the large rolls in his hand. "Look at it! Have you ever seen anything so perfect?" She watched him caress the warm bread. He ripped off a piece and gave it to her. "Here," he handed her the olive oil and she dipped the bread and ate it and felt the oil running down her hand to her wrist. He motioned to the server to bring more. "It's so simple. All bread should be this good. It's not fucking rocket science."

"Here we go," Candace said. "Social commentary by Joe Golding."

"When you go to Italy even the poor people have good bread. But here in America the people with nothing eat shit. It's a simple thing, this bread."

"I want to move to Italy," Greta said.

"I often ask the question: Is it impossible to have a simple life?"

"The world is not simple," Claire said.

"The world is not simple." Joe repeated the phrase like the line of a great poem.

"There are too many people, there's too much stuff, too many choices. Even a trip to the supermarket's a challenge," Claire said.

"Too many choices," he agreed.

"But you can't go backward," she said. "You can't just take it all away. You can't take away things that people have gotten used to, even the bad things. Things like cars. Lawn mowers. Disposable razors. It's not like people are going to start happily walking five miles down the road just to get their simple loaf of bread. It's not like we can take all the computers and dump them someplace and go back to actually talking to each other."

"We're too used to pressing buttons," Greta said.

Joe smiled. "It's too bad, isn't it? All the stuff that comes between us." He looked at Claire. She had an impulse to touch him, to take his hand. They were connected somehow, more than the others at the table. She'd felt it earlier, at the wine tasting, a rift of desire that broke through from someplace dark.

The waiter came with the wine and poured it all around. Another server brought more bread, ceremoniously pouring the olive oil onto the plate. It was a bustling dining room, full of interesting people— different than L.A., Claire thought. In L.A., people had their projectors running 24/7—she called them the *I'm ready for my close-up* crowd— and that included everyone you saw, from the hoity-toity to the bum on the street—they were each a starring player in their own precious little movie. But here the people seemed less pretentious, a heady, intellectual crowd, the men in tweedy blazers, the women in linen dresses and Birkenstocks. They seemed eloquent and cultured, like her parents had been.

She was glad to be out of L.A. It was better here for Teddy. Her father had been right after all; she only wished she could thank him.

"Let's have a toast," Joe said. "To simple pleasures." He looked at her.

"Hear, hear," she said.

They brought their glasses together. Everyone drank and looked at their menus.

"What are we ordering?" Candace asked.

"I was thinking of getting the lamb," Golding said.

"I'm getting the lamb too," Claire said.

"It's very greasy here," Candace warned. "I wouldn't get that, Joe."

"Maybe you're right," he said.

"We'll have the fish tonight," Candace decided, closing the menu.

The waiter came over to the table. Claire watched as Candace ordered their fish. She found herself smiling.

"And you, ma'am?" the waiter asked.

"I'm having the lamb," Claire said. *The more grease the better.*

The waiter left and another server came and replenished their wineglasses. Joe asked her what she did for a living.

"I'm a sculptor," she said. "It's not much of a living, though."

"That depends on how you define living," he said.

"How marvelous," Candace said. "What sort of sculpture?"

"I do figures, mostly women."

"Have you shown your work?"

"There's a gallery in L.A. that shows my work."

"Not New York?" She said it in a *poor baby* voice.

Claire shook her head and for some reason felt ashamed. "No, not right now," she said. *She had never shown in New York.* "But soon, I hope."

"I know you," Greta announced importantly. "I read about you somewhere. You're one of the 'New Feminists.'"

"As opposed to an old one," Claire said, wryly. The article had been about her and four other women artists whose work explored issues that related to being female. Aside from the fact that being deemed a feminist was the kiss of death for any artist these days, the article had been published in *Artforum,* which in itself had been something of a career feat.

"What the hell *is* feminism, anyway?" Joe said. "Would somebody please explain it to me?"

"Feminism?"

"It's a seventies term," he said with distaste. "I don't see anybody out there burning their Wonderbra."

"I'll tell you about feminism," Greta said. "It's supposed to protect us from assholes like you."

Candace blurted a laugh.

"I'm serious," he said. "What does it actually *mean*—feminism?" He spit the word out like soggy bread.

"Equality," Claire said simply. "Basic provisions for women, like fair pay."

"Respect," Greta proclaimed.

"The word's a relic," Joe said. "Our kids, for example—I would bet they don't have a clue what it means."

"I would probably agree with that," Greta said, then leaned into Claire's ear and whispered, "My daughter's too busy giving blow jobs to feel discriminated against."

The comment put her off—she remembered Teddy describing Monica Travers as the girl with the "big mouth," which Claire had naively misinterpreted as a girl who wasn't shy about speaking her mind—perhaps times *had* changed. She found herself wondering if Teddy had ever had a blow job—they'd never discussed it—it wasn't something she liked to think about. She'd never admit to it, of course, but the idea of her son's penis in some girl's mouth made her extremely uncomfortable.

Joe shrugged. "The world is different now, the economy, the politics. Everything's different. It's a different playing field."

"Oh, yeah, it's different all right," Claire said. "Not good different, just different."

"I know I'm generalizing," Joe continued, "but the truth is people don't like words like *feminism* anymore. It sounds, oh, I don't know, *pedestrian*."

"Yeah, like the word *vagina*," Claire said. "Most people don't like that word either." Claire and Greta laughed, and Candace laughed too.

"Solidarity!" Greta said, raising her glass.

"What makes you think men and women are equal in the first place?" Joe said.

Some of the other men at the table snickered.

"You're in a mood tonight," Candace said to him.

"Sexual tension 101," Greta muttered to Claire.

"Look," he said, backpedaling. "You know it just as much as I do. Look at yourselves—look at the way you starve yourselves, the way you dress, the shoes you wear with the skinny heels. Your tit jobs, your Botox. You think that makes you equal?"

"It's complicated," Claire conceded.

"Yeah, it's complicated all right. Just for argument's sake—and at the risk of sounding misogynistic, which I'm sincerely *not*—let's say a war broke out right here, right now. Who do you think would take control?" He didn't wait for an answer—apparently he didn't want one, and finished off his glass of wine. "You girls would be running around like ants in a puddle, waiting for someone to tell you what to do. It's biological. Protection of the species and all that—but you know I'm right." He poured himself another glass of wine then held up the empty bottle, signaling to the waiter to bring another. His face was flushed, he'd broken a sweat. "We're not the same," he said, looking right at her. "You're weaker. Admit it."

"On the defensive is perhaps more accurate," Claire said, but it was not the robust comeback she'd been hoping for. "Equality is in the head, not the body. It shouldn't matter who has more physical strength. That's entirely the point."

"But it does matter. That's the trouble. It matters a lot. Men are stronger," he insisted. "It's how we're made. It gives us an edge. You know it's true."

She had nothing to say to him—or perhaps there was too much to say—the restaurant was not conducive to the sort of argument she would have to put forth. Golding helped himself to more bread and dipped it in the oil and put it in his mouth. He licked his oily fingertips. "You think it's easy for men?" he said, chewing. "You so-called," he made quote marks with his fingers, "feminists have turned us into a bunch of confused eunuchs."

"Poor baby," Greta said.

"You say one thing then do another. That's not equality—it's manipulation. We're so fucking confused we'd rather have sex with the computer."

"Speaking from experience, no doubt," Greta said.

"You girls are just a small part of the female population," he said. "You want to know why women are still the inferior sex? You can bitch and moan all you want about getting fair pay, fair benefits—but when it comes right down to it, there are still plenty of women out there who are perfectly happy to suck dick with the meter running, just as long as they get paid."

"*What?*"

"In other words: They're perfectly happy to run up a tab, as long as somebody else picks up the check."

What an asshole, she thought.

Working in the barn the next morning, Claire found herself stew- ing over Joe Golding and their conversation at the restaurant—maybe he was right, maybe feminism was passé. Maybe people couldn't relate to it anymore. And it was for that reason too that she hadn't liked the article in *Artforum*. She didn't like being labeled as an artist of one kind or another, and now that she thought about it, perhaps "feminist" indeed had a shopworn connotation—not to mention that, as an artist, being dubbed a "feminist" wasn't going to sell tickets, as her father would say. Her father had always been contemptuous of critics. Years before, Waldo Klein, the theater critic for the *New York Times*, had owned a house in Egremont and, out of the goodness of his heart, as her father put it, always reviewed Eddie's plays—more often than not, abysmally. Eddie would read them aloud at breakfast in a cockney accent, pretending it didn't hurt—but even as a child she knew it did. She felt a fresh surge of anger and asked the room, "Who *are* these people, anyway?" Writing their wicked little articles. Who were they to judge her work? Did any of them know it was the single thing, aside from Teddy, that kept her alive, that made her want to get up every morning? It was what had gotten her through all the other bullshit. It made her whole. And what did their work do for them? She imagined her critics as the goody-goodies in high school, so eager to bestow their brilliance upon the ordinary folk that they could barely sit still, their hands flapping in the air with the desperate enthusiasm of freshly caught fish. *Pick me! Pick me!* They were the "experts," always ready to dish out the bad news. While the artist was down in the dirt getting her hands dirty, the experts were pulling on white gloves. When you were locked in the stocks of critical opinion, it could take years to wash off a comment hurled in haste. Being branded as a "feminist artist" conveyed a certain subliminal message to the public that perhaps what she had to say in her work was, in fact, old news. Somehow it didn't have the same lofty ring to it as being, for example, a Postmodernist or a Realist. "Feminist" was her art with parenthesis around it, as if it were separate or removed in some way from the work that the other artists did, the *real* artists.

Recently, she'd read an article about some young male artist who'd put his own semen on a piece of paper and called it art, and the critics, relying on their substantial knowledge of art history, had heralded the boy a genius. But when female artists painted with menstrual blood, the critics pursed their lips and called them "Feminists," satisfied that the word, with all its dowdy implications, would suffice.

Still, she could not separate her work from her politics—the word *politics* had become a catchall phrase, another kind of category that inveigled your hidden dreams and fears. She couldn't separate her *needs* as a female person from her art. She had to wonder: How could you be female and not be a feminist? Joe had called the word a relic—but to her it was more important than ever—an emblem that needed to be raised up high in the air for all those blow-job-giving girls to see. Not that she had any issue with oral sex, but what were those girls getting in return? Certainly not the handy orgasms of their partners.

What woman didn't want equality? The question seemed preposterous to her—yet there were still women out there who were indifferent to their own rights and powers. It made her angry and, indeed, it fueled her work. What if a war *did* break out, she readdressed Joe's question. What about all those women who'd been raped in Afghanistan—would that happen here? Could it? According to Joe Golding it was a definite possibility.

18 ⌯

Golding was a superstitious man and it was superstition that made him go to temple on the High Holidays, not religious devotion. You went to temple to get written into the Book of Life and if you didn't go, you risked insulting God, which was never a good idea, no matter how remarkable your excuse. Even Candace, who had not been born a Jew and had converted when they'd married, went to temple on the High Holidays. That morning the sun was bright and the air smelled of apples and horses and wood smoke. Joe felt the promise of survival in his bones. He felt unbearable gratitude.

Driving with his wife and daughter to the synagogue, he reflected on the years that had come before, the rituals they'd shared as a family. On every Rosh Hashanah, they used to take Willa apple picking after services. They'd wander through the rows of trees, filling their bags. *Look, Daddy, look at this one!* She'd hold the apple up in her perfect little hand. Later, in the kitchen, she'd stand on a stool at the counter, dipping her apples in honey. Would the year be sweet? he wondered now. For some reason, he felt a sense of doom when he looked at his daughter. Her aura of mystery. Her morbid sartorial inclinations. He supposed it was natural, inevitable; she was growing up. Sometimes he'd look at her and do a double take—he hardly recognized her. This was not *his* Willa. This Willa had breasts, hips. She'd taken to wearing dark eyeliner. She wore patchouli oil and tea rose and those awful black sneakers with the broken shoelaces and she made noise like a Hindu dancer when she walked, her bracelets up to her elbows. And she wrote lines from rap songs on her arms and legs—at least they weren't tattoos, he reminded himself. "Not yet," his wife had said. Their daughter was becoming a stranger. He glanced at her in his rearview mirror, not surprised to find her on her cell phone. At least she was wearing her tallit, he thought.

Candace sat beside him in a black Chanel suit. His wife looked like she was going to a funeral, but most of the women dressed like that on the High Holidays—more so on Yom Kippur. Everybody felt guilty, or at least looked like they did. Although he'd asked her not to, she'd brought the cane. It had been two weeks since the mare had thrown her and she was still using it. They'd been to the doctor, she'd had an MRI, nothing was found. When Joe had discussed her condition with the doctor in private, the doctor had said, "It's not uncommon for women of menopausal age to experience psychosomatic symptoms."

He looked at his wife now as she adjusted her makeup in the

vanity mirror. No amount of makeup could cure her expression of perennial discontent. Joe knew it had something to do with the fact that when she was two years old her mother had left her in a bus station locker and disappeared—luckily, somebody had heard her screaming. After that, it was one foster home after another until he'd met her, when she'd showed up at his office in New York, hoping to work as a typist—he'd taken one look at her in her Catholic school clothes, *St. Theresa's* stitched on her breast pocket, the knee socks, the *feed me* look in her eyes, and that was it—she was hired, and not just to sit behind a typewriter—her shrink at Riggs said it wasn't uncommon to have flashbacks of the bus station ordeal, even now. Post-Traumatic Stress Syndrome, he'd called it. Joe tried to be understanding, he tried to indulge her, but still, it irritated him. *Get over it already,* he wanted to shout. But instead, he said, "You look pretty."

She offered him the slightest of smiles. *No I don't.*

"I'm glad you came. Thank you." *Such civility!*

To his surprise, Candace reached over and took his hand and squeezed it. He knew he was supposed to interpret the gesture as some meaningful symbol of her devotion, but he could not.

The temple had its origins in a large brick house on Crofut Street, but after a major capital campaign, of which he'd been a major contributor, a new, larger temple was erected just north of town. The new building had been designed by a congregant, a well-known local architect, and resembled a modern Noah's Ark. Whenever he entered the building, walking first through the glass, light-filled annex from the parking lot, then into the enormous foyer, he felt an unmitigated sense of pride knowing that his money had found its way into every brick and beam that had made it. The head rabbi was a woman, which bothered him slightly, although he could never speak of it to the others. As a boy in Queens, he went to the narrow crumbling shul on his block, of which the aged Rabbi Pilchick had been its wizened leader. With his sprawling white hair and imposing forehead glistening with the sweat of his great intellect, Pilchick was a *real* rabbi. But this woman, this Rabbi Zimmerman, who was all of forty, seemed, well, ordinary.

Still, he went to temple with an open mind, eager to feel something, eager to feel, what—*resolved?* He had not married a Jew, and in the beginning, when he had gotten himself embroiled with Candace, he hadn't thought it would make a difference in the long run, but it had. Although she had done her best to maintain a Jewish home, lighting the candles on Shabbat and making elaborate holiday meals, his wife was not a believer and he detected in her compliance a simmering contempt. He often wondered if he died first—and he was nearly certain that he would—if she would even bother to have a funeral for him or would simply cremate him and throw the ashes out in the next day's trash. This was entirely possible and no amount of discussion on the subject made him feel any better. Candace did not like discussing the subject of death, and he knew that, regardless of what he put in his will, she would do what she liked.

Willa, on the other hand, was a good Jew, and this phenomenon was more than he could have ever hoped for, knowing that her biological parents had been Catholics. She had become a bat mitzvah, not because he'd told her to, but because she'd chosen to on her own. At the age of twelve, with her picket-fence teeth, she'd come into their bedroom to deliver the earnest declaration—she didn't care if her blood was green as a four-leafed clover, *she,* Willa Golding, was a Jew! Joe had never been the sentimental type, but he had to admit, that was one of those parenting moments that really got to him. It made him believe that, even with all the other crap in his life, at least he'd done something right. Not that he was religious—not that he was even a believer—he wasn't. He was a true skeptic and, in general, the concept of religion gave him the creeps. But somehow this was different. He guessed if he had to pinpoint when things had started changing for him, religion-wise, it would be then, when they'd go to temple regularly in preparation for the bat mitzvah. He'd never been comfortable going before, but Willa had a way of making everything easy, and before you had a chance to freak out, you were there, doing it, mumbling prayers in some close approximation of the actual Hebrew. Her fearless nature frightened him too, because he knew, eventually, it might get her into trouble. He would try talking to her about it from time to time, when he'd drive her back and forth to her meetings with the rabbi, but she'd just roll her eyes at him and shake her head and say, "Oh, Daddy." The months passed and they grew accustomed to hearing Hebrew in the house, her melodic hafto-rah wandering through the rooms, and soon the day arrived. Candace had risen to the occasion by planning a magnificent party, inviting two hundred guests to the black-tie event. To the distaste of many of the locals, they'd had the party at their country club, which had very few Jews as members, taking over the ballroom of the club-house, which was an original Berkshire Cottage—a place so staunchly cultivated you'd think the cushions were stuffed with hundred-dollar bills. For her mitzvah project, Willa had spent the year working at a local barn with abused racehorses. All the hard work had been worth it when she finally saw her present, a black Dutch Warm Blood named Boy.

Late as usual, they had to park in the lot of the Greek Orthodox Church down the road. The church and temple shared an understand-ing and reciprocated to each other as needed. You always saw Jews walking along the road in all their finery during the High Holidays, and during Easter you saw Greeks in the temple lot all dressed up for church. Services started at ten; it was ten-twenty now, and he parked in the only spot that was left, deep in the farthest corner of the lot under the drooping branches of a chestnut tree; he hoped the little brown pods it dropped wouldn't scratch his car.

It was a windy morning, but the wind was not cold. It swept up the hem of Candace's skirt, showing her pretty legs, and she jumped around trying to contain herself, grappling with the cane. Willa came up and took his arm and together they entered the synagogue behind his wife. Walking with his daughter arm in arm, he imagined her fu-ture wedding day, and his eyes went misty. He couldn't imagine lov-ing anything more than this child, who had miraculously come into their lives and brought them such joy. He held her tighter, wishing that he could protect her somehow from the banquet of tainted deli-cacies that awaited her rapacious appetite. Of course, he knew he could not.

They entered the sanctuary and were ushered into a pew in the back and another congregant handed them each a prayer book. Rabbi Jonathan, the assistant rabbi, was standing at the pulpit. Rabbi Jonathan was young to be balding, and had a strong, reliable face. Other members of the congregation had told Joe that he was gay. He didn't *look* gay to Joe, but people said he lived with his partner and that they had moved to the state of Massachusetts so that they could eventually get married. Jonathan had something of an old soul about him. With his squat, sturdy frame the young rabbi might have been a warrior in ancient times—Joe could easily picture him in one of those short white togas and sandals, wielding a shield that looked like a sledding saucer. He wondered if he'd played football in high school, and if he had, what it was like to play football if you were gay *and* Jewish. There had been few Jewish boys on the football team at his school, but that was a long time ago, things had changed; now you found Jews all over the place, on every conceivable team. There were even Jewish figure skaters, Jewish boxers. There were Jews who rode horses and raced cars. He wondered distantly if there were any *gay* race car drivers or gay boxers and he assumed that there were. Carlos, their horse trainer, was gay, of course. Joe had no quarrel with homosexuality, but he'd made a decision a long time ago not to produce gay movies. Often his films included scenes between two women or even three or four women, but that wasn't really *gay* sex—and generally it was a device of titillation for men, not for women. Men liked watching a woman take it up the ass—anal was a requisite element of a good gonzo film. But the industry was changing. There were more and more amateurs getting into it, thinking they could produce decent compilations with a video camera—and they could get girls as long as they paid. They'd get the addicts, girls so addicted to crystal meth they'd do just about anything to get some— and they'd rent a big house somewhere and feed the girls drugs all weekend. It wasn't the way Joe did business. They generally used contract girls. Most of their girls were reliable and were more into coke than meth. In the old days, it was mostly Italians making porn. But now there were squeamish Jewish lawyers who'd sidestepped into the business to get rich quick, and they did. They had. These days there was so much competition you had to be on the edge to stand out. The Internet had opened up the business to ordinary people who'd shoot home movies in their living rooms and try to pass them off as professional product, which pissed off the *real* professionals who followed the rules. The raunchier the better—that's where the money was. It's what the customers expected. His brother, Harold, who was fondly known in the business as the Shakespeare of Porn, had to rack his brain to come up with more and more violent scenarios. Harold lived in California, in Chatsworth, with his third or fourth wife, he'd lost count. Their father had died when they were in grade school. Born less than two years apart, they'd always been close. And they'd had to take care of their mother, always finding some kind of work after school. In high school, they'd both gotten interested in film, and then Harold, who was older, took a job working for Jimmy Salerno, who taught him everything about the business. Salerno was old-school porn and became a kind of father-figure, and when Joe graduated from high school, he started working there too. "It's like any other business," the old man had told them. "No different than selling shoes. You'll see."

Eventually, they scraped up enough money to buy the old man out, and the rest was history. It took them a few years to get going, but once they did, rivers of money poured in. Rivers, lakes, an ocean. It was almost too much to believe. They opened stores all over the country that sold adult product, videos and sex toys—that's where they'd made their money—and they'd built a reputation and people trusted them. In high school, Joe had dreamed of being a film director, but once he'd stepped into the swampy waters of porn, there was no getting out.

People in the Berkshires didn't know what he did for a living. The truth was he and Candace shared it like some forbidden addiction. It sustained their lifestyle, but like every kind of dependency known to man, it had certain requirements and secrecy was one of them. Not even Willa knew. Like everyone else, the rabbi thought he made commercials and had no idea that a huge portion of the funding for the new temple had come from him, which when you boiled it down stunk of pussy. People liked to degrade the porn industry. From time to time, he'd stumble upon a conversation about it at a cocktail party, knowing all along that the naysayer likely had a stash of vibrators at the ready, or crept down to wank off in front of the computer when all the kiddies were sleeping. But Golding had made his peace with it—he used to care, but not anymore—well, not really. It was why he and Candace had moved up here in the first place—where nobody knew them—where they could buy their freedom and a life for their daughter. People liked to believe that porn was a deranged pastime expressly reserved for perverts, but Golding's wealth had proved otherwise. Like a cure for the common cold, he and Harold provided ordinary people with a remedy for lackluster romance—bad sex. That's what it was, wasn't it? In his opinion, unique was the marriage with long-lasting eroticism. People needed to shake things up once in a while, and plenty of people did just that. In fact, to his and his brother's amazement, their hottest-selling title last year was a movie about a transvestite and the highest percentage of viewers turned out to be straight men.

He suddenly thought of Claire Squire—the feminist—and scoffed out loud. *Feminists.* Uptight bitches. They used to show up outside his studio in Chatsworth with their picket signs—as if shutting down the multibillion-dollar industry was even a remote possibility—and even if they *did* shut it down, there'd still be a plethora of women with the decency to offer their bodies for the good of mankind. And most of them weren't complaining. The women who performed in porn films were a spectacularly complicated breed of female; they didn't mind getting their butt spanked for eighty grand a year, plus benefits.

He looked over at his wife, and then at Willa, who waved to a group of friends sitting across the aisle. Rabbi Jonathan signaled for the congregation to rise and they all stood together while he opened the ark. The gold doors opened, revealing the luminous chamber where the Torahs were kept. The rabbi held the Torah in his arms like a small child and said a prayer in Hebrew and they all stood there watching him, three or four hundred of them, waiting for him to open the sacred scroll.

19 ∽

Candace tolerated going to temple for Joe and Willa's sake, but she may as well have been watching the Home Shopping Network. She was not moved; she did not feel exalted. In truth, she had little faith in religion. Her foster parents had raised her as a Catholic and she had tried very hard to love Jesus, but she did not think that He had loved her back.

She'd grown up in East Orange, New Jersey, in a two-family house on Willow Avenue. Her foster father worked at the Pabst Blue Ribbon Brewery in Newark. With only one car, they'd have to pick him up every night after work, driving down South Orange Avenue in the old station wagon. They would sometimes have to wait, parked at the curb, and while her foster mother fixed her makeup in the rearview mirror Candy would look out the window. Sometimes the door was open and you could see the men inside, lining up to punch out. They'd smile or crack jokes or light cigarettes. It was good to work, she surmised, it was something men did. She would put her head out the window and look up at the gigantic brown bottle on top of the building, with a shiny blue ribbon on its gold label. Driving home, there were things she noticed: black men on the corners on broken chairs, just sitting and smoking or sometimes playing cards or maybe drinking out of brown bags. Her foster father would shake his head at them, complaining how awful pleased they looked to be sitting around doing nothing and wasn't it a fine thing, but Candy didn't think they looked pleased at all, and over supper he'd complain some more about it until the plates nearly quavered with hate.

They made her go to church. She had the one dress, even though it had grown too tight, and Mary Janes that gave her blisters. Her foster mother would yank a comb through her hair, complaining about the knots, and then tug it back in a pony tail with an elastic band. She'd cover the elastic with a red ribbon that she kept between the pages of the Bible, where it stayed clean and flat. The church was the prettiest building in the neighborhood. It had a bell tower and Candy liked the sound of the ringing bells as they walked down the sidewalk. Pigeons lined up on the ledge like old ladies in gray kerchiefs, gossiping. Inside, the ceiling went all the way up to heaven, and it was painted exactly like the sky, with clouds and angels. The paint was chipping off and sometimes she'd see pieces of it in people's hair or on their shoulders, like little pieces of heaven, and when the sun poured through the colored glass their faces turned yellow. Sitting between her foster brothers in her too-short dress, her pale thighs sticking to the pew, she always felt like a charity case—the way people looked at her, their eyes hollow with pity. The boys would shove her back and forth, from one shoulder to the other— *baby, baby, stick your head in gravy*—stifling laughter, and she was the one who got in trouble. They were cruel, hateful boys. At night, they held their dirty hands over her mouth. They threatened her if she told. Once, they blindfolded her and marched her into the woods behind the junkyard. They dug a hole while she waited, trembling, in her nightgown, and then they took off the blindfold and showed it to her. "We'll put you in here if you tell," they said. From down in that grave, she could remember looking up at the trees and wondering if Jesus could see her. The trees stretched their long black branches out, making a canopy—a chuppah she thought now, like the one she'd been married under. Only, where was Jesus then? He had seen her down in that shallow grave, and He had seen the boys with their guilty hands, but He had done nothing to help her.

By the age of twelve Candace had had enough of Jesus.

Years later, when Joe had asked her to marry him, she agreed to convert. It was the least she could do for him; he had saved her life. In her mind, she thought if she devoted herself to Judaism, God might finally take an interest in her. Although Joe was a reformed

Jew, Candace was so determined to feel Jewish that she elected to have a mikvah. She had wanted so desperately to be clean, to clean away her past, and she prayed (like a good Catholic) that the bath would purify her so that she could begin a new life, nascent as an infant.

But you couldn't really start over. That was a huge, modern lie invented by talk-show hosts. Sure you could change things that improved your life, but all the bad stuff lingered. It lingered in your body, compromising your organs. It lingered in her still.

For Joe, she had done her best to become a good Jewish wife. She wanted to make him happy and if it meant lighting the candles every Shabbat, and inviting his brother, Harold, for Passover every year, so be it. Joe's brother, Harold, who'd bring his latest wife—Sigourney was his fourth—no children, thank God—and stay for too many days afterward, complaining about what the matzo was doing to his stomach. Harold, who pinched her ass whenever he got the chance, or cornered her in the kitchen, her hands trapped in oven mitts, gazing longingly down the flushed V of her cleavage. When she'd first met the two brothers, they were gangly, handsome boys from Queens who'd backed their way into the "film business" through a family friend. She could remember meeting their mother for the first time in their tiny apartment. The mother, whose name had been Ella, was the kindest woman Candace had ever met. On their first evening together, Ella took Candy into her bedroom and gave her a gold locket—Candy still had it. Ella had cooked stuffed cabbage and served cream of mushroom soup from a can. It was one of the most memorable meals she'd ever had.

The rabbi motioned for them to sit down and she was glad, her Manolo Blahnik's were killing her. As the women in the pew in front of her sat down, smoothing their dresses and skirts to keep them from wrinkling, they glanced back at her and nodded solemnly; Candace nodded back with equal solemnity. People knew who she was. They knew they had money and plenty of it and sometimes that was enough. None of them would guess that Joe and Harold were among the top-grossing porn producers in the country. *Who knew?*

her husband had said once when the money started gushing in. Neither Harold nor Joe had ever guessed they'd be so rich.

The small choir began to sing. *May the words of my mouth, and the meditations of my heart, be acceptable to You, O Lord, my rock and my redeemer . . .*

People wanted to be redeemed, she thought. Everyone did. *We're only human.*

Willa nudged her and offered her a LifeSaver. This was the part she liked best about being in temple, sitting next to her daughter for an hour or two without her running off like usual to be someplace else. Just sitting there together. It was lovely. Candace admired her daughter. She was bold, stylish; she had a way about her. Candace liked to think that, as her mother, she'd had something to do with it.

Willa gathered her tallit around her shoulders, pushing her hair over to one side so that it undulated like fire down her arm. Over the years, her hair had darkened and it was full and thick. Candace glanced at Willa's face as she sang a prayer in Hebrew. Her voice was sweet and fine—it made Candace proud. Unlike Candace, her daughter didn't question her faith. It was simply a trait, like her hair or her long tapered fingers. It belonged to her. Gratefully, Willa didn't seem overly concerned about her biological roots, but Candy sensed it wouldn't last. As her daughter grew older, she would want to know more. It was only natural. They had told Willa that her birth parents had been young and unprepared to raise a child, and they'd answered her questions when she had them, but Candace knew it might not be enough. On the day Willa came into their lives, her biological father had handed Candy an envelope. This was after the mother had died, after the coroner had taken the body away. To this day she could not remember the man's name—she'd blocked it out—but he'd sat out in the car for over an hour. At the time, Candace had worried that he'd changed his mind. Eventually, he came to the door holding an envelope. "I wrote this for her," he'd said. "Give it to her when she turns sixteen. She'll probably need it by then." He'd looked at her, a young's man's face that was already old. "Will you do that?" She'd promised that she would.

But she hadn't. Willa had turned sixteen last November; she would be seventeen in less than two months.

Although she'd wanted to, she'd never opened the envelope. Instead, she and Joe had put it in the safe and tried to forget about it. And for a long time they did. Willa was such a good, sweet baby, an easy baby, and those first few weeks Candace rarely put her down— Joe had to coax the infant out of her arms. In her happiness, Candace decided that perhaps there was a God after all. He had finally come around for her, and this child, this miracle, was His apology for all those years she had suffered.

Early in their marriage, when they'd tried to conceive, Candace had somehow known it wouldn't happen. As a result, their intimate life was overshadowed by a burgeoning sense of failure. They went to doctors, a fertility specialist, even an acupuncturist, but none of it worked. In her mind, she believed it was her own fault. God was punishing her for her past. The films she had made for Joe, although they were few, and the awful things that her foster brothers had done to her, when she was still a child. In the great court of heaven, God had deliberated the evidence, then pounded his gavel and cried: *Your womb is a gutter! A gutter full of dirty things! Your womb is not suitable for an infant!*

Then a friend of Joe's, an adoption lawyer, heard about a baby out in California. The lawyer's brother was a doctor in an AIDS clinic— miraculously, the baby showed no signs of having the disease. They deliberated and Joe convinced her. Arrangements were made; the birth parents requested to drive the infant there themselves—it was highly unusual—generally there was a third party—but, considering the mother's ill health, they agreed to it. Since the baby was already three months old, Joe and Candace promised to keep her name. Candace could remember borrowing the Willa Cather book from the library and reading it through the night without stopping. After she'd finished it, she'd decided that she liked the idea of the child being named for a woman with a powerful voice and even now it pleased her whenever she spoke the name aloud. It had happened so fast, so suddenly. One day they were childless, the next day they were not. They'd rushed out to buy a crib, a car seat. Tiny little clothes. Musical toys. She had wandered the aisles of the baby store with the lightheaded fascination of an astronaut on the moon.

It had rained that day. When their car pulled up, she'd run out with an umbrella, her feet getting soaked. She didn't care—she would walk a thousand miles in the pouring rain just to have that child in her arms. Her love for Willa had already bloomed. It had stretched out inside her like some kind of beautiful flower. But still, in those first moments after they'd arrived, in the time it took to get to their car, she felt completely alone, more alone than she'd ever felt, and consumed with doubt. She didn't know if she could *be* a mother, if she could be *this child's* mother. She was terrified. Joe had come up behind her and she could hear him saying something to her, muttering instructions, and there was the shock of the white sky and the awful rain and the strange car in their driveway and the shadows up front, where the woman sat, unmoving. And then the door opened and the man got out, stretching like it had been a long drive, and he gave Candy a little wave, unconcerned about the raindrops splattering on his forehead and running down his face, and then wordlessly, stoically, he took the infant out of the car and brought her up under his chin the way you'd hold a kitten, as if he was breathing her in for the very last time. And then he handed her to Candace and she felt this warmth—a feeling so strong it was like the breath of God pushing through her, and she knew, right then, that it was meant to be.

The lawyer had told her they were junkies, but even at the time it had seemed an ungenerous description, because she could sense in the father a certain dignity and intelligence and pride. The father worked part time in construction and he was built that way, wiry and strong and tall and he had that particular electric energy that drug addicts get, teetering on the cold edge of need, and she remembered the sleeves of his borrowed suit were too short. He had the same lovely color to his hair that Willa had now, like the leaves outside, reddish brown. And the eyes of a sailor, gray as the ocean in winter.

Their eyes had met only once, she recalled, when he'd handed her the baby: *Take care of her.*

And she had nodded that she would.

Over the years, especially when Willa was little, people would squint at her face, comparing her features to Candace's and Joe's, and they'd make that irritating, humming sound of confusion and say, "Let's see, who does she look like?" To which they'd respond, "Willa's adopted. She looks like herself." And the person, chagrined, would reply, "*Well,* isn't *that* nice!"

Inevitably, whenever she told people that Willa was adopted there was a pause—not necessarily an awkward one—maybe *thoughtful* was a better word. And people generally felt the need to express their feelings about it. Some were naive enough to ask what had prompted them to adopt. *How good of you to take a stranger's child into your hearts,* some would say, as though it were a kind of pitiable charity. *What a marvelous thing adoption is. It's so wonderful.* But underlying the sentiment they never let you forget that you were raising someone else's baby. It was a subtlety that seemed to separate her from the other mothers, even now. And it wasn't only evident in conversation. Often the newspapers would print the phrase *adoptive parents* or *the adopted child of . . .* which burned Candy up. Willa was *her* daughter, no one else's—and *she* was Willa's mother—the whole adoption thing had become irrelevant.

Filled with sudden emotion, she inched her hand over and took hold of Willa's and squeezed, but Willa gave her an imploring look, apparently mortified: *What's your problem?* So Candace let go, reminding herself not to take it personally. Adopted or not, Willa was a teenager. She was supposed to disparage her mother.

The minute they got into the car after services, Willa took off her heels and stockings and put on her high-tops. On the way home, they stopped for apples—it was Joe's idea. Candace stayed in the car while Joe and Willa went up the hill into the orchard, pulling apples off the trees. She watched them climb the hill, eating apples as they went, and she wished now that she had joined them. She imagined running barefoot through the wet, muddy grass, the feeling of the cool grass under her feet. She watched them for a long time, weaving in and out of the trees, laughing, filling up their bags, until the afternoon sun became so bright that she had to look away.

20 ✑

They would talk in the van. Mr. Heath would look at her in the rearview mirror and she would look at him and she imagined that she could see beneath his headmaster's façade into the person underneath. They talked about all sorts of things. He confided in her, she thought. He trusted her. The idea of him whirled up in her dreams. Sometimes she'd imagine him touching her, recalling the way he'd brushed her knee that night in his car, by accident of course, when he'd opened the glove compartment. It had sent a thrill up her leg, like the sting of a yellow jacket. Sometimes, when she was bored, she'd try to imagine him with Mrs. Heath. She would bet Mrs. Heath didn't give blow jobs. God Forbid! Willa knew she was no expert, but she couldn't imagine a man who would refuse that. In a way, it made her feel a little sorry for him, having a wife like Mrs. Heath. He was trapped, he'd told her, like a mime in a glass box.

Ada had been bugging Willa about helping her paint her room. She made it seem like Willa owed it to her, not as a favor, but as a payback. Why she owed Ada, Willa didn't know, but she thought it might have something to do with Teddy Squire, who obviously liked Willa better. Ada wanted to paint each wall a different color, something Willa's mother would never allow. Ada was not especially creative, and whereas she did better in the regular classes, Willa always did better in art. Willa felt sorry for her because her parents were weird and because she wasn't pretty and tended to put on weight. Plus, Ada had a mean streak. She was the kind of person who fought for things regardless of whether or not she wanted them. It was the competition that drove her, the idea of winning, and when it seemed like a futile pursuit, she'd get depressed and go on an eating binge. When she'd found out that Willa had gotten the Sunrise Internship, she'd stopped speaking to her for three days. Later, she'd admitted to Willa that she'd eaten four boxes of Yodels and a bag of beef jerky before throwing up.

Their house smelled faintly of cigarettes and something else, dirt maybe. In Ada's room, they painted one wall yellow, one pink, one blue. Ada's mother didn't use a decorator like Willa's mother did. Ada's room was small and messy. She had a double bed, lumpy with tattered, defected stuffed animals. Her closet door was plastered with pages from magazines, another thing her own mother did not allow, and the boy from Polo, the enormously cute one, was smack in the middle. He was the boy Willa had chosen when they were looking through magazines, picking out who they wanted to marry one day, but it was Ada who'd put him on her wall.

He was probably gay anyway.

"You like?" Ada held up a new pair of earrings. They were pretty, but Willa didn't wear dangly earrings. She thought they were trashy, but said, "Nice." She only wore posts, tiny black stones. They did their nails and Willa told Ada what she'd done to Teddy Squire. Ada only shrugged as if she didn't care, as if she was above it, but Willa figured she was jealous. She used Ada's bathroom and saw that it was filthy with little hairs all over the place and all of Ada's beauty products, none of which Willa recognized. Ada bought most of her beauty supplies at the drugstore, whereas Willa bought hers at Gatsby's. Willa had a Mason Pearson hairbrush, like all the models, and used Kiehl's, and she'd had her own personal scent designed by a perfume company in the city. Her skin was better than Ada's, and her mother was prettier too and knew so much more about clothes and makeup and style than Mrs. Heath did, whose skirts hung down her hips like a pillowcase.

She heard Ada downstairs, fixing a snack. She glanced into the Heaths' bedroom and saw an unmade bed, books scattered across the floor, dirty clothes piled up on a chair. In contrast, her parents' bedroom was always neat, the bed always made, the small pillows her mother's decorator had ordered from Turkey strategically placed.

Downstairs in the kitchen, Ada had put out chips and salsa. They sat together at the table pigging out. As they ate, Willa couldn't help wondering if Ada was going to make herself throw up afterward. The kitchen was messy, dishes in the sink. There were some plants on the windowsill that needed watering. Willa's kitchen was always spotless, thanks to Argentina, their housekeeper. After they ate, Ada said, "I'll be right back," and went up to her room. Willa figured she was going to throw up. It made her queasy. She sat there, waiting. She leafed through an L.L. Bean catalog. A few of the women's items had been circled with pen: a pink cardigan, a pair of woolen clogs, a dorky pair of khakis. A car drove up and parked and a minute later Mrs. Heath came through the door in her pillow-case skirt, flushed and rumpled. Willa closed the catalog and put it back where she'd found it while Mrs. Heath hung up her coat and her keys and bustled in. "How nice to see you, Willa," she said.

"You too." Willa smiled brightly.

"Where's Ada?"

"She's upstairs." *Puking her brains out. It isn't easy having a mother who's two sizes smaller! How could you be so cruel?*

Her mother looked confused, then called up the stairs, "Ada!"

Willa heard the growl of the flushing toilet. A moment later Ada appeared on the stairs. Aside from the fact that her eyes looked teary, you couldn't tell if she'd done it or not. *Your fingertips are yellow.*

"Willa's helping me paint my room," she told her mother.

"That's very nice of you, Willa," Maggie Heath said. "I've heard some very good things about your work this year. Congratulations on the Sunrise Internship by the way."

"Thank you."

"I imagine you've been working especially hard."

"Yes, ma'am."

"Well, good for you."

Say it like you mean it.

"Would you like to stay for dinner?"

"I have to call and ask."

"Go ahead, honey."

No wonder he's not into you.

Mrs. Heath's bones were sticking out. You could see the bones in her back, the knobby knot at the base of her neck. Her cheekbones seemed distorted, too big for the rest of her face. How had things become so messed up? Willa wondered. There were people starving in foreign countries, their bellies swollen from malnutrition, and here in America there were smart women like Mrs. Heath who refused to eat. She was on a hunger strike, Willa thought, but it was unclear what she was protesting.

It made Willa want to get fat as some kind of political statement. She wanted to fight the world sometimes. She imagined herself on a galloping horse, holding a spear like Joan of Arc. She just wanted to be different. She wanted to be free. She wanted to travel. To wear long skirts with bells on her ankles. She wanted to go to India. She wanted to fall in love. She wanted to fall madly in love with someone who would whisper to her and write songs about her. She wanted to have babies, lots and lots of babies, and live on a farm somewhere and grow her hair down her back. She would be very beautiful. These things would happen, she knew. One day.

When Mr. Heath came home, he seemed surprised and glad to see her. He kissed Mrs. Heath, a peck on the cheek, but she could tell he didn't really mean it. When Mrs. Heath was out of the room, Mr. Heath studied her face and asked, "What's different about you, Willa?"

She shrugged; she couldn't help smiling. "Nothing."

"Something's different." He squinted, deliberately perplexed.

She laughed. "Nothing! Just the same old me."

Ada appeared in the doorway with the paintbrushes and started washing them in the sink. "And how's my Ada Potata?"

"Fine." But she didn't sound fine.

He put his hand on Ada's head and she shook him off. "I have to wash these."

"How'd it come out?"

"It looks really good," Willa said.

"Nothing like a fresh coat of paint," Mr. Heath said. "I wish the rest of the world were so easy to fix."

Ada smiled at him, but it wasn't a real smile, Willa thought, just a mean flash that conveyed to Willa that she thought her father was an asshole. Mr. Heath made himself a drink, first ice then gin then some tonic, and took the glass down the hall and disappeared inside a small room, his office. A moment later, Willa could hear him on the phone. Ada rolled her eyes.

"What's wrong?" Willa asked.

"He's talking to his girlfriend."

Willa felt a little stab in her chest. "What do you mean?"

"Nothing. Forget it."

"Should I go?"

"No," she said, and tried to smile. "Stay."

Mrs. Heath served baked fish and sweet peas. She was a good cook, but Willa had lost her appetite. *He's talking to his girlfriend.* Ada ate quickly and drank her milk noisily. The food seemed very bright: the yellow fish, the green peas, the vivid lemons. Mrs. Heath poked peas with the tines of her fork. She looked as if she were someplace else, far away from there. In a way, Willa hoped she was. She thought of those coloring books she'd used as a child, which would ask: *What's wrong with this picture?* And you would circle the answers with your pencil. She would circle Mr. Heath's glass of gin, which he repeatedly replenished, and Mrs. Heath's distant gaze, and their daughter's eager appetite. She would circle the pasty white bread, the tub of margarine, the cheesy bottle of salad dressing. Nobody talked, just ate and drank. It felt like they were part of a strange play and everyone had forgotten their lines. Mr. Heath used his silverware strategically, foraging his flounder for tiny bones. Sometimes he had to use his fingertip, just to be sure. He drank his gin, squeezing half a lime into the glass. Like her mother, Mrs. Heath did all the serving and all the clearing. There was the strong smell of fish in the kitchen. Mr. Heath smiled at her across the table and she smiled back, even though she'd decided, right then and there, that she didn't really like him. Still, he captured her eyes and wouldn't let go and it was awkward. It was as though they were above the others, floating in a privileged space, speaking their own private language without words.

21 ⌒

They all became friends, Claire and Greta and the Goldings and the Fairchilds and the Liddys and the Witherspoons and James Alden, a neurosurgeon who had recently lost his wife to cancer and would sit on the periphery, drinking and speaking to no one. They would meet at parties on weekends and drink entirely too much alcohol and flirt with one another, married or not. It seemed typical to her that the one person in the group who might be available for a relationship had absolutely no interest in her. Claire hadn't had a real group of friends since CalArts. Except for the occasional bed partner, she'd been alone for a long time, too busy trying to pay the rent and raise Teddy to have lasting relationships. These people were smart, interesting, accomplished. They all had kids in the school. Most of them lived in beautiful, unusual homes. Even Greta had a simple and lovely cottage on the lake. She'd had coffee with Greta in Lenox a few times and they'd shared their secrets with each other like expensive party favors.

Golding had a fabulous wine cellar. Elaborate meals were planned and cooked, a filet, perhaps, with roasted potatoes and asparagus, whatever vegetable happened to be in season, and after the meal, a little drunk, they would walk outside into the field, ankle-deep in mist, and you could hear the horses stamping the dirt and the distant train. The men would smoke cigars out in the field, while the women stood together with their arms linked to ward off the chill, and they would all look up at the sky, either splattered with stars or moonless and black, and each one would sigh with appreciation, knowing just how good they all had it. There was such openness there in the Berkshires, such *freedom,* and she would spread out her arms and let her head drop back and think: *This is it! This is life!* And then inside more drinking and sitting on the old furniture, antiques that creaked and complained whenever you moved, upholstered in weary velvet, or fabric sprawling with pheasants or horses or dogs, and it would occur to Claire how they were all just borrowers—of the furniture—of the old beautiful houses—and of the moments, even, because she was certain that they had each come before, the husbands and wives, the unattached spinster—the divorcée—even the heady conversations about books and politics and art, and poetry, yes, that too had come before, lines of famous poetry exchanged like spoonfuls of rich desserts. Someone would begin reciting a poem—Joe, or Diane Fairchild, who'd gone to Wellesley, something like Milton, *fucking* Milton, and then someone else would snicker and laugh and recite another, Neruda perhaps, or often Yeats—Yeats of course was a favorite among the women—and it created a rhythm in the room, an appreciation of beauty, of the richness in life.

And it was on one such occasion, they were at *her* house this time—her father's house—and she had passed around hats, all different kinds of hats, and she was wearing an old Turkish hat, and it was all of a sudden very cold out, very damp, and they were out on the porch, all eight or ten of them, and they were all quietly drunk, had been drinking for hours, and the stars were enormous and the sky incredibly black, and Joe touched her on her back, he *touched* her on the small of her back, her most elegant mysterious place, and that was it—she *knew.*

The next morning he came to the barn. He pulled up in a little car, an Austin Healey. She'd been working all morning, her hands thick with plaster. She washed her hands and dried them on a towel, then went to the door.

"I thought you might be looking for this," he said, holding up Teddy's backpack. "You might want to look inside it."

"Why, did you?"

"I thought it was Willa's." He shrugged, apologetically. "There's some very powerful stuff in there."

"Really?" She opened the pack and dug around and discovered a Baggie of weed.

"It's not something they should be doing."

"I know," she said, but Teddy had been smoking pot for years. He went to great lengths to disguise it, spraying his room with Lysol. "It's better than drinking," she offered.

He stood there with the chimes clanging.

"Do you want to come in?"

"You're working."

"But you're a very nice distraction." She held out her hand as if to a child. "Come see. Come see my *feminist* art."

He glanced up at her sheepishly. "I feel sort of bad about that. It was stupid, wasn't it?"

"It wasn't stupid," she heard herself lie. Even now, at her age, she could feel herself sliding into old habits from her youth, the way she'd been encouraged to behave around men she found attractive. Making it easier for them, not wanting to hurt their feelings, more than willing to compromise her own. "Maybe that's not the right word for it. It's a difficult subject and, as you can see, it's one that's had my attention for a while." She gestured to the room, her work. "Anyway, it's complicated. Men and women. The way we define ourselves. It shouldn't be. It shouldn't be complicated, but it is." She looked at him. "I guess we can't seem to get our story straight."

"It's certainly open to interpretation," he said. "It all depends on how you see things, where you come from, your background, what your life experiences have been. It's impossible for everyone to agree, don't you think?"

"Maybe, but then everyone's justified in their thinking, and there's no right and wrong. Laws become arbitrary decisions. That doesn't work either. Then you have teams. You're either on one team or another, right or left, Red Sox or Yankees—even the judges on the Supreme Court. It becomes more about the teams and the players than the issues."

"I hate politics, don't you?" He smiled at her. "But I happen to love baseball."

He looked at her work. He walked around the sculptures in the way that people do, contemplatively tilting his head to one side then the other. "These are very good." He looked at her. "You're very talented."

"Thank you."

He lingered over her sculpture called *Spanking Machine,* the inspiration of which had been stirred up years before, watching children on a playground.

"Still one of my favorite games," he said.

She laughed as he pondered *Road Map,* a naked woman standing in a puddle of tar.

"She looks sad," he said.

"I know."

"Are you?"

"Sad?" She shrugged. "Sometimes. There's a sense of loss in people's faces that interests me. In their bodies. The way the shoulders roll forward, the spine, the heavy head. Gravity. The way you get pulled down over time."

"These are really good. I like the way you think."

"Do you want some coffee? I was just about to have some."

"I would." They walked outside. The trees shook off their leaves.

"That's some car. What is it?"

"A '57 Austin Healey. A bunch of us are in a club. We share vintage cars."

"It's adorable."

"A great car. A work of art."

"What is it with men and cars?"

"They're like women, but they don't lie." He smiled and held up his hands, as if to defend himself.

"Don't worry, I won't hit you. Not yet anyway."

They went into the kitchen through the side door. He sat in her father's old Windsor chair and she put more wood in the woodstove. "It's impossible to heat this place," she said. "The stove helps."

"It's quite a house."

It was still early, a windy day that gossiped of winter. The trees scratched against the glass. The sun roamed the wood table. Joe rubbed his hands together. "You look hungry," she said. "Do you want to eat?" She poured him coffee.

His dark eyes caught the sunlight. He shook his head. "Would you mind very much if I kissed you?"

"What?"

"I've been thinking about it for a long time." He held his hands out before her like a criminal caught in the act. "I just want to hold your face," he said.

"But you're married."

"We haven't had sex in years. Half the time we sleep in separate rooms."

Now she was feeling sorry for him, which, she imagined, was exactly what he wanted. "It's important, sex. It's good for the soul."

She nodded. She couldn't help agreeing with him. "But it's not fair to Candace."

"Is it fair that she doesn't sleep with me?"

"Why doesn't she?"

He shrugged. "I don't know. Menopause."

"That's not why."

He looked at her. "It's not about the sex anyway. It's something else. We're," he paused, trying to find the exact words, "out of synch. When I'm with her, it's like watching a movie without sound. You only get half of what's going on. The other half, the important half, is this huge mystery."

"So you're not communicating."

"We don't speak the same language."

"Maybe you need a translator."

"What, a shrink?" He scoffed. "We've been down that road before. I'll be sitting in the guy's office thinking: What the fuck is *his* problem."

She smiled, she understood.

"I don't believe in shrinks," he said. "They'll take your money. Misery is very lucrative."

"As much as I'd love to, it's not a good idea."

"What the fuck does that mean, 'as much as I'd love to'?"

"It means it's not a good idea."

But Golding was a salesman. "When was the last time you got laid?"

"Excuse me?"

"Don't pretend to be prim. I know you're not."

She was aware that her heart had begun to beat very hard and very fast. "How do you know?"

"Your work, for one. We have a lot in common, you just don't know it yet. And anyways, sex is good for you, healthy. People should be having more of it."

She stood there; she didn't know what to say.

"Come sit on my lap."

"What?"

"I want to feel you in my arms."

"I can't."

"You know you want to."

She opened the door. "I have work to do. You should go."

He got up. "Did I offend you?"

She nodded and he came right up to her ear. "Good, because anyone as uptight as you deserves it. Let down your hair, Rapunzel." He pulled out her clip and her hair spilled down. He put his hands through her hair and he kissed her. She hadn't been kissed in a very long time and she was reminded of her loneliness and she almost started to cry. Her heart opened like an old wound with the blood rushing through.

"Out," she said. "I can't do this."

But he kissed her again and the kiss was good and she went deeper into it. They did a kind of crazy dance through the kitchen, turning through the hall, into the living room, up the stairs. They were on the landing in the bright wind of the open windows. They were down the hall, they were in her room, they were rolling across the unmade bed. Afterward, she told him, "This is crazy."

"It's the sanest thing I've done in years."

She pulled on her white blouse. "You're married."

"You're gorgeous," he said. "I'm in love with you."

"Don't be stupid."

He came over to her and kissed her again and they fell back down onto the bed. They rolled around kissing while the bed springs squealed. "I feel like I am."

"You love your wife."

"Out of obligation I love her."

"Love is love. You have to work at your marriage."

"Yes, doctor."

"Ve must shrink your head!" she said in a German accent.

"If you're such an expert, tell me this. What's a nice girl like you doing without a husband?"

"I don't know." She told him about Billy, how he'd gotten busted and gone to jail, how she'd never told him that she was pregnant. "I should have, but I didn't. We haven't spoken in years. I don't know if he's still there, in Mexico, or if he got out. Truthfully, I just wanted to forget about him. Does that sound awful?" He didn't answer her. She sat up on the edge of the bed. He put his hand on her back. She could see herself in the mirror across the room. It was a scene from a movie, she thought, the two of them half naked on the bed, her shirt open, her breasts falling heavy. "I guess I've never been in love," she said finally.

"You're beautiful," he said. "And so intriguing."

"It's a relief to know you don't just want me for my body." She laughed. "I mean, *look* at this body." She grabbed her amble buttocks, her drooping breasts.

"You are like my friend's good bread," he said. "Warm and soft. I want to get very fat on you."

She rolled on top of him, her face inches from his. "Eat," was all she said.

———

They began an affair. It was vigorous and raunchy and incredibly satisfying and it surprised them both. They'd meet in the morning and walk in the woods behind the house. They'd walk on narrow trails, fighting the branches, or along the lake where there was always wind. You would hear the wind all the time. It was too loud to talk, so they would kiss instead. They walked and kissed under the watchful trees. They kissed with the wind loud in their ears. They'd make love on the old beds in the barn. Years before, when there was a farm, they'd been used by the help, to rest after lunch. There were two rickety old beds that he pushed together. You smelled straw, dirt, and plaster, and the old beds squealed and complained. They made love as her sculptures looked on impassively. They made love as the mice went about their business of being mice. They made love as the wind shook the flimsy wood siding. Although Joe was rich, he made love like a peasant, with his sturdy square hands, his barrel chest, his swarthy face, his brown eyes dim with longing. He sweated, he stunk up the place. Guilt had sewn lines of regret in his forehead. His fingertips were callused, fragrant with tobacco. He'd made so much money, but seemed to regret it, and his fucking was a method of diligent penance, a way of showing her that he was no different than the man on the street.

It was a kind of love, not married love, something else. They had made a pact, and it was sacred in its secrecy, it wound itself around them like rope, it bound them together, tighter and tighter, until it seemed there was no escape. They knew each other in one way, but in another they remained strangers. She knew nothing of his work, his marriage. She only knew that he loved his daughter, he was completely devoted to her. Everything he did, he told her, was for her happiness.

One morning she said to him, "Don't you work?"

"Of course I work. What kind of question is that?"

"Where's your office?"

"Where's my office? California."

"What exactly do you do?"

"I make money," he said. "Lots of it. I'm a money-making machine."

But this didn't satisfy her. "How do you make this money?"

"Why does it matter to you?"

"It's what you do," she said. "It's part of you. It's who you are."

He seemed angry suddenly. He stood up and took out his wallet and showed her a wad of cash—hundreds of dollars' worth. Impulsively, he threw it up in the air like a handful of confetti and the bills tumbled down.

"What are you doing?"

"That's who I am." He left the money like that and walked out.

"Where are you going?" she ran after him. "That's not very nice."

He turned around, his face angry. He hit himself on the chest. "This is me, Claire," he said. "This is who I am. Right here, right now."

"I'm sorry."

He waved her off. He got into his car and pulled away. She stood there, watching him disappear in a cloud of dirt.

22 ∽

Golding couldn't bring himself to tell her what he did. And for good reason, because he knew she would stop seeing him and even worse she would begin to hate him. But it was too late now, because she would demand to know. What had started as a whim was now something else, something complicated. He didn't like having feelings for the women he fucked, but he had feelings for her.

He admired Claire. She was elegant in the way of a forest, how you will come upon moss or the startling beauty of a white birch and become transfixed. After making love they would eat something in her kitchen. Using a very sharp knife, she would slice apples or pears, the good smoked cheese in the green wax. Springwater with lemons. There were mannerisms she'd inherited from her mother, a woman he had seen in photographs around the house, regal, elegant, her neck wrapped in strands of pearls. Claire knew certain things that his wife did not—how to fix a martini, how to set a table, how to use the silver, how to place the knife on the plate when she'd finished using it, at precisely the right angle, how to read *Ulysses*. He would watch her work sometimes, if she let him. In the chilly barn, she would vanish before his eyes, her face soft in a kind of dream-state. She made a woman and scattered feathers at her feet. She wrote on the woman's body with Magic Marker. It seemed to him that she was a true artist. He had never met one before, and there was something exciting about watching her work. Although his conscience told him he was wrong for wanting her, he did not feel that it was wrong, but he knew it could not last.

In her work, she made connections about the body and sex and desire and, in a way, he did the same thing in his work. His work was considered illicit, and they were on opposite ends of the decorum highway. In art, you could present a naked woman and a dog in the same scene, but when you did it in porn, it was considered obscene. It was something he would have liked to discuss with her. In her work, you could put the images out there and ask the public to make their own connections, banking on the fact that those connections would venture into the lurid and perverse—or you could show them porn and do it for them—and sometimes the porn was *less* perverse, just people fucking. Either way, the images came from the same dirty place. On the other hand, maybe it wasn't dirty—maybe they'd all been sold a bill of goods by a couple of uptight Puritans and their lives, incredibly, still adhered to the same rules.

One afternoon they went for a drive. They took the convertible, and the sun shone on her hair. It reminded him of the fields of sunflowers in Provence, where he and Candace had spent their honeymoon, and he felt the same pleasant disturbance of being in a foreign place, at the mercy of so much beauty.

She had on a linen blouse, a gauzy black skirt, little black boots. The magenta scarf around her neck she'd woven herself on a loom. They went to the museum in North Adams, MASS MoCA, and walked around the sprawling space and Claire explained some of the art to him, the more modern pieces that seemed to him elliptical and abstruse. One artist she had known at CalArts. Joe was struck by her confidence, her knowledge, and when he compared his own expertise in business, she seemed smarter. It came to him rather abruptly that he'd gone soft, that his money, nice as it was, had made him lazy. He was essentially a salesman; he took little pride in it. He envied her passion for her work.

They ate in the small café and shared a bottle of wine. On the way back to Stockbridge he said to her, "I haven't been totally honest with you."

She looked at him, waiting, and he was grateful for the wind, the roar of the engine. Maybe he hoped she wouldn't hear him.

"I'm in the porn business," he said. "It's a business. It's what I do."

She just sat there with her sunglasses on, he couldn't see her eyes. He told her how he'd gotten into the business, by accident. How he and his brother had worked to build the company.

"Nothing is by accident," she said.

He turned onto Prospect Hill and pulled up to her house. She sat there a moment. He could feel his anger kicking around inside his chest like a sneaker in the dryer, that clumsy thud was the beating of his heart. He had to concentrate very hard on keeping his mouth shut. He suddenly realized that it had been foolish to lie about what he did—not just to Claire, but to the community. It was a mistake that he and Candace shared. They'd done it for Willa, to protect her, not because they were ashamed of porn, but because the rest of the world was in fucking denial. And denial brought out the worst in people. Willa would have been the one to suffer for it.

And then, proving his point, she said, "It's a despicable industry. It's the most demeaning thing how you use women."

"It's not like we *use* them against their will. They're on the payroll. In fact, it's the only business I know of where the women routinely make more than the men. And furthermore, the girls love the sex. That's why they do it."

She balked. "Yeah. Right. I'm sure they do it because they love it. They just can't get enough of it."

"Look, you're entitled to your opinion."

"You're damn right I am." She got out of the car and he followed her and grabbed her wrist.

"I don't get you, Claire."

She pulled her arm away. "What's not to get?"

"I thought you were so liberal, so progressive."

"This has nothing to do with my politics."

"No? Then explain to me why you're so mad."

"Because you weren't honest with me."

"I was ninety-nine percent honest."

"That's not enough. What you do defines you. It's who you are." She shook her head, incredulous. "You're in the fucking porn business!"

"It's only a part of who I am."

"I can't accept that."

"Look. Nobody knows what I do, not even Willa." She looked surprised. "I was afraid to tell you because I knew this would happen."

"Well, you know what? You're smarter than you look."

She left him there and went into her house. Still, he followed her. She stood at the sink, drinking a glass of water.

"God, you're tough."

"You want the truth? What you do, how you make your money— I'm repulsed by it. Not for some creepy moralistic reason, but because it continues to reinforce the century-old idea that, when you come right to it, every woman's a whore and deserves to be used—now if you'll excuse me I have work to do."

But he wasn't ready to go. "What about you?" He took hold of her arms, pressed her against the counter. "You know you're going to miss me, admit it. Your highbrow pussy's no different." He kissed her neck. He could smell her sweat, the faintest orange blossom cologne. Just when he thought he had her, she pushed him back, hard.

"Get out."

"What about your work? I wouldn't exactly call it prim. It's okay for you to be suggestive, but not for me?" He shook his head. "What you don't seem to get is we're in the same business. Granted, what you do is all dressed up in intellectual bullshit, and what I do is the processed-cheese version. But you know what? As much as you don't want to believe it, we've got the same customers."

"Are you finished?"

"Yeah, I'm done." Almost relieved, he walked out.

23 ᥴᥳ

In the morning, while the television flashed the morning news, the camera gliding languorously over dead people in body bags on a street in Baghdad, Candace thought: *Oh, god, oh, god, oh god.*

She could almost remember the smell of that tight place, the darkness, and the thread of light through which came the sounds of the world beyond the narrow rectangle where her mother had put her. The smell of old shoes. They had been following her. And sometimes, she would wake in the night hearing footsteps.

She and Joe had stopped having sex. At first it seemed almost natural. There were always plenty of good excuses. Either she was too tired, or he was too tired. Once a month, he flew to California to check on Harold and the business, and he was always very tired and drained when he returned. The work was difficult; there was more competition; the customers wanted different things. She had the feeling he'd lost interest in his work. Making money used to be enough. Now, she wasn't so sure.

They'd get into bed at night and turn away from each other, desperate for sleep. She found it difficult to relax. Her body felt strange, alien. Her hips, her tender breasts. She'd put on weight. It dragged her down. It made her feel unattractive. The last thing she wanted was to be touched. She felt somehow disconnected from the person she once was, as though all her colors were fading to gray. She felt, as the days went by, that she was gradually disappearing. She'd look at her husband's broad back in the darkness and think: *I'm lost.*

She'd read numerous books on menopause; she knew, like some menacing criminal, it had taken her against her will and would do what it wanted. It would be a slow, tortuous descent, she thought. As a young woman, she'd had a kind of striking beauty, at least people had told her so, and now, quite suddenly, she did not. Her face had gone soft like an overripe peach. The corners of her lips turned down, as if in a frown, yet she was not frowning. Her eyes, like the windows of an abandoned house where something awful had happened, seemed coated with dust. A deep crevice had crept down the middle of her forehead, forking off into two symmetrical ruts on either side of her mouth. She supposed it was natural. It's what happened in your fifties, it happened to everyone and it was happening to her.

Greta Travers had told her about a terrific plastic surgeon in Albany—Greta had already had her eyes done and was ten years younger than Candy. Candace had made an appointment eight weeks ago and the day had finally arrived. She hadn't discussed it with Joe until that morning, when she asked him if he would drive her there. "Of course," he said.

They took his Mercedes. Candace didn't like to drive; Joe was always the one behind the wheel.

"What are you thinking of doing?" he asked.

"We'll see," she said. "Let's see what he says."

"For what it's worth, I think it's unnecessary." He glanced at her. "You're beautiful to me, you know that."

She tried to smile; she didn't believe him for a minute. *If I'm so beautiful, what are you doing with Claire Squire?* As if she didn't know. She'd known for weeks. How stupid did he think she was? When she focused on it she became very angry, to the point where she could almost feel the anger, like spurs, kicking her insides. But, the truth was, she didn't want to sleep with her husband, and maybe, somehow, he sensed it. Sex was the furthest thing from her mind. She wasn't attracted to him, but perhaps that wasn't fair, she wasn't attracted to anyone.

She just wanted to be left alone.

Sometimes she thought of leaving him, but when she weighed all the aspects of divorce, splitting up the house, sharing custody of Willa, she doubted her ability to manage. Her husband had been having affairs since the beginning of their marriage, but somehow this one was different. For one thing, she knew the lover in question, Claire Squire, and she liked her. She considered her a friend.

Don't shit where you eat, she wanted to tell him.

The doctor's office was on Hackett Boulevard. It was a modern glass building. The waiting room was decorated in brown and gold, and the nurses were pleasant and friendly. It wasn't the first time she'd had surgery. When she'd first met Joe, he'd convinced her to get her breasts enlarged. For her film career, he'd told her, offering to pay for the operation. As it had turned out, the film career fizzled after only two films. She was too nervous on the set. "It's not for everyone," Joe had said, trying to comfort her that first day. When she'd felt her partner's penis enter her anus, she'd felt like she was being split in half. It took every ounce of her physical energy to pretend that she liked it. The man behind her had a particularly large penis, and, even though she'd had two enemas the night before as instructed by the director, she could feel herself losing control. There were the hot lights, the members of the crew, it all blurred together as she started to cry, she couldn't help it. She'd never felt so humiliated—all those people just standing there watching her *taking it up the ass.* She'd cried so hard her face had turned crimson; they had to cancel the shoot.

The nurse called her name and led her into a room. The doctor was Indian, a handsome man in expensive clothes. On his wrist a beautiful gold watch. She liked him immediately. *Make me beautiful,* she wanted to say. He took pictures of her, Polaroids that made her look like a criminal in a lineup. He looked closely at her face, observing the details, the various flaws. With his soft fingertips he outlined the soft tissue-paper skin around her eyes, explaining how he could help her. He ran his fingertips over her closed eyelids and it made her very sleepy. It was like a magic blessing and she thought if everyone would just leave her alone she might finally be able to get some sleep.

24 ⌒

Teddy put the blame on his hands. For almost everything. He had a poor pencil grip, that's what Mrs. Heath had told him. "Why didn't they ever teach you how to hold a pencil?" she'd said, and he focused on the little hairs on her lip and the coffee stains on her teeth as she attempted to manipulate his hand. It was a rude dance, his hand under hers on the pencil, making crude marks. Like duck shit. He held his pencil like a retarded person. He held his pencil like a caveman holding a weapon you might use to poke something. *Poke.*

It was hard to block out Mrs. Heath, although he tried. She'd lean over him, gliding her fingertip down the page, pointing out his myriad mistakes. She was not concerned about his feelings and on some occasions he would feel a blast of heat rising up his neck. He would give her a look, and she'd balk a little bit like she was afraid. She was like one of those little dogs you just want to kick across the room. *Yap yap. Yap yap.* The way she treated him, slowing down the way she spoke to a remedial decibel, like he was too stupid to understand when they both knew that he wasn't. In class, they were reading *The Odyssey*, and his tutor had given him a tape so he could hear it, which made a big difference for him, all the words popping in his mind like bubbles, *pop,* and with his newfound confidence he had raised his hand, noting the look of surprise on her face, but she never called on him, not once. She'd almost smile, then turn her attention across the room and pick on someone else, someone reliable. If she really wanted his opinion, which she obviously did not, he would tell her that her precious *Odyssey* was like some kind of amazing fucking acid trip, and maybe the old bard Homer wasn't blind at all—but some kind of acid-tripping fucking genius stumbling over his own sandal straps, who never imagined that all these totally lame *high school* students would be ruminating over his brilliance a thousand years later. From a purely pedagogical point of view—not to be confused with *pathological* or *pedophile*—which, he had to remind himself, often camouflaged themselves as such—he knew what Mrs. Heath wanted as a teacher. Mrs. Heath wanted to sprinkle their minds with grass seed and watch the blades spike up through the earth, flat and predictable as a golf course. She wanted dependable students, well fed but not necessarily nourished. But he was not in that category. Admittedly, he could not count on his perceptions of letters and words, and he was not always accurate. He misused words most when he liked their sound. A sentence had a kind of music, and the word *sounded* right. The definitions were never as interesting as the sound they made coming out of your mouth. He rolled their flavors around on his tongue, tasting every nook and cranny, but he could not be trusted to deliver the right answer and she would never give him better than a C, no matter what genius work he produced. The way he saw it, his mind was a big unruly field of wildflowers. One day he would shower the world with blossoms.

When he eventually got bored, he'd give in to distraction and notice other things. The windows. The big squares of perfect glass. The yellow shades quivering just a little. Everything came down to the body, that's what he thought; it's what his mother had taught him. How he felt sitting there in the chair, a prisoner. The joy he always felt, getting out. It's why he liked certain buildings, certain modern houses. He would build them one day, it was his dream. There was a house he liked on the mountain. Sometimes he'd go there. It belonged to an architect who only used it in the summer. Teddy had figured out how to climb up onto the deck. The deck was suspended over the mountain with metal cables, and when you sat on the edge of it with your feet hanging over you felt as if you were flying. It was the sort of house he would have one day. He had made his decision; he was going to be an architect.

Ada raised her hand. She wanted to show them what she knew. Her cheeks brimming. She was like one of those fuckable blow-up dolls, any moment she might burst. He could smell her. She was a corn muffin. She was potatoes with butter. *Pick me, pick me!* The way her pink snow-cone tits pushed up against her shirt made him hard. The roll of flesh around her middle, cylindrical as a snake, revealing itself sinisterly whenever she moved. She had a kind of scowl on her mouth. The girls in his class were like members of an exclusive club. *Keep out!* His mind would drift upon them like smoke. Not ordinary smoke, but the wet mist that settled on the fields at night. He had compared all the breasts of the girls in the class and given Monica the highest marks, but it didn't make him want to touch her, although he knew he would if she offered. The only one he wanted to touch was Willa Golding. She made his stomach ache. He would look at her and feel pain, *loss*. She was the blue woman by Modigliani with her legs in a triangle; she was the quince bush near the kitchen door, with its fiery orange fruit; she was the black teeth of the ocean. Ada was yesterday's bread thrown to the ducks. *Quack, quack!* Mrs. Heath had paired them as study buddies, which he found mildly interesting—the smartest with the dumbest always made a happy pair, him being the smarter of course even though she thought it was the other way around. They'd go into town to the library, up on the balcony overlooking the old ballroom, up in the stacks with thousands of dusty old books that nobody ever read, and she'd take out her notebooks, her perfectly sharpened pencils. She had the most perfect handwriting he'd ever seen. He'd just look at her sitting there in her kilt, her not unpleasantly chubby thighs, her coconut white skin jiggly as pie filling, her slightly thick ankles, the quivering crucifix at her throat. She had devoted herself to Jesus, she'd told him, which turned him on somewhat, mainly because when she talked about Jesus she got a look on her face, like she was hot. He would sit there thinking: What would happen if I touched her? *Would I singe my fingertips?* She wore itchy wool crewneck sweaters, thick white socks, clunky Doc Marten's. There were the usual onlookers, cotton-brained people with nowhere else to go, let out from the halfway house down on Housatonic Street. This numb nut in a red sweater, who'd sit in the corner, always the same book on his lap, the spine cracked, the yellowed pages never read. A few moments of freedom in the arcade of inquiry before strained beef and succotash.

"Are you even listening to me?" she'd say, exasperated by his apparent stupidity, to which he'd answer, gazing into her narrow black eyes, "I'm hanging on every word, gorgeous."

After school, Willa took him home. She wanted to show him how she rode. She wanted to introduce him to Boy, her horse. He waited for her in the kitchen while she went up and changed. Her housekeeper was there, Argentina. She didn't speak any English. She gave him a Coke and smiled and nodded while he drank it. Then her mother came in. Teddy thought she was nice. Her breasts were hard to miss. It embarrassed him; he couldn't look her in the eye.

He went out with Willa to the barn. Her horse was big and black. It was a beautiful creature, he thought, stroking its side. "He likes you," she said. He watched her tack up. She moved quickly, wrapping its ankles, putting in the bit; she knew her way around that horse. He sat up on the fence while she cantered around the ring, practicing jumps. Rudy came over to say hello. Teddy hadn't seen him since that night at the Men's Club. "You're a good card player. I admire that."

"Beginner's luck." Teddy shrugged.

"I underestimated you, you're smart. You got to be real smart to play cards like that."

He'd never been called smart by anyone, maybe just his mother but that didn't count. "Thanks."

"Hey, I got something for you," Rudy said, reaching into his pocket. "Close your eyes and open your hand."

"What is it?" He felt something drop into his palm.

"A little souvenir is all."

Teddy looked: Dale's tooth. He didn't want it, but he stuck it in his pocket.

"You sure as hell earned it." Rudy leaned on the fence and they both watched Willa on the horse. "You're wasting your time, brother. She don't need you, she's got the horse." He laughed, shaking his head. "Teenaged girls *love* horses."

Teddy watched Willa sail over a jump.

"I got a remedy for what ails you," Rudy said. "You interested?"

"Maybe."

He told his mother he was going over to Marco's to study, which is what he should have been doing. Instead, he went out with Rudy. "I'm taking you under my wing, son." Rudy grinned at him, and handed him a can of beer. "Go ahead, enjoy yourself."

The sun was setting in the back window of the truck. They drove over into New York State, down empty roads, through wide-open fields. They had the windows open and you could smell the earth. The long grass hissed at them as they rolled past. The late sun cut a glare across the glass. The air was fresh and clean. If his mother hadn't told him about his father that morning, he might not have taken the trip with Rudy, but over breakfast she'd shown him a letter she'd gotten from a Mexican prison, confirming that a man named William McGrath, otherwise known as his father, Billy, had been an inmate there for ten years. He'd been released, his whereabouts were unknown. When he'd asked her what he'd gone in for, all she said was, "Drugs."

"That was pretty stupid," he'd said to her.

"Nothing about doing drugs is smart."

"I didn't mean the drugs. I meant getting caught."

That got her. "You get yourself home after school today," she'd told him. "I think you need to spend some time up in your room, thinking."

Fuck that.

You couldn't judge a man because he'd gone to prison. Rudy had gone to jail and he was all right. When he asked him about it, Rudy told Teddy that he'd made a mistake. "I'm not going to lie to you, it was fucked up. But I did my time and moved on." Maybe his dad, wherever he was, had done the same. It came to Teddy that he was drawn to people like Rudy, people who lived hard and true; they didn't waste time on the bullshit. It was how Teddy wanted to live. And whether she believed it or not, it was how his mother had raised him.

As darkness fell, they drove deeper into the country, so far out you didn't see any houses, only a farm or two, and you could smell manure in the air. Then he pulled off into a field where other cars were parked. In the distance, he could see a huge bonfire and a group of men standing around it. Rudy parked and they got out and walked over. Some of them had brought beer and Rudy had taken his. They walked over to the fire and stood there looking down into a valley, where a shallow pit had been dug out of the field. There were flaming torches all around it, and people were standing behind the thin ropes, getting ready to watch. He and Rudy walked down to the pit and joined the crowd. There were cages of dogs, pit bulls, and some of the dogs looked sick and others were whimpering. Some of the dogs looked too weak to get up, their ribs poking through, their muzzles covered with blood.

"Look who's here," Rudy said. He nodded toward somebody over by the cages. It was Dale. "You better keep your distance. He's got a real short fuse."

"I'm not afraid of him."

Dale had on black rubber gloves up to his elbows. His dog was in a cage, panting hard. It was an ugly dog, Teddy thought. Unlike Luther Grimm's dog, Dale's dog looked scrawny and weak. The men standing along the ropes were shouting now, placing their bets. A couple of women stood off to the side, smoking. There was a big crowd around the pit and the people had mean, hungry eyes. They had come to bet, they had come to win. Dogs were going to die. There was the smell of blood in the air. You could hear the howling, the whimpering. They saw Dale bring over his cage; his dog was going to fight. The second he opened the metal door, the dog went tearing into the pit after its opponent as everyone watched, their faces dumb with glee. The two dogs became a jumble in the dark, and then you could see that one dog had the other by the neck and blood was spurting out like a fountain. "Look at you." Rudy grinned and shoved Teddy on the back. "You're not scared, are you?"

Teddy shook his head, but he was.

"Those animals are bred to fight," Rudy explained, as if it were all right. "They want to fight. It's all they think about."

"I don't know."

The people were shouting as the one dog maimed the other, and you could see the fur torn off and the raw flesh underneath and the organs inside busting out. The fight was over. Dale's dog had lost. It cowered in on itself, whining miserably. Money went back and forth from hand to hand. Dale yanked the animal out of the pit as it yelped for mercy and Teddy could see Dale making a big show of his anger and knew he was going to make it pay. He kicked it along with his boot away from the group and doused it with lighter fluid, joking as he did it, wanting everyone to see, then flicked a match at it. The crowd watched as the dog caught fire and some people even laughed, watching it run around in the field, covered in flames.

"Let's get out of here," Rudy said.

They were quiet in the truck. "That was fucked up," Rudy said. "There's something wrong with that man."

They smoked a joint to calm down. Rudy asked him if he wanted to meet his sister, a nurse in Troy. They waited for her down in the hospital lobby, watching people coming in and out of the sliding glass doors. Her shift ended and they went to this Polish bar, below street level, and they had good sweet pickles and wheels of cheddar cheese and Ritz crackers. Teddy didn't say much, but he watched the other people, men mostly, hunkered over the bar in tweed coats, with pointy red chins and bulky, swarming hands. Rudy's sister had long red hair down to her hips and wore fake eyelashes and she smiled a lot. She had a baby too, at home, a boy. They went back to her apartment and he was a little drunk and they peered into the crib and watched him sleep.

They smoked some more pot with his sister then said good night. It was late, and he knew his mother was going to be pissed. She would probably try to ground him or something futile like that, as if she could. On the way back to the Berkshires, they drove through Spencertown and Rudy asked him point blank if he wanted to get laid. Teddy figured why not—he didn't want to seem lame—and he didn't want Rudy to know he'd never done it. You couldn't lie to a man like Rudy. They went up a road called Angel Hill, and took a turn down a dirt road. They drove along that way for a while and he cracked the window and he could smell manure again and he could hear the crickets. Then this house appeared. It was a farmhouse with the shades pulled down over the windows, dim lights behind them. There were some cars parked in the grass. Rudy pulled a comb through his hair and handed it to Teddy and Teddy used it and licked his palm and pressed his hair down in back. Then they got out and started up through the wet grass. Somebody came out. It was a man who looked familiar, something about the way he walked, the subtle hunch of his shoulders, but Teddy couldn't see his face. The man walked around back out of sight and a moment later a car started up. While Rudy was looking for his key, Teddy turned to watch the car pull out. It looked like a Volvo, he thought, a station wagon, but it was dark, he couldn't be sure. Rudy pulled a skeleton key from his pocket and unlocked the door with it. As they stepped into the foyer, Rudy put the key away. You could hear people up in the rooms. Then a girl came out in one of those Japanese robes and you could see her tits sliding around underneath. Teddy started to sweat. His hands felt clammy. Rudy whispered in her ear and she looked at Teddy. Her smile was a wicked flash. He shrugged, he felt weird, but she took his hand and they went up the dark, narrow staircase. At the end of the hall, she knocked on a door. There was a girl in there. The woman in the robe nodded for him to go in.

The room was dark save for a candle. The girl was sitting on the bed. He thought she might be crying. But then the door closed and she got up and put out the cat.

"Are you okay?"

She nodded, but he didn't think she was. "What's your name?" She had an accent. He told her his name and she said, "I'm Pearl."

"Where are you from?"

"Poland." She was lighting a joint. "You smoke?"

"Not now."

She went to the window and opened the shade. "You like the moon?"

He could see it full in the sky. "Yes, I like it."

“You’re romantic, yes?”

“I guess.”

He felt a little sick and his mouth went dry. She came and stood by the bed and took his hand and swept it up her belly to her breasts. She let him touch her all over. She took his hand and put it on her and he moved it around. Then she made him lay down.

It was almost light when Rudy came and got him. He had fallen asleep and the windows had gone to white. They went down the stairs, holding their shoes, and even Rudy was trying to be quiet. Down the hall, Teddy could see some of the girls in the kitchen, drinking coffee. They went out to the car, his bare feet getting wet in the grass, saying nothing to each other, and eight geese crossed over the sky.

25

It is only a matter of time before a man betrays his wife. This is what Maggie Heath’s mother had told her when she was just a girl. Her mother had told her a lot of things, and most of them had come true—don’t swim after eating or you will get a cramp; don’t go out in the winter with a wet head, you will catch cold; don’t believe for a minute that your husband will be faithful to you—he won’t.

On an ordinary Thursday afternoon after school, Maggie discovered an envelope on the seat of her car. She never locked her car, nobody did. It was probably an invitation to something, she assumed, and opened the envelope with anticipation, but instead of a card she found a tidy pile of letters that had been cut with meticulous precision out of a magazine—a clever invitation, perhaps, which did not surprise her, the parents at Pioneer were a very clever bunch. She would have to look at it more carefully at home, she thought, pulling out of the lot. Turning out of the driveway, she caught sight of her husband on the soccer field, coaching the boys’ game against Waverly. The sun was bright and his features were blurred, but his posture gave him away, the slightly stooped shoulders, the forlorn keel of his spine. On the adjacent field, the girls’ field hockey team was practicing scrimmages, Ada among them; Maggie was grateful to have a few hours to herself. It was only a short drive home to their little cottage. The Head's house was like a beautifully wrapped present—the box was nicer than its contents—and had been home to many families before them. Maggie pulled into the driveway and gathered up her things, stacks of papers to correct and the envelope that had been left on the seat, and went into the kitchen to make tea. She had eaten very little that day and now she felt weary and her belly rumbled with hunger—a not unpleasant feeling that she'd grown accustomed to and rather liked.

Inside, she put on the teakettle and sat down and poured out the contents of the envelope: To her surprise, there were only seven letters, and now the idea of an invitation seemed less likely. She had a knack for word puzzles—she could do the Sunday *New York Times* crossword puzzle in less than an hour. Her father had nicknamed her Wordsmith, when she was still in elementary school. She had always loved words, and loved to write—she'd won a poetry prize at Amherst—the Emily Dickinson Poetry Prize—and she'd written her senior paper on Sylvia Plath. It had been Nate Gallagher's father, in fact, who'd encouraged her to write—but it was Nate who'd become the writer. When she'd received his application in the mail, she'd been so happily surprised that she couldn't resist calling him in for an interview. His parents had lived on the outskirts of campus in a little white cape. On some evenings the house would be all lit up like a storefront, people coming and going, smoking and drinking out in the yard—she'd always longed to go inside, but had never been invited—none of the students were. Through the open windows, you would hear someone bellowing the words of Chaucer or Shakespeare in the voice of a practiced actor. *Get thee to a nunnery!* As a teenager, Nate had been shy and aloof. She could still picture him walking the black paths on campus, his loping, long-legged stride, long arms hanging down, hands shoved in his pockets. People had said he'd gotten hooked on drugs. A few years later, after he'd dropped out and disappeared, Maggie's roommate had gone out west on vacation and visited San Francisco. Walking on Fisherman's Wharf, she'd seen Nate Gallagher with a girl, strung out, a tiny baby in his arms.

Maggie wondered whatever happened to the girl and the baby. She didn't have the courage to ask.

After Nate had left home, the Gallaghers' house became a quiet, dull place, the curtains drawn, the windows dark. And his father was never the same.

The teapot whistled, interrupting her reverie, and she made herself a cup of tea and returned to the table and brought her attention to the letters, pushing them around on the surface like pieces on a board game. There was an E and an A and another E. There was a T and a C and an H and an R. Immediately, she made the word *teacher*. Well, that made sense, but what was the meaning of it? It seemed a silly thing for someone to do. She studied the word. Perhaps there was another possibility. Moving the letters around on the table, another word took shape. C-h-e-a-t-e-r. There. *Cheater*.

Cheater?

She sat there studying the word. Had Ada cheated on a test, she wondered, last week's Latin test perhaps? Had someone *seen* her cheating? Almost immediately, she refuted the idea. First of all, her daughter didn't cheat—she didn't *need* to cheat. She was one of the best students at Pioneer. Furthermore, cheating wasn't something that Pioneer students did. It wasn't part of the school's culture. In fact, trust was instilled in the students from their first day on campus, allowing them the freedom to leave their backpacks outside in the halls during classes without fear of anyone taking them. People respected one another's belongings. There was no thievery of any kind at Pioneer.

She dumped her tea in the sink and poured herself a glass of gin. She left the letters where they were and walked into the living room and looked out at the lake, something gnawing at her mind. Something highly unpleasant—Maine, the incident at Remington Pond, the awful scream she'd heard in the night. She'd been dreaming about loons. *Cheater!* The word taunted her. Again she looked out at the lake. She could be anywhere, she thought. The lake, the endless rows of trees. She felt stranded, abandoned—the way she'd felt up there.

Cheater!

They'd found the girl in the lake. When they'd pulled her out, her skin was the color of violets.

Things didn't really go away. You just learned to push them deeper.

There was the dream of happiness and then there was what was real. Happiness all lined up in a row, like the houses in Hilltop Acres, lined up like tissue boxes at the supermarket, their pale colors as predictable as the lives inside. Well—who was *she* to talk? Anyway, those weren't their customers—those children went to public school.

She sipped her drink and lay on the couch as the gray sky grew dark. The girl had been depressed, she reminded herself. She'd had issues. It was a school for kids with problems. They used behavior modification. The girl suffered from aquaphobia, a fear of water, since early childhood. Her parents had never been able to teach her to swim, which of course, for safety reasons, was essential. But she was not a normal girl. Maggie could picture her, touching her toe on the surface of the lake. They'd tie a rope around her waist and lead her to the shore. She was a scrawny girl, knobby-kneed. *Don't splash me, the water's cold!*

She and Jack had put Remington Pond behind them and moved on.

Jack was late getting home. Wanting to avoid him, she'd gone to bed early. He came heavily into the room. In the darkness she watched him unbutton his shirt. A fragrance wafted off him, the smell of lilacs, but perhaps that was the new laundry detergent. He went into the bathroom to get washed. He coughed, urinated. Then the bathroom door opened, spreading light across the bed. He stood there a moment looking at her as she feigned sleep, her heart beating loudly in her ears. If she didn't move perhaps he'd leave her alone. But that wasn't the case. He pushed up her nightgown and fumbled his way between her legs and thrust inside of her. His mouth smelled of gin. It did not take long. Then he turned away and began to snore.

But sleep would not come so easily to Maggie. She lay awake all night, the word *cheater* jingling in her brain.

In the morning, Ada stormed into her room. "I'm out of uniforms," she complained. "How do you expect me to go to school without any clothes!"

"That's impossible," Maggie defended herself. "I just did the laundry." She went to the girl's bedroom and opened the closet, expecting to find the plaid skirt where she had hung it the day before, but it was gone. "That's odd," she said. "I could have sworn . . ."

"You're really losing it, Mom," Ada said cruelly, grabbing the skirt she'd worn yesterday from the hamper.

"What's all the commotion?" Jack asked when they came into the kitchen. He was sitting at the table drinking coffee and grading his students' history papers.

"No commotion," Maggie said. "Ada needs to order some more uniforms, that's all."

"So order them," he said, uncharacteristically generous. "And hire a cleaning lady while you're at it, this place is a mess."

"I'm trying my best," she said to him.

"Your best doesn't cut it." He looked at her hard. "You're obviously overwhelmed."

The insult chilled her. She went into the bathroom and shut the door. For several minutes she sat there on the edge of the tub, trying to catch her breath.

When she came out, it was obvious to her that no one had noticed she'd been gone. Ada was looking over his shoulder, trying to see into his grade book. "What did I get, Dad?"

"You'll get your paper back like everyone else."

Ada rolled her eyes and finished her juice and put her toast in her mouth and pulled on her coat. "I'm going to walk," she announced, grabbing her lunch bag before Maggie had even finished filling it. A moment later she was out the door.

Maggie pulled on her green crewneck sweater and brushed her

hair in the mirror. Her skin was pale and dull. She had dark circles under her eyes. Behind her, in the reflection, she caught Jack staring. "What are you looking at?"

"Nothing."

"Is there something wrong with my outfit?"

She stood there before him. He shook his head. "You look fine."

But she didn't believe him. "I've put on some weight," she admitted, although it wasn't really true and they both knew it.

He looked at her blankly. *You can lose all the weight you want, I still won't love you.* He got up from the table and dumped his coffee into the sink then stepped into the side hall to put on his coat. He stood there looking out at the day. "I don't know why she couldn't wait," he said. "She's always in such a goddamned rush."

"She wanted to walk."

"Her paper was weak."

"Really?"

"Let me put it this way: I've seen better."

The way he said it made it her fault. Everything was always her fault: the missing uniform, the untidy house, the bitter coffee. She turned on the tap and rinsed the dishes, stacking them in the dishwasher. The door slammed. To her surprise, Jack had walked out, leaving behind his grade book. "Jack," she called. She went to the door, but he was already in the car, backing out. There had been a frost, and the windshield was clouded. His face was obscured behind the glass. She ran outside, across the cold grass, waving his ledger in her hand, but the back windshield was cloudy too. He hadn't even said good-bye. It occurred to her that she was barefoot. She stood there, as though it were her punishment, almost relishing it. Maybe she'd catch cold, she thought. Maybe she'd get so sick she could no longer work and would have to go to a hospital where she could get the proper kind of care. *The proper kind of care.* The words lingered a moment in her mind.

The book felt heavy in her hand. She brought it back inside to the table and flipped through it, curious to see what he'd given Ada on her paper. Maggie ran her finger down the row of names. There were only fourteen in Honors History—the brightest of the group of juniors. Ada had gotten an 80 on the paper, which was respectable enough considering the challenging subject matter—her overall average was a 90, which was, in fact, highly respectable. Meticulous about handwriting, Jack listed all the averages in a trim row, yet still something didn't look quite right. It took her a moment to pinpoint it, but then she observed that Willa Golding's row of grades was smudged with erasure marks—apparently Jack had changed her numbers. Willa had gotten a 97 on her paper, which was inordinately high for her— she was, at best, a mediocre student and wouldn't even have been placed in Honors History if it weren't for her meddling father. The only reason she was in Honors anything was because her father would complain if she wasn't, and Jack didn't want Golding complaining. Jack always did what Golding wanted, no matter what, including losing at golf, and Golding always showed his gratitude with a substantial check to the annual fund. It was what Jack called a symbiotic relationship.

She supposed it was possible that Willa was improving. But to this degree? Possible, but doubtful. An ugly feeling stretched up her spine.

Time for breakfast, she thought. Time to eat. She poured herself a bowl of Shredded Wheat and sat down. On her second spoonful, something hard and strange rolled across her tongue and instinctively she spit it out. There on the table, in a puddle of milk and chewed-up wheat, was a Scrabble piece, the letter E to be exact. *What in the hell?* Wielding her spoon like a weapon, she poked around in the bowl and discovered three more little wooden squares, then dug into the box and found three more, seven in all. A quick glance at the letters told her what they spelled, but she moved them into place anyway, as though seeing the word again would somehow secure in her mind its intended meaning. *Cheater!*

The idea that someone had come into their home and done this— one of Ada's friends perhaps—but *who?* Someone knew *something,* but *what?* It was all too familiar. There was a pattern here, she could see that now, a perverse sort of logic, and in her most rational mind, in that cold little place where even the worst sort of news could be assimilated and processed, she understood that there was the very likely possibility that her husband was sleeping with someone else.

That Jack, in fact, was the *cheater*. And worse, that someone in the community knew about it.

Headmasters didn't have affairs, everyone knew that—but her husband hadn't seemed to grasp that particular concept. Not only was it against the law, it was against their moral code. Even if it weren't true, the mere suspicion of an affair would be enough to ruin him—and her too. Trust was what made people send their children to Pioneer; it was the essential ingredient. Without trust, you had nothing. Moreover, Jack's position as Head was only half the equation. He was a distinguished member of the community. People knew him, they looked up to him, they sought him out for advice on a variety of subjects. And the *church!* What would Father O'Rourke say? What would he *think?*

Sweat prickled her skin. Was it possible? Was it *true?*

"Are you all right?" Nate Gallagher asked her during lunch. "You look pale."

"I'm fine." She tried to smile.

"You're not eating very much."

"Of course I am. In fact, I eat a very balanced diet." But she made no effort to put anything in her mouth.

"I want to show you something," Nate said, fishing out one of his student's papers. "It's a story by Teddy Squire. I thought you'd like to see it. It's quite good. I was pleasantly surprised, given the boy's deficits."

He handed her the story and she detected the slightest tremor in her hand as she reached for it. She could feel Nate watching her as she pretended to read the first paragraph.

"It's pretty ingenious," Nate said. "Told from the point of view of a pit bull."

"Can I take it with me? I'd like to finish it. I have some time now."

"Of course. Just put it back in my box when you're done. I think you'll be impressed."

She smiled at him. *I doubt it.*

"Well, I'm late. See you later." He gathered his things and stood up. "Take care of yourself."

She nodded that she would. Of course she would.

For reasons she could not entirely explain, she went back to her office and read the boy's story. The story detailed the dog's escape and subsequent attack of its owner, ripping the man to pieces with his teeth. Although it was highly irregular, as she was not the boy's writing instructor, she took it upon herself to make corrections, using her red Sharpie like a scalpel, cutting open sentences and ridiculous metaphors with such vigor that the marks all over the paper resembled blood.

She couldn't help herself.

After she'd finished, it came to her that perhaps she wasn't well. She shoved the paper into Nate Gallagher's box and walked out.

The sun was very bright. It flooded the windshield. She wanted to be alone. She wanted to go somewhere, to be anonymous. The bookstore in Pittsfield was a good place. It was enormous; she often hid there among the books, losing herself in the possibilities they presented. She spent an hour in the Self Help section, flipping through books on dieting. There were books on how to manage your metabolism, and she herself had experimented with laxatives from time to time, but that took too long and you always gained the weight back. She wanted to find something that was quick. All the books warned that you had to be patient. It took time to reach your ideal weight.

Behind her, she could feel the presence of the cookbooks. Wooed by a vivid cover, she picked one up and leafed through it. She loved the way it smelled, the ink, the fine paper, the oversized photographs. Ordinary vegetables looked glamorous—the violet tips of the artichoke, the bulbous flesh of the leeks, the pulpy womb of an acorn squash. And the pastries. The raspberry tarts, the éclairs bursting with custard. She gazed longingly at the pictures of couples in their kitchens, or sharing wine on Nantucket decks. They all looked so happy— they were *enjoying* life. Life wasn't just something to get through, like a series of narrow tunnels. That was how she had begun to feel, like she was inside a tunnel trying to get out, trying to get to the light, but the more she tried the longer the tunnel seemed. Why did Jack hate her so much? What had she ever done to him? She'd been a good wife, the *best* wife. She'd given everything to him. She'd gone against her parents' wishes for him; a mistake.

She turned the page and saw a beautiful dining room that resembled the one she'd grown up with. Her mother had been a marvelous cook. She'd entertained all the time in their big white house in Andover. Maggie had been the one to set the long shiny table in the dining room, and she'd polish the silver and put out the crystal, setting each glass down ever-so-carefully under her mother's owlish gaze. Her mother would make cream of spinach, her favorite as a child, and roast beef, and potato pudding, and always elaborate desserts with crazy names, Baked Alaska, Cherries Jubilee. Maggie turned the page to a photograph of an omelet and found herself wondering what could be more perfect than a cheese omelet, its cheddar filling oozing languidly over the plate. Standing there in the cookbook aisle Maggie could almost taste it, and then the taste turned awful, wretched, like something dead in her mouth, and she ran to the bathroom and threw it up.

Later, in the car on her way home, she felt a little better. The sun was sinking below Mount Greylock and she told herself that in time things would improve. It was not unusual for her to be upset, but it was important to keep things in perspective. They were off track, she realized. It happened sometimes, in marriage. But she would make Jack see that he still loved her. She would. She would do whatever it took. And Jack would love her again, and he'd want to make love to her like he had when they were young, patiently and gently instead of the way he touched her now, like an old suitcase that had been tossed around, buckled and unbuckled and buckled again.

What she'd told herself had been a mishap—an accident—was something else, something ugly and deep. It was *private!* They had tried to put it behind them, he'd *promised her,* but now she could see it was happening again.

The week crawled by. She focused on her work, she stayed out of

Jack's way. She had nothing to say to him. She couldn't bring herself to meet his eyes. On Friday, as she was leaving work, she discovered another envelope on her windshield, firmly secured under the wiper blade. It was the exact same envelope as before, carefully sealed, but this time her initials had been written on the front in clunky black crayon, in what looked like a small child's hand. Maggie snatched the envelope and got into her car. She sat there a moment. Most of the students had gone home for the day, or were on the playing fields. It was dreary and overcast and the air stunk of rain. Maggie placed the unopened envelope on the seat beside her and drove out of the school lot. On impulse, she drove into Lenox and parked in the Loeb's parking lot. She sat there for several minutes with the envelope on the seat beside her. An older couple brought their cart over to the car next to hers, an old gray Cadillac. They were slow-moving, quarreling as they unloaded their bundles into the trunk. There was a little dog in their car, a Chihuahua, yapping. Maggie held the envelope in her hands as she watched them. She felt almost weary with grief. The old man had liverwurst skin. His body swam inside his coat. His wife wore a blue scarf tied under her chin. Her skin was very white, with two blotches of blush on her cheekbones, and her lipstick had been applied with a wobbly hand, like a child's coloring book drawing that has gone outside the lines.

Maggie opened the envelope carefully, retrieving a single sheet of paper, neatly folded. With some degree of trepidation, she unfolded the paper and saw the phrase *Everyone Knows* written menacingly in black crayon. Her hand began to shake, the words throbbed with affirmation. The sun glinted off the cars. It shone in her eyes and they began to tear. She would confront him, she decided. Tonight, after dinner when Ada was upstairs doing her homework. It was the only reasonable thing to do. *Innocent until proven guilty,* she defended him.

She got out of the car and went into the market and yanked free a cart and jerked it through the narrow aisles, carelessly, bumping into things. She chose items randomly, letting them tumble into the cart. She'd cook him a meal, she thought.

At home, she cleaned the house. On her hands and knees she washed the floor. In her rubber gloves, she scoured the bathrooms. The smell of Clorox made her brain sing.

When he came home that night, she poured him a drink. He took it into his study, as he did every night, and she heard him on the phone. She went to the door and stood and listened. "I have to go now," she heard him say. "My wife is waiting for me."

He opened the door and found her standing there. "Dinner's ready," she said.

"Then let's eat."

Everything about him annoyed her. His twinkly eyes, his smile, his clumsy hands. She'd made his favorite: meatloaf and lima beans, a meal he'd grown up on in army-base mess halls. They ate in silence. She watched him as he chewed, the lump of food passing down his throat. When they finished, Ada went up to do her homework as predicted. She gave Jack a bowl of strawberry Jell-O and he sat there and ate it with the intent concentration of a five-year-old boy, while she cleared the table.

"I think you should know something, Jack," she said, furiously scrubbing the dishes.

His spoon clanked the bottom of the bowl. "What should I know, Maggie?"

The plate slipped from her hands into the sink. It cracked in two, but she didn't tell him. She stood there for a moment with the water rushing down. She'd cut her finger, it was bleeding. She watched the blood streaming down into the drain. It made her a little dizzy. Still, she didn't tell him about that either. She took a towel and wrapped it around her finger. Then she turned off the faucet.

"These notes," she said. "Someone is leaving them in my car."

"Notes? What notes?"

She showed him one and a little blood got on it.

He snatched the paper out of her hand. His eyes opened wide. "What the hell is this?"

"Somebody left it on the car."

"What are you talking about?"

"On the car, Jack. Someone left it there."

"What?" It was as if she were speaking a foreign language. "What the hell?"

"Are you having an affair, Jack?"

Deliberately, he put down his spoon. He looked up at her face and for a minute she thought he was going to tell her that, yes, he was having an affair and he was terribly sorry about it, but he didn't. He stood up and took her hand. "Why would I do a thing like that, Mag?" His eyes began to water. "What kind of a monster do you think I am?"

She shook her head, tears springing to her eyes. "I didn't think . . ."

But he wouldn't let her finish; he wasn't listening. He was already down the hall, leaving her in his cold wake. A moment later she heard the door to his study firmly close.

26 ⟶

On Yom Kippur, his wife refused to go to services. She claimed she wasn't well, her eyes grim. *I'm not guilty like you,* her eyes proclaimed.

Maybe she wasn't well, he decided. Truthfully, he didn't mind going without her. He preferred it. He wanted to stand there in the presence of God and repent. He wanted to stand there in his Armani suit that had suddenly become too snug, begging the highest power for forgiveness.

The sky was dark, it was going to rain. The weather suited his mood, the darkness of it, the longing of the heavy clouds. On this holiest of days, they deserved a good storm.

He woke Willa and they dressed and together they drove to the synagogue. "Your mother isn't herself," he explained as the rain started to fall. There was a turtle in the road. They had to stop, and Willa got out and moved it onto the grass, a line of cars waiting without complaint. People had more patience when it came to animals than they did humans, he thought. More than once, when he'd gone running on this very same road, he'd nearly been run down, people cursing him for being in their way. *Get out of the road, asshole!* But for a turtle, they had all the time in the world. Willa got back into the car with raindrops dripping down her face, smiling at him, victorious.

"Your mitzvah for the day," he told her.

In temple, they were seated up front. For once, they'd arrived on time. Along with the usual choir, there was a cellist and a violinist. Whenever he heard the violin in temple, something seemed to dislodge inside of him and he felt his connection to all the Jews who had come before, their history as a people, the suffering they had endured. He took out his handkerchief. He felt weary, moved. Just being in the synagogue among his fellow congregants was a symbol of survival, of continuing, moving forward, whatever forward meant, no matter the consequence. And the prayers, the Hebrew, whatever the hell it all meant, came down to simply that. *Continuing.* The music was mournful, soulful. In his regular life, he rarely used the word *soul,* it felt pretentious and didactic, but here it was what mattered most. He tried to imagine what his soul looked like and a picture came into his head: his heart on a platter, being eaten by rats.

He had been a Jew from birth, it was all he knew. *I am Your humble servant,* he thought, glancing toward the heavens. In the last election, his Jewish friends had persuaded him to reelect the president, who had promised to protect the interests of Israel. Israel was important to him, and that alone had bought his vote. But, as it turned out, the enticing carrot had been coated with poison, and he regretted the decision, as if, somehow, he was in collusion with an administration he now distrusted. Admittedly, living in the Berkshires had removed him from the chaos of the larger world. The grim news in the papers made him anxious, paranoid. Over the years, his ability to trust people—close friends and strangers alike—had become a test of judgment, and his confidence was so compromised that he was not certain that he could trust his own. He felt disconnected from his own country, let alone Israel and the Middle East, and he longed to feel connected, right here, right now, with the people around him, people like him, who on this Day of Judgment, had shown up to be redeemed.

Rabbi Zimmerman said, "Everything can be found in the Torah. There's every possible story here, of good people and bad people, the wretched and the beautiful, the deceptive and the generous. You can read the Torah and know our world, it's all right here. It's all here for you." The rabbi looked up and met Joe's eyes, as if she were speaking directly to him, as if the words had been especially chosen for him, and he felt a chill all the way down to his feet. The moment lasted only a matter of seconds, but it was meaningful to him. It occurred to him that life was, quite simply, a quest for meaning, in any possible shape or form, and he sensed that, somehow, he might find it here—today—a small piece of meaning that could sustain him. Without religion—the belief in God—people had no hope, no reason to dream. Without God, there was no future. It was very simple, he realized. People needed to believe in some higher power, the possibility that there was a larger presence that could overrule an awful or even mediocre destiny. People could not bear the idea that their fate was strictly in their own hands and neither could he. Joe shut his eyes and prayed fervently for mercy. *Inscribe us for a blessing in the book of life!*

Willa took his hand and squeezed it and she smiled at him. *Such a beauty!* On the day they'd adopted her, he'd made a promise to himself that he'd never leave his wife. It didn't seem right to adopt a baby then get divorced—looking back on it he saw the delicate intricacy of such a promise, and now he'd come to a point in his life where he questioned his ability to keep it. Regular people got divorced all the time, he told himself. Just because they'd adopted a child didn't mean they loved her any more or less—and it didn't mean they were any better than the next person—or worse for that matter. People were flawed, that was all there was to it, and *he* was flawed too. He could fuck up just as supremely as the son of a bitch sitting next to him.

But his wife had become a stranger to him. He'd done what he could for her, to make her happy, yet none of it seemed to matter. Whatever she wanted was hers, all she had to do was ask—and it was his pleasure to give it to her. She had wanted a pool, he'd had one built. She wanted this horse or that one, this piece of jewelry—he deprived her of nothing. They had the cook, the trainer, a full-time housekeeper. Whatever her heart desired. Sometimes he'd find her in the house, staring out the windows, and he'd think to himself: *What could she possibly want now?* Did he love her? Had he ever really loved her? Yes, yes, of course he had. At the time, when they'd met and begun dating, she saw him for who he really was, a poor boy from Queens who'd lost his father, who dreamed of making real movies; not some asshole in the porn business.

He thought: *I will give away all of my money; I will walk in the streets in torn clothes; I will take my meals at a soup kitchen; I will show God. I will show Him!*

Our Father our King, hear our prayer!

Was it so wrong, what he did for a living?

His stomach grumbled; he was already hungry. In an attempt to appear particularly repentant, he'd been determined to fast. For not only had he and his brother made more money than ever by exploiting the God-given wonders of the female anatomy, he had betrayed his wife—not with a stranger, which he had done numerous times before—but with a woman from the community, a *friend.* But today all would be forgiven! He would sit there all day and repent, crammed in with the other guilty Jews, repeating the prayers, unanimously asking the Lord for forgiveness. *Forgive me for being a total schmuck! Forgive me for lying for convenience. Forgive me for giving stingy Christmas bonuses. Forgive me for my indifference. Forgive me for not totally believing in You.*

Joe imagined God deliberating the severity of his guilt, holding his grizzly white chin in his hand, nodding with understanding or shaking his head in judgment. *You will suffer the consequences, Joe Golding!* He imagined the Great Ruler shaking his finger at him.

He was suddenly desperate for a cigar. The rabbi motioned for them to rise. They were about to do the mourner's kaddish—he didn't know anyone who had died—it was a good time to take a break. Shaping his face into a solemn expression, he excused himself and shuffled out of the pew. *Yit'gadal v'yit'kadash sh'mei raba.* The words rang in his ears as he walked outside.

The air was crisp. He walked around to the back of the temple and saw a group of kids talking in a circle. He recognized some of them as Willa's friends and he nodded at them cordially, lighting his cigar, then walked toward the parking lot and took out his cell phone, wanting to give the impression of having some important business to attend to when in truth it was just an excuse to smoke. He loved a good cigar. It was something that still made him feel like a man. A *ruthless* man in some ways, yes, but you had to be in his business— and what was so wrong with that? He had a broad chest covered with hair and he was proud of his swarthy Hungarian face, his dark eyes, and he knew how to make love to a woman—and Claire Squire had loved every minute of it! He thought of their argument and felt a fresh burn of anger. Then he thought of her breasts, her gorgeous ass, and felt a twinge of remorse. *Fuck her! Fuck Claire and the high horse she rode in on. And fuck all of those full of shit fundamentalists.* He'd had it up to here with the antiporn people—he refused to take the blame for their hypocrisy. Fucking liars! Lying to Jesus with a straight face— as if He didn't know! If that didn't take you straight to hell, he didn't know what did.

Joe believed in sex; it was one of the best things in life. In fact, there were few things better. And yes, he had indulged himself; it was his right as a sexual male. If God hadn't wanted men to enjoy sex, he wouldn't have done such a knock-up job inventing the penis, the blessed erection, the vicious thrill of an orgasm. And why shouldn't he take care of himself once in a while? What was so wrong with it? Was it a *crime* to have a little pleasure once in a while? He could have any woman he wanted! Why should he feel guilty? It wasn't like he had invented it.

He refused to apologize for the choices he'd made! If people wanted to make a living fucking for money, so be it—he would be there to put it on film. They weren't the first of the sacrificial lambs— people had been wading in pools of spilled blood since the dark ages. And if people wanted to pay to watch, then he was happy to reap the benefits.

Filling his chest with air, he stood taller, proud. He and his brother, Harold, had built that business from scratch. They had nothing to be ashamed of.

All the kids were pouring out of the temple into the grassy backyard: The rabbi had begun her sermon. Rabbi Zimmerman's sermons were particularly thought-provoking, he gave her that. Like most women, she got straight to the point. On his way back inside he saw Willa and her friends dancing in the parking lot. They weren't her regular friends from school, but rather the kids she'd grown up with in temple who'd been bar and bat mitzvahed the same year. Now they wore tallits around their shoulders to symbolize their adulthood; their braces were off; the boys had facial hair and deep voices and the girls bought their underwear at Victoria Secret. He couldn't help noticing his daughter's shapely legs, the playful bounce of her breasts. Feeling a sudden heat in his chest, all his liberated theories about sex instantly evaporated. He swore he'd kill anyone who tried to touch her—Claire's son, Teddy, included. He would! He'd beat the hell out of him!

On the way home, he admitted to Willa that he worried about her. "You're beautiful, honey, do you know that?"

"No," she said. "Far from it."

"Willa. The boys—this Teddy."

"I know, Daddy." She rolled her eyes.

"Be careful, that's all I ask."

"I know," she said. "I will."

"Talk to your mother," he said.

"Don't worry. I know everything. I know what to do."

"But you don't *have* to do anything."

"I know, Dad. *Okay!*"

"You have the rest of your life to have sex. Don't rush into it."

"I won't," she muttered.

Later, when they got home, Willa wanted to ride. She raced up to her room to change. Together, they went out to the barn and he watched her tack up then stood at the fence to watch her ride. Although he'd spent three hours in temple and had deprived himself of food since the night before, he still didn't feel absolved. He wore his guilt like a heavy coat, the pockets stuffed with worms. He felt light-headed, weary. His fingers burned.

Several days before, Harold had sent him their newest feature, *Totally Blown Away*. In one scene, a girl who looked to be about Willa's age (the actress was twenty-four) was on her knees, surrounded by six or seven men, he couldn't remember now, who were all getting blown by her, one after the next, and coming all over her face. Of course she was loving every minute of it. He'd flown to Chatsworth for the shoot and he remembered when they'd done that particular scene the girl had vomited several times. In the film, she made it look easy, she was a real professional, but it had been a difficult shoot. To show their appreciation, he and Harold had taken the girl out to Morton's for a steak dinner.

His daughter's horse had been named by its previous owner and Willa had decided not to change it. He couldn't help seeing a certain irony in the name—Boy—and he couldn't easily overlook the sexual aspect of riding—people had done studies of its attraction to adolescent girls. He'd once overheard his stable manager saying that girls rode till they could fuck for real. Thinking about it now, Joe suddenly felt overcome with regret. He felt uncertain about almost everything. He felt at a loss.

Willa rode by, the horse's hooves beating the dirt. His daughter had a perfect seat. From the time she was a small child she had wanted to ride and took to the sport naturally. He could remember her playing with little toy horses, making them jump over her blocks. They'd hired the best trainers for her and whenever she showed, she generally placed well. There was something fine and aristocratic about a young girl in show clothes, the tight chaps, the jacket, the helmet, the shiny black boots. She was wearing jeans and a T-shirt today, and her half chaps and paddock boots were covered with mud, but she was all blue-ribbon in his book. She took the jumps easily, gliding over them with what seemed little effort. She had a woman's body now, he noticed, hips and thighs and breasts, and she moved with a newfound elegance. Again he thought of the boys who would want her and felt queasy. Maybe it was because he hadn't eaten, but he felt weak. Dizzy. He thought he had better lie down.

He walked back up to the house, suddenly eager to see Candace. The house was quiet; he didn't think she'd come down. In the bedroom, the curtains were still drawn. His wife was in bed, her face red and swollen, as if she'd been crying. "What's wrong? What's the matter?"

She shook her head. "I'm not myself."

"Tell me."

"I just feel . . ." she couldn't seem to finish.

"What?"

"Everything's dark."

He lay down with her, pulling her into his arms. "Come here. Let me see you. Let me look at you."

She looked up at him like a child. "Do you still love me?"

"Yes, of course I do." He kissed her. "Yes, *yes!*"

She cried and he held her and he cried too. He didn't think that either could say what they were crying about, but it was something they needed to do, right now, together, and then, quite suddenly, they were laughing, hard, brash laughter that came up from someplace deep.

He held her gently, as if to protect her. He did love her, he would love her forever. He began to kiss her, tenderly, almost afraid she might break in his hands. He looked at her face, her dark gaze, sad and beautiful and pale, like a Stieglitz photograph. There were things he could not explain. Why he cheated on her, why he simply couldn't be honest, faithful. These were mysteries to him. He loved women—younger women, older, he loved her most of all and he hated her too, he couldn't help himself. He hated her past, her unfortunate childhood. Her memories were heaps of old clothes that stunk of mildew, they needed to be burned. They took up space in their marriage. He hated that his wife had experienced terrible things and there wasn't a thing he could do about it. He kissed her, thinking of the girl in the movie, who, like Willa, was somebody's daughter and deserved better.

27 ↶

On the Thursday before Halloween, Willa waited with the others for the community service van, but Mr. Heath never showed up. It was Mr. Gallagher who appeared, wrestling with his knapsack and a ring of keys, explaining that he would be taking over as driver. "Sorry I'm late," he said.

Willa was relieved. She had been considering quitting the internship, but now, perhaps, she wouldn't have to. Last week, after dropping the others at Solomon's Table, Mr. Heath had asked her to sit up front. She had detected the odor of gin on his breath and he drove erratically, cutting people off, swerving around slower cars. Out of the blue he asked her where she wanted to go to college and, jokingly, she'd said, "Harvard, of course." He had replied, seriously, that getting into college wasn't always about the grades, that she had to be strategic, and he could help her with that. He had connections at Harvard, he told her, then put his hand on her knee and slid it up her thigh. It had happened so fast, like a wasp landing on her skin, that she'd been too frightened to brush it off. Without taking his eyes off the road, he had moved his hand under her kilt and put his fingers in her underpants. "I know what you want," he said. Then he'd pinched her there and she'd felt a throbbing up inside her and a wash of heat.

It had seemed to take forever to drive the short distance to Sunrise House and for a moment she had not been able to move. "Go on," he said, his voice flat. "You don't want to be late."

She had felt at the time that she could hardly make it to the door and when Regina let her in she said in a voice that was not her own, high-pitched and quavering, that she needed to use the bathroom. "Right through there, honey," Regina had said, and Willa had gone into the small bathroom, grappling for a paper towel to wash herself off with. She had told Regina that she was sick, and had called her mother to pick her up, but her mother was taking a riding lesson and sent Rudy in her place. Regina made her walk down to the corner to wait and when she saw his truck she whimpered with joy. "Don't puke in the truck," was all he said.

She hadn't wanted to admit it, but she'd felt something with Mr. Heath, something awful and intense. It made her feel sick, despicable. Rudy had dropped her off and she'd run inside the house, up to her room. She'd kneeled over the toilet, but nothing came up. What Heath had done to her had made her *wet*. Wanting to wash it away, she'd gotten into the shower and scrubbed herself. It was a flaw, she realized, something in her blood, and she decided right then that what had happened to her in that van was nobody's business. She'd put it out of her mind. She'd never tell a soul.

"Hey, you okay back there?" Gallagher said.

Their eyes met in the rearview mirror. He was almost squinting at her, as if he were intent on reading her mind.

She nodded. "I'm fine."

Mr. Gallagher had a beard. As a rule, she didn't like beards and wondered if food got into it while he ate. He was the only teacher at school who wore blue jeans. Every day he wore the same thing: a white buttoned-down shirt with blue jeans and red suspenders. In the beginning of the semester, when the weather was warmer, he wore fisherman's sandals, the sort she'd seen on the men in Greece, when her parents had taken her to Corfu last year on spring break. But now he wore scuffed-up work boots, like a construction worker. In class, he would roll up his shirtsleeves as if to symbolize getting to work. She had never met a real writer before, and she was always a little nervous around him, like she might say something stupid.

He pulled on his seat belt and glanced at her in the big rearview mirror again and said, "All ready, mademoiselle?" in a pretend French accent that made her smile and she told him that she was. But she wasn't. Not really.

It was hard going there. The faces of the women. Their hardened bodies, their bruises. The sadness that lingered in their eyes. You could see how they'd suffered in their smallest gestures, the way they'd light their cigarettes, a ritual, a stolen pleasure, having survived some ordinary terror. You could see it in the slightest tremor of their hands, the vague longing in their eyes, the words *I have nothing, I am no one,* ringing in their ears.

It came to her suddenly. *I'm one of them.*

A door had opened in her mind, luring her into a blurry place, the place where she'd started out, the murky womb of a stranger. She didn't know what it meant, if it defined her in some way. Other kids could look at their parents' faces and see aspects of their own; she could not. She had no blood relatives. Her parents had told her that it didn't matter, but what if it did?

When she was little, her mother used to take her for blood tests every few months. It had something to do with her biological mother's blood, something that could have been passed down to her. Not AIDS or anything like that, her mother had assured her, but something else. Of course, she'd been fine. But still, it had frightened her at the time. Sometimes she tried to imagine her own birth, forcing her brain to go back into that dark, anonymous tunnel. With her eyes closed very tight, she'd try to feel the snug, plush walls of the woman's (her mother's) vagina as it pushed her out. Sometimes she imagined it when they went through the carwash, when those long, black spaghetti strips swished across the windshield. It reminded her of birth, what it must have been like passing through that dark opening into daylight. Whose hands had caught her coming out? Had they been gentle? Or had it been some nurse at the end of a long shift, handling her with perfunctory care. Who had wrapped her in a blanket? Who was the first person to lay eyes on her? Who had been the first to feed her—her birth mother? And what had it been like for her, that woman, knowing she would be giving her baby away? After carrying her for all those months, then suffering through the birth, how was it possible that she could give her away? This was the part Willa could not begin to understand.

Thinking about it now she felt guilty. She had no business even questioning her good fortune. She had wonderful parents. She loved her mother, and she loved her father, and she couldn't imagine being raised by anyone else. But when she went back to that single day, the day of her birth, she couldn't help feeling sad. It hurt, the way a scar hurt when it rained.

She looked out the window at the people on the street. Most of the storefronts had been decorated for Halloween, but they still looked drab.

Mr. Gallagher said, "You're awfully quiet back there."

She sat up taller in her seat, pushed her hair behind her ears. "Just thinking."

"What about? Halloween? You gonna dress up?"

"I'm going to be a witch. But I'm always a witch. Every year. It's boring."

"It's not boring."

"I have a good costume."

"You'll make a splendid witch."

"What about you?"

"I'm too old."

"No! You should be a pirate," she told him.

"Aargh!"

"You'd make a good pirate. How long did it take to grow your beard?"

"A long time. What do you think, should I shave it?"

She shrugged and asked, because she was intensely curious to know if he had one, "What does your girlfriend think?"

"Don't have one."

"Why not?"

"I had one once. Then there were a few insignificant relationships."

"What do you mean, insignificant?"

"Well," he hesitated. "Let's just say I wasn't in love."

"Well, you should find a girlfriend and ask her about your beard." She tilted her head from side to side, trying to figure out how he would look without it. He had high cheekbones and gray eyes with little yellow flecks in them and he had a wide mouth that reminded her of a hammock. *A smile you could sleep in,* she thought.

"You know, that's a very good idea. I think I'll do that."

"I think you would miss it, though," she said.

"No doubt." He stroked his beard contemplatively. "It's kind of like having a pet."

"On second thought, maybe you should shave it. Unless, of course, you have a chin issue."

"No, not that I know of, no chin issue. In fact, I have a rather respectable chin." He held it up for her to see, dignified-like, in profile. "But I think you're right. Beards are totally out."

"Off with your beard!" she proclaimed, and he laughed, but they both seemed to doubt that he would ever shave it.

He turned the van into the street. They passed small houses with tidy green lawns. People had put out pumpkins and skeletons and some had made gravestones out of Styrofoam that said R.I.P. on them. "How's this thing going for you? The internship. Is it hard?"

Her throat went tight and she admitted that it was.

"You're very bold to do it."

They'd reached the end of the block, but for some reason she hesitated about getting out. She wished she could just go home, where everything was beautiful and orderly, unlike Sunrise House, where everything was not. They sat there another minute, looking at the small brown house. He didn't rush her. Slowly, she gathered her things and got out. "Thanks for the ride, Mr. Gallagher."

"You got it."

There were two new children at Sunrise House, five-year-old twins. They were very shy, a boy and a girl, and said nothing to anyone. Their mother had snuck out of their apartment in the middle of the night and they had walked six miles into town—the mother had been beaten up by her husband. She was barefoot, the children only in socks and pajamas. Willa took the twins and Gracie and Tyrell out onto the back porch. Regina had bought small pumpkins for them to decorate. The grass was very green in the yard and beyond the high fence you could see the distant mountains. Willa liked how the mountains surrounded the town—all of the Berkshires were surrounded. They were like the walls around a castle, she thought, or like Regina's big, open arms around the children. Regina was a big mountain of a woman, she thought. Willa spread out newspaper on the porch floor, which had been painted a gritty, tree-trunk brown. She put the pumpkins out in a row. "Everybody pick a pumpkin," she said.

The children considered the pumpkins carefully. Tyrell chose the largest and Gracie chose a lumpy, deformed one. The twins decided to share the smallest one. Willa set up the paint and the children got busy. Most of them made faces. The most prominent feature on each pumpkin, Willa observed, was the smile, and it came to her that children always drew a smile on a face, no matter what. She thought about it a moment, eager to derive some deep conclusion. *People just want to be happy,* she thought.

She could remember making jack-o'-lanterns with her dad. It was her favorite thing about Halloween, the two of them at the kitchen table, cutting shapes out of the pumpkin, crazy faces with jagged teeth and wicked eyebrows and triangle noses. When she was little, her dad always took her into town to trick or treat, while her mother stayed home just in case someone showed up—which was rare on their rural road. Her dad would put on his old pea coat from high school and a sailor cap and put a pipe in his mouth and he'd hobble around, calling himself a drunken sailor and she'd laugh and laugh. They'd light their pumpkins on the doorstep and watch the jack-o'-lanterns come alive. Later, when they returned home, she'd dump out her loot on the kitchen floor, strategically taking inventory. It made her smile, thinking of it now.

When they had finished their pumpkins, Willa brought them inside to have a snack. They sat at the little children's table in the dining room. Someone had put a bird feeder outside the window and they liked to watch the birds. Bobolinks, Regina had called them. Usually, somebody spilled and she would have to go into the kitchen for paper towels and come back and clean it up and tell the child not to worry, but so far that afternoon nobody had. A car pulled up out front. A girl was getting out of a taxi. She ran toward the house as if the sky were raining bullets. Immediately, Willa went to the stairs and called up for Regina, then went to the door to let the girl in. The girl was tall and scrawny with brown hair streaked with gold. She had on a raincoat, a Burberry, Willa noted, but she didn't seem like the kind of girl who could afford one. The girl glanced over at the children, her face raw, her eyes wild. Regina came down and Willa went back over to the children, who were watching the stranger with fascination, no doubt comparing her with their mothers. The girl turned her back on them, furiously unbuttoning her coat while Regina stood there, waiting, her eyes narrowed with anticipation. When the girl opened her coat, showing Regina what somebody had done to her, Willa caught the flash of her skirt—it looked like a Pioneer uniform— a green tartan kilt—and a chill throttled her insides.

Regina said, "You ought to go to the hospital, Petra."

The girl shook her head. "I don't have any money." She spoke with an accent. "I have no insurance."

"You know you don't need any. They'll take care of you. You need to put this on record. You need to talk to the police."

Willa noticed the blood dripping on the floor.

"I can't," the girl cried. "You know I can't."

"You need a doctor, honey."

"Doctors ask questions," she muttered. "The cut is not deep. Please."

"I thought we'd made some progress last time, but now I don't know." Regina held her hand out to the girl. "Let's go upstairs and clean you up."

Regina led the girl upstairs, murmuring tenderly to her, and Willa felt humble down to her bones.

"She's bleeding," Gracie said, pointing to the small puddle of blood.

Willa hurried into the kitchen and wet a paper towel and went and wiped the blood up. When she got back to the table Tyrell said, "She got cut up."

The twins just stared.

"Do you like the cookies?" Willa said to them, gesturing, and they nodded their heads grimly.

"Mama got cut too," Tyrell said. "He had a knife," he held up his hands, "this big."

Willa felt something go tight in her throat. "It's good for your mama to be here," she told the boy, "where she won't get hurt anymore."

"She cry every night." The boy looked at her doubtfully. "She say it her fault." He started to cry.

"It's not," Willa said. "It's not her fault."

He cried and cried, rubbing his eyes with his fists. She took his small body into her arms and held him tight. "It's okay," she said, over and over, but it was such a lie she had trouble getting the little words out of her mouth.

Later, Regina asked her to bring the new girl up some tea. She handed her a tray. "See if she'll explain the uniform."

The girl was in what they called the lounge. It was just a small room with an old green couch and a TV. She had her feet up on a coffee table and she was staring without expression at one of the soaps. The girl watched Willa's every move, entering the room, placing the tray on the desk, as if she were protecting something Willa might steal.

"We're wearing the same skirt," Willa said.

The girl said nothing. Willa stood there.

"Where did you get it?"

The girl hesitated, looking as if she were translating in her head, but they both knew she spoke perfect English. She smiled a little. "It was a gift."

"It's my school uniform."

"A friend of mine. He likes it."

"That's gross."

"Why?"

"It just is."

The girl shrugged and lit a cigarette. "It is not unusual. He is very respectable gentleman." She spit out a laugh.

"You're not allowed to smoke."

The girl got up and went to the window and opened it and blew the smoke out through the crack. "Do you have any money, rich girl?"

Willa shook her head. She watched the girl as she smoked. "What happened to you?"

"Do you want to see?" The girl lifted her shirt. Someone had scratched the word LOVER into her abdomen with a knife.

"Does it hurt?"

The girl nodded. "I have a lot of marks." She shrugged. "They are my stories."

Willa took one of her cigarettes and lit it and the girl cracked a smile, as if Willa was her new accomplice. The two of them smoked out the window.

"What do you do?" Willa asked.

"You don't know?"

"Are you a student?"

Again the girl spit a laugh. "No. I work." She grabbed her crotch. "Step into my office."

"Why do you do that?"

"Why?" She seemed surprised by the question and shrugged as if Willa were stupid. "I'd prefer to clean toilets, but I can't make so much money."

Willa noticed a tattoo on the back of her ankle, a heart wrapped in chains. "It's pretty," she said, wanting to keep the conversation going.

"For my mother," the girl said, her eyes lit with pride. "She's dead already."

28 ∽

When Jack Heath had asked Nate to take over the responsibility of driving the community service van, he'd gladly accepted, knowing it would give him more time alone with Willa. Heath had found him just before lunch and said he needed to talk, it was a matter of some urgency, would he come outside, and Nate wondered if he'd been found out. Maybe the Goldings had recognized him. But, as it turned out, that wasn't the case. They walked down to the lake, where Heath confided in him about his wife. "She's having some personal issues," is how he put it. His wife was prone to depression, he explained, and suffered from spells of paranoia. He had serious concerns about her well-being; he wanted to spend more time at home. Heath looked out at the lake, squinting in the bright sunlight. "It's a shame, really," he said. "The toll it's taken on her."

"I'm sorry to hear it."

"The academic life," Heath went on. "It can be hard on the family. I'm assuming you can relate to that?"

"Yes, sir. Yes, I believe I can."

"It's something we all share." He looked at Nate meaningfully.

As much as he was one of them, he felt distinctly apart, as though there were a thin piece of glass between them. "I hope she feels better soon," Nate offered.

He too had observed certain peculiarities in Maggie Heath. Her lunch menu, in particular, had become nothing short of bizarre. From a small, plastic container, she'd extract her lunch with the precision of a doctor about to perform a procedure: eight cashews, ten carrot sticks, two radishes, a cheese stick, and a can of prune juice, all consumed methodically like forms of medication. Nate guessed that she'd lost at least fifteen pounds since his arrival at Pioneer. But these things he kept to himself. His other concern, which he informed Heath about, was her treatment of Teddy Squire, which verged on the extreme. To give an example, Nate described how she'd marked up the boy's story with a blatant disregard for his feelings. "I tried to talk to her about it," Nate said. "I didn't get very far." Quite frankly, he told Heath, it was unprofessional. He went on to explain how she'd pushed the paper into his mailbox with such force that it crumpled like a piece of trash. Nate had been unwilling to hand it back to the boy in that condition and had made up a story about accidentally spilling coffee on it. To his relief, Teddy had shrugged and said it wasn't a big deal. He had another copy on his hard drive.

Heath listened patiently, nodding his head. There were several variables to consider, he told him, speaking slowly, but he did not elaborate, and they walked back up to campus in silence and went their separate ways.

"I'll be driving the community service van from now on," he announced to the students, who shrugged noncommittally as they climbed into their seats—except, he thought, for Willa, whose eyes seemed to soften with relief. Nate was especially grateful for the seven minutes they had after dropping off the sophomores at Solomon's Table. Seven minutes of time to just be together in the same place, breathing the same air. It was all he wanted. The more he came to know her, the more he saw little pieces of himself in her mannerisms. Her hair, her bushy eyebrows, her long fingers, the way she shook her hair over one shoulder in the exact same way Catherine had, the way she moved, curling herself up into a square on the seat, the way she always took off her shoes just like he did, preferring to be barefoot—it seemed unfair that she didn't know who he was, that he couldn't possibly tell her, yet it probably didn't matter, after all. She had a life here. She had her parents, grandparents; they were her family tree, not he and Catherine. She'd done just fine without them.

Moreover, how well did he know his own relations? He had met Cat's mother only once, when he'd gone to tell her that Cat had died. He'd tracked her down in a trailer park in Sacramento. She lived alone, long divorced. She'd cooked him supper, and packed all of Cat's childhood mementos in a suitcase for him. "You knew her better," is what she'd told him. He'd taken a train back east, a seven-day journey across the country. He recalled the ride as an excursion through purgatory, shooting dope in the train lavatory as the world flashed by through the tiny window, the smell of urine in his nostrils, the sound of the train cutting up the air.

At six sharp, as instructed, he pulled the van up in front of Sunrise House to wait for Willa to come out. It was already dark and the air was cool. When the door to the house opened, he saw a brightly lit foyer, four small children at Willa's hips hugging her good-bye. It choked him up a little and he coughed. She climbed into the back. "How'd it go?" he asked.

She seemed upset. She told him a story about a prostitute who'd come in wearing a Pioneer skirt. He waited for her to go on, but she didn't. He watched her in the rearview mirror and saw that she'd begun to cry.

"What's up, what's the matter?"

"It's not fair. How people treat each other. It's very sad."

He didn't know what to say to her. The things that came to mind were all clichés and would do her no good. The world was full of pitiful people—he himself had been one once—and she was getting her first taste of it. "People can change," he said, but the words sounded false—platitudes from a clueless man.

"I don't know," she said. "I'm not so sure."

"People get into stuff. For a while it defines them. Drugs and stuff. It gets the best of them. But it can end."

She said nothing. The car swelled with silence. At last she said, "I just want to go home."

They drove the rest of the way in silence. He thought of the letter he'd written to her on the afternoon he'd given her up. It was after her mother had died, after they'd taken the body away. For several hours, he'd sat in the car outside the Goldings' home, unable to move—stuck—and he'd found the paper and a pen and started writing. When he'd finally finished it, he'd felt a little better. He'd gotten out of the car and walked to the door and it was like walking halfway around the world, his body weighed down, as if with sand, and he caught a glimpse of them through the window, the new parents celebrating their baby, holding her up, cooing at her, doing all the silly things parents do around babies—and he knew it was time to go.

It was Candace who'd come to the door, wearing an expression of confusion, of feral determination, as though she would do whatever it took to keep the baby—and he shook his head that, no, he hadn't changed his mind, nothing like that, he only had a request, and he'd held up the letter in his trembling hand.

It's the truth, he'd said. One day, their daughter would need to know it.

Maybe that day had come.

He turned onto North Street then circled around to Solomon's Table where the group of sophomores was waiting out front. They climbed in and he drove them all back to school, the whole noisy lot of them, where their parents waited in the muddy horseshoe driveway in their respective cars. He watched Willa as she ran to her father's car. Although he didn't want to, although he knew it was inappropriate, he felt a tug of jealousy when she got in and kissed Joe Golding's cheek and they drove off together, father and daughter, oblivious to their remarkable good fortune.

Halloween was a big deal in Stockbridge. The Hopper Inn had a party every year. It was a grand old place, boasting the extravagant architecture of the twenties. It sat on ten pricey acres at the end of a long gravel driveway on Main Street. Larkin had told Nate that the inn's owners, a married couple in their forties, were amateur trapeze artists and had set up a trapeze in their backyard. Every year on Halloween night they put on a trapeze show and everybody in town was invited. Nate had a few drinks at Hardy's then walked over to see what was going on. A big crowd had gathered in the backyard to watch the act. Torches had been staked all around the property, giving off the smoke of kerosene, and there was a woman in circus clothes leading a baby bear around on a leash. Small tents had been set up with people doing tricks: there were card tricks, a snake charmer, a fortune teller, a man swallowing a sword. A band of drummers, maybe fifteen or twenty in all, were drumming a tribal beat, and Nate could feel the vibration in his feet, coming up through the grass. They were known in the area, bare-chested men with bongos and women too, in long skirts and halter tops, their bellies showing, their bodies gleaming in the cool night air.

She was there. Claire. She was sitting in a lawn chair drinking something out of a paper cup. In the torchlight her face had an orange glow, and her eyes shone and glittered. He went over to her and sat on the ground. "Trick or treat," he said.

"Where's your costume?"

He thought she looked pleased to see him. "I'm wearing it."

She cocked her head. "Don't tell me." Squinting. "You're a struggling writer."

"You're good. What gave it away?"

"The beard, of course. Can I touch it?"

"Be careful, something might jump out and bite you."

She grinned. She reached out and tugged on it.

"Ow."

"I thought it was part of your costume."

"Very funny. What are you drinking?"

"Punch," she showed him. "It's black."

"That's a surprise. What the hell is it?"

"Here." She handed him her cup. "It tastes like ouzo."

He took a sip. "It's actually pretty good. Are my teeth black?"

She grinned. "Are mine?"

They both had black teeth.

"Look," she said, "they're starting."

The beat of the drums got louder, faster, and all eyes were on the scaffold. The man and woman climbed up on opposite sides to their platforms. They were wearing skeleton costumes, black leotards with glow-in-the-dark bones stitched into the fabric. There was a net below, yet it vanished into darkness, compounding the sense of risk and danger. The woman began the act, perched on her little swing like an exotic bird. She did a few tricks, hanging upside down, doing somersaults the way kids do on the monkey bars in a playground. Then the man started swinging. He did some tricks too, then hinged at the knees and hung upside down. Simultaneously, the woman dropped through the air, swanlike, and he caught her around the ankles. The crowd ooed and ahhed in terror and Claire gripped his arm. Delighted, Nate looked over at her and she smiled, gratefully, he thought, and he held her gaze, and then suddenly everyone was

cheering. The man and his wife were back on the platform. "I think
I need a real drink," Claire said.

They went to Hardy's. She ordered scotch, and he had a beer.
"That was amazing," she said. "Talk about trust."

"Yeah, I know what you mean."

"Imagine just flying through the air like that? Trusting someone to
catch you?"

"I know." He shook his head. "I couldn't do it."

"If that's not true love, I don't know what is."

He watched her as she looked around the room, her eyes like
magnets, pulling at life, drawing it near. There was a crowd at the
bar. It was peak leaf-watching season and the place was packed with
tourists, some of whom were in costume. They took their drinks to a
small table in the corner. It was too noisy to talk; they had to shout
at each other across the table. She finished her drink and glanced at
her watch. "I need to get home. I gave Teddy a curfew. Can you give
me a lift?"

"Sure."

They walked outside, down the sidewalk with its leering jack-o'-
lanterns. "I have a confession," he told her. "It's about my truck."

"Your truck? What about it?"

They walked over to it. "Does this truck look familiar?"

She walked around the truck looking it over. "My father had a
truck like this."

He told her how he'd bought it from Otto. "I'm pretty sure it was
your father's."

"Oh, my God, that's so weird." Excitedly, she started pointing
out things she recognized, a tiny dent on the rear panel, the remnants
of a bumper sticker that had some antiapartheid slogan on it. "I
put that on right before I went to college. This is so amazing. Can
I get in?"

"Please." He opened the door for her and she climbed up onto the
seat, jumping around like a kid, opening the glove compartment, un-
rolling the window. He pulled down the visor and showed her the

photograph. "It was right there when I bought it," he explained. And then added, a bit awkwardly, "I didn't feel right about taking it down. And then of course I met you."

She sat back, shaking her head. "Life is so weird."

"I wasn't sure how to tell you. I thought it might seem very odd."

"What's odd is that my father and I weren't close, we hardly spoke to each other, that's the truth. I would never have thought he'd do something like this."

"You were his good luck charm." He handed her the picture. "Here, you keep it."

She studied the Polaroid, shaking her head. "I made that skirt. We had Home Ec back then—sewing. I made it out of my favorite pair of jeans. Look at me. God. That's my rabbit, Bonnie. She had hundreds of babies. You'd walk out in the back field and see all these fluffy white bunnies, like snowballs in springtime. It was crazy."

He watched her face, her eyes shining even in the darkness of the truck.

"You know what they say? Things happen for a reason."

"I know. I believe that." She looked at him.

"It's got to be fate. There's no other explanation."

"Fate or coincidence," she said, grinning.

"Ah, you're a skeptic."

"I guess it all depends on how you look at it."

"I'm going with fate."

She looked down, almost shyly, and said, "I'm glad you are."

He would have liked to have kissed her then, but he had no right. She gave the picture back to him. "Keep it up there, okay?"

"Are you sure?"

She thought for a moment. "Unless you mind?"

"No. I don't mind. I've gotten kind of used to you up there."

He slid the picture back under the elastics. Then he started the truck and took her home.

29 ∽

They stole pumpkins from Maynard's pumpkin field and you had to carry the heavy thing back into the little clearing, through the alley of hulking pines, and you carried your pumpkin like a baby. Hers was fat and round and orange and she was already in love with it. Marco had handed out the pills that his friend so and so had sent him all the way from Seattle, and the pills made them feel wicked and bright and toxic all at once, buzzing up in her head like neon, and they were all viciously happy. *Dear mother, dear mother, dear mother. Ha ha ha ha ha ha!* So the object of the game was to roll your pumpkin to the finishing line, and the grass was thick and wet and terribly green and you could smell the dark earth beneath it, the cold funk of mushrooms, and she got down close to her pumpkin with its cold bumpy skin and wished it good luck. Whoever won the race got to use the ax. Teddy had brought the ax from his grandfather's barn and had made a show of it, dragging one of his feet like the hunchback of Notre Dame. The pumpkins were wet and slippery and it wasn't easy rolling one through the grass. The pills had turned them into ravenous donkeys, braying and snorting and laughing all the way up to the finishing line—*finishing line or firing squad,* Willa thought, drifting behind because she didn't *want* to win. Ada would be the winner. Ada couldn't help winning; it was what she did best. Ada stood up in her Ugg's and smoothed out her clothes. The laugh burst out. "Ada gets to use the ax," Teddy declared, his eyes bugging out maniacally. "But first we have to decorate." He handed out Sharpies and everyone drew faces of people they hated on their pumpkin, mostly teachers, emphasizing various imperfections like Mr. Miller's hooked nose, or Mrs. Riley's mustache, or Mr. Jernigan's horse teeth, or Ms. Hancock's unibrow, and Willa did Mr. Heath, because she *did* hate him now for what he'd done to her, she hated him terribly, and Teddy did Mrs. Heath, because her every waking moment seemed dedicated to making his life miserable, and when they were done they backed away and appraised their work, guffawing because it *was* terribly funny. Teddy went for the ax, walking in his loping way,

and handed it to Ada and said, "It's up to you, Ada." Ada seemed uncertain, as if she now regretted winning, and she studied the pumpkins carefully, trying to figure out which one to pick. Not one but
both her parents had been represented, the Lord and Lady of their illustrious school. Ada staggered forward like some deranged princess,
the ax a burden in her scrawny hands, and everyone started to cheer
her on. *Chop, chop, chop!* She chose a pumpkin, putting her foot
down on top of it, and you could tell it was Mrs. Heath because of
the mole Teddy had drawn on it—he'd made the mole unnecessarily
bulbous, with a few hairs shooting out of it like porcupine quills—
and everyone went silent because it was a surprise and not a surprise
that Ada would pick her own mother. In a way everybody hated
Ada's mother and in another way they loved her too, because she
was a really good teacher and everybody did pretty well in her class,
aside from Teddy, who couldn't read very well and refused to use
punctuation and talked back to her every chance he got—but *she* had
done well, she had gotten A's, and if you had a problem like you
didn't feel well or couldn't concentrate, Mrs. Heath always let you
out. She would say something like, "Go and sit in the sunshine for a
few minutes, maybe you'll feel better." And so Willa felt sorry for Mrs.
Heath because her daughter didn't appreciate her and her husband
was a creep. Ada brought up the ax and swung it down, but the
blade missed and curled open a hunk of grass and it heaved open
like a gash. Undeterred, she brought it up again, heavy in her arms
like it might pull her over backward, wobbly-legged, and *whoosh* it
came down again through the air into the pulpy flesh of the pumpkin. *Thwack.* It made a dull sound when it hit, like a body gushing
open, revealing its glittering belly of seeds, the pale, slippery jewels,
and little pieces of pulp flew up into their eyes. Ada hacked that
pumpkin up and she laughed and laughed and she hacked it up and
up and up some more and she laughed again. *I hate you I hate you I
hate you!* she cried. She cursed it. She muttered terrible things.

"Ada," Willa said. "Ada, you can stop now. Ada, *please, please* just
stop!"

And Ada turned, her eyes dim and vacant, and she smiled a little and threw down the ax. "She deserved it."

They watched her walk away. Willa called after her, but she didn't turn. She just kept walking, into the greedy dark.

They went after her. They followed her through the trees and caught up and took hold of her and helped her walk. Teddy said the pills weren't good, it was Marco's fault, and Marco said to go fuck yourself, and he went off with Monica and it was just the three of them, her and Teddy and Ada. Then they went along the lake to bring Ada home and they could hear the sound of loons. It was a crazy sound, Willa thought, and she felt that things could never be the same.

There was a thick fog. They walked along. She saw the moon bright upon the water and she heard the birds swoop down. Ada muttered. Something about an accident on a lake. A girl, her babysitter, who'd drowned. "I saw her dead," she said. "I saw her when they pulled her out. She looked so cold. She was blue." She pulled on the sleeve of Teddy's coat. "We found a little kitty once in the woods. It was so cute. We used to feed it. I tried to find it. After she died, I went to the woods. I looked for it. But it never came . . ." Her voice trailed off. Her eyes were distant, vacant. Then she looked at Teddy. "Why don't you love me?" she said to him, walking backward into the lake. "Why don't you love me?"

And Teddy tried to grab her.

"Why don't you love me? I'm too ugly for you!"

"No, Ada. Get out of the water."

"I'm so ugly I could puke."

And then she did. She puked in the water. Teddy grabbed her and pulled her out and they waited for her to stop. They walked on. Finally, the Heaths' house appeared, the little cottage, as in a storybook, only it was dark, just the dim light over the door, blinking like an eye full of dirt.

They went in. It was very late. The house was dark. A band of light ran under the door of Mr. Heath's study and up the narrow opening.

Willa could see him bent over his desk, the floor littered with crumpled papers. They crept upstairs to Ada's room and put her to bed. Down the hall, emanating from the master bedroom, was the blaring tone of the TV, indicating that the station had gone off for the night. Willa thought of going in and shutting it off, but now they could hear Mr. Heath downstairs, walking across the creaky wood floors, then the crash of ice on the counter, then the cubes tumbling into his glass. She thought he might be an alcoholic and it made her sorry for him, but then her pity was replaced with anger. Stealthily, she and Teddy descended the staircase and crossed the living room to the door. Teddy made it out, but just as she was about to cross the threshold Heath grabbed her wrist.

"What a nice surprise," Heath said, almost gravely.

"We brought Ada home," Willa managed. "She's sick."

Heath stood there. "I hope there wasn't any drinking involved. I wouldn't want to have to suspend you."

"No."

"I've been wanting to speak to you." She could hear the liquor in his voice. "I have things to say to you."

"I have to go," she said.

He staggered backward slightly with his arms open like a man asking to be shot. "I want to explain."

"Don't."

"I made a mistake."

"It's okay," she said, even though it wasn't.

"Please," he whispered. "Forgive me."

She shook her head. "I can't." The words came out silently, and she doubted that he had heard her. She pulled free of him and ran out the door.

"What was that about?" Teddy asked.

"Nothing."

They walked up the hill under the black trees. Willa debated telling him about Mr. Heath, but couldn't bear the thought of uttering the words. They went to his house. Outside, in the wind, he kissed her. "You can stay here," he said. She was too messed up to go home. It would upset her parents. For Teddy's sake, she was a good actress; she looked his mother in the eye. I need to call my parents, she said, but Claire said she'd do it for her, why don't you just get in bed. Claire took her hand and brought her to the guest room and helped her into bed. She covered her, like a mother, pulling the covers up. "Good night," she said, and turned off the light and closed the door. Willa lay awake, her mind reeling. In the room next door, she could hear Claire talking to Teddy about the Ecstasy. Claire said she didn't like him doing pills, she expected more from him, and it would only get him in trouble and hadn't he been in enough trouble already? "How do you expect to get into college?" she asked him.

"I'm sorry," Teddy said. "It was stupid."

But Willa knew Teddy didn't really mean it. Doing the drugs had been fun.

She could hear Claire on the phone, calling her parents, but thank God she didn't say anything about the pills. Teddy's mother was cool; she wouldn't do that.

Tomorrow is Saturday, Willa thought, closing her eyes.

In the morning, they had breakfast with his mom, buttered toast and hot cocoa. She thought Claire was very beautiful and Willa decided she was going to grow her hair long like hers and wear it in a braid. Teddy had a chocolate mustache. He smiled at her across the table. Then, out of the blue, Mr. Gallagher showed up. He drove a truck. He pulled up and came to the door in his scraggly wool sweater, an oatmeal-colored hat with earflaps. He was like an overgrown boy, she thought. In his arms was a big white rabbit.

"I couldn't resist," he said, grinning, and Claire started to laugh.

"Where on earth did you find it?"

"Over in Richmond. I couldn't believe it—some guy selling rabbits on the side of the road. It felt like destiny."

"Yes, yes, it was clearly destiny." Claire took the rabbit in her arms.

"He's so cute," Willa said, petting the bunny. "What are you going to name him?"

"How do you know it's a him?" Teddy said. "Do we have scientific evidence?"

They all looked at the rabbit, trying to determine its sex, but none of them could.

"How about Bonnie," Gallagher suggested.

"Bonnie is such a good name for a rabbit." Claire put the rabbit down. It jumped all over the house. "Oh, my goodness. Bonnie, you get back here!"

"Bonnie he is," Teddy said.

Claire scooped up the rabbit, then went over and kissed Mr. Gallagher on the cheek. "Thank you for this."

"It's my sincere pleasure," he said, and did a little bow.

They spent the afternoon together, all four of them. Teddy and Mr. Gallagher skateboarded in the old pool. The pool had been drained years before and was full of cracks and piles of dead leaves. Teddy was good on the board. He could do all sorts of tricks, but Mr. Gallagher was pretty hopeless. His incredible height made him wobbly.

It was a wonderful day, the last good day, she would remember later, that they would have together.

The sun lit up the sky. The grass was long and tickled her calves. Claire made cookies and Willa and Teddy got to lick the bowl. They were like puppies, licking the big wooden spoons, their fingers. She hadn't felt so good and happy in a long time, and she could almost forget what Mr. Heath had done to her in the van. She could almost pretend her life was normal.

It got late and Mr. Gallagher offered to drive her home. In his truck, he played the radio, the classic rock station. "Brown Eyed Girl" came on and they sang it together, extremely loudly, out the windows of the truck. At the house, her mother came out and invited Mr. Gallagher in for a drink, which, to Willa's surprise, he accepted. He looked a little shaky at first, and when her mother asked him if anything was wrong he said, no, just a little light-headed from a day out in the sun, it was surprisingly warm for the first of November, was it possible that this was a version of Indian summer? And her mother said, yes, it seemed like Indian summer indeed, and they went out onto the porch and drank lemonade and watched the sun sink down into the field while the horses slept on their feet, swatting flies with their tails.

Part Three

✐

Attachment Disorder

[sculpture]

Claire Squire, *Suffer the Consequences,* 2006. Plaster and gauze, 60 x 24 x 18 in. Collection of the artist.

The figure of a naked pregnant woman standing alone, her belly full and round and crawling with graffiti: cunt; pussy; auntie; ho; doggie; mama; baby; punta; chica; chick. The expression on her face is one of caution, fear.

30 ✑

On the day Luther Grimm's dog escaped, it ran into a school playground and took off the ear of a five-year-old girl who'd come out for recess. Teddy and his mother had seen the report on the morning news. They showed the child in the hospital, the hysterical mother. They still hadn't found the dog. They were offering a reward.

After school, he walked through the woods behind his grandfather's house to see for himself. This time, the woods were quiet, save for the groaning of the old trees. When he got to Grimm's yard, there was no sign of the dog. A police cruiser was parked behind Grimm's pickup truck. The door of Grimm's house opened and the cops came out and Luther Grimm was with them. He brought the cops over to see the tree where he used to chain up the dog. Grimm's face looked blurry and wet. He was clutching a handkerchief. He kneeled down and showed the cops how the chain was broken. "He's a good dog," Grimm was saying. "He's just a puppy. He don't mean nothing. He don't mean it."

Teddy stood there and watched Grimm go back into his house. Something didn't seem right. He wondered where the dog was now.

On the Wednesday before Thanksgiving break, the school did its own version of Thanksgiving, and everyone had to contribute to the meal. Three long tables were set with real china on white tablecloths and it was like a big deal and people were supposed to dress up. Teddy wore the jacket he'd worn to his grandfather's funeral. Even Mr. Gallagher had put on a tie and he'd trimmed his beard. Teddy sat next to Willa and they held hands under the table, their hands twisting together like two desperate spiders. He could feel her needing him. "You make me feel safe," she said into his ear. She seemed distracted, he thought, like she wanted to be someplace else, all jittery in her seat. Her face so pale and this nervous look in her eyes that hadn't been there before. He wondered if she were in some sort of trouble. On Halloween, when they'd taken Ada home, he'd overheard Heath asking her to forgive him and she'd stood there shaking her head. Forgive him for *what,* he wondered. And she'd walked up the hill with tears streaming down her cheeks.

Mr. Heath stood up at the head of the table next to his wife. Even though he was all dressed up, there was something ragged about him, Teddy thought. He caught Mrs. Heath staring off into space while her husband gave a speech about the importance of being thankful. Teddy knew it was good advice, but somehow, coming from a douche bag like him, it felt watered down.

Later that afternoon, Willa took him riding. They rode her horse bareback and he got on behind her and held her around the waist. He could smell her right at the neck, a sweet baby scent, and felt like their bodies were one. He held her tight. They galloped across the wet field.

Over break, she went to Barbados with her parents. His mother invited Mr. Gallagher for Thanksgiving dinner. It was becoming obvious to Teddy that Gallagher and his mother had the hots for each other, even though they went to great lengths to hide it. That morning, his mother bought a fresh turkey from the farmer down the road and plucked the feathers off herself on the back steps, saving them in a shoebox to use in her work. Teddy liked Gallagher all right, but he wasn't sure how he felt about him hitting on his mother. Whenever he was around, she'd get this look on her face, this kind of radiance. She was a beer poured too fast, her golden liquid spilling over the edge.

It started snowing that afternoon. Gallagher showed up in a corduroy blazer, his beard neatly trimmed, his hair combed back behind his ears. He held an armful of yellow tulips and his mother took the flowers in her arms like a fussy infant and brought them into the kitchen and laid them on the table. She stood on a chair to get down a white pitcher and put the flowers in the pitcher with some water and brought the pitcher to the table. While the turkey was cooking, the three of them put on boots and walked out into the back field. The snow fell heavily and dazzled in the cold sunlight like a shower of sequins. After a while, they came upon a coyote with something dead in its mouth, a woodchuck maybe. For a moment none of them moved, and he noticed how his mother squeezed Gallagher's arm. It occurred to him that he was used to having his mother to himself and compared the moment to other times when they'd confronted the possibility of danger and it was just the two of them. Those times she didn't need anyone protecting her. The coyote lifted its head slightly, as if to be polite, and ran off with its supper.

Teddy helped his mother set the table. First, they whipped up the linen cloth like a parachute and watched it settle down on the surface. They set each place with the old china plates that had been her grandmother's. She took the silverware out of an old wood box with a red velvet lining, and placed the tarnished silver candlesticks in the center. His mother put on dangly crystal earrings that made little shapes on her cheeks whenever she laughed. There was something almost formal about the way she moved in front of Gallagher, something contained. Teddy compared it to the beginning of a symphony, when you don't really know what to expect, but the music lures you gently and you get pulled in. Somehow there is no letting go. You want to follow it. You want to get to the end.

Last year on Thanksgiving she'd had to work. Teddy had stayed in the apartment, getting stoned, eating Fruit Loops out of the box.

After the feast, they played Scrabble and listened to his grandfather's ancient records. It was kind of fun, though. Gallagher was pretty exceptional at the game and used words like *mirth* and *boon*. He changed Teddy's *ant* to *antipathy* and his mother's *gent* to *effulgent* and got too many triple word scores to name. Teddy decided that playing Scrabble with Mr. Gallagher wasn't such a good idea after all, even though, in truth, he kind of liked it even though most of his own words were pretty lame. For dessert, they had ice cream and fresh raspberries and whipped cream and he fell asleep on the couch after midnight, hearing the sounds of muffled delight coming from the darkened hall.

Some of the workers at the Goldings' barn had gone home to Bogotá for the holiday and Rudy asked if Teddy wanted to help him out in the barn. Teddy was glad to have something to do. The pay wasn't much, but the work wasn't all that demanding; it was good lunch money, Rudy tried to joke. "I assume there's a cafeteria at that country club school of yours, or do you get served on tablecloths?"

"Yeah, there's a cafeteria," he said, wryly. He didn't really like Rudy talking about the school like he was some spoiled rich kid. He didn't see himself that way, but Rudy hadn't known him last year, when he was a dirtbag kid in L.A., hanging out at the skateboard park, shooting the big roaches in his mother's apartment with a BB gun.

To get to the barn, Teddy had to wake at five, which wasn't easy— he wasn't a morning person. Half-asleep, he rode his bike to the Goldings' barn under the grim clouds. His mother had promised to get him a car in the spring, if he got decent grades, but he wasn't sure that was possible, so he thought he'd better save up on his own. Rudy showed him where everything was and what he was supposed to do, mostly shoveling out the stalls. He didn't mind the work. He liked using his body, pushing the wheelbarrow, dumping the manure in the pasture where Rudy had shown him and he liked working outdoors and he liked the smell of the farm.

After work the first day, Rudy invited him up to his room for a beer. They drank Coronas and Rudy showed him his porn collection. "Here, check this out," he said. "You can take it home, just don't let your mother know." He laughed. "Incidentally, it's what he does."

"What who does?"

"Golding. He's in the porn business."

"Really? Willa never said anything."

"She never said anything because she doesn't know. It's a big fucking secret." He pressed the DVD into Teddy's chest. "This one's my favorite. Take a good look at the star, you just might recognize her."

The movie was called *Drive-In*. It didn't have much of a story, but he supposed few of these films did. It went like this: A man and a woman were at a drive-in movie, watching a science-fiction flick, sitting on the hood of the car. The man starts fucking the girl on the hood of the car, and he's questioning her, asking her if she likes his big fat dick inside her and she squeals and says, yes, she likes his big fat hard dick fucking her, and then two other men come over and ask her if she wants them to fuck her too and she says yes, she wants to be fucked in both places at once, they can fuck her at the same time while the third fucks her in the mouth, then they can all be happy. She just wants to make them happy, she says. Teddy watched the girl's face and she looked like she was in pain, which was part of the turn-on, he realized, and he saw a tear running down her cheek.

Stupid cunt, he thought, coming into his own hand. *You deserve it.*

It didn't occur to him until later that night, when he was lying in bed, that the girl in the movie was someone he knew. He got up and looked at the picture on the cover. It showed the woman lying on her stomach in a leather G-string. Her hair was platinum blond; a wig, he decided. Her face seemed wildly familiar. *You just might recognize her,* Rudy had said. And then, in a spectacular revelation, it came to him: It was Willa's mother, Mrs. Golding.

Sure, she was much younger, and she was hot as summer pavement—but it was her. He'd put money on it.

Over that week, when Willa was away, he went up to see the girl on Angel Hill. He felt bad about it; he felt despicable, yet he couldn't keep away. Like a drug he felt hollow when she wore off. When he'd gone into her that first time, he'd remembered a visit to the science museum as a small boy, sticking his hand into a mysterious cavern to try to guess what was inside—his fingers had encountered the soft, tepid chambers of a sea sponge.

He felt in a struggle with himself. Every time it was like being in a dream, you never knew what to expect. She was a mystery to him. She might put on a black veil. She might have on makeup or not.

Every time she'd pull up the shade so he could see the moon, if there was one, and they'd lie together very close on the bed, smoking, talking, and then she'd start to touch him. She reminded him of one of the old china plates from his kitchen, ringed in blue. She was like a thing of beauty from another time, a ghostly beauty that scared him. He guessed she was maybe eighteen or nineteen. Sometimes he'd find bruises on her thighs, scratches. She had scabs on her belly from something; she wouldn't let him see. She said one of her clients hit her sometimes. "He likes to punish me," she said dully. "He says I'm no good. I need to pray. He makes me get on my knees." She laughed, trying to make a joke of it, and dug around in her box of trinkets. "He gave to me this." She showed him a rosary. "He wants to reform me." She had a broken rib. Her room was full of flowers. "He sent me flowers," she told him. "Chocolates."

"Who is he?" Teddy said.

"I can't tell you." She shook her head. "If I tell you, he will kill me."

Teddy took all the flowers in a heap and brought them outside and made her watch as he set fire to them. They stood there watching them burn.

Once, as an experiment, Teddy pushed her head down, hard, like he'd seen in the film, making her gag, and he thought in his head: *You know you want it like this, you deserve it.* But she reared back. "Don't be like that," she said, her eyes tearing. And he held her. Told her he was sorry. He didn't know why these things came into his head and sometimes he worried that there was something wrong with him, that he was a bad person, like maybe his father had been.

She was hooked on crystal meth. It was her whole world. She'd do anything just to get some. He asked if he could try it, but she wouldn't let him. "You stay away from it or I won't love you anymore." He'd watch her hunch over her glass pipe like an old bag lady that's pulled something out of the trash. He didn't like fucking her when she was high and now she was high all the time. Once, when he was kissing her, her tooth fell out in his mouth. He spit it out in his hand. The tooth was gray, almost black. It was rotten. He felt sick.

She got up and looked inside her mouth in a mirror. "Look what's happening to me."

"You have to stop."

"I can't."

"I'll make you. I'll lock you up." He said it like he meant it, but he knew he didn't care enough. He looked away from her. He needed to get out of there. He didn't want to be with her anymore. "Don't be sad." She tried to kiss him, but he didn't want her kisses.

"You shouldn't be here. It's not right."

She gave him her crazy smile and shook her head and messed up his hair. "I'm okay, Teddy Bear."

He pulled on his jeans. "I have to go."

She grappled for her stash, made an ugly face. "Then go."

His mother was waiting for him when he got home. He could tell by the cold look on her face that she was pissed. She made him sit down with her at the kitchen table. "I cleaned your room today," she told him. "Look what I found." She held up his box of rubbers. Worse, she had found the movie Rudy gave him. "What's going on?"

"Nothing."

"I assume you're sexually active?"

"So?" He saw no point in lying to her. He had never lied to his mother in the past, why should he start now. But for some reason he could not explain, he started to cry. He cried like a little child. His mother came over and took him in her arms. She held him there.

"It's okay, honey, whatever happened. You can tell me anything, you know that."

He cried a little more, then she sat back down, waiting for him to explain. "She's someone I met," he told her. "It just happened." He felt so stupid. "I don't want to go there anymore."

His mother looked at him. Time seemed to pass very slowly. Finally, she said, "Who is she?"

"She's a prostitute," he admitted.

His mother sighed. He could tell she was disappointed. "Please tell me you used a condom."

He nodded miserably. "I'm not an idiot."

She hesitated. "What's with this?" She held up the movie. "Where did you get it?"

"Someone gave it to me. I didn't even watch it," he lied.

"It's not real," she told him. "It's not the way it really is. I hope you know that. It's not how women should be treated."

"I know," he muttered, but he didn't know. Not really.

"You'd better," she said. Then she tossed the movie into the trash. "That's where it belongs. Tell your friend you lost it." She started up the stairs. "And get your homework done."

31 ⌒

Being a single mother had its challenges. Claire had always imagined that, as Teddy got older, it would get easier. But that's not what had happened. It had gotten harder, more complicated, and she sometimes doubted her abilities to properly guide him. What did she know about adolescent boys? As embarrassing as it was to admit, the fact that he'd lost his virginity was upsetting to her, even though she'd lost hers at the same age. Just those words: *losing your virginity*. As if something were lost, not found. Why wasn't it something to celebrate, she wondered. Why couldn't *she* celebrate it? After all, sex—making love—under the best of circumstances, represented the ultimate connection between two people. Why shouldn't she be happy for him that he'd embarked on this thrilling aspect of adulthood?

But he'd lost it to a prostitute.

That upset her. Deeply. What in the world had possessed him?

Couldn't he have waited for someone he loved? Someone like Willa.

Why was everyone in such a goddamn rush?

And what about love?

What about love? a voice echoed. She hadn't loved Joe Golding, yet she'd slept with him repeatedly. Their affair had been substantial, salacious, passionate. Typically, and with no shortage of irony, when someone like Nate Gallagher appeared, someone who made her positively *weak* with longing, the possibility of sex terrified her.

Moreover, when it came to her son, she was fairly emphatic that a person of his age had no business having sex for the simple satisfaction of having it, *without* love.

She was no prude. In fact, she considered herself to be quite liberal when it came to the subject. She fully supported sex education in schools, including the dispensation of condoms. Animals naturally mated when the time was right; why shouldn't humans? And what was so wrong with sexual gratification, anyway? But in truth, her conversations with Teddy about intercourse had been limited to clinical mechanics, and, quite frankly, they had made her squeamish.

Maybe Joe Golding had been right about her after all; maybe she was the worst sort of hypocrite.

But a *prostitute?*

Why?

And what was he doing watching porn? *That* infuriated her. That she could not abide. *What in the hell was wrong with him?*

"It exists in our culture," Joe had said to her, as if that made it all right. "There must be a good reason for it."

On an impulse, she called Golding's cell phone. When he answered, she could hear the ocean in the background. He was on a beach in Barbados. "Rough life," she said.

"Somebody's got to do it."

"I need a male opinion," she said, and told him the story about Teddy. "I figured I'd ask an expert."

"It's not uncommon for boys of his age. What movie was it?"

She told him and he sighed, obviously familiar with it.

"Have you seen it?"

"Yes," he said. "I've seen it. It's an old film, where did he get it?"

"Some friend of his."

"I would confiscate it if I were you."

"I already have."

Joe hesitated a moment too long and said, "I don't want that thing getting around."

"Okay."

"And do me a favor," he said. "Don't watch it."

"Why not? Maybe I'll learn something."

She had said it as a joke, but he didn't laugh. "Promise me, Claire."

She wasn't about to promise him anything. Instead, she changed the subject. "By the way, I've decided there's no such thing as a simple life. It's futile to even pursue one."

"I've come to that conclusion myself," he said.

"I wish there was."

"Me too."

"I wish the world were different." He didn't say anything. Again, she heard the waves, the sound of happy voices in the background. "I'm sorry I was such a bitch."

"You have strong feelings. You shouldn't apologize."

"For someone with such a sheltered life," she told him, "you're a very accomplished lover."

He laughed. "Coming from you, that's a compliment."

"I actually miss you."

"I miss you too."

"I guess I'm more conservative than I realized," she said uncertainly.

"*Conservative* is not a word I'd use to describe you."

"I need to find someone who's available for a change."

"Yes, you do. And you will, Claire. I'm sure of it."

"Are things okay with Candace?"

"Yeah, they're okay," he said. "Aside from a little collateral damage. I appreciate what you did, actually. You inspired me to work on my marriage." He laughed a little then said, as if to make it official, "I am attempting to honor my commitment to her."

"Good for you." She used the German accent. "A little head shrinking can go a long way, yes?"

"I know it's hard to believe, but I just might be cured."

"Ya, it's good."

"It's good to be away, as a family."

"Good boy," she said. "I'll let you go."

"I'll see you."

It was a nice conversation and she was happy they'd talked, but she felt a little lost when she hung up. It always came down to her being alone. That's just how things worked out for her. She'd give a lot of herself to people, men, and end up empty-handed. She didn't blame them, it was her own doing. She had no one to blame but herself for being unattached. But now she wanted someone in her life. She didn't want to be alone anymore. She wanted to live out the rest of her days with a man she adored.

She thought of Nate Gallagher driving around in her father's truck with her picture on the visor and laughed out loud. He had called it fate. It occurred to her that she wouldn't mind riding around with him for a while, *years,* maybe.

She wondered how he'd look without that beard.

She went downstairs and fixed herself some tea. *A simple life,* she thought, dunking the teabag, lifting it up on a spoon, wrapping the string tightly around it to squeeze the water out. Her mother had taught her to do it. And her father would scoop the sugar and hold his spoon on the tea's surface, letting the tea seep into the sweet mound gradually, so it would evenly disperse. She could almost imagine him sitting here now, doing it. "The sweet things in life take time," he used to say. "You have to be patient."

On the way up to bed, the DVD in the trash caught her eye. In the interest of parental surveillance, she decided to have a look. She took it from the trash and went upstairs to her room. She studied the box, the picture on the cover, noting, with amazement, that the actress bore a striking resemblance to Joe's wife. In illegibly small print, the credits revealed it as a *J & H Production.* "As in Joe and Harold," she announced to the room. "Well, what do you know?"

Joe had failed to mention that his wife was an—ahem—actress. Claire felt an irritable mixture of feelings, one of which, regrettably, was jealousy. Because even though a certain part of her hated Joe Golding, and regretted sleeping with him, it could not be disputed that, with his lovely peasant hands, he had vigorously turned her on.

Mustering an open mind, she pushed the disc into the machine and watched the film, trying to imagine how the images translated in Teddy's teenaged brain. The fact that the actress was indeed Candace Golding thirty years younger was highly disconcerting. Claire felt clammy and a little strange, feverish. *Did people really do this stuff?* As the men entered all three of her orifices at once, Claire tried to comprehend the physical ramifications of such a position. It made her feel terribly sorry for Candace, it made tears spring to her eyes. How was it possible that she'd ever done this? No wonder Joe hadn't wanted her to watch it. Yet still, she couldn't take her eyes away. It was like watching some kind of bizarre circus act. She sat there, her heart pounding in her chest. Was this normal behavior, she asked herself, or was it abnormal? Was it instinctual, stirred up from some primal place? *No,* she thought emphatically. She couldn't help remembering Joe's words, *We're bigger, stronger.*

What was it about men that made them like this?

Claire had taken her share of Women's Studies classes in college and she'd learned that feminists were divided on the issue of pornography. Some were ardently opposed to it. Others categorized porn as an aspect of freedom that was protected by the first amendment and therefore permissible. It was better to allow it than censor it, they argued, because censorship was a tactic of repression, but it seemed to Claire a stupid rationale. Yeah, she didn't like the idea of censorship either, but no matter how you sliced it, getting fucked three ways at once was *getting fucked.* No matter what sort of free speech you used to describe it.

32 ∽

It was an honest mistake. After his mother had gone to bed that night, he'd gone down to the kitchen and retrieved the disc from its plastic box, then put the box back into the wastebasket. In the morning, she'd emptied the wastebasket into the large plastic bag in the kitchen, which in turn went out to the curb for the garbage trucks to take away. She never suspected that he'd taken back the disc.

He'd put it in a ziplock bag in his backpack, fully intending to return it to Rudy that afternoon, but during study hall Willa had asked to borrow a pencil, and she'd gone digging around in his backpack. She'd pulled out the disc, examining it in her hands, curious about the title, "What's *this?*" she'd said, wide-eyed. "Is it contraband?" Then Marco had grabbed it, announced the title, and started making fun of him, and then Monica took it and wouldn't give it back. A huge ruckus ensued, one that Teddy could do little about, and everyone was laughing and accusing him of being a pervert. After school, Willa came up to him and asked him about the film. "I want to see it," she said.

"No you don't."

"Why not?"

"Because, you won't like it. It's not for girls."

"What? That's ridiculous."

He shook his head. "You won't. Trust me."

"Where did you get it?"

He started walking.

"Answer me!"

"Rudy, all right? I got it from Rudy. And I'm bringing it back."

They rode the bus together, as usual. He got off at her stop and walked over to the barn. She barged into Rudy's place and said, "Show me that film or I'll tell my father."

"Tell him what?" Rudy said. "I don't really give a fuck." But then he said, "Show it to her, then. She's going to find out someday. May as well be now."

"Find out what?"

Rudy took the disc and put it into the machine. Willa sat there and watched it. "Is that—?"

But before they could answer she ran out.

33 ∽

She ran for a long time. She ran into town. The sun was sharp. She found her reflection in the dark window of a shop. There were two of her looking back, identical outlines of a girl in a stupid uniform, someone she was supposed to know yet who seemed like a stranger. The lines could not contain her, she thought. She was spilling over into someone else.

Who am I? she thought.

She had some money. She bought a pack of cigarettes. She didn't care. She went into the park and sat on the swings. She smoked. The sun was falling down behind her back. Time passed, an hour, maybe more. It was getting cold.

She felt something wrap around her shoulders, a coat. She looked up. Her father was standing there. She ignored him, but he said, "Let's go home."

In the car, he told her what he did for a living. "It's a business," he said. "Like anything else." He told her how he'd met her mother when she was only eighteen. "It was a hard time for her. She didn't have many options."

"That's so gross," she said. "I can't believe she did that. What's wrong with her? I would never do that."

Her dad squinted into the setting sun. "We all have things that we regret, Willa. That's one of your mother's."

"I don't," she snapped. "I won't. I won't ever. I won't make mistakes like that."

"I hope you don't, honey," he said. "But you might. Sometimes you get into a situation. Sometimes things just happen. You open a door and walk through it and suddenly there's no getting back. I'm not trying to make excuses. It's just the way it is in life. It's just how things turn out."

She thought about Mr. Heath and started to cry.

"I don't like what you do," she said finally.

"I don't like it either."

She looked over at him and felt her heart breaking a little bit. *He's my daddy,* she thought, and touched his arm. His eyes were teary, she realized he was crying.

"It's okay, Dad. I'm not mad anymore."

But he kept on crying, mopping his eyes with a handkerchief. "I just want you to be happy," he said. "That's all I've ever wanted."

"I know."

"I would do anything for you, Willa. I want you to know that. Your mother too. She loves you very much."

They drove the rest of the way in silence. The road was getting dark. He pulled up in front of the house.

"I'm not going to say anything to her about this," she said. "It's in the past. It should stay there."

"Okay." He touched her cheek, gently, and kissed her forehead. Then they got out of the car and went in for dinner.

34 ∽

Candace's husband was like a man under a spell. It was as if he'd been struck by lightning or, as in a Shakespearean play, had drunk some intoxicating potion, and when he'd woken up from a murky sleep, it was her, once again, that he loved. When he looked at her, she saw desire in his eyes, and it made her shy sometimes and uncertain. Often, when they made love, her eyes would tear. Her love for him had been buried for a long time. It had languished under layers of dirt and now he was digging into her, grasping what was left and blowing off the dust. There it was, their love, it shone in his hands like some archaeological treasure.

On the one hand, she was grateful that he still loved her, on the other, she trusted none of it.

The trees were black and bare, the fields the color of cornmeal. That morning, Willa had woken her to ride. Together, they rode the trails in silence as the sky came to light. The sky was pink, the blush of carnations. It was almost winter. Steam flowed out of the horses' mouths. Her daughter's skin was flushed with health.

Over breakfast, Willa told her about a girl she'd met at Sunrise

House. "She's a prostitute," she informed her, darkly. She seemed to be watching for her reaction.

Candace shifted in her chair. "I'm all for community service, Willa, but I'm not so sure I'm comfortable with you having a friend like that."

"Why?" she said, her voice verging on antagonism. "She's just a person like you or me. She made a bad choice, that's all. She opened a door and walked through it."

"Okay," Candace said, sensing some subtext to the conversation. That was one of Joe's lines, about the door.

"She needs some money," Willa continued. "I told her I'd give her some."

"How much money?"

"Not very much. She's in a bad situation. I want to help her. She doesn't have anyone else."

"What will she do with the money?"

"She wants to go home. She's from Poland."

"Ah, she's from Poland," Candace said, as if that made a difference. "Well, of course I'll give you some money." She reached for her purse and gave her a hundred dollars. "But be careful. You don't want her to think there's more where that came from. You never know with these people."

"Yeah," Willa said. "You never know."

"Just don't forget that she's a stranger, that's all I'm saying. You have to be careful."

"I know, Mom," she said, but Candace wasn't so sure. She looked across the table at her daughter, wanting to tell her about her own life when she was her age, but she couldn't push the words out. "It's sad," she said finally. "The things people do, *women,* to get by."

Willa met her eyes. Candace took a deep breath, trying not to cry. Sunlight filled the windows. The trees moved in the wind. The kitchen gleamed and sparkled. "We're so lucky," she nearly gasped.

"We are." Willa came over and put her arms around her and gave her a kiss. "I'm the luckiest girl in the whole world."

They could hear the bus coming up the hill, its squealing gears. Willa grabbed her backpack and ran out. Through the window, Candace watched her running down the driveway, remembering her little girl in her various stages of growth. Now she was tall and gangly and her feet were too big for the rest of her and her hair was long, down to her hips. She was a woman now, Candace thought almost mournfully. It was only a matter of time before the world rushed in and had its way with her.

Joe had flown to California that morning. It was parent/teacher conference day and Candace wasn't looking forward to going alone. Not that she had anything to worry about. Willa was a good student; they always had good things to say about her. But it was hard for Candace going down to the school. In truth, she felt intimidated. Just pulling down the long driveway made her nervous, finding a place to park on the field of expensive cars, many of which had the names of colleges affixed to their rear windows. *Bates, Colgate, Princeton.* Today, the school was all dressed up for the occasion. The dead mums had been replaced with holly bushes and there were pretty wreaths on all the doors. Inside, humble Hanukkah and Kwanzaa decorations had been placed strategically on the walls. In the auditorium, there was a special meeting about college taking place for the parents of juniors; Greer Harding was already on the stage. Candace slipped inside as silently as possible and sat off to the side. In her usual supercilious twang, Greer Harding detailed the horrors of the application process. "Applications are at a record high," she warned. "It will be a sincere challenge for your children to get into their first-choice schools."

Candace had not gone to college. Although Joe had offered to send her, she had declined. She had never been much of a student. This whole college thing was out of her league. And it was one of the reasons she kept quiet when they had company, often other Pioneer parents, who would launch into lengthy discussions about government and politics, subjects that she did not fully understand—

usually she'd clear the plates. Of course, Willa was going to college, it was simply assumed she would go and would want to go, but Candace could offer her daughter little guidance. Already, Willa had long surpassed Candace in academic terms.

She looked around the room at the other parents. Some of them were taking notes. Claire Squire was sitting across the room, slouching in her chair with her knees up, rather rudely, on the back of the seat in front her. She seemed to be half-listening, sketching on her appointment schedule. Based on what Willa had told her, Claire's son didn't have much of a chance of getting into college. He had academic issues, Willa had said. Rumor had it that the only reason he was at Pioneer in the first place was because his grandfather had built the gymnasium, and it was the only reason he hadn't gotten kicked out. For several months, Candace had been under the impression that her husband had fallen in love with Claire Squire. She would see them at parties, all wound up with a kind of electricity, as if someone had tied them up in Christmas lights. Claire had a certain sloppy beauty that appealed to her husband and that Candace almost envied. She supposed it made him feel younger, being with a woman like her as opposed to with his wife, who'd taken on middle age with a certain anguished diligence. For years, her husband had betrayed her with other women, she knew it, she had known it all along, yet she had done nothing to stop him. When she thought about it now, she came to the conclusion that her husband cheated because it reinforced his contention that sex could be casual, especially for men, and that, because of what he did for a living, he was entitled to casual sex as one of the recreational perks of his industry. Unlike other heterosexual men, whose sexual habits were about as daring as painting by numbers, he could enjoy sex without any hang-ups. "Men need sex more than women," he had told her once. "It's in our DNA."

At first, she'd been hurt by his philandering. She'd threaten to leave, he'd promise to stop. But he didn't; he only got cleverer about hiding it. In truth, she didn't really want to leave him. She saw no point. When she was young, her body had been used for sex, with little regard for her feelings on the subject. She had shoved all those memories into the darkest, deepest parts of her. And even now when Joe made love to her she couldn't completely let go.

For a long time in the marriage, she too had been under a kind of spell. She'd pulled away from him; she'd retreated, as if in defeat. Defeat was like an instinct to her, a place to rest. Yet now, after all this time together, the world was suddenly brighter, her senses sharper. It was as though she had been lost, for years, in a shameful foreign city and had finally, at long last, found her way out.

"The word *packaging* comes to mind." Greer was answering another parent's question about what to do if your child was a mediocre student. "Try to find a way to make your child stand out, a certain trait or talent you can emphasize." More hands went up. People were fixated on the SATs. Candace recalled taking the test in high school at St. Theresa's—she'd gone to the lavatory and when she came back she found her pencil broken in two, the girl behind her snickering. It had upset her so she could barely finish the test. "I'm afraid that's all the time we have," Greer said. Parents began to file out of the auditorium, judiciously holding their schedules. Mr. Heath was standing on the side, greeting people as the group came out, a kind of impromptu receiving line. Whenever Candace saw Heath she found herself fumbling, nervously, as if he were the president. He seemed like a perfect man, she thought, if that were possible. His good, clean looks, his impeccable clothes. The way he'd take his wife's hand whenever she came near, or whisper in her ear, or guide her gently from room to room, his hand perched on her back. He spoke gently, in the sort of voice people used with very young children. The Heaths were an ideal couple, it seemed, and very much in love. Candace wondered what it would be like to have a husband like him, so devoted, a true partner.

It had been Joe's idea to send Willa here. On the day he'd taken Candace to see the school for the first time, she'd been impressed with the campus, the buildings, the lush green playing fields and the woods beyond. There was the lake, on which the crew team competed, and the fully equipped boat house. It was spring at the time and the dogwoods had been in bloom, sugaring the air with their blossoms. In the Main House, on an antique table in the over-sized foyer, there was something called The Kindness Jar. The enor-mous glass jar was the sort of thing you'd find at Costco with pretzels in it, and it was filled with little cards on which the students had re-corded their routine "acts of kindness."

"Our first goal is to produce good citizens," Jack Heath had told them on their tour. Candace remembered feeling particularly warmed by the idea—it was a far cry from the tirelessly evil antics of her old classmates. And unlike the somber, punitive atmosphere she'd endured in high school, the teachers at Pioneer actually seemed happy to be there. Everyone walked around with a dazed and pleasant expression on their face, as though they were all members of an exclusive cult.

She found herself wondering if her life would have turned out dif-ferently if she'd gone to a school like Pioneer, if an education like the one their daughter was getting would have made her into someone better, someone more confident, smarter. But she couldn't imagine it without recasting the other people in her childhood, her ineffectual foster parents, and her mother, who could think of no better solution than to leave her in a bus station locker and throw away the key. If she had her druthers to do it over again, she'd choose a father like Joe, who stopped at nothing to give his daughter everything he could. After years of therapy, Candace had finally come to terms with her childhood. Joe had taken her away from all that. Like two thieves, they'd fled the city. Joe had brought her up here to get away from her past. And she had; they both had. She'd gone from having noth-ing to having more than she'd ever dreamed of, no questions asked. And yet, after all these years, she couldn't fully relax. The truth was, she'd never felt like she'd deserved it. Even now, she walked with the unsettled gait of a fugitive, as though, at any moment, a hand would come down on her shoulder and proclaim her guilt.

Her first appointment was with Mr. Gallagher, the writing instructor. Gallagher's class was held in Walden House, a free-standing structure that had been built years before by some students as some sort of existential experiment, whatever that meant—she'd never understood that term and she still didn't, even though she'd heard conversations about it at her own dining room table. Apparently, Walden House was a special place at Pioneer and Gallagher was a special sort of teacher. When she stepped into his classroom, she was struck with an uncanny sense of déjà vu. Something about his eyes seemed so familiar.

"Come right in, Mrs. Golding," Gallagher said.

She sat down at the large round table. The school touted itself for teaching at tables, and not at desks, but sitting there so close to him made her nervous. At St. Theresa's, they'd sat in chairs with one-armed desks, she'd been left-handed and they didn't have any left-handed writing desks and the nuns made her use her right hand instead. *Stop causing trouble,* they'd admonish. *Learn to write with your right hand like everyone else!* One nun, a Sister Belinda, seemed to derive pleasure from watching her struggle, erasing so hard the paper inevitably tore and she'd have to start again.

Unlike the nuns, Mr. Gallagher had on a blue work shirt and jeans, red suspenders, a skinny black tie, and his hair was longish, a bit too long for her taste—and that beard—he had the wild glare of a man who'd walked out of the woods. On his feet were heavy work boots. His hands were large and sprawling, a working man's hands. His eyes flashed like a good storm.

"Your daughter can write," he told her. "She has an ear for language."

Candace beamed with pride, but then the pride turned bitter and she started to cry. Gallagher looked troubled and reached across the table and touched her hand. "What's wrong? She's doing fine, you don't have to worry."

Candace shook her head, that wasn't it. "Please, forgive me. I feel so silly." He placed a tissue box before her and she took one and blew her nose. "I don't know what hit me," she apologized.

"It's the room. Everyone cries in this room. It's okay to tell the truth here, that's what I tell them. We say what we feel."

"That's great. That's really great." She blew her nose again. She couldn't seem to articulate what she was feeling. She didn't tell him that her smiling little girl had vanished and someone else had taken her place. "I know it's her favorite class," she said finally. "She's always writing in her journal."

"The journal helps them organize their thoughts," Gallagher explained. "My hope is that the students find out something new about themselves, through writing. That's the goal."

"It's been a hard year," she said. "She's changed a lot. It may have something to do with the Sunrise Internship."

"How do you mean?"

"I think it's been hard for her. Going there, I mean."

"Why's that?"

"Well . . ." She thought about it a moment. "The women there, for one thing, with those sorts of problems. I think it's alarming to her. Frightening."

Gallagher nodded. "It's not easy, I agree."

"I think it has to do with the fact that she's adopted."

"How so?"

"I could be wrong, but I read somewhere that adopted children often make the assumption that they come from terrible circumstances. That their birth parents didn't have the wherewithal to raise them. It's not necessarily true, but in her case it was. The birth parents were indigent."

He frowned. "Indigent?" He spit out the word like something foul.

"She may identify with these women somehow."

"You're making the assumption that *they* come from terrible circumstances, socioeconomically speaking—as if money accounts for happiness. As if in families with money women *don't* get battered, which we know isn't true. But that's a totally different conversation."

"Yes, I see your point," she said, feeling slightly patronized. "I know. And you're right, it's not true. Money has very little to do with happiness."

"An easier claim to make, of course, when you have it. Money, I mean."

She looked at him. "Yes, that's true too."

"You may be reading into it. How much does Willa know about her biological roots?" he fished.

"Not very much," Candace admitted. "We weren't sure it was nec-essary for her to know. She's always known she was adopted, she's grown up knowing. We've always tried to give her the feeling that it's a special thing, a wonderful thing."

"Which it is," he said. "Her birth parents—what do you mean by *indigent?*"

"Well . . ." She didn't really want to get into it and regretted bring-ing it up. It wasn't the sort of information she should be sharing. "They were poor. The father was into drugs, heroin. They both were. The mother had AIDS."

Nate Gallagher shifted in his chair. He couldn't seem to look at her. Perhaps he was distracted. Perhaps she was taking too much of his time. "Go on," he said.

"He didn't have a steady job. They had very little. They were liv-ing in a tenement in San Francisco."

Gallagher looked down at his hands. He didn't say anything for several minutes, which she thought was somewhat odd. "I'm not a psychiatrist, Mrs. Golding, but I don't think it matters all that much," he said, finally. "People make mistakes. They get into stuff that they shouldn't. Things happen." He looked at her very carefully, his eyes tinted with his own brand of wisdom. "It's nothing to be ashamed of."

"You're right. I know."

"As corny as it sounds," Gallagher said, "life is very long. You're supposed to mess up when you're young and other people some-times benefit from your mistakes—as you did in this case. But things rarely stay the same. People grow up and change. They move on. The truth is that you probably know close to nothing about those people who gave birth to your daughter. We're told certain things, information that pushes us into tidy little categories, but they're just words. We're rarely told the whole story and the story is always changing."

She looked at him and held his gaze. For several seconds they were perfectly still, staring at each other. Something seemed to be knocking at her brain, she didn't know what, an old scrap of memory that she couldn't quite grasp. She felt like he was almost angry with her. *You're too stupid for him,* Sister Belinda mocked. But then he smiled, warmly. He'd been intent on communicating something to her, some essential information that might help her with Willa, and she appreciated his effort. She could understand why the students liked him so much. He made the world make sense.

"Maybe you should ask her," he suggested. "Ask her if she wants to know."

"I will," Candace said. "She's old enough now. She has the right to know."

"It's been my experience, Mrs. Golding, that teenagers seem to yearn for the truth in the same way that adults yearn to ignore it," he said. "If nothing else, it's always liberating. But you should remind her too that people change. Her birth parents, I mean. The fact that they were indigent. It's not a reflection of her. It's who they were at the time, not who *she* is now."

There was a knock at the door; his next appointment was there. "I'll get going," she said, but she didn't move. Gallagher took her hand and looked at her intently.

"Your daughter's a fine girl. You've obviously done an excellent job with her."

She felt herself blushing. "Thank you for saying so."

"Enjoy this beautiful afternoon, Mrs. Golding."

And she thought to herself: I will.

35 ↩

Nate went home that afternoon feeling drained. He was badly in need of a drink. In his apartment, he fixed himself some bourbon and lay on the couch, listening to Beethoven on his stereo. He considered packing his things, leaving—being here had become unbearable in its own way. Surprisingly, seeing Willa, getting to know her, had been harder on him than he'd predicted. Not because he wished he could take her away, nothing like that. Not because he even thought of himself as her father, because he knew he was not. Their only connection was their blood, which, when you came right down to it, didn't mean all that much. The genetics did, perhaps—he could see traits in Willa that he saw in himself—good things, mostly, but the bad things were probably there too.

What he'd said to Candace Golding had been an idealized version of the truth—suggesting that people really did move on and change. But what if it wasn't true? What if he were still the same person he'd been back then? A man who couldn't get it together to finish anything he started. Someone who couldn't commit.

36 ⌒

Her son seemed beleaguered by something beyond his control. Distracted. He seemed aloof, uncertain. Claire tried to talk to him, but he'd shrug, disinterested, and change the subject. That morning, after he got on the bus, she went up to have a look in his room. There was nothing so revealing as a teenager's room, she thought, breathing in the woody reek of stale pot. The room was its usual mess, piles of dirty clothes on the floor, the unmade bed. Pinned to the back of his door was a photograph of Maggie Heath, presently employed as a dartboard. With festive penmanship he'd colored in all her teeth. He'd crudely drawn snot coming out of her nose and little cockroaches coming out of her ears. In his wastebasket, she pulled out several papers he'd written for Mrs. Heath's Language Arts class, each one with a glaring red D on its front. *Where's your topic sentence?* one declared. *Sophomoric,* read another. *Poorly organized. See me!*

With a sinking heart, Claire read over the papers and found herself agreeing with the teacher to some degree. He'd used little or no punctuation and many of the words were misspelled. He still confused certain letters, writing B where it should have been D, or P where it should have been F, and vice versa. He'd been doing this ever since first grade; they'd told her at the time that he'd grow out of it and eventually catch up—he obviously hadn't. His handwriting was sloppy. Instead of using an eraser, he had simply written over the wrong letter, seemingly satisfied that a messy jumble of pencil marks would suffice, as though he were too busy to take the time to redo it. In truth, she couldn't blame Mrs. Heath for her criticism, but the teacher's method obviously wasn't working and Teddy showed no signs of improving. Like most kids, he would retract like a snail if you embarrassed him, and Mrs. Heath had clearly done a good job of that.

"We're putting him on academic probation," Mrs. Heath told her that afternoon during their parent/teacher conference. "It's for his own good."

They were up in her classroom and she was showing her Teddy's grades, offering them as proof. "We'd like to see more effort on his part," she said, frowning. "That's the sort of thing we expect here at Pioneer."

But later, Nate Gallagher took a different tact. He told her outright that Teddy was dyslexic. "I'm surprised nobody ever suggested having him tested," he said.

When she thought back over all the years in L.A., switching from one overcrowded, understaffed school to another depending on where they lived—plus the fact that she wasn't the type of mother who had the time to sit around doing homework with him—*if* he was even home to do it—he was on his own at fourteen, basically, with her always working—but still, it seemed amazing to her that he'd been pushed through year after year without so much as a phone call from somebody. Teddy would tell her he was bored, he couldn't concentrate—and his report cards remarked that he wasn't working up to his true potential. Which was basically what Mrs. Heath was saying, accusing him of being lazy and indifferent, which was not entirely untrue, but—and it was an important exception—after so many years of being labeled a loser, she couldn't really blame him. And when you compared his work to the other students in his class, it probably *was* unacceptable, but what if he couldn't help it? It was clear to her now that the apathy her son so dazzlingly displayed came from a dark place inside of him, a place that, until now, he'd dealt with completely on his own.

"We moved around a lot," she said morosely. "He always seemed smart; he had an attitude. They thought it was behavioral." *It's all my fault,* she thought. *I'm the worst sort of mother.* She shut her eyes to keep from crying and sighed.

"Hey." Nate hugged her. "It's okay. He's a really smart kid. It's not too late to get him what he needs."

"Which is what?"

"Testing, for one thing. One of the many things you'll discover is just how smart he is. He's relied on that intelligence to get him this far, without any help. I'll find out who's good around here and we can set it up.

"In the meantime," he reached behind him and pulled a stack of photocopies off the shelf, "I want you to have these," he said, handing them to her. "These are some of the stories I've published in journals. Just so you know he's not a lost cause."

She held the stories in her hands, impressed, honored. "You're dyslexic?"

He nodded. "Once I finally figured out how to write a decent sentence, which took me about twenty-five years, I couldn't seem to stop. As it turned out, I had an awful lot to say."

She looked over one of the stories. "Thank you for these."

"You're welcome."

She wanted to say more, to tell him what she was feeling and how moved she was by his honesty, but the next parent had come to the door.

"I'll see you," she said.

"Soon."

He was on her mind. In the barn, when she did her work; when she stood at the counter peeling apples. She wanted to cook; she wanted to bake pies. Her body was firm; her breasts ached. She wanted to be in love.

She read his work. She sat in the old wingchair full of horsehairs. Sometimes she would read a paragraph and wait, thinking, looking out at the field. His words came into her head like a good cold wind. She would make a fire and sit before it in the chilly house that was too big for her and imagine what it would be like to have him there.

One afternoon, he called. He asked if she wanted to go for a drive in her father's old truck. She had learned to drive in that truck. The shift was up on the column, and you had to roll the windows down. When you played the radio, it always crackled, no matter how clear the reception. It had that old truck smell, of gasoline and vinyl, a smell she had known well as a child. It was a moody Sunday and Teddy was sleeping in. Nate came and picked her up and they slipped out of the house, silently, not wanting to wake him. They stopped at the café and bought a picnic lunch and drove into New York, into Chatham, under the low heavy clouds. There were great farms out there, with cows and sheep and pigs. You could park and walk for miles. It was cold and the sky was dark. They walked through somebody's sheep field to the shores of a wide creek. They sat on the large flat rocks and ate their lunch and shared a bottle of wine while the sky played its gloomy étude. "I read your stories," she told him. "They're wonderful. I read every word of them."

He thanked her, shy with pride.

"This is going to sound weird, but—" She suddenly stopped herself.

"What? What's weird?"

She looked at him. "I kind of have a crush on you."

"Really?"

"Do you mind?"

"Do I mind?" He grinned at her.

"It's kind of serious. I'm totally smitten."

"Smitten?"

"As in besotted, obsessed, head-over-heels." She spoke dramatically.

He stroked his beard like a mad scientist. "A rather old-fashioned condition, wouldn't you say?"

She nodded.

"I think it's quite serious." He put his hand on her forehead. "You're burning up. It wouldn't happen to be contagious, would it?"

"Very. It's a highly communicable disease, I'm told."

He shook his head. "That explains it."

"Really? You too?"

"Oh, yes. The symptoms are intense. I've really been suffering. I can't eat. Can't sleep. I have this pressure right here, in my heart."

"Me too." She looked up at him and he pulled her close and kissed her. "I'm totally terrified," she whispered.

"That makes two of us."

The clouds pressed down and the light turned sharp and it thundered. She felt something let loose inside of her. She could smell his clean smell. He had on a worn flannel shirt, old jeans, a duck-hunting coat with millions of pockets. His hands were large, his fingers long. He was like a man from an earlier century. He could plow a field; he could make a fire; he could build his own house. It started to rain. She wanted to climb inside him. He kissed her again and they stood there in the rain kissing, the rain running into their mouths.

They had to walk back to the truck. The sky turned yellow as the rain fell, the road was empty. Suddenly, there was hail. He held her hand as they ran through it. They were like the last people on Earth, she thought.

Later, shivering in his apartment, she let him undress her. It was as if their bodies were whispering to each other and neither of them could bring themselves to speak, and she was aware of the sound of his breath as it came close to her face and the distant prickling of sleet on the windows. "God, you're beautiful."

"I'm not," she said. And she wasn't, not really, not anymore. She had a crooked, intelligent face and a body battered by work, by late nights with no sleep, by a certain variety of neglect, but somehow right now, here in this place, his touch made her so. Then he took off his clothes and laid all the wet things, his and hers, on the clanking pipes of the radiator and the room filled with the smell of wet wool, the smell of childhood afternoons of ice skating and sledding and wool mittens left to dry. *My poor little kittens have lost their mittens,* she thought, and he kissed her. They climbed up on the old bed with its cranky springs, sliding under the cold sheets, and she wrapped her body around his and held on, as the saying goes, for dear life.

37 ᶜᵒ

They shot their movies in a rented McMansion in Chatsworth. Their film crew was comprised of film school graduates who couldn't get work in L.A. They used contract actors and usually things went pretty smoothly. Over breakfast in his brother's office, he told Harold he wanted out. "What the fuck for?" Harold said.

"I've had enough."

"Who is it?" Harold asked.

"What are you talking about?"

"There's a woman in this equation somewhere because all of a sudden A plus B does not equal C, am I right? I'm right, aren't I? She obviously gave you a good dose of conscience. I'm sure you feel a whole lot better for it." He lit a cigar. "Next time you want to come clean, get yourself a high colonic."

"Harold, I'm done."

"Don't be an idiot, business is better than ever."

"It's different for me."

"What's so different?"

"I have a daughter."

"Let me tell you something, choirboy, daughters cost money. Women are very expensive."

"I want you to buy me out. It doesn't have to happen right now. Over the next five years or so."

Harold shook his head. "You're serious about this?"

Joe nodded. "I've got a call in to the accountant. I'll have him call you with the numbers."

Harold shook his head. "It's been a good life for you. You have everything you want."

"I know. I know that. But I want out."

"Yeah, sure. Do me a favor. Call me when you're over your midlife crisis, because that's obviously what this is. I'll send you some Neil Young CDs in the meantime."

Joe ceremoniously kissed his brother's cheek. "Thank you for your blessing."

"It's like a gallstone. You'll pass it. It's painful, I know, but you'll get over it."

The phone rang. "Take it, Harold. I'll talk to you later."

Harold waved to him as he stepped out into the hall. They were shooting a scene in the living room and there were people standing in the hall, gesturing for him to be quiet. He didn't give a shit. As he passed the doorway, he glimpsed the actors in the scene. The woman was on her knees, blowing a guy while another guy fucked her from behind. He walked out of there for the last time, the exultations of counterfeit love filling his ears.

Back in the Berkshires, when he told his wife that he was leaving the business, her reaction surprised him. "What are you going to do with yourself?"

"I'm sure I'll think of something."

"You're not that young," she said. "It's not so easy to switch careers."

But he could see that wasn't the issue. When you grew up poor, you never stopped worrying about money. "If you're worried about money, there's no need. We'll be fine. We'll make it work." He took her in his arms. "I'm getting out for Willa, for us."

"What about for Claire?"

The question hung in the air. He could see in her face that she knew.

"I can't help thinking she's had an influence on you."

"Is that such a terrible thing?"

"I don't know," she said. "I don't know anymore."

"It shouldn't have happened," he said.

"But it did. Like all the other times. They shouldn't have happened either."

"I know. You're right. I don't know what to say." He looked at her. "I'm sorry, Candace."

"What did you think? Do you think I'm stupid?"

"No, of course not."

"Because I'm *not*. All your little tricks. I saw right through them." He nodded. "I'm sure you did."

"I should hate you for it, but I don't."

"I want you to. I'm awful. I don't know why I do these things."

"It's my fault too. It's both of us. I know I've been distant. It's been a hard time for me. I've had physical issues. I've been somewhere else." She looked at him, hard. "But I'm back now."

He kissed her neck, her face. "You're the only woman I've ever loved." He took her hand and put it against his heart. "You're the only one right here."

He did love her; he did. He loved his wife. He couldn't imagine living with another woman. Yet he wasn't certain he could fully commit himself to her. Even after all this time, *especially* after all this time. He couldn't be sure he could be faithful. The truth was he doubted that he could.

Later that afternoon he went for a run. He wanted to sweat out his jet lag. He wanted to breathe in the clean air of the Berkshires. The road was empty and black. The clouds were gray. On an impulse, he ran to Claire's house. Like a schoolboy he wanted to tell her about his decision to leave the porn business. As childish as it was to admit, on some level he wanted her approval. But when he ran up her driveway he saw an old Ford pickup parked near the house. He knew he should turn around, leave her alone, but something made him continue, a part of him that felt like he had the right. It was absurd of course, he had no claim on her. He glanced into the barn. At first, he thought she was one of her sculptures, naked and pale, sitting astride her new lover's hips. She looked up and caught his eye and his throat went tight. He had no right to be jealous—and he'd just sworn his loyalty to his wife—but he couldn't help it, he still had feelings for her. Embarrassed, he jogged back down the driveway. He could hear her calling his name. She had thrown on a big wool coat and her silly Turkish hat, oversized boots, her father's probably, untied. He wished he was in a position to love her properly. If he'd met her years ago, perhaps, he would have tried to. Everything came down to chance in life. She was out of breath. "Stop, for God's sake!" Her eyes were a vivid blue, her lips chapped. He could remember the lazy grin she'd get when he'd kiss her.

"I see you're busy," he said. "You're a sucker for distraction."

"I'm sorry." She touched his cheek in her pauper's gloves, her fingertips warm and flat.

"What for?"

She shrugged. "I don't know. For this. For right now."

"No hard feelings," he said. "I'm the one who's married, remember?" By now, Nate Gallagher had gotten dressed and was leaning in the doorway of the barn.

"I'm told he's a good man," Golding said.

She smiled like a woman in love.

He kissed her anyway. "Still friends?"

"Always."

His hand on her cheek. "Be happy, Claire. You deserve it."

38 ⌒

On the morning of her seventeenth birthday, Willa's father made waffles with fresh raspberries and whipped cream. Her mother gave her a necklace from Tiffany's. She put it on, thrilled, and admired herself in the mirror. Her father gave her a new saddle.

"Sit down for a second," her dad said. "We want to talk to you about something."

She sat down, terrified that her parents had somehow found out about Mr. Heath, about the despicable thing he'd done to her. Her mother was holding an envelope. Perhaps the school had written them a letter.

But her mother said, "This is for you."

Willa took the envelope and opened it and pulled out a letter. It was about twelve pages, handwritten on lined notebook paper, and it was addressed to her. There were smears of ink, little blue blossoms, from where the paper had gotten wet. "What is this?"

"It's a letter from your birth father," her father told her. "He wrote it when you were a baby. He gave it to us on the day we got you."

"We think it's time you had it."

Willa read the first sentence. *We left San Francisco that morning, even though your mother was sick.* Her stomach went tight. She looked at her parents. "Have you read it?"

"No," her mother said. "Never."

"It's yours," her father said. "It's been in the safe all this time."

Her hands began to tremble. Her whole body felt jittery. She felt a mixture of feelings, both happiness and dread. Here in her hands was the truth, she thought, here in her hands was her identity. It was proof, she guessed, of her existence, of where she'd come from, her genetic link to the human race. But not really. Her parents were right here, in the flesh. Her mother and her father. They'd taught her to walk, to read, to ride a bike. They'd been the ones to take care of her when she was sick. *They* were the proof. They'd been here all along.

"I want to read it out loud," she said.

Her parents looked surprised. Her mother looked up at her father. "Should we go into the living room?" he asked.

They went into the living room and sat down on the couches. Her father stoked the fire. She thought he might have tears in his eyes and didn't want her to see. She waited until he sat down.

The first thing she said was, "I love you both."

"We know you do, honey," her dad said.

"We love you very much," her mother said, her eyes brimming.

"It's okay, Mom," Willa said. "I'm okay."

"I know, sweetie." She wept softly.

Willa went over to her and hugged her. "You're my mommy."

In a wavering voice, she read the letter out loud. It was harder than she thought it would be; the hardest thing she'd ever done. Her parents listened. The chairs and the crackling fire listened. The beautiful heavy drapes listened. And the horses outside, standing at the fence, they were listening too. Even God was listening, wherever He was.

When she had finished, the three of them sat there for several minutes staring into the fire. It felt like the end of something. It felt like the beginning.

"I didn't know it was AIDS," she said finally.

Her mother nodded. "You're very lucky. We didn't want to tell you because we thought it might upset you."

She looked at the letter, the handwriting—it seemed familiar to her. "Whatever happened to him?"

"We don't know," her father said. "We'll be happy to help you find him, if that's what you want."

She looked at her father and at her mother. How could she possibly tell them how much she loved them? She held the letter in her hands. She looked at it, the anonymous handwriting of a person she would never know.

Then she put it in the fire and burned it.

On Tuesday afternoon, when Mr. Gallagher dropped her off at Sunrise House, the Polish girl was sitting on the front steps, smoking. "What are you doing?" Willa asked her. "Aren't you going in?"

"Waiting for you," she said.

Mr. Gallagher called from the van, "You okay, Willa?"

"Yeah." She smiled and waved and stepped onto the porch. "I'm going in," she said.

"No, you're not," the girl said.

"What?" Willa smiled, strangely flattered by her attention.

"See you later!" Gallagher called, and drove away.

"Do you have any money?"

Willa nodded. "So you can go home. Back to Poland."

The girl snorted, shaking her head. "Look, do you want to get high with me?"

"I have to go in," Willa said.

"Why?" The girl coldly appraised her. "Aren't you tired of doing what everybody else wants?"

Now that she thought about it, she was. "Maybe."

It occurred to Willa that there was a phone number on the girl's hand, a number she herself knew by heart: Teddy's. "Do you know him?" she asked.

"Why, do you?"

"He goes to my school."

"Is he your boyfriend?"

"No," she muttered.

"He's nice boy. He comes to see me. He's my Teddy Bear."

Willa swallowed hard. "What?"

"It's no big deal."

It occurred to her that she was on the brink of doing something stupid. She could feel it lurking around her shoulders. She could feel it blowing her up, like a balloon, bigger and bigger until she went *pop!* She would make a very big mistake, yet she could not stop herself from making it. The letter had upset her more than she thought. The journey her poor mother had made. Sick, dying. The awful car. The rain. She had died in their driveway. It was a world Willa could barely imagine, one that she'd found on the pages of books— *my poor mother,* she kept thinking. And poor her too. She pictured herself as an infant, riding in the backseat of that car with the rain beating down. *Her hands brittle with rage.* Had she known in her baby mind that, in a matter of minutes, her entire link to the universe would be gone? Thinking about it made her sad.

Her mother, Catherine, had been beautiful, yet she'd known it all along in her heart, where all adopted children know things. But it was her mother Candace that she loved. It was Candace whom she cried for when she was sick, Candace whom she longed for those long summer nights away at camp, Candace whom she relied upon for advice, Candace who was her emotional barometer, her touchstone, her life. She could not imagine a day without her.

But still, she owed Catherine something.

She wanted to pay homage to her. Her mother the drug addict.

So she went with the girl. They walked down the street, away from the shelter. She felt like a person leaving the scene of a crime, as if any minute Regina would run out and shout, "You! Stop!"

Pearl knew where to go to get the meth. It was a narrow house, shoved between two others. Willa gave Pearl some money. "You splendid girl," she said, and kissed her on the cheek. "You will not be disappointed." There was a man on the porch in a broken chair, counting cars. He had on a dirty T-shirt and trousers and his feet were bare, even though it was cold. He muttered numbers as they climbed the steps and she could still hear him inside, *thirty-eight, thirty-nine,* like a metronome. It was dark inside and stunk of cats. There were cats wherever she looked, scrawny whining cats. Empty cans littered the floor. A TV was on somewhere, coming from a back room. "Wait for me," Pearl told her, and walked off down the hall. She stood there alone with the cats. The cats watched her with their creepy yellow eyes. One came and rubbed up against her ankles. When Pearl came back she was smiling. They went into the park. There was a huge cement whale and they walked through its mouth and sat in its belly. "You shouldn't do it," the girl warned. "You don't have to." She touched her face. "I'll still love you if you don't."

"It's okay. I want to."

It was what bliss was—a way of getting there—inside the cottony seclusion of a cloud. Her body sparkled. She was a movie star. She watched the girl chop the powder with a blade. She thought about it; she didn't know what would happen and she didn't care anyway. She wanted to put her face in it. She wanted to turn her mouth inside out, her mouth, her teeth, her nose, her throat. To feel it rushing through her. It was cold and warm, it was syrupy, it was the smell of hyacinths. She watched the girl snort it. She shook her hair like it was full of rain. "My real mother was a junkie," she heard herself say.

The tattoo shop was empty. The man in the leather vest knew Pearl. "I want one just like hers," Willa told him. "For my dead mother."

Pearl laughed so hard it sounded like crying and Willa almost peed in her pants.

She had to lie on her stomach. He told her to rest her head, to just relax. It would hurt a little. He was drawing on the back of her calf— her Achilles' heel, she thought ironically, remembering the poster of Achilles in Mr. Jernigan's class. He did a heart, in chains.

It got dark and it started to snow and she had missed her ride with Mr. Gallagher, who had probably found out by now from Regina that she had never shown up. He probably would call Mr. Heath, and her parents.

It was a mess. She felt bad.

They walked all the way to Lenox as the snow fell down in big sloppy flakes. At the arcade, they met up with Teddy. He looked at Willa's face. "What's up? I've been trying to call you for days."

"Nothing."

"What are you doing with *her?*"

She shook her head. "I don't know."

"Did she give you drugs?"

"Why did you do it? Why did you sleep with her?"

He stood there looking down at his feet. He had no answer for her.

"I hate you now," she whispered. "You're disgusting. I loved you before, but not now."

He tried to grab her. "Willa."

"You could have had all of me. But now you get nothing."

"Please, just come over here. Let me talk to you."

"Leave me alone," she said.

"What have you done to her?" he said to Pearl. Pearl's smile smeared across her face and suddenly Willa didn't trust her. But she felt a tug of need for her, for her little tin of drugs. "What did you give her?" Teddy kept saying, and when she wouldn't answer he grabbed her and shoved her hard against the wall, much harder than was necessary, and then he made a big mistake. He hit her. She made a grunting sound when she hit the wall, then looked at him and smiled, so he hit her again.

Everyone saw. They were looking at him. He saw that they were looking and ran out.

A little while later, Mr. Heath showed up. "Willa Golding," he said. *You're under arrest!* "We've been looking all over for you."

Pearl started to laugh. She laughed and laughed. "Stop it," Willa said. "Stop that laughing."

"Yes ma'am." Pearl jumped up and did an army salute and moved her hips like a hula dancer. "At your service, Captain."

"Let's go, Willa," Mr. Heath said quietly, tight-lipped, grabbing her arm roughly, opening the door.

He had his car, an old Volvo station wagon. "I've notified your parents," he said like a cop. "I told them I'd be bringing you home."

"Oh," she said, almost like breathing.

He pulled out of town onto the main road. "I spoke with Regina," he told her. "She was worried when you didn't show up."

"I'm sorry."

"We all expected more from you."

They drove into Stockbridge in silence. Finally, he said, "Do you know that girl?"

She shrugged. "She knew you, didn't she."

He kept his eyes on the road, his jaw tight.

"She knew you," Willa goaded him. "I could tell. It was so obvious."

"Many people know me in this town." But his voice wavered.

"She wants to go home. She wants to go back to Poland."

He laughed and shook his head. "And you offered to help her, right?"

She nodded.

"She's not the sort of girl you should associate with."

"Why not?"

"Because girls like that—" He stopped himself.

"Girls like what?"

"Girls like that bring out the worst in people."

"What do you mean?"

Mr. Heath squinted into the darkness like a man with a toothache. "They deserve what they get," he said. "That's what I mean."

He turned down her road. They didn't speak, but she could feel something between them, something ugly. She had the feeling he'd been to see Pearl, that he was one of her customers. She wondered if he'd been the one to give her the kilt.

"I haven't said anything to your parents about your little adventure this afternoon," he told her. "But I will if I have to. At this point, information like that could jeopardize your chances of getting into college. I'm afraid Harvard's a bit out of reach." He looked over at her.

She sat there a moment, trying to think. Her brain was a jumble of wires and plugs. "I don't get you," she said, finally, swatting her tears. "I don't understand what you want from me."

He jerked his head like she'd made a preposterous statement. "Why would I want anything from you?"

"You don't?"

"Of course not," he said. "Why would I? I mean, I'm very flattered, my dear, but I'm not that kind of man. I would never betray my wife."

She shrugged, confused. Her head was pounding.

"I don't know what gave you that impression." He smiled like he felt sorry for her.

Her father was coming out of the house, his face elated. For some reason, he always treated Mr. Heath like royalty. "You might want to pull up your knee socks," Heath muttered, getting his headmaster face on. "Tattoos are against school rules. I suggest you keep it covered. I don't want to have to suspend you."

She reached down and pulled up her socks and got out of the car, stumbling a little. Her legs were shaking. Her ankle hurt where she'd gotten the tattoo and she experienced a sudden terror that the needles the man had used had been contaminated. Everything seemed dim and strange. She had almost forgotten how to walk. Her teeth hurt. Her gums were stinging.

"Talk about service," her dad said too loudly, and she understood that Heath had called him with some phony story.

"I'm afraid that van's on the fritz," Heath said. "Sorry to hold up your dinner."

"No, no. Not to worry. How about coming in for a drink?"

He shot her a look, letting her fully understand that he was the one in control and could do what he liked. "No thanks, Joe. I've got my family waiting." He emphasized the word *family,* and she felt a rush of shame.

Her dad put his arm around her as Mr. Heath pulled out of the driveway. "You must be starving," he said, as they went inside. "Your mother's got your dinner in the oven."

The drugs had worn off, she felt ragged. She felt like she'd crawled home on her hands and knees. She didn't want to eat. Her mouth felt sticky and prickly. What she needed was more. She had to have it. She was like a dog with mange. She scratched and shook. Her mother frowned. "My skin is pink," she said to her.

"What? Don't be silly. Are you all right?"

Crack an egg, watch it run down. Her hands on her head, her hair. She tucked it back behind her ear. *Leave it, leave it.* She tucked it back again.

"Maybe you're coming down with something." Her mother put her hand on her forehead. "Why don't you go up to bed?"

Willa took a shower and put her nightgown on. She wanted to feel clean and innocent; she wanted to forget everything that had happened—Mr. Heath, Sunrise House, Pearl and her terrible stories, the meth. Mr. Heath didn't like her anymore; maybe he'd never liked her. Maybe she'd made it up in her mind. It embarrassed her to think about. Maybe it was her doing, she didn't know, she couldn't tell. Maybe she'd been asking for it.

What kind of slut are you, anyway?

She didn't know what to do about it. It made her feel ugly. She didn't know how to manage all the feelings. She closed her eyes very tightly. She shoved them deep down inside of her, where no one could see.

39 ⋍

Jack admired reserved women. Reserved women were refined, her husband used to say. Women like his mother. He used to say that he admired his mother because she was self-possessed, and even as smart as Maggie was she never understood what he meant. The word *possessed* always threw her. His mother didn't have to blab her ideas and opinions all over the place, Jack had clarified. She was content to sit and listen. Demure, he'd said. Everything about her was demure and dignified. When Maggie had met Jack's mother for the first time, the words that came to mind were less flattering. Remote, detached. Repressed. She hadn't been the same, Jack's father had explained, since the accident that killed little June. When Maggie had asked what had happened, the question simmered in the air, making the room seem ten degrees hotter. "Our little girl was asphyxiated," the captain had told her. The four-year-old had been playing dress-up with dry-cleaning plastic.

Repressed, she thought, pulling apart the word in her mouth like a mealy piece of meat. She could almost feel its weight on her tongue.

"You never get over something like that," Jack had told her.

That Sunday after church Jack took Ada up to Miller's farm to buy a Christmas tree. It was something the two of them did together every year, and Maggie always stayed home to be surprised. "That's the most beautiful tree we've ever had," she'd say.

With only a week left before Christmas break, she had a stack of exams to correct and essays to read and comments to write. There was laundry to be done, bathrooms to clean. There were presents to wrap.

Looking around now, she felt at odds with the disarray, the

routine of chaos that characterized their lives. Of course she was the one to do the cleaning. It would never occur to Jack to pick up after himself, or Ada either, for that matter. Ada was becoming so distant, so aloof, and she blamed her husband for it. He was always putting her down in front of the girl. That sort of sentiment wore off on people, like second-hand smoke or cheap perfume, and Ada would treat her with the same eye-rolling antagonism that Jack did, as though Maggie were some sort of housemaid, some servant to be neglected and abused.

What about me? She couldn't help thinking it. What was she getting out of the situation? Not much. Yet she felt she was a good mother, a good wife—she'd held up her end of the bargain. Her mother had raised her to be good and loyal and patient, to make the best of things. But now she felt detached from Jack, as though he had a whole life that existed without her, and her happiness had grown less and less important to him. Everything they did together—meals, work, even sleep, was somehow out of context, as if they were just filling in temporarily, substituting for the real married couple they once were.

She vacuumed the first floor. In the corridor outside Jack's office, she took a moment to study the framed photographs on the wall as if they might have an answer for her. The pictures chronicled their history as a family, living the life of nomadic academics—a front porch here, a city stoop there, a deck, a terrace. Clapboard and brick. Amherst, Somerville, Hadley, Maine, this house here at Pioneer. Vacation scenes on display, tedious family trips; the Thanksgiving table; Ada and Jack on the blanket at Tanglewood. Nothing is what it seems, she thought. The way they were on the outside. And the way it really was in here.

Snarls of dust, piles of mail, toppling stacks of books. An ashtray had fallen off the coffee table and now there was a pile of ashes on the carpet. Smoking was another of her husband's little secrets. He only smoked in the house, of course. God forbid anyone should see. It occurred to her that the goldfish had died. It lay on its side, drifting around the bowl. She hated the fish; she was glad it was dead.

She left it there and went to do the laundry, pushing the dirty clothes into the machine, pulling the clean ones out, folding them into stacks. Ada favored padded bras, which were harder to fold and always toppled over in the basket. She wore thongs too, tiny insectlike pieces of satiny fabric purchased with her babysitting money. They certainly didn't look very comfortable, Maggie thought, holding up the skimpy garment between her fingers like a dead rat.

Later, as she was putting away Jack's clothes, she discovered a small box in his bureau, concealed under a stack of undershirts. The box was long and slim, wrapped in shiny black paper, with a pink bow. She shook it gently: jewelry. She tried to think. It wasn't her birthday or anniversary, and Christmas wasn't for two weeks. A tiny card had been slipped under the ribbon, but it was blank.

He'd bought her a gift, she realized. Perhaps he planned to give it to her tonight. Perhaps it was his way of apologizing.

How sweet.

She returned the little box to his drawer in precisely the way she'd found it. He loved her, of course he did! She almost felt guilty for mistrusting him. It was *she* who should be apologizing to *him*.

Traditionally, the week before Christmas break was a festive time at Pioneer, with choral concerts and the exchange of Secret Santa gifts, and this year was no exception. There was a plethora of baked goods around campus, platters of brownies and blondies and lemon bars made by the more industrious homemakers. Of course Maggie ate none of it. Toward the end of each day, Maggie would tingle a little in anticipation of the evening that lay ahead, when she would likely receive her husband's gift. So light was her spirit during that time that she'd make casual jokes with the other faculty members, or treat the students with exceeding kindness, and people took notice of her in a new way, and told her how well she looked. But the nights came and went with routine indifference, and at the end of the week there was no gift or celebration, only the impenetrable silence of the house. Then one morning, while Jack was in the shower, Maggie checked to see if the box was still there; it was. The pretty box grinned at her like some kind of cruel joke. While Jack whistled away in the steam-filled bathroom, she took it out and carefully removed the tape along the paper seam. Gently, so as not to rip the paper, she unwrapped the box and opened it. Inside, she found a gold necklace with a single white pearl.

There, now you've seen it. Now put it back.

With great care, she rewrapped the gift and resealed the tape and returned it to its place inside the drawer. It was a lovely Christmas present, she thought, and very generous, and of course she would pretend to be surprised when he gave it to her. But Christmas came and went, and the slim box did not appear. Instead, he gave her a blender. When she went up to check on the box the next day, it was gone.

Over the years, Jack had bought her gifts for special occasions, the usual birthday and anniversary presents, but she couldn't remember one that she'd especially liked. Choosing gifts for people wasn't easy, she knew, and she usually succumbed to traditional choices on Jack's birthday or Father's Day, things like ties or hand tools or golf accessories, which he always seemed to like. Once, early on in their marriage, she had knitted him a scarf for Christmas and he'd been so touched that his eyes actually produced tears—he was not the sort of man who revealed his feelings, even to her, and she'd never once seen him cry. As a young boy, his father would criticize any display of weakness, tears included, even after he'd broken his arm playing football. On the way to the hospital, his father had threatened to break the other arm if he saw as much as one tear run down his face.

Now that she thought about it, she couldn't imagine Jack being comfortable in a jewelry store, trying to pick something out for his lover, whoever she was. It dawned on her that being who he was in a very small town, he wasn't about to purchase a necklace in one of the local shops, as he would run the risk of being judged for the purchase. Tongues were always wagging about one thing or another, and it stood to reason that tongues might wag over the Head of Pioneer School, whose parents paid close to twenty grand a year per student, purchasing a less than spectacular necklace for his incredibly selfless, hardworking wife. Maggie closed her eyes, picturing Greer Harding's tongue wagging about it all over the place and laughed out loud.

The fact that he'd given her a blender confused her. It was an insulting gift, really, a hefty piece of machinery, bulky, painfully domestic. But the necklace was just the opposite. The necklace had been delicate, *feminine.* She could almost imagine the tiny pearl between her fingertips.

He'd purchased the blender at Sears. If she knew Jack, he'd purchased the necklace there as well.

He was, after all, a very practical fellow.

It had begun to snow and the roads were slippery. The parking lot was crowded and the mall was bustling with people returning unwanted Christmas gifts. Maggie entered Sears on the lower level, and wandered through the balmy serenity of the furniture department, tempted to lie down on one of the mattresses for a little nap. The jewelry department was upstairs, on the main floor. She took the escalator. The jewelry cases were lit from inside and her hands felt warm on the glass surfaces. It didn't take her long to find the necklace, and her heart began to beat very fast. A saleswoman came over to see if she needed help. "That one," she tapped the glass impatiently. "I'd like to see it, please."

The woman took it out, handling it the way one might maneuver a small slippery snake, and gave it to her.

"Is it a real pearl?"

"Yes, it's real."

"How much is it?"

"I believe it's eighty-nine dollars." The woman reached back into the case and turned over the little ticket pinned to the pink velvet to check. "Yes, that's right. Would you like to try it on?"

Maggie fastened the chain around her neck and looked at herself in the oval mirror. The chain felt light, the small pearl hit her at the throat. "I'll take it."

On the way home, she stopped at Loeb's and bought lamb chops and mint jelly and cauliflower. To start, she would make soup. In her sparkling new blender, she would beat her famous vichyssoise till it had the consistency of milk.

That night, her husband and daughter ate hungrily. He was so busy eating that it took him nearly an hour to notice the necklace around her throat.

He did a marvelous double take, then his face turned all sorts of interesting colors. He excused himself, as she knew he would, and went into his office and shut the door and did not come out for the rest of the night. He was so quiet, in fact, that you could almost believe he wasn't even there.

She took her time cleaning up. Standing at the sink washing the dishes, she could hear the snow coming down like a hundred people whispering the same two words: *Everyone knows.*

"I'll be at Monica's," Ada said, going out the door with her overnight bag.

"Have a good time," Maggie called. She glanced out the window and watched her daughter get into Greta Travers's car. The car pulled away.

She could feel her old strength returning, the same courage she'd summoned during that terrible week at Remington Pond, after they'd found the girl.

She dried her hands on a towel. The kitchen was neat and quiet and a small lamp glowed in the living room. For a moment she lingered with expectation outside his door, like an acrobat about to do a life-threatening trick. Then she knocked.

"Yes?" came his voice.

She pushed open the door. "I want to ask you something."

He took off his glasses and looked at her, waiting.

"Who is she?"

A flush rose to his cheeks, as if he'd been slapped. He turned back to his desk.

"I'm losing my patience, Jack."

"She's just a girl I met," he said finally. It was a simple sentence, she thought, with an ordinary noun and verb, yet to her it was as esoteric as some obscure poem. "She's a prostitute, actually," he said almost casually, as if that made it all right. "Since you want the facts."

"Yes, I do. I want the facts."

"Look, Maggie."

"Don't you *look Maggie* me."

"I'm sorry, I know it's unforgivable."

"You promised me, Jack," she said. Her voice sounded whiny. "You said never again."

He looked down at his guilty hands.

"Liar!" The word shot up from someplace deep and she said it again and again.

"Maggie, please. Keep it down."

"What's the matter, Jack? You worried somebody's going to hear? Huh? You worried somebody's going to find out? Everyone knows, Jack. Everyone knows about you."

He glanced up warily, as if the very sound of her voice caused him pain.

"The notes," she reminded him.

"You're paranoid." He got up and walked past her, nearly pushing her out of his way, and went into the kitchen. "Nobody knows." He took out a glass and poured himself some gin. He drank it warm.

"Someone does. Someone out there knows."

He shook his head, he didn't believe her. He drank the gin.

"Fix it, Jack."

"I can't. It's too late."

"This school is our life," she said. "This was our chance to have a life. And look what you've done."

"I know."

"How is it possible that a smart man like you could be so stupid?"

He took his drink into the living room and sat on the couch. She stood in the darkness, watching him. "I don't know what to say, Maggie. I made a mistake."

"This is just the sort of thing that could ruin you, *us*."

"She's pregnant."

It wasn't something she expected to hear and it took her several minutes to process the admission.

"She's just a girl, really," he said, gently.

"Just a girl," she repeated, breathlessly.

"I'm not quite sure what to do about it." He looked at her. "It's been on my mind for some time now. It's always on my mind. She is," his voice faltered, "on my mind. I've been distracted. I can't seem to concentrate."

He set his drink down soundlessly. He began to cry. She went to him.

"You are not going to ruin our lives over some stupid girl, do you understand? I didn't marry you for this. I didn't bring our child into the world for *this*."

"Yes, yes, I know." He began to whimper.

"We are going to have to think about this very carefully," she said.

"I know," he muttered. "You're right, Mags." Then he took her hand and sank to his knees. "Please forgive me. I'm a fool. I can't seem to help myself."

She ran her hands through his thick hair and raised his chin so that he would look at her. Tears of guilt ran down his face.

"We'll figure it out, won't we, Mags? Just like the last time?"

"Yes," she spoke in a whisper. "Yes, Jack, yes. Just like the last time."

Part Four

cꝋ

Panic Disorder

[sculpture]

Claire Squire, *Hunger Strike,* 2007. Wax, pigment, papier-mâché, horsehair, 5 x 14 x 14 ft. Collection of the artist.

Five female figures on their hands and knees in a circle, licking Splenda off the floor, their faces feral in their determination to feed on the sugar substitute as though it will sustain them. Their bodies are nearly emaciated, their ribs exposed, the hip bones and shoulder bones exaggerated.

Hunger Strike addresses a woman's lifelong obsession with her weight—depriving herself of nurturing in both the literal and figurative sense of the word.

40 ∽

He had come to a point with Claire. It was a kind of ache he had for her, a kind of pain in his gut. He had begun to tell her that he loved her. He would look at her. He would say, "I'm in love with you."

It began to snow late in the afternoon and they'd made a fire and opened some wine. He'd stopped at Guido's earlier for 'groceries and she'd spread all the ingredients out on the counter, wild salmon, a baguette, red potatoes, tomatoes. She was good with the knife, chopping the salad, preparing the potatoes. He watched her as she worked, sipping the wine. "Claire," he said, because he loved to say her name.

She looked at him and smiled. "Yes, Nathan."

"I need to tell you something," he said. "I've wanted to tell you for a long time."

"So tell me."

"I'm afraid to. It's something from my past, from another time."

"Don't be afraid. It won't change anything." She put down the knife and waited.

"When I was a much younger man, I lived in San Francisco with a woman. I was just a few years older than Teddy. Her name was Catherine. She was someone I loved. We did a lot of drugs, mostly heroin. She was—we were both addicts. It was a lifetime ago." He stole a look at her. She was watching him, listening intently. "Anyway, she was sick; she had AIDS. I loved her. It was a difficult time."

Claire's face went gray. In a matter of seconds she looked fifty years older. He could see the fear in her eyes.

"I was spared," he said. "I used to get tested every month—I'm fine, you don't have to worry—and I'd never put you at risk, I hope you know that about me."

The color came back into her cheeks. She nodded, she kissed him.

"But being spared only added to my guilt."

"I'm sorry, Nate." She took his hand.

"We had a child," he admitted. "A daughter."

Claire flushed, surprised. "What happened?"

"We gave her up."

"For adoption?"

"We had to." He looked away, guilty. "I was in no position at the time to be anyone's father."

"That must have been so hard," she said. "It must have been awful."

"It was."

"Was the baby all right?"

"She was perfect," he said simply. "It was miraculous."

He told her about that day, how Cat had died in the car, and then, abruptly, he stopped himself. He had planned to tell her everything, but he suddenly realized that Claire didn't need to know it was Willa. It would change everything—the way she looked at the girl—the way she thought about Joe and Candace—it wasn't fair to any of them—it wasn't fair to him.

"I just couldn't do it alone," he said finally. "I wasn't ready to be a father. For a long time, I felt terrible about it, miserable. I felt so guilty, like I was the worst sort of person. But I don't anymore."

"I'm glad." She kissed him. "You'll have another baby one day."

He took her in his arms and whispered in her ear. "Let's go up and try making one right now."

Later, in bed, he stayed up for a long time watching her sleep. The wind howled outside. The whole house seemed to be moving, creaking, and he could feel the wind coming through the cracks in the walls. After dinner they'd gone outside with Teddy and made snow angels. They'd laid in the snow catching snowflakes the size of pigeon feathers in their mouths. It had been the most fun he'd had in years. Later, in the shower, she'd tugged on his beard and dared him to shave it off and in the heady blur of passion he'd told her he would. They'd made love in the half-dark room and he'd watched her as she rode his hips, her mouth open, her breasts swaying like heavy summer fruit, her loose hair spilling down her back. He finally fell asleep, conscious of the world outside, the fury of the weather.

He woke early, before her. The sky was empty and white, quiet now, as if it had exhausted itself. He looked over at his lover, her sleeping face, her lips pale as clay. Oh, how he loved this time with her. She'd had a lot of wine last night, he thought. Maybe she'd forget about his beard. He could understand Claire wanting him to shave it off, as though his true self might be revealed. It would draw attention to his face, he realized. And, even though it had been many years, there was still a chance that the Goldings might recognize him. If it was what Claire wanted, though, he decided, it was a chance he was willing to take.

He got dressed and went down to the kitchen to make coffee. Teddy was sitting at the table, eating a bowl of cereal. "Living in sin," Teddy said, shaking his head.

"The snow," Nate tried to explain. He and Claire had been careful not to be too intimate around Teddy, unsure how he'd react to their relationship. "Your mom didn't want me to drive."

"Yeah, right."

Nate looked at the boy. "Are you okay with this?"

"What if I'm not?"

Nate stood there, trying to come up with something to say to make the boy feel better about the situation, but Teddy smiled, shaking his head. "Relax, Gallagher. It's okay, man. I'm glad it's you."

He got up and put his bowl in the sink and Nate said, "Hey," and pulled him over and bear-hugged him. "Thanks for your blessing."

"I love you too, Gallagher." Shaking his head, Teddy went out.

Nate made coffee and sat there for a moment, drinking it, imagining Claire as a young girl in this crazy house full of stuff. Claire came down a little later, smiling in that mysterious way of hers, that grin, and she took his cup and set it down and kissed him, a long slow wonderful kiss, then led him back upstairs, ignoring his complaints. She took him into the bathroom and sat him down on the toilet seat and put a little towel around his shoulders. "Welcome to my leetle shop," she said in an Eastern bloc accent. "Ve give you a shave, ya?"

She held up a pair of scissors and wiggled her eyebrows menacingly and said, in her regular voice, "Do you trust me?"

He looked at her carefully. "Yes, I trust you." In fact, she was the first woman he had ever fully trusted.

"Good." She kissed him again and when their lips came apart he repeated her question.

She looked at his face, her hand on his cheek. "Yes," she said. "I totally trust you."

He brought her chin down and kissed her. "Good."

She stood back up. "You are ready, ya?"

"Ya," he said. And then she picked up the scissors and cut off his beard.

Instinctively, his hand went up to feel the fur that was no longer there. He felt a little worried. But Claire was confident. Like an artist, she stood back appraising her work. "Better already," she said.

Then she took the can of shaving cream and shook it up—she was enjoying herself immensely—her power over him—her breasts in his face as she sprayed a creamy pile into her hand and patted it on his cheeks. It was turning him on. He gripped her waist, pulling down her boxer shorts, suddenly curious to know if it was possible to shave and fuck at the same time.

It just might be, he thought.

"Look at you," she said later. "You're gorgeous."

She handed him the mirror. Reflected there, he saw his old self, his father's square chin, his mother's wide cheekbones. His face had been beaten up over time, the beard had hidden some of the lines. He'd been hiding behind it for too long. He was glad to be rid of it.

He caught Claire staring at him like a long-lost relative. She couldn't seem to keep her hands off him. They stayed in bed all morning, finally stumbling downstairs at one o'clock to find Teddy eating lunch. "Man, what happened to you?"

"I got a shave."

"You look naked." Teddy looked at him. "How does it feel?"

"Smooth."

"You look different, man. Younger."

"Same old me," he said.

Teddy wanted to go snowboarding and Nate offered to take him. With years of practicing on a skateboard, Teddy was an avid snowboarder. Nate had learned to ski as a small child, when his father would take him to Killington every Christmas. They rented a small chalet there. It was the only time Nate could remember his father actually being proud of him. The slopes were crowded with tourists who'd come up for the day. There was a long lift line. He heard a lot of New York accents. Riding on the chairlift, Teddy seemed anxious to talk and when he asked Nate if he'd ever been with a prostitute, Nate understood that the boy's sudden urge to go skiing was about more than getting his exercise.

"Not intentionally," Nate said. "Not that I know of."

"What do you mean?"

"When I was younger, I did some stupid stuff. Drugs. I slept with a lot of women."

"I know this girl," he said uncertainly. "She may be a prostitute." He warily glanced at Nate, who translated the admission: *She's a prostitute.*

"We did it, you know? We had sex. I just wanted to see what it was like."

It wasn't Nate's place to start lecturing the boy on the risks of sleeping with a prostitute. "Why are you telling me this?"

"She's into drugs," he said. "I don't trust her."

"Are you doing drugs, Teddy?"

"No, but Willa is." He blurted it out, as though he'd been holding it in for a long time. "I'm kind of worried about her."

Nate felt himself tightening his grip on the handrail. He looked down at the ground and suddenly felt dizzy. "What kind of drugs?"

"Meth. The girl, her name's Pearl, turned her on to it." Teddy explained how Willa had met the girl at Sunrise House. "I tried to ask Willa about it, but she won't talk to me. I think she hates me."

"I doubt that."

"I thought she loved me." He looked at him.

"Maybe she does. Hate and love get tangled up sometimes."

"I want to make her stop," Teddy said. "I want to—" But he couldn't finish, it was time to get off the lift and within seconds Teddy was halfway down the mountain. Nate went after him, but he wasn't a daredevil like the boy. It was very icy; he wanted to take his time. And all the way down, he couldn't shake the feeling that he'd left something behind.

The next morning, he went into school early to finish reading the journals. He was anxious to see if Willa had mentioned anything about the drugs. He couldn't help feeling responsible, as if there were some genetic reason for her wanting the meth, as though the hunger for it ran in her blood.

Pulling onto campus, into the empty faculty lot, he noticed a young woman sitting on a bench outside the main office. It was nearly seven and the place was deserted, but in less than an hour the buses would arrive. Nate had never seen the girl before, but she was young—too old to be a student—but pretty close. She sat there waiting, it seemed, for someone, and she was smoking. There was a no-smoking rule on campus. She had on a white coat, some sort of fake rabbit, and a skirt without stockings, her white calves shaking slightly in the cold, unsuitable white pumps on her feet. Nate went over to her. "Hello?"

"Hello." He detected an accent. She grinned, showing off a grim set of teeth.

"Can I help you with something?"

She dragged on her cigarette, squinting in the smoke. "Maybe."

"You're not supposed to smoke, there's a rule."

"There's nobody here."

"Not now, but soon. The buses will start pulling in."

She shrugged and put it out, twisting the butt into the bottom of her shoe.

"Are you waiting for someone?"

She showed him a newspaper advertisement. "Greer Harding."

"I see."

"There is job," she said. "I want to clean."

"It's cold. Do you want to wait in my office?"

"No, I wait here."

"Are you sure?"

"She is nice lady?"

"Ms. Harding?" Nate hesitated. "You could say that."

"She will give me job?"

"Yes, I think so," he said, wanting to reassure her.

She folded her arms over her chest. "I will wait. It's okay."

He left her there and went into Walden House and took the stack of journals off the shelf and began with Willa's:

When I'm with her, I sometimes imagine the ghost of my dead mother. I watch her getting high, smoking the pipe, her eyes yellow like a wolf's. The girl is my friend, but we are from different lives. I have money, parents who love me, and she does not. Her parents died in a car crash when she was little. Her uncle raised her. She is a dancer. What I like about her is this: I can tell her things; anything. I can be free. I can be myself.

We went into the belly of the whale. You could make sounds and they'd echo off the walls and I thought of Pinocchio when he gets swallowed up by the whale and I thought of Moby Dick. My dad took me to see that movie at the old Capitol theater when I was little and I can still remember the taste of that popcorn. I remember feeling sorry for the great fierce white whale and not understanding why they wanted to kill it. And then my dad took me to Melville's house to see the little room where he'd written it and I thought about what it might be like to be a writer and to sit in a chair day after day putting down your thoughts. You can find places in your mind. I try to imagine the place I lived as a baby, after I was born. I try to picture my sick mother. I don't know, I can't remember it. But sometimes I think I can see her face looming over me, her sad smile.

I don't know. Maybe I'm crazy.

Sometimes when I look in the mirror I can see a glimmer of her shining through, like a ghost. I sometimes think she's watching over me.

288   *We snuck into the old ballet studios on North Street, just before they closed. We could hear the class finishing, the girls clapping for their teacher, the tapping of their wooden toes. We huddled in the janitor's closet, giggling, and I felt close to her, like she's my sister or something, this trust between us. I always wanted a sister anyway. When it was quiet we crept out into the studio. It was still light enough outside to see. We pulled open the curtains. Through the window you could see a brick building, a secretary sitting at her desk. I thought about that woman watching the dancers all day and wondered if she thought about them when she went home at night, if she ever dreamed of dancing when she was sitting at her desk. Pearl knew about ballet studios; she knew where to find the music and how to turn it on. It was Chopin, I think. She played it softly, then found some toe shoes and put them on. "When I was small, my mother used to sew my shoes," she said. "Shiny pink ribbons."*

Pearl danced for me. She was amazing, twirling around the room. She made me get up and dance with her. I could smell her sweat, the perfume she always wears. The way she walked with her legs turned out, penguinlike. The way she stood there breathing hard with her hands on her hips, her back slightly curved, contemplating herself in the mirror. She would be pretty if it weren't for her teeth, the sores she gets on her face.

We sat for a while, very close, and we could see ourselves in the mirror across the room. We almost look the same. We have the same legs, the same hair. It's just the faces that are different. Anyway, that's when she told me she was pregnant. She fell asleep for a few minutes on my shoulder. I stayed up all night, worrying about her. She is the type of person you can easily worry over. We just sat there and I watched the sky turn from purple to gold, like an old bruise.

Willa didn't come to school that day and Nate felt at a loss. Against his better judgment, he drove over to their house after school. Pulling up the long driveway, his mind reeled back to that day full of rain. It had been like a dream, he recalled, with the windows all fogged up. Nothing had seemed real.

He parked and walked to the door. It was a wide door from another century, painted a glossy black. He used the brass knocker. Joe Golding opened it. His face was cold, and for a moment Nate thought he'd recognized him. Instead, he shook his hand. "You shaved," he said.

"Yeah."

Joe looked at him again with that same cold expression.

"Teddy told me about the drugs," Nate said.

"She's in her room. We had to lock her in."

They stood for a moment in the foyer. Nate could hear her upstairs like a caged animal, throwing things against her door.

"Is there anything I can do?" Nate asked.

"No," Joe said, his eyes hooded, dark. "She'll be all right."

It was not his place to be here, Nate realized. Whatever was going on with Willa was none of his business. "If you need anything . . ."

Joe nodded his thanks and closed the door.

In the truck, Nate had a memory of Cat, sitting on the floor of their apartment, sick. They hadn't been able to score; they didn't have any cash. Her body shook. She cried out, she wept for it. He had to talk her through it. It wasn't easy. She hit him, she bound herself up in his arms. He had tried to contain her like some kind of watery creature. Finally, as the sun was coming in, they'd fallen asleep. When he'd woken later, he saw what she'd done to him, his body mottled with bruises.

On the front lawn of Larkin's place, a group of kids were making a snowman. Nate was glad to be home. He pulled into the back and parked in the old carriage house. It occurred to him that he wasn't well, he was covered with sweat. He thought he might have a fever. He went up to the apartment, hearing his neighbor's somber cello, and poured himself a drink. He lay on the couch, drinking, watching the snowflakes drift outside the windows. He realized he'd begun to cry.

The phone rang, but he refused to answer it, even though he knew it was Claire. He could hear her voice on the machine, begging him to pick up. But he could not bring himself to talk to her. He could feel himself slipping into a familiar dark place, dark as a grave and cold, where nothing lived.

41 ↬

In her face, was a fitting expression for the girl, because everywhere Maggie went, that's who she saw. Dressed in a white cleaning uniform, a nurselike shift that buttoned down the front, and old white tennis shoes, the girl was the image of an ardent employee. With her stringy hair pulled back in a ponytail, she would wander around with her duster, her face flushed, her lips wet. There was no sign of any pregnancy, the girl was thin as a straight pin. Maggie walked in on her one afternoon in the girls' lavatory, smoking. She flicked the cigarette into the toilet, then dropped to her knees and started scrubbing. They did not speak to each other. Maggie had complained to Greer, saying that the girl was rude, insolent, but Greer had countered, "She's very thorough. She hardly speaks English! I don't know what you're talking about. *And* she's cheaper than the cleaning service. Besides," Greer added with relish, "Jack wants her."

"I don't know why you're doing this to us," Maggie hissed at him.

"Look," he said, giving her a wrinkled smile. "She needs help. Maybe the job will improve her circumstances." The expression on his face was familiar, one he wore to church or reserved for his favorite charities. Maggie wanted to slap it right off his face.

"She is not a charity, Jack."

His face darkened and in the fleeting moment she detected a smidgen of empathy.

The girl had figured out how to be a nuisance. Perhaps she'd decided that if she harassed them enough she'd actually get something for her trouble. She'd call the house at all hours of the day and night, either sobbing or giggling into the phone. Just last night, the phone woke her at four in the morning. Maggie picked it up and heard people in the background, noises that conjured in her mind the atmosphere of a bar—the girl's voice sounded raspy and worn. "Is Jack there?" she said.

"Who is this?"

"I need to speak with Jack."

"You most certainly cannot."

The girl laughed. "But I'll cry if I don't."

"You can cry your heart out, I don't really give a damn." Maggie hung up on her. The next day a package came in the mail. It was addressed to Jack, but Maggie ripped it open. Inside was a tiny outfit, the sort you'd put on a newborn baby. She held it up before her, its tiny shape moving ever so slightly, like the draft of a ghost.

They were two weeks into their unit on *The Scarlet Letter* when Maggie broke down in class. She had taught the book for so many years that, admittedly, she'd become numb to it, but for some reason on that morning it occurred to her that, regardless of time and space, the book's moral considerations echoed her own. She looked down at her notes, her shorthand of topics she'd planned to discuss, and the words throbbed with accusation:

Humiliation

Sin

Social identity

Shame

With irony, she considered the similarities between her husband's situation and Dimmesdale's—ludicrous as it was—the girl's name, Pearl, being another maddening coincidence—and she found herself taking on the gloomy preoccupations of an invidious wife whose dreams of revenge were not dissimilar to Chillingworth's.

Her head began to pound. Her lips began to tremble as she searched the expectant faces of her students, who had begun to giggle at her, nervously, then to whisper, feverishly, among themselves.

Everyone knows, their faces declared. Ada gave her a look, imploring her to offer an explanation, but Maggie couldn't find words, and simply left the room as an eager uproar erupted behind her.

In her car, she began to come apart as if some force of nature had busted her seams. Her heart was beating very rapidly and she wondered distantly if she were experiencing tachycardia and if, perhaps, she needed a hospital—but there was no time for that now. She pulled out of the lot, nearly running into Nate Gallagher, causing him to stumble and drop his knapsack, papers flying into the dirt. Through her rearview mirror, she noticed he'd shaved his beard; he had not quite outgrown the gloomy, taciturn expression she remembered from Choate. She made a mental note to open the letter she'd received from her old high school roommate.

Turning onto the main road, her tires squealed. She took back roads across the border into Austerlitz, then over the mountain into Spencertown. She'd been out this way once or twice before. A handful of students lived out here and took a bus over the border to attend their school. New Yorkers bought weekend homes here. There was a country store that sold fresh pies, and the lofty Spencertown Academy, which offered art classes to small children and had a gallery; she'd been to some of their openings and they'd been quite good. The town of Chatham, which was cosmopolitan by comparison, was just up the road. Along the main drag there were charming little houses, side-hall colonials that had been built in the early part of the nineteenth century. The people who lived here had money. They had high-powered jobs in the city. They came up here to escape.

Angel Hill was a dirt road that ran deep into the country. Stately old homes were mixed in with ramshackle farms. She traveled several miles, eight or nine more, until she came to a small farmhouse. It was up on a hill, the way Jack had described it to her. It was two in the afternoon and the place looked deserted. She parked out front and sat there a moment, wondering what she would do once she got inside. She had her pepper spray, just in case. You never knew with women like this.

She crossed the wet lawn up to the front door. There wasn't a sidewalk, only a few flat stones that had been laid years before and were half covered with grass. The door was slightly ajar, as if they were expecting her, but of course that wasn't true, they had no knowledge of her visit.

Although it wasn't cold, and the snow had almost entirely melted, the woodstove was roaring in the living room. She stood in the foyer a moment, just listening. She could hear people upstairs, the muffled sound of laughter. At the end of the narrow hall was a kitchen where an older woman was putting away groceries. A cat was playing with the empty grocery bag, crawling inside of it, jumping on top of it. There was a glare inside, sunlight streaming through the dirty windows. She walked down to the kitchen and asked the woman if she knew where Pearl was. "We're closed."

"I'm a friend," she explained.

The woman expelled a gust of sour air and went down the hall and called up through the banister. "Pearl!"

A moment later, the girl put her head over the banister and looked down at her, the necklace Jack had given to her swinging back and forth like a pendulum. "What do you want?"

"I just want to talk."

"What about?" She sounded annoyed. "I'm busy now."

"It won't take long."

The girl shuffled down the stairs, noisily, in baggy sweatpants and a T-shirt. Maggie tugged on her necklace, the pearl, and said, "We have the same necklace."

The girl's hand went to her throat, a reflex. She fondled the pearl contemplatively. "It was a gift."

"From my husband."

The girl shrugged. "I get many gifts. There are many husbands."

"Can we sit somewhere?"

The girl ushered her into the living room. They sat on the couch together. She was pale. Her teeth looked gray.

"Why won't you leave him alone?"

The girl scowled, arrogant. "Why should I? He promise me things."

"What things?"

"I need money."

"We have a daughter," Maggie said.

The girl lit a cigarette. "Good for you. I am happy for you."

"I want you to stay away from him. I want you to leave us alone. Will you do that for me?"

"But he loves me," she said, her eyes glittering with spite.

"He doesn't love you," Maggie said.

"He says he will help me, he will take care of my baby."

Maggie doubted the girl was even pregnant. "He's just using you."

The girl shook her head. "You don't know. You don't know anything."

"Don't you talk to me like that."

She shrugged again. "Look, I don't make the rules. If he comes, I can't say no. He has a key."

"What do you mean, he has a key?"

"You have to buy one to get in. They cost a lot of money."

Maggie felt a burning in her chest. "Why can't he see someone else?"

"He wants only me."

"How old are you?"

She smiled. "Old enough."

"What do you do, when he comes?"

"We go upstairs. I have a room."

Maggie shook her head. It was full of static. "What does he want?"

"He likes to pretend."

"I don't understand."

"He likes me to dress up like a schoolgirl."

A wave of nausea went through her. "I don't believe that."

"I will show you." The girl stood up and held out her hand. "Come, we go up."

Like a child, Maggie allowed herself to be led up the stairs. It was an old house with crooked floors. There was the smell of coconut oil.

They went into the girl's tiny room. It was messy, just like Ada's room. On the nightstand was a candle, a pipe of some sort. A small TV blinked some idiotic program. The girl opened her closet, revealing the green tartan plaid of a Pioneer skirt. "Here, I'll put it on for you." She yanked the skirt off the hanger. Maggie looked away while she put it on, but the girl showed no modesty. "There, see?" She shuffled into a pair of fuzzy pink slippers and modeled the skirt for Maggie.

"I'm feeling sick," Maggie said, clutching the bedpost for support. "I need some air."

The girl lurched open the window. Maggie stumbled toward it, gulping the cold winter air. The girl went out into the hall and came back a moment later with a glass of water. "Sit down."

Maggie sat on the bed. She felt very strange. The floor seemed to tilt. "Drink," the girl said.

Maggie drank the water and the girl watched her.

"I don't know how you stand him," Pearl said.

"I . . . I don't know what you mean."

"The things he likes." The girl seemed to wince. "He has a problem."

"He doesn't mean it," Maggie said. "We don't—"

But the girl had taken her hand, interrupting her lie. "You should be careful," she said. "He's a very dangerous man."

42 ⌒

Claire hadn't heard from Nate in three days. She'd left several messages, and he hadn't returned them. Even Teddy had noticed his absence. "Go down there," he urged her. "Maybe he's sick." So she did.

He came to the door in his bathrobe.

"You look awful."

"I've been sick," he apologized.

"I've been worried about you. I tried to call."

"I know. I'm sorry." He took her in his arms. "Come in."

They sat on his green couch and she made him some tea and he made a fire in the fireplace. He told her about Willa, about the drugs she'd been doing, about his guilt over it, and then he said, "There's something you should know about Willa Golding."

She looked at him, waiting.

"She's my daughter."

They made love as the snow fell all the way into evening. He made her a drink and they sat in the dark living room before the fire. Now that she looked at Nate she could see similarities in their faces, the shape of their eyes, their mouths. "I'm not planning on telling her. I know it seems devious, but I don't mean it to be. I don't want to hurt the Goldings and I think it might."

"If it becomes important to Willa to find you one day, she will."

"Do you think I'm despicable?"

"No," she said. "I think it was something you needed to do."

"When we gave her up, I wasn't in a place where I could judge. I never knew if I'd done the right thing or not. It was like this hole in my heart. I had to come back here. I had to see for myself."

"And how do you feel now? Was it the right thing, giving her up?"

"Yes. I believe it was."

43 ∽

Willa had always been pretty good at math, but after three days without eating much of anything she thought her judgment might be off. She estimated that it was a twenty-foot drop from her bedroom window to the ground below. It was half past six in the morning and the house was still quiet. It had snowed the night before and now the ground looked fluffy and white. She jumped.

The jump was thrilling, and when she landed on the ground, hard as it was, she felt elated, free.

Free at last, she thought, and ran into the woods, where no one would ever find her.

44 ✍

It was Joe Golding who called the house with the news about Willa. He'd wanted to speak to Teddy's mother, but she was at Gallagher's. "It's Willa," Golding had said. "She's gone." When Teddy asked what had happened, his heart beating a million miles a second, Joe said, "We thought she was over it. She seemed better. But she climbed out her window."

"Did you call the police?"

"They're out looking for her now."

Rudy showed up in his truck and they drove out to Spencertown, thinking she might have gone out there to see Pearl, but he doubted it. He didn't think she even knew about that place. The roads were thick with snow. Still, Rudy drove quickly. There were only a few cars on the road, crawling along as the snow accumulated. When they got up Angel Hill, it was like being inside a feather pillow, the big white flakes coming down.

They went inside and Rudy said he'd wait in the living room, but within minutes he was coaxed into one of the rooms downstairs. Teddy started up to Pearl's room, but the old lady grabbed Teddy's arm and said, "She's with a customer."

He went up anyway. If anyone knew where Willa was, it was Pearl. But after he opened the door, it only took him a second to realize he'd made a mistake. And when Dale was lumbering toward him with his pants around his ankles, he didn't exactly get out of his way. The punch came hard and fast. He hit Teddy so hard the whole room tipped over and before he knew it he was on the floor, with Dale's boot kicking his ribs.

"Here's what you get, you son of a bitch. You think you can fuck with me? Huh? You think you can get away with that? I had to have fucking mouth surgery. You fuck. You *fuck!*" He kicked him a few more times, in the same way he'd kicked his dog, and then he held his head like a bowling ball and banged it repeatedly against the floor. Blood came up in his throat and he started to blubber.

"Stop it, stop it!" Pearl was screaming. "You will kill him!"

Teddy could hear them scuffling, and he had her back on the bed and finished what he'd come for, and they made a sick awful sound with her whimpering all the way through it, and all Teddy could think of was that dog Dale had set fire to, and that Pearl was in awful danger. But he couldn't move. There wasn't a thing he could do about it.

Distantly, he could hear Dale pulling her up off the bed, shoving her across the room. Through his one good eye he watched Dale's boots as they walked out into the hall, pushing her on her back. "Move," he said to her. "Your boyfriend wants to see you."

Then the boots stopped, like he'd forgotten something, and came back. They were steel-tipped construction boots and when they made contact with his ribcage all the air flew out of his mouth and he thought he was going to die.

But he came to moments later. The house was suddenly quiet. He discerned the sound of a car door closing. He crawled across the floor and then, with great difficulty, pulled himself up onto the bed. Everything swirled. He saw the world smeared with yellow. He looked out the window and saw a car starting up, some kind of old vintage car. It was creepy, he thought. He couldn't make out the driver, but as it turned down the road he saw something he recognized. The face of a white pit bull pressed up against the glass.

45 ∽

Nate's conversation with Claire the night before had filled him with a deep sense of resolve. And as the firelight had played across her face he'd experienced a vivid revelation. He was going to marry her.

That morning, Lloyd Jernigan, the Latin teacher, had called to see if Nate would mind taking out the girls' cross-country ski team; he was sick in bed and there was a practice scheduled on the trails over by the lake. Nate could think of nothing better than skiing before work and told him he'd be happy to do it.

The girls on the team were well-equipped skiers in brightly colored parkas and they were a good team, having won several races already that year. Some of the trails were on school property, but many wandered off into the woods and some reached as far as Hawthorne Road. The trails were open to members of the community, and were used often, but on that morning Nate observed that the woods were eerily serene and vacant. They'd finished their route, which Lloyd had expertly laid out, and were on their way back to the boathouse for hot chocolate and scones when something caught his eye. He held up his arm for them to stop. "Hold up a second," he said. "Wait here." The girls immediately began to chatter as he took off his skis and went down the incline on foot. It was the skirt that caught his eye, the unmistakable tartan plaid. There was a girl down there, he realized, down near the water, in a bed of bloody snow.

He told the girls to wait there, not to move, then went down to get a better look, coming upon her twisted legs, the black high-top sneakers, the rumpled knee socks, a small tattoo on the back of her calf. There was the tangle of auburn hair, her slender white arms stretched over her head as though she'd dropped out of heaven. Her face was turned from him, concealed by a layer of blood. He couldn't see her, but he'd know those sneakers anywhere. He staggered to her side, reaching out his hand, but there was too much blood. Pieces of flesh seemed to be missing. Part of her ear, a wound on her neck like a jellyfish. Two fingers raggedly severed at the knuckles. Her clothing almost entirely shredded.

He backed away. His head began to pound. It wasn't possible. *This isn't happening.*

She wasn't moving. She was cold, her body twisted. He took off his coat and covered her, then started screaming for help, his voice rising up through the trees, over the tree tops, then echoing back to him across the black surface of the lake.

Within minutes, the cops arrived. An ambulance. Yellow streamers were stretched between trees, barricades were put into place. The EMTs kneeled at her side. Having determined she was gone, they backed off, respectfully, looking down at her like fallen prey.

Nate borrowed one of the girls' cell phones and called Jack Heath, but he didn't answer. He called Greer Harding, who screamed something into the phone about insurance liability and lawsuits; he couldn't make it all out and he didn't understand a word of it. He hung up on her. Dazed, he watched from a distance as photographs were taken of the body. The detective was a man named Croft, distinguished, in the crowd of police personnel, by a brown felt hat. He wanted to ask Nate some questions. "This is my partner, Judd Whalen," he told him. The three men shook hands. They went along the trail, then down the incline to the body. Nate explained how they'd been out skiing. Croft kneeled at her side, a knight to a princess, pulling on plastic gloves. "Do you know her?"

"I don't know," Nate muttered. "I can't tell. There's too much blood. I'm assuming she's a student." His voice quavered.

"She's got the uniform on, doesn't she?" Croft said.

"Yes, sir." Nate's eyes burned.

"Looks like an animal got to her," Whalen said. "Maybe a bear. Man, that's a damn shame."

"There were some sightings of bear last week, but that was over in Washington County," Croft said. "And these puncture marks are too small for bear. It looks more like a dog to me."

"I'll tell you what," Whalen said. "That ain't no ordinary house pet."

"Could be the same animal that attacked the little girl a couple of months ago. We never did find that dog. Offered a big reward too."

"Not big enough," Whalen said. "We've had problems with people fighting pit bulls. Some of those dogs are worth big money. But this, I hate to see this. This is a damn shame."

More cops were coming through the woods. Nate saw Jack Heath in the distance. He was talking to his wife, who looked distraught. She backed away from him, as if with disgust, hiding her face. Heath had on a white turtleneck under his standard blue blazer. He looked like a politician, Nate thought. He pushed his way through the throng to get to the girl, to get a look. "This is Mr. Heath, Detective," one of the cops said to Croft. "He's the school headmaster."

Croft shook his hand. "Mr. Heath."

Nate watched Jack's face go peaked as he looked at the body. He excused himself and ducked into the trees, retching. When he recovered, he returned to the group hovering around the body and apologized. "She's not ours," he said, barely audible.

"How can you tell? You can't see her face."

"That tattoo, for one thing. None of our students have tattoos. It's against school policy. We'd expel a student for behavior like that."

Croft's head tilted slightly, Nate noticed, as if he'd been stung by something but wasn't going to let it bother him. "Sounds like you run a pretty tight ship over there."

"We expect our students to follow the rules, Detective."

"No argument there," Croft said, picking up the girl's wrist, noting a phone number written in ink. "Can we get someone to check this number, please?" Then he took out his handkerchief and dipped the cloth into the lake. "If she's not a student, what was she doing in that uniform?" he said to nobody in particular. He wrung out the handkerchief then ran the cloth gently over her face. "Why don't you show us your pretty face, darlin'," he said to the dead girl. They watched as her face revealed itself in all its reckless beauty.

46 ⌒

When Joe had opened Willa's door that morning and found an empty room, he'd experienced a feeling of dread unlike he'd ever known. It was a physical experience, and he couldn't seem to breathe. They'd gone out looking for her, driving all over the place, but she was nowhere to be found and it never occurred to either of them to look at Sunrise House. They were up all night, waiting, hoping, then, the following morning, Regina called. Willa was there. Apparently, she was in quite a state. She had been walking all day, looking for her friend, Pearl, and hadn't been able to find her. She'd told Regina about the meth. And she'd told her about something else too. Something she could not discuss over the phone. Joe had agreed to come at once and he'd run out of the house in a hurry, slipping on his shoes without socks.

The roads were bad and it had begun to snow again. It was still early; people were on their way to work. He had to drive carefully. Down near the lake, there seemed to be a lot of traffic, and when he passed the school, and then the access road to the trails, he saw police cars parked along it. Something must have happened, he thought.

On Route 7, the traffic thinned. Still, he drove slowly, carefully, preparing himself for what would come next. It occurred to him that his daughter's relationship with the prostitute was about more than experimenting with drugs and that, in a profound way, they'd all been part of it, watching the events unfold. It seemed to Joe that, somehow, Pearl had become a symbol in Willa's mind of the sort of person she might have been had her birth mother raised her. Joe had gotten a glimpse of her biological mother—her name had been Catherine—in the car that day, just moments before her death. It had been a haunting vision he would never forget, but Willa could only imagine her and it had taken her into a dangerous world. In his daughter's mind, she had to find a way to be *like* her somehow, and, based on the information supplied in the letter, had seen in Pearl a girl akin to her natural roots. Joe reasoned that, in a deeply pathological way, Willa's charity to her was a kind of penance for getting a better deal in life, after all.

It had started with the letter, he realized. It was after that that she'd started pushing her limits, staying out too late, daring them to complain, to punish her, which they hadn't, knowing, as if instinctively, that she was testing them, waiting for them to step in and say *stop!* But, for some reason he couldn't quite fathom, they never did—until it was too late.

Perhaps they hadn't wanted to intrude, as if whatever she was going through was a natural rite of passage that they, as parents, simply had to accept. Perhaps they felt guilty, even, as though they were accessories to the crime of her destiny, as though adopting her had been wrong somehow—selfish of all the adults involved. They had to wade through all those feelings. They all had to, in their own way. It was something real yet awful and abstract. They couldn't define it, they couldn't discuss it. It was a dark feeling, heavy, amorphous. Desperately painful.

And then, that awful day, when he'd gone into her room and found her getting high, saw her stash and the small pipe, he'd grabbed her. "Don't you know how much I love you?" he'd demanded, flushing the white powder down the toilet. "Do you have any fucking clue how much you mean to me?"

But she was already a monster. "You can't control me!" she'd screamed at him, wiping her continuously running nose, her eyes distant, her face a mask. It was a side of her he'd never witnessed, and in a flash, just before the door slammed in his face, he'd seen the tattoo. He'd been so furious that he had to make a deliberate effort to restrain himself from hitting her. Because at that point, it was the only thing he'd really wanted to do.

He turned onto Montgomery Street, then wound down to the cul-de-sac. He had never actually seen Sunrise House and it came to him now that he'd relied on the school for too much—he'd trusted them, perhaps, too readily. He'd never met this woman, Regina, and had pieced together an image of her based on scraps of Willa's stories, but when she came to the door she was different than he'd expected. She had a big warm face, and was dressed professionally, in a wool suit. "Mr. Golding?"

"Hello, Regina."

"Please, come in."

He stepped into the foyer and stamped the snow off his shoes.

"I'd like to speak with you a moment in private."

"Sure."

He followed her into a small office and they sat down and she told him what Jack Heath had done to his daughter in the school van.

It would be hard for him to put the way he felt into words without sounding like a madman. A kind of primal energy rushed through his body. It was a natural instinct, he thought, that made killing Jack Heath seem like a perfectly reasonable thing to do, and it would take all of his concentration to tame it.

"I'm very sorry," Regina said. "I know it's a very difficult thing to hear."

They stepped into the foyer and she went up to get Willa. He could hear footsteps overhead, the creaking floors, and then the galloping footsteps of children. There were four of them in all, and they came down the stairs, apparently happy to see him. One little boy looked up at him and said, "Are you Willa's dad?"

"Yes, I am."

The boy studied him. "Hell-o. I'm Tyrell." He reached out his hand for a shake.

"I'm Joe. Nice to meet you."

Then he saw her. She had come down the stairs. Her hair was pulled back in a ponytail, and she looked as if she'd been crying. "Daddy," she muttered, and ran into his arms. He held her hard.

Driving home, he tried to focus on the road. He could feel his rage spilling over. He glanced at her, grateful that, at least on the outside, she seemed all right. He took her hand and tried to smile. He wondered how she had processed the violation. He could not be certain how he'd behave when he saw Jack Heath again.

In some way, if he read into it, he could interpret the incident as a bitter lesson, given his line of work, and one that, perhaps, he had needed to learn firsthand.

When they got home, Willa went upstairs to bed. She was very tired and needed to rest. Candace sat with her, holding her hand, stroking her hair.

He left the house, he needed some air. He needed to think. He walked in the woods and he cried. Every aspect of his life, he thought, had been tainted with compromise, the endless negotiation of what he had and what he didn't, what he deserved, and what was just out of reach. He felt betrayed by Heath, who he'd considered to be a friend. His life in general had been a neatly wrapped package of lies. As a younger man, he'd wanted to make films, to tell important stories that moved people, but he'd ended up limiting himself to porn. He'd wanted to live a good life, an honorable life, and, to some degree, he had, but it was shrouded with deception. He'd wanted to be a good husband, to respect and honor his wife, but he had not been faithful, and, as a result, he had deprived her of happiness. Until he'd met Claire, he'd been contemptuous of most women, insinuating himself into their lives with little consideration of their feelings. And as a father, he realized, he'd been distant, afraid perhaps that, because they didn't share blood, he had no right to try to influence or change her.

Later that night, when he heard about Pearl on the evening news, he understood how fragile they all were, that vulnerability was a human trait they all shared and needed to respect, and how, in a matter of seconds, based on the fickle inclinations of fate, your life could change forever.

47 ∽

Just like the time at Remington Pond, the news about the girl traveled fast and Jack Heath was keeping everything in line. He had always been especially capable in situations that demanded unprecedented strength and character. As a boy, his father would put him through drills of one challenge or another. Bomb scares, floods, fires. "Rise to the occasion," he was fond of saying, and Jack too liked the expression.

Jack called an emergency faculty meeting, ushering teachers and staff members into the large conference room, around the oval table. Because the attack had happened on school property, he said, it was the school's responsibility to address the tragedy as if the victim had been one of their own. He had informed the nearby psychiatric hospital, should any of their students need counseling, and members of the clergy were on hand to offer their support. They were on top of the situation, he assured everyone, and the staff, sheeplike, Maggie thought, in their willingness to comply, nodded their heads almost gratefully.

Maggie had put on her best suit, a buttercream Chanel that she'd found in a vintage shop in Sheffield. It was cheerful, like the sun, she thought. She tried not to think about the odd circumstances of the girl's death. According to the police, she'd been flying on drugs at the time—her pupils had been dilated—which Maggie interpreted as a blessing. They would know more, they'd told Jack, after they received the coroner's report.

Later that night there was an ice storm. The naked trees shook and broke like glass. She made dinner for her family *like a good wife,* but none of them could eat. Ada retreated to her room, and Maggie could hear her crying. She'd only been nine when the girl at Remington Pond was found. She'd been her favorite babysitter, Maggie recalled, and it was likely that it was all coming back. Maggie went up to her room and sat on her bed. "Are you all right?"

Ada gripped her stuffed panda bear and turned away. "Just leave me alone," she said.

That's what I'll do, Maggie thought. On the way out of the room, she noticed a Scrabble board under Ada's bed, the letters strewn across the carpet. It gave her pause. She met her daughter's eyes, but just now could not begin to address the sadness they contained.

She went downstairs and stood at the table looking at the food. *So much waste,* she thought, and left it there, and went into the living room and lay down on the couch. The fish bowl, she noticed, had been removed, and Jack had straightened up the piles of books and emptied the ashtray, no doubt preparing the room should anyone stop by, the police, for instance. Sleet rushed against the window. The whole world seemed to be breaking, she thought, watching the wild shadows on the ceiling. The night before, he'd brought her tea at bedtime; he'd sat there watching her drink it, then he'd helped her under the covers, pulling them gently under her chin. There'd been a moment between them, something in his eyes. She'd slept better than she had in months. When she woke with the sunlight on her face she'd felt refreshed.

It wasn't until she'd gone downstairs and seen his shoes, which were wet and muddy, that she understood he'd gone out when she was sleeping, and that he'd put something in her tea to make sure she stayed that way.

Now, even the gin couldn't touch her fear, the gnawing dread in her belly. She woke disoriented in the wild darkness. Her clothes were damp, her body coated with sweat. An awful foreboding consumed her. Where was Jack? With difficulty, she pulled herself up and wandered through the house, looking for him. There were things she noticed in the kitchen. The ice tray on the counter, scattered cubes of melting ice. The bottle of gin, nearly empty. She stood there for a moment, then poured some of it into a glass, swallowed it warm, coughed. A slow heat sank down her back. The wind gusted against the windows. She looked down the narrow hallway at the closed door, the stripe of light underneath. *What is he doing in there?* She walked to his office and opened the door. He was lying on the floor in a fetal position, his head resting on his hands, which were pressed together as if in prayer. Gratefully, she couldn't see his face.

Get up, you pathetic bastard, she thought miserably. *Get up!*

But she said nothing, and backed out of the room, soundlessly closing the door behind her.

In the morning the detectives appeared at Pioneer. From her office window, she watched her husband lead them around the campus. He seemed cheerful and solicitous, as if they were prospective parents and not cops. When they knocked on her door, she cleared her throat as if there were something jammed inside of it. Words crept out, weakly, like little bugs. Jack said, "They want to talk to you about Ted Squire."

"I see."

The detectives came in and sat down. The taller one, Croft, was holding a student's paper—it was Teddy's story about the pit bull. She recognized it because she'd been the one to make all the red marks on it.

"Edward Squire," Croft said his name. "What can you tell us about him?"

"What is it you want to know?"

"I don't know," Croft shrugged casually. "What kind of student is he?"

"Average," she said.

"Average?" Croft looked surprised. "You gave him a D-minus this quarter. That's significantly below average, wouldn't you say, Mrs.

Heath?"

"He's easily distracted. Attention deficit disorder. Not to mention that he's severely LD." She saw that he wasn't familiar with the term. "Learning Disabled," she clarified.

"So he doesn't read so good, is that what you're saying?"

So well, she thought, but only nodded.

"You read this? These are your comments?"

"Mr. Gallagher wanted my opinion."

"Uh huh. I see." He put on his bifocals and held up the paper and read her comments. "Far-fetched, implausible, disorganized, poorly structured." Croft looked at her pointedly. "That's some critique."

"I only wanted to help him."

"What do you think now?"

"What do I think?"

"Now that you know what these dogs are capable of. Do you think you'd still use that word?"

"I'm sorry, Detective. What word?"

"Implausible."

She shook her head, she couldn't look at him. "I don't know. I suppose not."

Croft took out a cigarette and just as she was about to tell him that smoking was not allowed, he lit it. "This Mr. Gallagher, that's his real writing teacher, correct?"

The way he said it, *his real writing teacher,* seemed deliberately insulting. Again, she nodded, noticing that there weren't any red marks on the story Nate had corrected. "I guess Gallagher had a different take on it," Croft said, showing her the grade he'd given the boy, an A.

"He was entitled to his opinion," she muttered. "I'm just wondering what you're getting at here, Detective."

"What I'm getting at?"

"Are you suggesting that the boy had something to do with this?"

"I might be."

"She was attacked by an animal, sir. That's not exactly something one can premeditate, is it?"

"Oh, you'd be surprised, Mrs. Heath."

"Forgive me, Detective, but, it sounds a bit—"

"Far-fetched?"

She nodded.

He squinted at her. "I guess it's a good thing I'm not getting graded."

He handed her back Teddy's story. "You might want to hold on to this. You never know, it might be worth something one day."

Croft started walking out, but the shorter detective, Detective Whalen, stopped and thanked her for her time. "Would it be possible to get a look inside the boy's locker?"

"I think, under the circumstances, it would be all right." She walked them out into the hall, down the stairs, to the row of lockers designated to the juniors. She stepped into the office to get the boy's combination. She could feel her heart turning dully. When she returned, Croft was talking on a cell phone, ignoring her. Perhaps she was being oversensitive, but she had the distinct feeling he didn't like her. She opened the locker for the men and stepped aside. There were photographs taped to the metal door, pictures of Teddy and Willa and Monica and Marco and even Ada, their little incestuous group— like an ad for Abercrombie, she thought with loathing. While Croft talked on the phone, Whalen dug around in the boy's locker. He found something and held it up.

"Look what we have here," he said, holding up a dog collar for everyone to see.

48 ∽

Claire was in the barn when the cops came looking for Teddy. They pulled their car up to the house and went to the door. She took off her apron and put on her coat. It had gotten cold; it was starting to snow again.

"Hello." She waved to them and they stood there waiting for her, their faces hard, grim. *This can't be good,* she thought.

"Mrs. Squire?"

"Yes?"

"I'm Detective Croft, Stockbridge police. This is my partner, Detective Whalen."

"Is there a problem?"

"Is your son at home?" Whalen asked.

"He's at school."

"We just came from there," Croft said. "He didn't show up this morning."

Claire tried to think. She'd been working all night; she hadn't seen Teddy come in. "He should have gotten on the bus this morning."

"He must have taken a detour."

"Is he in the habit of cutting school?" Croft asked.

"Not that I know of."

"A girl was attacked in the woods the other night."

"Yes, I heard. They're saying it was that dog, the one that attacked the little girl."

"Right." Croft took out a picture. "Did you know her? Did your son know her?"

Claire sighed. Tears rushed to her eyes. "I gave her a ride once. She was a dancer. I don't know if he knew her or not," she lied.

"She was a prostitute, Mrs. Squire."

Claire shook her head. "I didn't know."

Croft's eyes simmered with judgment. She could already tell he didn't like her. He'd heard things, she assumed. Rumors. Maybe he knew about Teddy's dad, that he'd gone to jail and would use it against Teddy, but she doubted it, and, anyway, Billy's criminal record had nothing to do with her. Maybe he resented the fact that she lived on Prospect Hill, with all the rich New Yorkers. She used to share the same resentment, but in her father's case it was different. Her father had earned his money the hard way, and had bought the house back when real estate was cheap. Of course she couldn't convince the cop of it now. And why should she have to? It was none of his business.

"We have a witness who says your son was her last customer that night," Whalen said. "Do you have any idea where he might be?"

"He has a cell phone." She took out her cell phone and dialed Teddy's number, but he didn't answer. "Are you saying my son's in- volved?" she asked, finally, not wanting to hear the answer.

"Let's hope not," Whalen said.

Claire tried to call Nate at the school, but the school's machine was on. On principle, Nate refused to carry a cell phone, which was the single thing that infuriated her about him. "We're living in the twenty-first century!" she'd complain. She pulled on her coat and drove down to the school. She found him inside Walden House, giving a class. She knocked on the door.

Nate grinned and excused himself. "Hey. You okay?"

"Have you seen Teddy?"

"No, he didn't show up today."

"The cops came looking for him."

Nate frowned. "What? They think he's involved?"

"He was with her the night she died. He was her last customer."

"Oh, God."

"They have a witness—they're trying to build a case."

"Not because of his story, I hope?"

"What story?"

"The one about the pit bull."

"I don't know about that, but he was seen at a dogfight somewhere. One of our neighbors saw him snooping around his property—a week later somebody stole his dog—a white pit bull."

"Sounds pretty circumstantial to me."

"It sure as hell doesn't *feel* circumstantial."

"Give me ten minutes to finish up here. Then we'll go look for him."

She had found drawings in Teddy's sketchbook of houses he liked and, if she'd found them under different circumstances, she would have been incredibly impressed. He had talent, she realized. There were several drawings of one house in particular. It was a famous house in the area, up on Lenox Mountain, which had been built by its owner, an architect from Boston. He only used it on weekends. "He told me once he sometimes goes there to think," she told Nate.

They pulled off the road, down a long narrow driveway. The house was a glass cube suspended dramatically over the mountain. You could see the reservoir down below. They parked and walked down to the house. A series of decks were stacked up the side. To their surprise, the sliding glass door opened and a man came out. He was Chinese, wearing a crisp white shirt and jeans. "Good morning," he said, holding a mug.

"Hello," Nate said. "This is rather awkward, but we're looking for someone. He's a boy; apparently he admired your house."

"He was here." The man looked distraught. "I thought he was a thief. I'm sorry. He's with the police now." The man set down his mug and came down the stairs. He was handsome, Claire thought. He had a kind face. "I'm Fred Chow," he said. "I live in Boston, this is my summer place. I came back this morning and found him sleeping in my bed. Imagine my surprise. He had a key, apparently. They found it in his pocket. He'd made a copy of the one I left under the flowerpot. I'll have to admit, he's clever."

Claire felt a stirring of dread. "I'm very sorry," she said. "If there's anything I can do—if he broke anything . . ."

But the man shook his head. "He liked the house," he said, almost flattered. "He wants to be an architect. This he told me as they were putting on the cuffs. An interesting boy, your son. He's done drawings of it, apparently. I'd like to see them sometime."

"I'm very sorry," Claire said. "This won't happen again."

The man nodded. "I'm not pressing charges. But they took him anyway. I think they wanted to frighten him."

"Thank you." Claire took the man's hand. "Thank you for being so kind."

The police station was on Main Street, an old-fashioned precinct, almost quaint. An enormous print of one of Rockwell's paintings,

Policeman with Boys, hung in the foyer. Claire wished her business here were so innocent. A cop escorted them down the hall and directed them to a bench outside Detective Croft's office. Claire could see the detective inside on the telephone. Teddy was nowhere in sight. Nate took her hand and squeezed. "It's going to be all right."

Croft stuck his head out the door. "Mrs. Squire."

He motioned for her to come into the office; Nate had to stay on the bench.

"Take a seat," Croft said, motioning to a chair. "The boy will be right out. I should warn you that he's a bit roughed up."

"What do you mean?"

"He claims somebody beat him up. We're looking into that now. I'm not going to be coy with you, Mrs. Squire, but I'm going to suggest you find yourself a lawyer."

"He had nothing to do with this, Detective," she said, but even she wasn't so sure.

"We'll get it all sorted out, Mrs. Squire. I can promise you that." Croft nodded at her gently, as though he pitied her. She wanted to tell him that her son was kind and good and didn't have a destructive bone in his body—he wouldn't even kill a spider when he found one in the house but would gently scoop it up onto a piece of cardboard and take it outside. Through the window Claire could see them bringing him in, Whalen holding onto his arm. He looked awful; beat up. He had a black eye. He had on her father's leather jacket and his black boots—she regretted letting him buy them now; she regretted a lot of things. He turned abruptly and caught her eye and his face withered somehow, like a wilting flower. A daisy like the ones he'd pull out of the ground when he was little and present to her as a gift. He walked in his loping teenaged way, all arms and legs and feet. She stood up as he entered the office, jaunty, defensive, arrogant. *Don't hug me,* his eyes warned.

"Teddy," she whispered, and then in a stronger voice, "are you all right?"

He didn't answer her.

"Take a seat, son," the detective told him.

Teddy sat down and crossed his arms across his chest. It was a familiar pose, one she'd seen many times in the myriad principals' offices of his youth. Whalen sat down against the wall and Croft sat behind his desk. "I know we got off to a bit of a rough start," he said to Teddy. "But we'll try this again."

Teddy shot Claire a look.

"Tell us where you were on the night of February third, Mr. Squire."

"I was home. My mother was out."

She tried to think: She was over at Nate's. "Yes, that's true."

Teddy explained how Joe Golding had called and told him about Willa, how she'd climbed out of her window. "Rudy and I went out to look for her."

"Rudy?" Whalen said. "I'll need his full name."

"I don't know it. Rudy. He works up there, for the Goldings."

"He's the barn manager up there," Whalen clarified.

"Rudy Walsh. He's got a record, don't he?" Croft asked his partner.

"Aggravated assault. He did four years."

"He had nothing to do with this," Teddy said.

"Do you want to tell us what you were doing over in Spencertown?"

"I told you. Looking for Willa. We thought Pearl might know where she was."

"They were friends?"

Teddy glanced at Claire, warily. "Willa had met her at Sunrise House." He explained her community service project. Whalen and Croft exchanged a look.

Croft said, "Gotta love that community service, teaching us all to be real good citizens."

"They were friends," Teddy went on. "But Willa wasn't there."

Abruptly, Teddy started to cry. "I was worried about her."

"All right, son. Settle down."

Teddy admitted that he'd slept with Pearl on several occasions, but he'd never done anything to hurt her. "She was just a girl I knew, all right? She was in a bad situation."

"You could say that."

Teddy looked confused.

"I guess she didn't tell you she was pregnant?"

Her son expelled some air. "No."

"Let's hope for your sake it isn't yours. I don't think a jury would be too happy to hear that."

"I didn't have anything to do with this," Teddy said. "Why don't you ask Dale? He's the one who was with her! He's the one who did this." He pointed to his eye. "He's the one who stole Luther Grimm's dog, not me."

"Oh, yeah?" Croft dug around in his files and pulled out a dog collar. "Then what was this doing in your locker?"

Claire shot a look at her son, his face white as paint. He didn't say anything; he didn't answer the question.

"I'd like to call my lawyer," Claire said.

The detective picked up the telephone and placed it in front of her. "Be my guest."

Claire dialed Lubin's number. When the secretary answered, Claire had to make a concerted effort to push the words out. When she told her it was an emergency, Lubin came right on. "What's the matter, honey?" he said and she was suddenly Teddy's age, pregnant and broke and begging him for a loan. "It's Teddy," she said. "He's in trouble. We're at the police station."

"I'm on my way."

49 ∽

The next morning, Joe got a call from Claire, asking him to meet her somewhere, anywhere. They met at the lookout on the mountain and walked the trails. Just being around her, alone, stirred his senses. His memories of being with her were still fresh. Almost immediately she started to cry. "What's wrong?"

When she spoke, her words came in spurts, breathlessly. "Teddy. They're charging him, Joe."

"With what?"

"Conspiracy to commit murder."

"On what basis?"

"They have evidence. A witness. They found a dog collar in his locker."

"So what? That doesn't make him a criminal."

"The girl was pregnant. They're claiming he had a motive." She shook her head, nervously lighting a cigarette.

"What motive? She was a prostitute. That sort of thing comes with the territory. Whatever happened to damage control?"

"Apparently she wanted to keep it."

"How do they fucking know what she wanted?"

"One of the girls in the house. I don't know." She shook her head. "It's a mess. His arraignment isn't till Monday and I can't make his bail. I don't want to leave him in there all weekend."

He knew she was going to ask him for money and he also knew that he was going to give it to her. "I'll figure out a way to pay you back," she said.

He reached out for her and she put her head against his chest. He held her there, breathing in the smell of her, which was at once disarming and familiar. "Don't worry," he said. "We'll get your boy out. We'll get him."

She looked up at him through her tears.

"I'd do anything for you," he told her. "You know that."

And the crazy thing was he would.

50

She went to pick Teddy up on her own. When they let him out, she wept with gratitude. They stood there in the large hall and she held on to him, crying into his neck. "It's okay, Mom," he said. "I'm okay."

He was hungry, so they went to the small café in town. He ordered a hamburger, but didn't eat very much. "I can't believe she's dead," he said. "Somebody killed her. It just wasn't me."

They were sitting in a booth near the big windows. He sat there with a toothpick in his mouth, staring sullenly into the dark. Then his face went pale. "There's the car," he said. "We have to go."

She paid quickly, leaving too much money on the table, and followed her son out into the night. He was walking quickly across the street to the market. The car in question was parked in the lot, the owner having gone in to shop. It was a vintage car of some sort, a big old sedan from the forties; it looked harmless enough. Teddy went up to it, trying to see in the windows. From the looks of it, the car was completely empty. "You're gonna have to go in there, Mom. Go in and see if you recognize anyone. I'll wait out here."

"All right. If that's what you want."

He waited in the shadows while she went in to look around. It was a small market, with narrow little aisles overflowing with merchandise. She wandered cautiously, pretending to shop, and turned into the pet food aisle, surprised to see a familiar face at the end of it. It was Jack Heath. Putting cans of dog food into his cart.

Her heart began to pound.

Gingerly, she backed out of the aisle and left the store.

They waited in Claire's car for Heath to come out. They watched as he loaded the bags into the trunk. Then he got into the car and backed out and they followed him, taking care to keep a good distance behind. As anticipated, he turned in to the school lot. Through the trees they could see his headlights climbing the private road that led up to the Head's house.

"If we follow him, we may be seen," Claire said.

"We'll have to go in on foot."

Claire turned down the access road that led into the woods. People came here to run and cross-country ski and, in summer, to swim in the lake. They walked through the woods, a horse-shoe trail that ran around the lake. The girl had been found near here, she realized.

In the distance, they could see the lights of the Heaths' cottage. As they approached, they saw that the car was parked, and the groceries had been brought inside.

They walked up the incline toward the house. It was easy to see inside—there were many windows—but they had to be careful. They walked around to the kitchen and could see Maggie Heath putting things away. She was talking to Ada. They could hear her say, "I'm going to feed the dog."

"See what I told you," Teddy whispered.

They waited, hiding in the bushes. Several minutes later the door opened and they saw Maggie come out, holding a puppy. "That's right, there you go." The puppy peed in the grass and barked. Then she scooped it up and brought it back inside.

"Quite the ferocious beast," Claire whispered.

Teddy looked dejected.

"Let's get out of here."

They started walking, but then a light came on in the cellar, making small rectangles on the snow. Silently, they crept down to peer through the window. Through the dirty glass, they saw Jack Heath coming down the stairs. They watched as he opened a can of dog food and put it into a bowl. Then he took a box of rat poison and sprinkled it on top. He disappeared for a minute then returned wearing thick black rubber gloves and carrying a baseball bat. Claire could see dog feces all over the floor. A moment later, Heath unlocked a closet and the dog came out to eat. It was a brawny white pit bull.

51 ✎

In situations of crisis, it was always best to rely on routine. Maggie had read this in a book somewhere, one of those best sellers that tried to explain inexplicable tragedies, like a track star who loses his legs in a car accident, or a famous mathematician who suddenly loses his mind. Routine was a dependable form of therapy when nothing else would do.

Every morning she got up, washed and dressed, and made the

bed. She went down the short hallway and woke Ada, who did the same. They went down for breakfast, each choosing their own brand of cereal. She made Ada's lunch, Jack tied his tie, and the day began. Unlike the beginning of the school year, she'd become a meticulous housekeeper, making certain that all the rooms were tidy, that the floors were scrubbed clean.

Under the circumstances, Maggie wasn't surprised when the detectives came to visit. They asked if she minded if they looked around. She said, no, of course she didn't. They smiled at her as she carried around the puppy. "He's teething," she told them.

They asked if they could see the cellar. "Of course," she said.

They went down and looked around. They saw the newspapers where the puppy had done his business. "We put him down here at night," she said. "We don't want him making a mess around the house. He's still learning, you know how it is."

"Sure."

One of them opened the small closet. "What's in here?"

"Just storage. Oh, is that bulb out? I've been meaning to replace it."

"I've got a flashlight," the one said.

He turned it on and stepped into the darkness. He wasn't going to find anything; Jack had made sure of that.

Remarkably, her family had made it through the week with little disruption, and as each day passed her fear gradually diminished so that it seemed entirely possible that they would get away with it and could get on with their lives, just as they had before. It had been a perfect murder, really, letting the dog do their dirty work—it had cost them twenty thousand dollars—Ada's college money. Dale had taken the money and left the country, leaving the cops with no other suspect but the boy, Teddy Squire. Of course, breaking into the architect's home hadn't helped the boy's situation, and the dog collar, well, she had to admit that was a nice touch on Jack's part. In Teddy Squire, the cops had clearly concluded, there were serious indications of a criminal mind, and she saw no argument there. It was the American way, of course, to incriminate a person on the basis of a moral deduction that had little more substance than a hunch. Sometimes it was all a jury needed. For the sake of her family, she hoped it was.

52 ⌒

The Head's wife, Maggie Heath, was afflicted with what his wife liked to call the "hostess with the mostest syndrome." In her pert little Talbots ensemble, she led Joe and Candace into her office, ushering them into club chairs covered in Cowtan & Tout. She sat in her chair, a black Windsor reproduction affixed with a gold plaque from her alma mater, Amherst College, and smiled at the two of them, waiting to hear what they had to say to her.

"Is Jack around?" Joe asked.

"I'm afraid he's ill. He's home in bed."

"Well, that's too bad. Somehow it doesn't surprise me."

"What?"

"I said it doesn't surprise me that he's sick. There's been a lot of bad things going around lately, lots of germs and viruses."

She frowned, confused, and pressed on. "Jack and I were so sorry to hear about Willa. I hope she's feeling better. It's really a shame, those awful drugs. They're highly addictive."

"Yes," he said, but he didn't want to hear it from her. "She's going to be fine. But we've come about another matter. I would have liked to discuss it with Jack too, but you'll have to pass along the information."

"I'll be happy to do that," she said, ever courteous.

"We thought it was only right to let him know before we took any legal action."

She looked confused. "I'm sorry, I don't know what you mean."

Joe hesitated, the way he used to do in business meetings when he was in the presence of crooks, making them wait, building up their anxiety so that when he finally broke the news it had a certain visceral impact.

"It has to do with your husband, I'm afraid."

"Yes?" He discerned a glimmer of fear in her eyes as her mind scrambled to process what he was about to tell her.

"It's about something he did to our daughter."

"Something he did?"

"He molested her," Candace said, matter-of-factly. "We're pressing charges."

"What? What did you say?"

"You heard her," Joe said. "In the meantime, as chairman of the board of trustees, I'm going to request that he resign, effective immediately."

She sat there a moment, stunned. "You'll have to excuse me," she said, and ran out of the office, covering her mouth as if to contain a scream.

Candace sat there with tears in her eyes. She was looking at the bulletin board behind Maggie's chair, covered with a collage of photos of students past and present, their babies, their pets.

"It's really such a shame," she said. "This is a wonderful place."

"It will be wonderful again," he said. "We'll find a new Head."

Wistfully, he glanced at the photographs of happy faces. It was then that he noticed a small snapshot, one that had been taken with an older type of camera, pinned in the lower right-hand corner. The picture had captured his attention because it was someone he recognized from his own past. Someone he never thought he'd see again.

He went over and took it down. He looked at it closely, like some priceless artifact. It had been taken on Fisherman's Wharf, he realized, observing the fish monger in the background, the tourists walking along the boardwalk. They were a little family, sitting on a bench, squinting up at the camera as though having their picture taken was the last thing they wanted. The man was tall, his hands stretching the width of the infant's torso. The infant was swaddled in a blanket, a newborn. The woman looked ill, caving into her lover's side. He turned it over and read the words: *Nate Gallagher, Fisherman's Wharf, 1989.*

Joe handed the picture to Candace and walked out, the sound of rain screaming in his head.

Maybe he wasn't thinking straight, but he walked quickly into Walden House, just as the students were filing out. Gallagher was pushing a pile of papers into his knapsack when Joe came in and grabbed him. The only thing on Joe's mind was beating the hell out of the son of a bitch, and he summoned every ounce of repressed anguish into an efficient and powerful assault. Gallagher was taller, but he was no fighter (it was likely, Joe thought, that he was some sort of hippie-pacifist, someone who'd read Emma Goldman religiously and had gone limp during protests of the Trident submarine), and Joe had grown up in Queens, he'd learned the dirty injustices of street fighting at an early age and he relied on them now. With relish, he felt the crack and gush of Gallagher's nose under his fist, blood splashing on the pristine white walls, his opponent's sweat glazing his knuckles. He would have kept going, if it weren't for Lloyd Jernigan pulling him off and shuffling him out of the room into the courtyard, where a crowd had gathered. He searched their faces, the gloomy, relentless consternation of teenagers, and thankfully, did not find his daughter's among them.

53 ᴄᴏ

Maggie had left campus and driven home and for several minutes stayed out in the car, wondering what to do next. What would she say to him? *How could he?* But when she walked into the house, no one was home. There was a white envelope on the table. She opened it and took out a piece of white paper upon which was written a single word. *Murderers.*

It came to her that the handwriting was familiar. Of course it was. It was Ada's.

She felt a little sick. She went outside for some air. She walked down the incline, then into the meadow where Jack had buried the dog. The snow had melted, and the ground had begun to thaw. Jack was standing there, alone, looking down into the empty grave.

"Jack?"

He just stood there, unmoving.

"Where's Ada?"

"It's amazing how soft the ground gets after a good rain."

Maggie stepped forward. She could see that someone had dug up the grave and taken the dog.

"All the snow's melted," Jack said. "Just like that."

"Who did it? Ada?"

He nodded. "Your daughter knows right from wrong. She has a conscience."

"She couldn't possibly have done it herself."

"Oh, no," he said lightly. "She had help."

He looked at her then, a cold look.

"The police?"

"We were so close, Maggie." He smiled at her, apologetically.

Tears ran down her cheeks. She let herself go. She wept bitterly.

He took out his handkerchief and handed it to her. "Dry your tears, my dear. Somehow, they don't become you."

He started walking back up to the house.

"Jack?"

She followed him inside. The kitchen was dark and clean. He sat at the table, staring at nothing.

Methodically, she took two glasses out of the cupboard and set them on the table, then brought over the bottle of gin and poured them each a glass.

"Clarity," he said. "It was Pound's greatest gift. To be clear, precise. I wanted to write too, like everyone else. I have," he gestured, making circles in the air with his hand, "plots in my head."

She sank into the chair. It was the end of something, she could feel it. It terrified her. She drank. The liquor burned her throat. She could never drink enough to temper the cold fear that had consumed her.

"My sister," he said. "Poor little June. Everybody was so sorry. It was a terrible accident." He drank his drink. "Lies," he said. "All lies."

Her heart began to beat very fast.

"They're handy little things, though, you have to admit. Parents do it, when they're desperate. My mother did. She couldn't bear to lose me too." A cold look washed over him. "June was Snow White. I was the prince. I just wanted her to be still. It was a glass coffin, if you remember. I said, *'Lay still, little June, lay still!'* The cleaning plastic made it look so real. It made her so quiet." He looked out the window at the lake. The black clouds moving in.

"Jack." She sighed. "Jack, please, listen to me."

"You never get over something like that."

She squeezed his hand. "We have to move on. We have to be strong."

He shook his head. "I can't. I was never as strong as you, Maggie."

It was then that she noticed the suitcase. He picked it up and walked out.

"Jack!" she shouted. "Don't you walk out on me, Jack! *Please, Jack!*"

But he did. He left her there. He just kept going.

54 ∽

Willa had told Regina that she wouldn't be coming to Sunrise House anymore for community service. Just going there reminded her of Pearl. To some degree, she felt responsible for her death. If she'd gone to Regina, for instance, two weeks before, and told her about the girl's drug addiction, that she'd complained about one of her regular clients threatening to kill her—if she had done that, Pearl might still be alive today. For her own selfish reasons, she hadn't done anything to help Pearl. She'd used her, like everyone else.

Regina had asked her to come one last time, to say good-bye to the children. They were going to have a little party for her, and she was looking forward to it. She was actually going to miss them. She'd been counting on Mr. Gallagher to drive her, but it was Mr. Heath who pulled up in his Volvo wagon. He leaned across the seat and opened the passenger door. "Regina's expecting you."

She stood there, confused. She didn't feel comfortable going in the car with him, but then she saw Mr. Gallagher coming though the crowd with a bloody towel on his nose. "What happened to Mr. Gallagher?" she asked.

"I don't really know," Heath said. "Come on and get in. Regina's got something special planned. You don't want to be late."

"Where are the others?"

"The others?" He thought for a minute. "The sophomores are in Boston today, at the museum." He smiled. "Come on, Willa, I promised Regina you'd be punctual."

Willa hesitated, watching Mr. Gallagher walk to his truck. She tried to catch his eye, but he seemed distracted by his nosebleed, holding the bloody towel over his nose.

She looked around for someone else to drive her, but the campus had swiftly emptied and there was no one else around. *Don't*, she thought, but she got in anyway.

On the drive, she concentrated on looking out the window, remembering the strange alleys and dark corners that Pearl had taken her to. The ballet studio where they'd spent the night. The strange house full of cats where they'd scored her drugs. "How've you been, Willa?"

"Fine, I guess."

"I haven't seen you in a while." He smiled at her. "I hear you're reading *The Scarlet Letter*. What do you think of it?"

"What do I think?" She hadn't done very well on the test. They'd been asked to write an essay and many of her ideas had been lifted from *Spark Notes*. "I don't think it was fair. What happened to her, I mean. The way she was treated."

"No, it wasn't fair. Of course it wasn't. But isn't that the point?"

"I don't know," she said. "I guess."

"Love is a terrible thing." He shook his head. "It brings out the worst in people."

"Why are you crying?"

"I wasn't much of a student either," he told her, swatting his tears. "It was my father's pull that got me into Amherst. That's the way life is, I'm afraid. Everything's fixed."

"I don't understand."

"They don't tell you that, of course, but it's true. They make you believe you actually have a fucking chance."

"Chance at what?"

"It's all fixed," he said again, his voice a ragged whisper.

She wished he'd speed up. He was driving slowly, and it was getting late. The sun was low in the sky, reflecting off the windows of the houses on Main Street, reflecting off the shiny places on the dash. Sunlight came sharply through the rear windows, glinting off the side mirrors. Her eyes moved around the dashboard, fixing on a compelling gold glimmer in the ashtray. She narrowed her eyes, trying to focus, trying to ascertain what it was.

"My wife is much smarter than I am," he went on. "She is *fastidious*." He shook his head. "I can't do it anymore."

"Do what?"

"This. Everything. The school. I'm done," he said. "I wanted you to be the first to know."

"Why?"

"Because we have an understanding, you and I." He reached over and put his hand on her thigh. "She used to talk about you."

Her body turned to stone. "Who did?"

"Pearl. Petra. She had a very high opinion of you."

And then it hit her. It was a necklace, with a single white pearl on the end of it. It looked like it had a piece of hair stuck on it, and something else: blood.

"It was you?" she said.

"She was a prostitute," he said flatly. "She was asking for it."

"Let me out. Please."

"Oh, I'll let you out all right. When I'm good and ready. And I'm a long way off from ready."

He drove out of town, down long roads heaped with snow. The

snow was black with dirt. It was getting cold and he was driving very fast. He'd taken out a flask and was drinking out of it. He pushed in a cassette, an old man speaking in a gravelley voice. "Pound," he said. "The Cantos. The only thing that's ever made any sense." The tape made a whirring sound as it played. It was somewhere in the middle, the man's grave voice reciting: *Palace in smoky light . . . Troy but a heap of smoldering boundary stones. ANAXIFORMINGES!*

"Aurunculeia!" Heath shouted, spraying spit. "Hear me!"

It was then that she knew he was going to kill her.

He drove into the woods. There was a thin road, what was called a carriage trail, they'd learned about them in history, and there were small huts along the way that had been used for victims of smallpox in the eighteenth century. As he pulled into the woods, branches scratched against the car. He parked in a jumble of overgrowth. In no particular hurry, he took out a gun. It was a small handgun. "My father taught me how to use it on my ninth birthday," he explained. "There's lots of things I've done in my life nobody knows about. Things that were meaningful, that made a difference. You don't realize it, but I've already made a difference in your life. I suspect you'll never forget it."

She sat there, looking straight through the windshield. She could feel him looking at her—she knew he was going to touch her.

"It's a gift," he said. "Knowing people the way I do. Knowing how people think, what they want. Intuition, you might call it." He did something to the gun and lowered it and sat there for a moment, looking straight ahead. "People don't say what they really think. But you and me, we know better. We see through it. I knew it that time, when I drove you home. I knew what you wanted." He looked at her and smiled, then played with her hair. "It's okay to admit to it. I'm not going to tell anyone."

"Please," she said. "Leave me alone."

But his voice came sharp. "Let's get out."

They walked along. It was getting darker by the minute. All the trees were moving. The branches were bare and black. She glanced up at the sky. He walked behind her. Her feet were cold in her sneakers, which were wet from the snow. A chill went all through her body. They were like two soldiers entering into something, some kind of war. She surveyed the woods before her; she could run. But where? She could run back to the road, she thought. She turned her head slightly, trying to see where he was, and, to her surprise, felt the hard ridge of the pistol on the back of her head. "Walk," he said.

55 ☙

Somehow, watching Willa drive off in Heath's car didn't sit well with him. Heath had told him that community service had been canceled indefinitely. He was sitting in Claire's kitchen while she administered first aid, gently wiping the blood from his face. "He did some job on you," she said.

The phone rang. Somewhere in the house, Teddy picked up. A moment later he came into the room. "That was Willa's dad. She didn't come after school. He wanted to know—"

But Nate didn't wait around for him to finish. "Call the police!" he shouted. "Jack Heath's got her."

He drove over to the Goldings' house and went to the door. "She's with Jack Heath."

Joe's hard glare broke. "I'll get my coat."

They took Nate's old truck. It was just the two of them, the two fathers, he thought. "I'm sorry about before," Joe said. "For what it's worth."

Nate nodded. "You can throw a punch, I'll say that for you."

"Why did you come up here?"

Nate repeated the question inside his head. "I guess I just needed to see her. She doesn't know, of course. I wasn't planning on telling her. That's something you need to understand."

"I'd like to keep it that way, if that's all right."

"Yes," Nate said. "Of course. I never intended for anyone to find out. It was a personal thing. And I'm sorry."

Joe nodded. "I understand. I might have done the same thing in your place."

The men looked at each other. Nate felt resolved.

They pulled up in front of Jack Heath's house. The door was open. The house seemed empty. They ran up the stairs and looked in the bedrooms. The beds were unmade, the drawers empty. They went back downstairs into the living room. "Where would he go?" Joe said.

But Nate could hardly hear him, for something else had caught his attention. The last rays of sunlight, shattering the surface of the frozen lake.

The roads were dark now, no lights, and a fog had rolled in, a thick layer of mist that clung to everything in sight. It was not unusual. Like dancing ghosts, the mist haunted the land. Nate pulled down the access road and parked. "His car isn't here," Joe said.

"He might have come in from the other side, north of here."

They got out. For several minutes they stood there, listening. It was quiet. They stood in fog up to their knees. They started walking north. They walked together, side by side. The trails were dark, it was hard to see. What at first sounded like the cry of a bird came again, and once again, and they realized it was a scream. They wandered deeper into the darkness, trying to locate its source, and then they heard a shot.

56 ∽

He'd shot her in the leg. She could hardly believe it. And now her leg was throbbing with excruciating pain. Her leg went numb, as if it had fallen asleep. Blood flowed out of her with surprising speed. She felt his arms around her, pulling her through the dirt. It made her think of Pearl, of what she'd gone through. It terrified her so desperately that she lost all ambition to move and she fell to her knees and began to pray.

He dragged her several feet and laid her on her back. Her eyes were fluttering and the world came in flashes, like a film playing on a broken projector, all you see are flashes of white light. She thought she might pass out and tried very hard not to, but it was the only thing she wanted to do. Sleep, like a velvet tunnel. She wanted to curl up inside of it. Mr. Heath stood above her, the gun in his hand. Looming over him was a sort of tower. It was for hunters, she realized. A place to wait for deer.

"You shouldn't have tried to run like that," he said.

But now someone was calling her name. She could hear her name flying through the darkness like some great bird.

Heath cursed. He seemed frantic. He kneeled down and pushed his hands beneath her and lifted her in his arms. With great difficulty, he climbed the ladder, hauling her up to the high dark place. He was making sounds, breathing very hard. And now her name came again, rising up and falling down. There were two voices now, but she was too tired to call back. They wouldn't know that Heath had a gun, that, like two unassuming deer, he was waiting for them.

Heath clicked off the safety. He was taking aim. She turned, she screamed. And something very hard landed on her ear, the barrel of his pistol. He'd hit her there to make her quiet. And her ear rang and rang. It was very dark and she suddenly felt very tired. Perhaps if she could just rest a moment. A little sleep, she thought, was all she needed. Then she would climb down from there and find her way home.

57 ↩

For Joe, it was like being inside a nightmare, the darkness, the naked trees, the fog—and the gunshot that came out of nowhere. Instinctively, he zipped up his coat, as if to protect himself from what he knew was about to occur, and when he felt the bullet enter his arm, a vigorous burning sensation overtook him. For several seconds he could not move, even as it became clear to him that the bullet had kept going and had made a big hole in his flesh. His arm was falling asleep. Gallagher and Heath were fighting, rolling around on the ground, and Gallagher had rolled on top of him and was grappling for the gun. He got it and threw it someplace. Noises curled out of their bodies as one man overpowered the other. Then Joe gripped Heath's coat, binding it up in his fist, and hit him very hard. He went down, out cold.

They left Heath on the ground and ran over to the tree stand. Pain rippled through him, but in truth the wound was of no real consequence. His face was wet, freezing in the cold wind, and he realized he'd been crying. They approached the tree where a crude ladder led up to a small tower, made for hunters.

Joe felt Gallagher's hand on his back. "Go get your daughter," he said.

But Heath was on his feet; he had found the gun. He staggered toward them. "You think you're so clever. We've had you pegged from day one."

"Put the gun down, Jack," Gallagher said.

But Heath was in no mood to be told what to do. He put the gun to his temple and fired. They watched him drop to the ground.

Joe climbed the ladder. Willa was lying on the small platform. It occurred to him, with horror, that perhaps she was dead. But then he saw the rising and falling of her chest. "Willa?" he said. "Willa, honey."

"Daddy? Is that you?"

She turned into his arms.

"Yeah, it's me, honey. I'm right here."

Part Five

◦〜◦

Assessment and Interpretation

[sculpture]

Claire Squire, *Her Own Good,* 2007. Paper, methylcellulose, horse-hair, tartan kilt, Victoria Secret bra and thong, knee socks, 67¼ x 18 x 50 in. The Abby Wexler Collection, Los Angeles.

The girl stands alone in her school uniform, showing off her underwear. A tattoo across the small of her back reads IN YOUR DREAMS.

58 ✑

Shortly after Maggie Heath's arraignment, Nate went to visit her in prison. It was a minimum-security facility in Lancaster, a two-hour drive from Stockbridge. He felt he owed her somehow, some remnant of prep school loyalty. They visited in a large open room full of other prisoners and their guests. There were children. The walls were lined with soda and fast-food machines. In her gray smock, she was calm, pale. She'd put on a little weight. "How's Ada?" he asked.

"She's all right. She's with my parents."

"Are you all right?"

"I'm fine," she said. "Really."

She could say it a million times and he'd never believe her.

"I wanted to give you this," she said, handing him a small snapshot. He studied it, amazed by his own youth, the greenish glow of Catherine's skin, Willa's tiny little face. The picture was responsible for the scar over his right eye, where Joe Golding had punched him, but he still wanted it. It was the only photograph he had of Cat.

"Who was she?" Maggie asked.

"Someone I knew once." He looked at her; he didn't want to get into it. She was the last person who deserved any of his secrets. He put the picture in his pocket. "Thanks."

"You're welcome." She cracked a smile. "I suppose you hate me, now."

"No," he said. "I don't hate you, Maggie."

He squeezed her hand, more out of pity than anything else. He had known her before Jack Heath had come into her life and swept her up in a squall of bad luck.

"And you, what will you do? Did you finish your novel?"

"Not quite," he said. "I've got some other things I need to do first. I'm planning on doing some traveling."

"Where do you have in mind?"

335

"Mexico," he said.

"That sounds wonderful, Nate. Good for you."

A buzzer sounded, indicating that visiting hours were over.

"Good-bye, Maggie."

She raised her palm. And then, within seconds, she was gone.

When he got home that evening there was a note on his door from Larkin, asking him to stop by. "Someone left this for you," he said, handing him a cardboard box. "It barks."

"What?"

There was a puppy inside, a little yellow mutt. The note said, "He's for Teddy. He earned it." It was signed Ada Heath.

59 ⌒

Enchanting was a word people used to describe the Berkshires in springtime. And it was true. As if overnight, the fields had suddenly turned green. The trees shimmied with new leaves and sprouted fruit. The air smelled sweet.

Claire had been working in the barn all night, trying to finish the new piece. It was a sculpture of Petra. She washed her hands and dried them on a towel and stood back, appraising the work. She'd built her out of plaster, a dancer in a pink tutu, her long legs slightly turned out, her arms down at her sides. Her face bold, arrogant, the way Claire remembered her. It was a gift for her, an apology. Things could have been different for her; they should have been.

"She's beautiful," Nate said from the doorway.

Claire nodded her thanks.

"I think she'd be pleased," he said.

"I hope so."

"She looks . . . almost innocent."

"Good," she said. "I wanted that. I wanted that for her."

They stood there a moment, looking at it. Claire felt a flutter of pride.

"Oh, I almost forgot." He handed her an envelope. "This came for you. I thought it might be important."

It was from her gallery in Los Angeles. Eagerly, she opened the envelope and read the letter. They were opening a new space in New York. "They want some of my pieces!" She started jumping around. "Oh, my *God! Thank you!*" She threw her arms around her lover's neck and kissed him over and over and over again, and she did not think that she would ever stop.

60 ⌒

The sun had decided to shine brightly on their wedding day.

They'd set up a tent on the back field. It was to be a small wedding, with only a few people attending. Afterward, they would have a feast at the long table. From where she stood in her beautiful dress she could see Joe and Candace and Willa sitting in the front row. She caught Joe staring at her, admiring her in the dress with his dark, gypsy eyes. He smiled at her meaningfully, then mouthed the words *Mazel tov*. Candace gave her a little wave. Except for a small scar on her thigh, Willa had fully recovered from the gunshot wound. She was wearing a short dress and sandals and Claire could clearly see the tattoo on her ankle. There seemed no point, she'd told her, in trying to hide it. Anyway, she'd said, it was permanent—it was part of her identity now. A few rows behind her was Rudy, Teddy's illustrious cohort, who was all dressed up in a suit and sitting very tall in his seat, putting her in mind of Abraham Lincoln. Across the aisle, on the other side, Greta was sitting with her new boyfriend, the bereft neurosurgeon, and some of Teddy's friends, Marco Liddy—whose mother had made their wedding cake—and Monica and several others. Nate's father had come with a nurse attendant and sat off to the side, in a wheelchair. Irving Lubin had come with his wife, Sheila. Old Mr. Larkin had come too, and had brought them two lovebirds as a gift, in an old-fashioned birdcage. They'd hired the cellist who lived on the third floor of Larkin's house; she was playing the Bach Suites. The minister was waiting patiently, holding his Bible. From her position under the magnolia tree, she watched her lover walk down the flower-strewn path. In his black tuxedo, he looked exceptionally dignified, she thought. She loved his long legs and arms, his broad shoulders, the way he moved, with grace, like Gulliver the gentle giant. After the wedding, the three of them were going to Mexico. They had reservations at a small resort on the gulf owned by a man named Billy McGrath, Teddy's father.

Teddy walked over and gave her a hug. "Now, are you sure you don't have any questions about the wedding night?" He wiggled his eyebrows meaningfully.

"Yes, I'm sure."

"Because I'm happy to explain things to you."

"I don't think that will be necessary."

He looked at her with pride. "You look beautiful, Mom."

"Thank you, Teddy."

"Are you ready to be given away?"

She thought a moment and looked across the field at Nate Gallagher. She looped her arm through her son's. "Yes," she said with certainty. "I'm ready."

"Then let's go."

the poker scene; Chuck Goodermote; Rabbi Don Cashman for his inspiring sermons; Becky Marvin; Sue Baum; Officer Miles J. Barber of the Pittsfield Police Department; Sue Turconi for her artistic creativity and advice; and Paula Lippman, Beth Appelman, and Beth Pine.

My heartfelt appreciation to the following people who held or inspired special events on my behalf: Joan and Lyle Brundage, Dorothy Silverherz, Birdie and Stanley Brundage, Lisa Brundage Shapiro, Beverly and Ed Robbins, Alison Gould, Millie and Marty Shapiro, Pat Van Gorp, Judy Pincus, Janet Zuckerman, Lisa Fishman, Barbara Palmer, Barbara Falkin, Rhoda Derman, Natalie Derman, Lynn Leonard, Fran Manne, Linda Radowitz, Gloria Colacino, and Barbara Vink.

Deep personal thanks to Robin Porter, and the members of JHA Riding Academy for their horse advice, including Wendy Halsdorf, Leah Halsdorf, Julie Halsdorf, Kim Luftiber, Chris Cameron, and Jeremy Mitchell.

IN MEMORY

Nina Payne
Barry Lippman
Stephen Barr
Sanford Rosenberg

Acknowledgments ᥴᥩ

I want to thank my brilliant editor, Carole DeSanti, for being the single person on this earth who drives me to write; my agent, Linda Chester, for her integrity and certainty and intelligent guidance; Clare Ferraro, Carolyn Coleburn, Ann M. Day, Courtney Greenwald, Karen Anderson, Kristin Spang, Sharon L. Gonzalez, Marlene Tungseth, and Paul Buckley, and everybody else at Viking for their incredibly hard work on my behalf.

My profound thanks to my husband, Scott Morris, for staying the course, for being the *one,* and to our children, Hannah, Sophie, and Sam, for their patience, honesty, and creativity in all matters that encompass the novel-writing process.

Sincere thanks to Peter Stine for publishing Nate Gallagher's letter in *Witness: Exile in America,* Volume XX, 2006, which inspired me to write this novel, and to Michelle Gillette, who included a short excerpt in the Summer Fiction supplement of *The Women's Times,* 2006.

I want to acknowledge the article "A Cruel Edge," by Robert Jensen, Ph.D., that appeared in the Spring 2004 issue of *Ms. Magazine,* which gave me extraordinary insight into the experience some women endure in the production of pornography. I owe my deepest gratitude to Anthony Simone and Kelly Erikson for sharing their stories, as well as to Grace Dugan for connecting us. Thanks also to Leah Tyrrell for sharing her experiences with her beautiful baby, Emily.

Many thanks to the following individuals for their continued interest and support of my work: Kyra Ryan for her editorial expertise; Gary Jaffe of Linda Chester and Associates; Susie Landau Finch; Lee K. Abbott and the members of his writing workshop at New York State Summer Writer's Institute 2006, where I first workshopped

Elizabeth Brundage

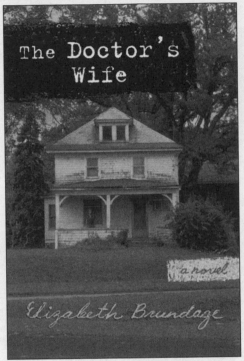

ISBN 978-0-452-28691-7

"Appearances are deceiving in this
psychological thriller... a compelling read."
—*The Boston Globe*

Available wherever books are sold.

Plume
A member of Penguin Group (USA) Inc.
www.penguin.com

A taut and terrifying thriller about the lengths
we will go to make our dreams come true

Coming in August 2010

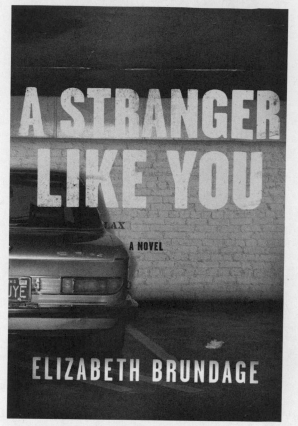

ISBN 978-0-670-02200-7

Available wherever books are sold

www.elizabethbrundage.com

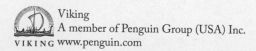